REGENCY

Rogues & Runaways

Two tantalisingly scandalous Regency
romances from Margaret Moore

D0414867

Unknowingly pursuing her destiny, award-winning author **Margaret Moore** graduated with distinction from the University of Toronto with a Bachelor of Arts degree. She has been a Leading Wren in the Royal Canadian Naval Reserve, an award-winning public speaker, a member of an archery team and a student of fencing and ballroom dancing. She has also worked for every major department store chain in Canada. Margaret sold her first historical romance, *A Warrior's Heart*, to Mills & Boon® Historicals in 1991. She has recently completed her eighteenth novel for Mills & Boon. Margaret lives in Toronto with her husband, two children and two cats. Readers may contact her through her website, www. margaretmoore.com.

REGENCY

Rogues & Runaways

Margaret Moore

MILLS & BOON

Mills & Boon, an imprint of Harlequin (UK) Limited,
Eton House, 18-24 Paradise Road, Richmond, Surrey TW9 1SR

REGENCY: RAGUES & RUNAWAYS
© Harlequin Enterprises II B.V./S.à.r.l 2011

The publisher acknowledges the copyright holder of the individual works as follows:

A Lover's Kiss © Margaret Wilkins 2008
The Viscount's Kiss © Margaret Wilkins 2009

ISBN: 978 0 263 89773 9

052-0612

Harlequin (UK) policy is to use papers that are natural, renewable and recyclable products and made from wood grown in sustainable forests. The logging and manufacturing processes conform to the legal environmental regulations of the country of origin.

Printed and bound
by CPI Group (UK) Ltd, Croydon, CR0 4YY

A Lover's Kiss

Margaret Moore

Chapter One

Considering Drury's life in general, I suppose I shouldn't really be surprised. It's unfortunate the young woman was French, though. We all know how he feels about the French.

> —from *The Collected Letters of Lord Bromwell*, noted naturalist and author of *The Spider's Web*

London, 1819

Panting, Juliette Bergerine lay on her bed in a tangle of bedclothes and stared at the stained ceiling above her.

It had been a dream. Just a dream. She was not in France, not back on the farm, and Gaston LaRoche was far away. The war was over, Napoleon defeated. She was in London. She was safe.

She was alone.

Except…what was that scuffling sound? It could be rats in the walls, but it seemed too distant.

And what was that noise? A shout? A cry of pain coming from the alley outside?

Kicking off her sheets and thin blanket, Juliette got out of her narrow bed and hurried to the window, raising the sash as high as it would go. Clad only in a chemise, she shivered, for the September air was chilly and tainted by the smells of burning coal, of refuse and dung. The half-moon illuminated the hastily, poorly constructed building across the alley, and the ground below.

Four men with clubs or some kind of weapons surrounded another man who had his back to the wall of the lodging house. She watched with horror as the four crept closer, obviously about to attack him. The man near the wall crouched, ready to defend himself, his dark-haired head moving warily from side to side as he waited for them to strike.

She opened her mouth to call out for help, then hesitated. She didn't know those men, either the attackers or their victim. Given where she lived, they could all be bad men involved in a dispute about ill-gotten gains, or a quarrel among thieves. What would happen if she interfered? Should she even try?

Yet it was four against one, so she did not close the window, and in the next moment, she was glad she had not, for the man with his back to the wall cursed—in French.

A fellow countryman, so no wonder he was under attack. Being French would be enough to make him a target for English louts.

Just as she was about to call out, the tallest of the attackers stepped forward and swung his weapon. The Frenchman jumped back, colliding with the wall. At the same time, another assailant, his face shielded by his hat, moved forward, slashing. She saw the glint of metal in the moonlight—a knife.

She must help her countryman! But what could she do?

She swiftly surveyed her small room, plainly furnished with cheap furniture. She had a pot. A kettle. A basket of potatoes that were supposed to feed her for a week.

She looked back out the window. As the Frenchman dipped and swayed, the first man rammed his club into his side. He doubled over and fell to his knees while the man with the knife crept closer.

Juliette hauled the basket to the window, then grabbed a potato. As the lout with the knife leaned over the poor Frenchman and pulled his head back by his hair, as if about to slit his throat, she threw a potato at him with all her might and shouted, *"Arrête!"*

The potato hit the man directly on the head. He clutched his hat, looked up and swore. Juliette crouched beneath the window, then flung another potato in his direction. And another. She kept throwing until the basket was empty.

Holding her breath, she listened, her heart pounding. When she heard nothing, she cautiously raised her head and peered over the rotting windowsill.

The Frenchman lay on the ground, not moving. But his attackers were gone.

Hoping she was not too late, Juliette hastily tugged one of her two dresses on over her chemise, shoved her feet into the heavy shoes she wore when walking through the city to the modiste's where she worked as a seamstress and ran down the stairs as fast as she could go. None of the other lodgers in the decrepit building showed themselves. She was not surprised. Likely they felt it would be better to mind their own business.

Once outside, she sidestepped the puddles and

refuse in the alley until she was beside the fallen man. He was, she noted with relief, still breathing as he lay on the cobblestones, his dark wavy hair covering the collar of his black box coat with two shoulder capes. It was a surprisingly fine garment for a poor immigrant.

She crouched down and whispered, *"Monsieur?"*

He didn't move or answer. Seeking to rouse him, she laid a hand on his shoulder. She could tell by the feel of the fabric that his coat was indeed very expensive.

What was a man who could afford such a garment doing in this part of the city at this time of night?

One answer came to mind, and she hoped she was wrong, that he wasn't a rich man who'd come to find a whore or a gaming hell. *"Monsieur?"*

When he still didn't answer, she carefully turned him over. The moonlight revealed a face with sharp cheekbones and a strong jaw, a straight nose and bleeding brow. His shoulders were broad, his waist narrow, his legs long.

She undid his coat and examined him the best she could in the moonlight. The rest of his clothing— white linen shirt and black cravat, well-fitted black riding coat, gray waistcoat and black trousers—were also of the finest quality, as were his leather riding boots. Mercifully, she saw no more blood or other injuries—until she looked at his hands. Something was not right…

He grabbed her arm, his grip unexpectedly strong. As she tried to pull free of that fierce grasp, his eyes opened and he fixed her with a stare that seemed to bore right into her heart. Then he whispered something in a deep, husky voice that sounded like a name—Annie, or something similar.

His wife, perhaps? *"Monsieur?"*

His eyes drifted closed as he muttered something else.

He had not grabbed her to hurt her, but out of fear or desperation or both. And it was obvious that whatever might be wrong with his hands, they were not crippled.

Whoever he was, and whatever had brought him here, she couldn't leave him in a stinking, garbage-strewn alley.

As long as he wasn't completely unconscious, she should be able to get him up to her room, where it was dry and there was a relatively soft bed.

She put her shoulder under his arm to help him to his feet. Although he was able to stand, he was heavier than she expected and he groaned as if in agony. Perhaps there were injuries she couldn't see beneath his clothes.

She thought of summoning help from the other people who lived in her lodging house, but decided against it. Even if they hadn't heard the attack, they already regarded her with suspicion because she was French. What would they think if she asked them to help her take a man to her room, even if he was hurt?

Non, she must do this by herself.

As she struggled to get the man inside, she was glad she had grown up on a farm. Despite the past six months sewing in a small, dark basement, she was still strong enough to help him into the building, up the stairs and onto her bed, albeit with much effort.

She lit the stub of candle on the stool by the bed, then fetched a cloth and a basin of icy water. Sitting beside him, she brushed the dark hair away from the man's face and gently washed the cut over his eye. A lump was starting to form on his forehead.

Hoping his injury wasn't serious, she loosened his cravat and searched the pockets of his coat, seeking some clue to his identity.

There was nothing. They must have robbed him, too.

He murmured again, and she leaned close to hear.

"Ma chérie," he whispered, his voice low and rough as, with his eyes still closed, he put his arm around her and drew her nearer.

She was so surprised, she didn't pull away, and before she could stop him or even guess what he was going to do, his lips met hers. Tenderly, gently, lovingly.

She *should* stop him, and yet it felt so good. So warm, so sweet, so wonderful. And she had been lonely for so long....

Then his arm relaxed around her and his lips grew slack, and she realized he was unconscious.

Sir Douglas Drury slowly opened his eyes. His head hurt like the devil and there was a stained and cracked ceiling above him. Across from him was a wall equally stained by damp, and a window. The panes were clean, and there were no curtains or other covering. Beyond it, he saw no sky or open space. Just a brick wall.

He didn't know where he was, or how he had come to be there.

His heart began to pound and his body to perspire. As fear and panic threatened to overwhelm him, he closed his eyes and fought the nausea that rose up within him. He wasn't in a dank, dark cell. He was in a dingy, whitewashed room lit by daylight. It smelled of cabbage, not offal and filthy straw and rats. He was lying on a mattress of some kind, not bare stone.

And he could hear, somewhere in the distance, the cries of street vendors. English street vendors.

He was in London, not a cell in France.

Last night he'd been walking and only too late realized where his feet had taken him. He'd been accosted by three…no, four men. They hadn't demanded his money or his wallet. They'd simply attacked him, maneuvering him off the street into an alley, where he was sure they'd meant to murder him.

Why wasn't he dead? He'd had no sword, no weapon. He couldn't even make a proper fist.

Something had stopped them. But what? He couldn't remember, just as he had no idea where he was, or who had brought him here.

Wherever he was, though, at least he was alive.

He tried to sit up, despite a pain in his right side that made him press his lips together to keep from crying out. He put his feet on the bare wooden floor and raised his head—to see that he wasn't alone.

A young woman, apparently fast asleep, sat on a stool with her head propped against the wall. Her hair was in a loose braid, with little wisps that bordered her smooth, pale cheeks. Her modest, plain dress with a high neck was made of cheap green muslin. Her features were nothing remarkable, although her lips were full and soft, and her nose rather fine.

She didn't look familiar, yet there was something about her that danced at the edge of his mind, like a whisper he couldn't quite hear. Whatever it was, though, he didn't intend to linger here to find out.

He put his hands on the edge of the narrow bed, ready to stand, when the young woman suddenly stretched like a cat after a long nap in the summer's sun. Her light brown eyes opened and she smiled at him as if they'd just made love.

That was disconcerting. Not unpleasant, but definitely disconcerting.

Then she spoke. "Oh, *monsieur,* you are awake!" French.

She spoke French. Instantly, he was on his guard, every sense alert. "Who are you and what am I doing here?" he demanded in English.

The arched brows of the young woman contracted. "You are English?" she answered in that language.

"Obviously. Who are you and what am I doing here?" he repeated.

She got to her feet and met his suspicious regard with a wounded air. "I am Juliette Bergerine, and it was I who saved your life."

How could one lone young woman have saved his life—and why would she?

He was well-known in London. Indeed, he was famous. Perhaps she hoped for a reward.

He rose unsteadily, the pain in his side searing, his head aching more. "Do you know who I am?"

Her eyes narrowed. "Don't you?"

"Of course I do. I am Sir Douglas Drury, barrister, of Lincoln's Inn."

"I am the woman who threw the potatoes."

Potatoes? "What the deuce are you talking about?"

"I threw my potatoes at the men attacking you to make them run away. And they did."

Was that what he'd been trying to recall? "How did I come to be in this room?"

"I brought you."

"By yourself?"

Anger kindled in her brown eyes. "Is this the thanks

I am to get for helping you? To be questioned and everything I say treated like a lie? I begin to think I should have left you in the alley!"

Trust a Frenchwoman to overreact. "Naturally I'm grateful you came to my aid."

"You do not sound the least bit grateful!"

His jaw clenched before he replied, "No doubt you would prefer me to grovel."

"I would prefer to be treated with respect. I may be poor, Sir Douglas Drury, barrister of Lincoln's Inn, but I am not a worm!"

As her eyes shone with passionate fury and her breasts rose and fell beneath her cheap gown, and those little wisps of hair brushed against her flushed cheeks, he was very well aware that she was not a worm.

She marched to the door and wrenched it open. "Since you seem well enough to walk, go!"

He stepped forward, determined to do just that, but the room began to tilt and turn as if on some kind of wobbly axis.

"Did you not hear me? I said go!" she indignantly repeated.

"I can't," he muttered as he backed up and felt for the bed, then sat heavily. "Send for a doctor."

"I am not your servant, either!"

God save him from Frenchwomen and their overwrought melodrama! "I would gladly go and happily see the last of you, but unfortunately for us both, I can't. I must be more badly injured than I thought."

She lowered her arm. "I have no money for a doctor."

Drury felt his coat. His wallet was gone. Perhaps she'd taken it. If she had, she would surely not admit it. But then why would she have brought him here? "You must tell the doctor you have come on behalf of Sir Douglas Drury. He will be paid when I return to my chambers."

"You expect him to believe me? I am simply to tell him I come on behalf on Sir Douglas Drury, and he will do as I say? Are you known for getting attacked in this part of London?"

Damn the woman. "No, I am not."

He could send for his servant, but Mr. Edgar would have to hire a carriage from a livery stable, and that would take time.

Buggy would come at once, no questions asked. Thank God his friend was in London—although he wouldn't be at home on this day of the week. He would be at the weekly open house held by the president of the Royal Society of London for Improving Natural Knowledge.

"Go to 32 Soho Square, to the home of Sir Joseph Banks, and ask for Lord Bromwell. Tell him I need his help."

The young woman crossed her slender arms. "Oh, I am to go to a house in Soho Square and ask for a lord, and if he comes to the door and listens to me, *he* will do as I say?"

"He will if you tell him Sir Douglas Drury has sent you. Or would you rather I stay here until I've recovered?"

She ruminated a moment. "Am I to walk?"

That was a problem easily remedied. "If you take a hackney, Lord Bromwell will pay the driver."

"You seem very free with your friend's money," she noted with a raised and skeptical brow.

"He will pay," Drury reiterated, his head beginning

to throb and his patience to wear out. "You have my word."

She let her breath out slowly. "Very well, I will go."

She went to a small chest, threw open the lid and bent down to take out a straw Coburg bonnet tastefully decorated with cheap ribbon and false flowers, the effect charming in spite of the inexpensive materials.

As she tied the ribbon beneath her chin with deft, swift fingers, a concerned expression came to her face now prettily framed. "I am to leave you here alone?"

Drury's crooked fingers gripped the edge of the bed as he regarded her with what his friend the Honorable Brixton Smythe-Medway called his "death stare." "I assure you, Miss Bergerine, that even if I were a thief, there is not a single thing here I would care to steal."

She met his cold glare with one of her own. "That is not what troubled me, Sir Douglas Drury. I do not like leaving an injured man all alone, even if he is an ungrateful, arrogant pig. But never mind. I will do as you ask."

Drury felt a moment's shame. But only for a moment, because even if she had helped him, she was still French and he had his ruined fingers to remind him of what the French could do.

Juliette marched up to the first hackney coach she saw, opened the door and climbed inside. "Take me to number 32 Soho Square."

The driver leaned over to peer in the window. "Eh?"

Her arms crossed, she repeated the address.

Beneath the brim of his cap, the man's already squinty eyes narrowed even more. "What you goin' there for?"

"I do not think it is any of your business."

The man smirked. "Bold hussy, ain't ya? Show me the brass first."

"You will be paid when I arrive, not before. That is the usual way, is it not?"

Even if she'd never yet ridden in a hackney, Juliette was sure about that. She thought the driver might still refuse, until his fat lips curved up beneath his bulbous nose. "If you don't have the money, there's another way you can pay me, little Froggy."

She put her hand on the latch. "I would rather walk," she declared, which was quite true.

He sniffed. "I'll drive ya—but I'd better get paid when I get there, or I'll have you before a magistrate," he muttered before he disappeared.

With the crack of a whip, the hackney lurched into motion. As it rumbled along the cobblestone streets, the enormity of what she was doing began to dawn on Juliette. She was going to a town house in Soho in a coach she couldn't pay for, to ask a British nobleman to come to her lodgings, to help a man she didn't know, who had been attacked and robbed by four ruffians in an alley.

What if Lord Bromwell didn't believe her? What if he wouldn't even come to the door? What if the driver didn't get his money? He could have her arrested, and she could guess how that would go. It wasn't easy being French in Wellington's London even when she kept to herself and quietly went about her business.

Biting her lip with dismay, she looked out the window at the people they passed, instinctively seeking Georges's familiar face. She had been looking for him for months, to no avail, yet she would not give up hope.

The buildings began to change, becoming newer and finer, although even she knew Soho wasn't as fashionable as it had been once. Now the haute ton lived in Mayfair.

The haughty, arrogant haute ton, full of men like Sir Douglas Drury, who had seemed so vulnerable and innocent when he was asleep and who had kissed with such tenderness, only to turn into a cold, haughty ogre when he was awake.

He must not remember that kiss. Or perhaps he did, and was ashamed of himself—as he should be, if he'd been trying to take advantage of her after she had helped him.

As for speaking French, most of the English gentry knew French, although he spoke it better than most. Indeed, he had sounded as if he'd lived his whole life in France.

The hackney rolled to a stop outside a town house across from a square with a statue in it. Though narrow, the front was imposing, with a fanlight over the door and a very ornate window above.

Taking a deep breath and summoning her courage, she got out of the coach.

"Mind, I want my money," the driver loudly declared as she walked up to the door.

Juliette ignored him and knocked. The door was immediately opened by a middle-aged footman in green, red and gold livery, with a powdered wig on his head.

He ran a puzzled and censorious gaze over her. "If you're seeking employment, you should know better than to come to the front door."

"I am not seeking employment. Is this the home of Sir Joseph Banks?"

"It is," the footman suspiciously replied. "What do you want?"

"Is Lord Bromwell here?"

The man's brows rose, suggesting that he was, and that the footman was surprised she knew it.

"I have been sent by Sir Douglas Drury," she explained. "He requires Lord Bromwell's assistance immediately."

"And somebody's gotta pay me!" the driver called out.

Juliette flushed, but met the footman's querying gaze undaunted. "Please, I must speak with Lord Bromwell. It is urgent."

The footman ran his gaze over her. "You're French."

She felt the blush she couldn't prevent. She was not ashamed to be French; nevertheless, in London, it made things…difficult. "Yes, I am."

Instead of animosity, however, she got the other reaction her nationality tended to invoke. He gave her a smile that wasn't quite a leer, but made her uncomfortable nonetheless. "All right. Step inside, miss."

"I ain't leavin' till I been paid!" the driver shouted.

The footman ran a scornful gaze over the beefy fellow, then closed the door behind her. Juliette prepared to fend off an unwelcome pinch or caress, or to silence him with a sharp retort. Fortunately, perhaps because of the person she had come to summon, the footman made no rude remark and didn't try to touch her.

"If you'll wait in the porter's room, miss," he said, showing her into a narrow room that was not very bright, even though the sun was shining, "I'll take your message to his lordship."

"Thank you."

He gave her a bold wink and said, "If only I was rich, what I wouldn't do with you."

At least he hadn't touched or insulted her, she thought as he pulled the door shut. Nor did she have long to wait in the cramped room that seemed full of furniture, although there was only two chairs, a table and a large lamp. Almost at once the door flew open and a slender young man stood on the threshold, his face full of concern. "I'm Lord Bromwell. What's happened to Drury?"

He was younger than she'd expected, good-looking in an average sort of way, and well-dressed as she would expect a nobleman to be, although more plainly than most. His morning coat was dark, his trousers buff, his boots black and his waistcoat a subdued blue. His brown hair was well cut, and his face was tanned, as if he'd spent the summer months in the country, riding in the sun.

"I am Juliette Bergerine. Sir Douglas has been attacked and injured near my home. He sent me to bring you."

"Good God!" Lord Bromwell gasped before he turned and started to call for the footman. Then he hesitated and asked, "How did you get here?"

"In a hackney coach. It is still outside."

"Excellent!" he cried. "I rode my horse instead of taking my phaeton. If we take the hackney, we can go together."

His forehead immediately wrinkled with a frown. "Damn! I don't have my medical kit."

"Are you a doctor?"

"I'm a naturalist."

She had no idea what that was.

"I study spiders, not people. Well, it can't be helped. I'll have to do what I can without it. Come along, Miss Bergerine. If I know Drury, and I do, he's probably a lot worse off than he's letting on."

Chapter Two

Should have foreseen that coming to my aid under such circumstances might have serious consequences for her, as well. Brix would probably say the blow to my head has addled my wits. Maybe it has, because I keep thinking there is something more I should remember about that night.

—from the journal of Sir Douglas Drury

When the surly driver saw Juliette leave the town house with Lord Bromwell, he sat up straight and became the very image of fawning acquiescence, even after she told him he was to take them back to Spitalfields.

Lord Bromwell likewise made no comment. Nor did he express any surprise as he joined her inside the coach.

Perhaps the arrogant Sir Douglas often came to that part of London to sport. He would not be the only rich man to do so, and the pity she had felt for him diminished even more.

As the hackney began to move, Lord Bromwell

leaned forward, his hands clasped. "Tell me about Drury's injuries."

She did the best she could, noticing how intensely Lord Bromwell listened, as if with his whole body and not just his ears. He seemed intelligent as well as concerned—a far cry from the dandies who strolled along Bond Street annoying Madame de Pomplona's customers.

When Juliette finished, he murmured, "Could be a concussion. If he's awake, I doubt it's a life-threatening head injury."

It had never occurred to her that the cut and the bump, even if he'd lost consciousness, could be fatal. She'd had just such an injury herself years ago, striking a barn post while playing with Georges.

Lord Bromwell gave her a reassuring smile. "I wouldn't worry too much about Drury. He's got a head of iron. Once when we were children, he got hit with a cricket bat and was unconscious for hours. Came to and asked for cake and wasn't a bit the worse for wear."

She managed a smile in return. She didn't like Sir Douglas Drury, but she didn't want him dead, especially in her room! She would be lucky if she weren't accused of murder if that happened.

"So except for his head, he wasn't hurt anywhere else? No other bleeding or bruising?"

"There was no blood," Juliette replied. "As for bruises, I could not see through his clothes, my lord."

Lord Bromwell's face reddened. "No, no, I suppose not."

"His hands…his fingers have been damaged, I think, but not last night."

Drury's friend shook his head. "No, not last night.

A few years ago. They were broken and didn't mend properly."

She also wanted to ask if Sir Douglas was in the habit of visiting Spitalfields, but refrained. What did it matter if he was or not?

"It's very kind of you to help him," Lord Bromwell offered after another moment. "I keep telling him to watch where he's going, but he gets thinking and doesn't pay any attention. He takes long walks when he can't sleep, you see. Or when he's got a brief. He can't write because of the damage to his fingers, so he can't make notes. He says walking helps him get everything ordered and organized in his head."

Then perhaps he had not come to her neighborhood looking for a woman or to gamble.

The coach jerked to a stop, and as Lord Bromwell stepped down onto the street and ordered the driver to wait, Juliette tried not to be embarrassed, although her lodging house, like most in this part of town, looked as if it were held together by sawdust and rusty nails.

Lord Bromwell paid the cabbie, then held out his hand to help her disembark, as if she were a lady instead of a French seamstress. A few ragged children played near the entrance to the alley and two women were washing clothes in murky water in wooden tubs. They scowled when they saw her and began to exchange heated whispers.

A group of men idling near the corner stamped their feet, their eyes fixed on Lord Bromwell as if contemplating how much money he might be carrying or the worth of his clothes. A poor crossing sweeper, more ragged than the children, leaned on his broom watching them, his eyes dull from hunger and his mouth open, showing that he had but two teeth left.

She quickly led Lord Bromwell inside, away from that driver and the people on the street, as well as those she was sure were peering out of grimy windows. No doubt they were all making their own guesses as to what such a finely attired young man was doing with her, especially going to her room.

"Take care, my lord," Juliette warned as they started up the creaking staircase. The inside of the tenement house was as bad as the rest. It was as dark as a tomb and smelled of too many people in close quarters, as well as the food they ate.

"Have no fear, Miss Bergerine," Lord Bromwell good-naturedly replied. "I've been in worse places in my travels."

She wasn't sure if he was just saying that for her benefit, but was grateful nonetheless. He was truly a gentleman, unlike the man who awaited them. No doubt if she had come to this man's aid, he would have behaved better.

She opened the door to her room and stood aside to let Lord Bromwell pass.

"Ah, Buggy! Good of you to come," she heard Sir Douglas say.

What had he called Lord Bromwell?

She entered her room, to find Sir Douglas Drury sitting on her bed, as calm and composed as if he had just dropped by for a drink or a game of chance.

"I should have known it would take more than a blow to the head to ruffle you," Lord Bromwell said with a relieved smile as he went to his friend. "Still, that's a nasty lump and you can't fool me completely. You're sitting up so straight, I'd wager you've got a broken rib."

"I don't believe it's broken," Sir Douglas replied

with barely a glance in Juliette's direction. "Cracked, perhaps, and likely I've got a hell of a bruise."

Ignoring him in turn, Juliette moved to the side of the room and took off her bonnet. Now that Lord Bromwell was here, there was nothing more for her to do except— *Mon Dieu,* she'd forgotten all about her work!

She would have to say she had fallen ill. She hadn't missed a day yet for any reason and wouldn't get paid for this one, but surely Madame de Pomplona wouldn't dismiss her if she said she'd been sick.

Juliette hoped not, anyway, as she returned her bonnet to the chest.

Out of the corner of her eyes she saw Lord Bromwell put his hand to his friend's right side and press.

The barrister jumped. "Damn it!"

"Sorry, but that's the only way I can tell if you've broken a bone," Lord Bromwell replied. "You're right. The rib's not broken, although it could be cracked. I'll bandage you before we leave, just in case. I wouldn't want anything to get jostled before you can be seen by your own doctor."

Lord Bromwell turned to Juliette. "Do you have any extra linen?"

She shook her head. Did it look as if she had linen—or anything—to spare?

"An old petticoat, perhaps?"

"I have only the chemise I am wearing."

"Oh," he murmured, blushing again.

"Buy her damn chemise so I can go home," Sir Douglas growled.

Lord Bromwell gave Juliette a hopeful smile. "Would that be possible?"

She didn't doubt he could afford to pay well, and she could always make a new one. *"Oui."*

He pulled out a tooled leather wallet and extracted a pound note. "I hope this is enough."

"*Oui.*" It was more than ample. Now all that remained was to remove the chemise he had purchased.

"Turn your back, Buggy, to give her some privacy," Sir Douglas muttered. "I'll stare at the floor, which will likely collapse in a year or two."

She would have expected Lord Bromwell to realize why she'd hesitated before Sir Douglas did and was surprised he had not. Nevertheless, keeping a wary eye on both gentlemen who looked away, she quickly doffed her dress and her chemise, then pulled the former back on.

She held the latter out to Lord Bromwell. "Thank you," he said as Sir Douglas raised his eyes.

She had the sudden uncomfortable feeling that he was imagining what she'd look like dressed only in the flimsy white garment.

Even more uncomfortable was the realization that she wasn't as bothered by that idea as she should be. If she were to be attracted to either of the men in her room, should it not be the kind, gentlemanly one?

Except that he had not needed her help, or spoken French like a native, or kissed her as if he loved her.

"Now then," Lord Bromwell said briskly, breaking into her ruminations. He had finished tearing her chemise into strips. "Off with your shirt."

Sir Douglas glanced at Juliette as if reluctant to remove it when she was in the room.

"If it is modesty that is hindering you, Sir Douglas," she said with a hint of amusement at this unexpected bashfulness, "I shall turn my back."

"It is not modesty that prevents me from taking off my shirt," he coolly replied. "It's pain."

"Oh, sorry!" Lord Bromwell cried. "I'll help."

Sir Douglas quirked a brow at Juliette. "Perhaps Miss Bergerine would oblige."

What kind of woman did he think she was? "I will not!"

"My loss, I'm sure. Well, then, Buggy, it'll have to be you."

With a disgusted sniff, Juliette grabbed the wooden stool, carried it across the room and set it under the window, determined to stare out at the brick wall across the alley until they were gone.

"I thought you were going to bandage me, not bind me like a mummy," Sir Douglas complained.

"You want it done properly, don't you?"

Juliette couldn't resist. She had to look. She glanced over her shoulder, to see Lord Bromwell wrapping a strip of fabric around Sir Douglas's lean and muscular torso. His shoulders were truly broad, not like some gentlemen who had padding in their jackets, and there was a scar that traversed his chest from the left shoulder almost to his navel.

"Not a pretty sight, am I, Miss Bergerine?"

She immediately turned back to the window and the brick wall opposite. "If that scar is from the war, you are not the only one who suffered. My father and brother died fighting for Napoleon, and my other brother… But I will not speak of them to *you*."

"I've not bandaged you too tight, have I?" Lord Bromwell asked quietly a little later.

"I can still breathe. But I must say, if this is how you tended to your shipmates, I'm surprised any of them survived."

Sir Douglas had to be the most ungrateful man alive, and she would be glad when he was gone, Juliette decided.

"They were happy enough to have my help when they got sick or injured," Lord Bromwell replied without rancor.

He truly was a kind and patient fellow.

"There. All done. Now let's get your shirt back on. Right, lift your arm a little more. That's a good lad."

"Need I remind you I am neither a child nor mentally deficient?"

"So stop complaining and do as you're told."

"I am not complaining. I'm attempting to get you to stop talking to me as if I were an infant."

"Then stop pouting like one."

"Sir Douglas Drury does not *pout*."

Juliette stifled a smile. He might not pout, but he wasn't being cooperative, either—like an irascible child.

"Do I amuse you, Miss Bergerine?" Sir Douglas asked in a cold, calm voice.

She swiveled slowly on the stool. Lord Bromwell stood beside the injured man, who was now fully dressed, his box coat slung over his shoulders like a cape. He had his arm around his friend and leaned on him for support.

"No, you do not," she replied evenly.

Sir Douglas continued to stare at her as he said, "Buggy, will you be so good as to pay Miss Bergerine for her time and trouble, as well as any lost wages she may have incurred? Naturally I'll repay you as soon as we get to my chambers."

Lord Bromwell once again took out his wallet and pulled a pound note from within.

"She'll need to replace that rag she's wearing, too. I bled on her right shoulder."

Juliette glanced at her dress. There was indeed a red

stain that hadn't been there before. But her dress was hardly a rag. It was clean and well mended.

Lord Bromwell obediently pulled out another bill.

"And some more for the loss of potatoes."

His brows rose in query. "Potatoes?"

"Apparently she used them to chase away my attackers."

Lord Bromwell laughed as he pulled out another bill. "Excellent idea, Miss Bergerine. It reminds me of the time I had to toss a few rocks to keep several unfriendly South Sea islanders at bay while my men and I got back to the boats."

"I trust that sum will be sufficient, Miss Bergerine?" Sir Douglas asked.

She took the money from Lord Bromwell and tucked it into her bodice. "It is enough. *Merci.*"

"Then, my lord, I believe we've taken up enough of this young woman's time."

"Farewell, Miss Bergerine, and thank you," Lord Bromwell said with genuine sincerity. "We're both grateful for your help. Aren't we, Drury?"

Sir Douglas looked as if he were anything but grateful. Nevertheless, he addressed her in flawless French. "You have my thanks, *mademoiselle.* I am in your debt."

"*C'est dommage,*" she replied, all the while wondering how his friend put up with him. "Goodbye."

The moment they were in the hackney, Buggy exploded. "Good God, Drury! Even if she's French, I expected better from you. Couldn't you have at least been a *little* polite?" He struck the roof of the coach with a hard smack. "She could have let you be killed or left you lying in a puddle."

Drury winced as the vehicle lurched into motion. "Obviously I am not at my best when suffering from a head wound and cracked ribs. I do note that she was well paid for her efforts."

Buggy leaned back against the squabs with an aggravated sigh. "You're damn lucky she cared enough to help you. What were you doing in this part of town, anyway?"

"I went for a walk."

"And got careless."

"I was thinking."

"And not paying any attention to where you were going. Any notion who attacked you?"

"No idea. However, since I am now minus my wallet, I assume robbery was the motive. I shall duly report this unfortunate event to the Bow Street Runners."

"Well, one thing's for certain. You've got to be more careful. Hire a carriage or try to confine your walks to Lincoln's Inn Fields."

"I'll try, and next time, if I am rescued by a woman, I shall attempt to be more gracious."

Buggy frowned. "You could hardly be any less. Honestly, I don't know what women see in you half the time."

Sir Douglas Drury, who was also famous for skills that had nothing to do with the law, gave his friend a small, sardonic smile. "Neither do I."

A fortnight later, Juliette decided to go the butcher's and buy a meat pie, the one thing she liked about British food and now could afford because of the money Lord Bromwell had given her. That windfall had made it worth enduring Madame de Pomplona's annoyance when she made her excuses for missing a day of work.

"And during the Little Season, too!" her employer had cried in her Yorkshire accent, her Greek name being as false as the hair beneath her cap.

Fortunately, that meant she had too much business to dismiss a seamstress who had, after all, only missed one day of work in almost six months.

Anticipating a good meal, Juliette started to hum as she crossed a lane and went around a cart full of apples.

The day was fair for autumn, warm and sunny, and she might actually get home before dark. The street was as crowded as all London seemed to be, so it was perhaps no wonder she hadn't been able to find Georges. It was like trying to find a pin in a haystack.

No, she must not give up hope. He might be here, and she must keep searching.

In the next instant, and before she could cry out, a hand covered her mouth and an arm went around her waist, pulling her backward into an alley.

Panic threatened to overwhelm her as she kicked and twisted and struggled with all her might to get free, just as she had all those times when Gaston LaRoche had grabbed her in the barn.

"What's Sir Douglas Drury want with the likes o' you, eh?" a low male voice growled in her ear as his grip tightened. "Got the finest ladies in England linin' up for a poke, he does. What's he need some French slut for?"

Desperate to escape, she bit down on the flesh between his thumb and index finger as hard as she could. He grunted in pain. His grasp loosened and she shoved her elbow into a soft stomach. As he stumbled back, she gathered up her skirts and ran out of the alley. Dodging a wagon filled with cabbages, she dashed across the street, then up another, pushing her way through the crowds, paying no heed to people's curses or angry words.

She got a stitch in her side, but didn't stop. Pressing her hand where it hurt, she continued to run through the streets until she could run no more. Panting, she leaned against a building, her mind a jumble of fear and dismay.

That man must have seen her helping Sir Douglas, which meant he knew where she lived. What if he was waiting for her there? She didn't dare go home.

Where else could she go? Who would help her?

Lord Bromwell! Except that she had no idea where he lived.

Sir Douglas Drury of Lincoln's Inn would have chambers there. And was it not because of him that she'd been attacked?

He must help her. Ungrateful wretch that he was, he must.

Besides, she realized as she choked back a sob of dismay, she had no one else to turn to in this terrible city.

Chapter Three

He was more upset than I've ever seen, although I suppose to the young woman and those who don't know him as well as we, he appeared quite calm. But I assure you, he was really quite rattled.
—from The Collected Letters of
Lord Bromwell

"Are you quite sure you're in a fit state to attend a dinner party?" the elderly Mr. Edgar asked as he nimbly tied Drury's cravat. "It's only been a fortnight. I think it might be best if you didn't go. I'm sure Mr. Smythe-Medway and Lady Fanny will understand."

"I'm quite recovered."

"Now, sir, no lying to me," Mr. Edgar said with a hurt air and the candor of a servant of long standing. "You are *not* completely recovered."

"Oh, very well," Drury admitted with more good humor than Miss Bergerine would ever have believed he possessed. "I'm still a little sore. But it's only a dinner party at Brix's, and I don't want to be cooped up in these chambers another night. I could, I suppose, go for a walk instead…"

Mr. Edgar's reflection in the looking glass revealed his horrified dismay at that proposal. "You wouldn't! Not after—"

"No, I wouldn't," Drury hastened to reassure the man who'd been like a father to him all these years, for he was *not* ungrateful, no matter what some French hoyden might think. If he had been rude or insolent to Miss Bergerine, she had her countrymen to blame.

Mr. Edgar reached for a brush and attacked the back of Drury's black dress coat as if he were currying a horse. Drury, penitently, kept silent.

As a general rule, a dinner party held little appeal for him, unless it was attended by his good friends. Then he could be sure of intelligent and amusing conversation rather than gossip, and nobody would hold it against him if he were silent.

At other parties, he was too often expected to expound on the state of the courts, or talk about his latest case, something he never did. It was worse if there were female guests. Most women either looked at him as if they expected him to attack them, or as if they hoped he would.

Just as Mr. Edgar pronounced him suitable to leave, a fist pounded on the outer door of his chambers, and an all-too-familiar female voice called out his name.

Juliette Bergerine's shouts could wake the dead— not to mention disturbing the other barristers with chambers here. And what the devil could *she* want?

"Saints preserve us!" Mr. Edgar cried as he tossed the brush aside and started for the door.

Drury hurried past him. He fumbled for a moment

with the latch, silently cursing his stiff fingers, but at last got it open.

Miss Bergerine came charging into his chambers as if pursued by a pack of hounds.

"I was attacked!" she cried in French. "A man grabbed me in a lane and pulled me into an alley." A disgusted expression came to her flushed features and gleaming eyes. "He thinks I am your *whore*. He said you had other women, so what did you want me for?"

Shaken by her announcement as well as her disheveled state, Drury fought to remain calm. She reminded him of another Frenchwoman he'd known all too well who'd been prone to hysterics. "Obviously, the man was—"

"My God, I never should have helped you!" she cried before he could finish. "First you treat me like a servant even though I saved your life and now I am believed to be your whore and *my* life is in danger!"

Drury strode to the cabinet and poured her a whiskey. "It's regrettable—"

"Regrettable?" she cried indignantly. "*Regrettable?* Is that all you have to say? He was going to kill me! If I had not bitten him and run away, I could be lying dead in an alley! *Mon Dieu,* it was more than *regrettable!*"

She'd bitten the lout? Thank God she'd kept her head and got away.

He handed the whiskey to her. "Drink this," he said, hoping it would calm her.

She glared at him, then at the glass before downing the contents in a gulp. She coughed and started to choke. "What *was* that?" she demanded.

"A very old, very expensive, very good Scotch whiskey," he said, gesturing for her to sit. "Now perhaps we can discuss this in a rational manner."

"You are a cold man, *monsieur!*" she declared as she flounced onto a chair.

"I don't see that getting overly emotional is going to be of any use."

He sat opposite her on a rather worn armchair that might not be pretty or elegant, but was very comfortable. "I *am* sorry this happened to you, Miss Bergerine. However, it never occurred to me that any enemies I might have would concern themselves with you. If I had, I would have taken steps to ensure your safety."

She set down the whiskey glass on the nearest table with a hearty and skeptical sniff. "So you say *now.*"

He wouldn't let her indignant exclamations disturb him. "However, since it has happened, you were quite right to come to me. Now I must consider what steps to take to see that it doesn't happen again."

He became aware of Mr. Edgar standing by the door, an avidly interested expression on his lined face.

He'd forgotten all about his valet.

On the other hand, it was a good thing he was there, or who could say what Miss Bergerine might accuse him of?

Not that there would be any merit in such accusations, as anyone who knew him would realize. Although Juliette Bergerine was pretty and attractive in a lively sort of way, such a volatile woman roused too many unhappy memories to ever appeal to him.

The sort of women with whom he had affairs was very well-known, and they were not poor Frenchwomen.

"If you can provide me with details," he said, "such as the location and a description of the man who attacked you, I shall take the information to the Bow

Street Runners, as well as another associate of mine who's skilled at investigation. I've already got him looking for the men who attacked me. This fellow could very well be one of them.

"Until the guilty parties are apprehended, however, we have another problem—where to keep you."

"*Keep* me?" she repeated, her brows lowering with suspicion.

He shouldn't have used that word. It had a meaning he most definitely didn't intend. "I mean where you can safely reside. I would offer to put you up in a hotel, except that people might suppose our relationship is indeed intimate.

"As that is most certainly not true, I shall have the associate I've mentioned provide men to protect you. Since this is necessary because you came to my aid, naturally I shall pay for their services."

"You mean they will guard me, as if I am your prisoner?"

He tried not to sound frustrated with this most frustrating foreigner. "They will *protect* you. As you have so forcefully pointed out, I have put you at risk. I don't intend to do so again. Or did you come here only to berate me?"

He waited for her to argue or chastise him again, but to his surprise, her steadfast gaze finally faltered and she softly said, "I had nowhere else to go for help."

She sounded lost then, and vulnerable, and unexpectedly sad. Lonely, even—a feeling with which he was unfortunately familiar.

"Is something the matter with your hearing? I've been knocking for an age," Buggy said as he walked into the room.

Mr. Edgar, who had been riveted by Miss Bergerine's tirade, gave a guilty start and hurried to take Buggy's hat and coat, then slipped silently from the room.

Meanwhile, Buggy was staring at Drury's visitor as if he'd never seen a woman before. "Miss Bergerine! What are you... I beg your pardon. It's a pleasure, of course, but..."

As his words trailed off in understandable confusion, Drury silently cursed. He'd forgotten all about Brix and Fanny's dinner party, and that Buggy had offered to bring round his carriage to spare him the trouble of hiring one for the evening.

"Miss Bergerine had an unfortunate encounter with a man under the delusion she and I have an intimate relationship," he explained, getting to his feet. "Fortunately, Miss Bergerine fought him off and came to me for assistance."

"You fought the scoundrel off all by yourself?" Buggy cried, regarding Miss Bergerine with an awed mixture of respect and admiration. "You really are a most remarkable woman."

That was a bit much. "The question is, what are we to do with her? She can't go home, and she can't stay here."

"No, no, of course not. You'd be fined."

"There are more reasons than that," Drury replied, aware of Miss Bergerine's bright eyes watching them, and trying to ignore her. "I'd pay for her to stay in a hotel, but I don't have to tell you what the ton and the popular press would make of that."

"I agree a hotel is out of the question, and we can't let her go back to her room," Buggy concurred. "A child could break into that."

Wearing evening attire that made him look less like

the studious, serious fellow he was and more like one of the town dandies, Buggy leaned against the mantel, regardless of the possibility of wrinkling his well-tailored coat. "Given this new attack, which tells me you have some very dangerous and determined enemies indeed, I don't think you're quite safe here either, Drury. These rooms are too public, too well-known. Anybody could come here claiming to be a solicitor seeking to engage your services, and if he's well dressed, who would question him?"

"I'm capable of defending myself."

"As you did in the alley?"

Before Drury could reply, Buggy held out his strong, capable hands in a placating gesture. "Be reasonable, Drury. You know as well as I that this place is no fortress, and while I'm sure you can fight as well as ever against one man, you're not the swordsman or boxer you were."

No, he was not, and that observation didn't do much to assuage Drury's wounded pride.

Mr. Edgar appeared in the door with a tray in his hands. On it was a plate of thickly sliced, fine white bread, some jam and a steaming pot of tea. "For Miss Bergerine, sir," he said as he set it on the table.

"Please, have some refreshment," Drury said to her, waving at the food.

Miss Bergerine didn't hesitate. She spread the jam and consumed the bread with a speed that made Drury suspect she must not have eaten for some time. Her manners weren't as terrible as one might expect, given her humble origins and obvious hunger.

Mr. Edgar watched her eat with such satisfaction, you'd think he'd baked the bread himself. He also gave Drury a glance that suggested a lecture on the duties one owed to a guest, in spite of her unwelcome and unorthodox arrival, would soon be forthcoming.

Buggy suddenly brightened, as if he'd just discovered a new species of spider. "I have it! You must both stay at my town house. God knows there's plenty of room, and servants to keep any villains at bay."

That was a damn foolish idea. "Need I point out, Buggy, that the ton will make a meal out of the news that I've moved into your house with some unknown Frenchwoman? They'll probably accuse you of keeping a bawdy house."

His friend laughed. "On the other hand, Millstone will be delighted. He thinks my reputation is far too saintly."

"Obviously your butler hasn't read your book." Drury thought of another potential difficulty. "Your father wouldn't be pleased. It *is* his house, after all."

Buggy flushed. "I don't think you need worry about him. He's safely ensconced in the country playing the squire. Now I'm not taking no for an answer. You can come here during the day as necessary, but at night, you stay in North Audley Street."

Drury's imagination seemed to have deserted him in his hour of need, for he could think of no better solution.

"Upon further consideration, Miss Bergerine," Drury said, not hiding his reluctance, "I concur with Lord Bromwell's suggestion. Until those ruffians are caught and imprisoned, his house would be the safest place for you."

She looked from one man to the other before she spoke. "Am I to have no say in where I go?"

Buggy blushed like a naughty schoolboy. "Oh, yes, of course."

"Yet you talk as if I am not here," she chided. "And while I am grateful for your concern, Lord Bromwell, is it not Sir Douglas's duty to help me? I would not be in danger but for his carelessness."

Drury fought to keep a rein on his rising temper. "You chastise me for leaving you in danger, yet now, when we seek to keep you safe, you protest. What would you have us do, Miss Bergerine? Call out the army to protect you?"

"I would have you treat me as a person, not a dog or a horse you own. I would have you address *me,* not one another. I am here, and not deaf, or stupid. And I would have *you* take responsibility for the predicament I am in."

If she'd cried or screamed, Drury would have been able to overlook her criticism and wouldn't have felt nearly as bad as he did, because she was right. They *had* been ignoring her, and it really should be up to him to help her, not his friend.

However, it was Buggy who apologized. "I'm sorry if we've been rather high-handed, Miss Bergerine. The protective male instinct, I fear. Nevertheless, I hope you'll do me the honor of staying in my humble abode until we can find out who's behind these attacks."

"And if I don't invite you to *my* town house, it's because I don't possess one," Drury said. "If you have another suggestion as to how I may assist you, I'd be happy to hear it."

Miss Bergerine colored. "Unfortunately, I do not." She turned to Buggy, her expression softening. "I'm sorry if I spoke rudely, my lord. I do appreciate your help."

"Then please, won't you do me the honor of accepting my hospitality?" Buggy asked, as if she were the Queen of England and nobody else was in the room.

Drury ignored that unpleasant sensation. He was also sure she was going to accept, until she didn't.

"It is very kind of you to offer, my lord, but I cannot," she said. "I am an honorable woman. I may not belong to the haute ton, but I have a reputation I value as much as any lady, a reputation that will suffer if I accept your invitation.

"I also have a job. Unlike the fine ladies you know, I must earn my living, and if I do not go to work, I will lose that job, and with it the means to live."

"Since it's apparently my fault you'll be unable to work," Drury said, "I'm willing to provide appropriate compensation. As for keeping your job, if you tell me who employs you, I shall see that she's informed you are visiting a sick relative and will return as soon as possible."

Miss Bergerine wasn't satisfied. "You do not know Madame de Pomplona. She will not hold my place."

Having agreed to Buggy's plan, he wasn't about to let her complicate matters further. "I am acquainted with an excellent solicitor, Miss Bergerine. I'm sure James St. Claire will be happy to make it clear to her that there will be serious legal repercussions if she doesn't continue to employ you."

"There is still the matter of my reputation, Sir Douglas, which has already been damaged."

God help him, did she want compensation for that, too? He'd suspect she'd never really been attacked and had concocted this story to wring money from him, except that she'd been genuinely frightened when she'd burst into his chambers. Part of his success in court came from being able to tell when people were being truthful or not, and he was confident she hadn't been feigning her fear.

"I know!" Buggy declared, his blue-gray eyes bright with delight. "What if we say that Miss Bergerine is your cousin, Drury? Naturally, she couldn't live with you in your chambers, so I've invited you both to stay with me until you can find more suitable lodgings for her, and a chaperone. After all, the ton is well aware your mother was French and you had relatives there before the Terror."

Miss Bergerine regarded Drury with blatant surprise. "Your mother was French?"

"Yes," Drury snapped, wishing Buggy hadn't mentioned that.

On the other hand… "That might work," he allowed.

"You are saying I can pretend to be related to Sir Douglas?" Miss Bergerine cautiously inquired.

Buggy grinned, looking like a little boy who'd been given a present. "Yes. It shouldn't be too difficult to make people accept it. Just scowl a lot and don't talk very much."

Miss Bergerine laughed, exposing very fine, white teeth. "That does not sound so very difficult."

"Except for not talking much," Drury muttered, earning him a censorious look from Buggy and an annoyed one from her.

Why should he be upset by what some hot-tempered Frenchwoman thought of him? He was Sir Douglas Drury, and he had plenty of other women seeking his favors, whether he wanted them or not.

Miss Bergerine turned to Buggy with a warm and unexpectedly charming smile. "Because I think you are truly a kindhearted, honorable gentleman, Lord

Bromwell, I will accept your offer, and gladly. *Merci. Merci beaucoup.*"

And for one brief moment, Drury wished he had a town house in London.

Chapter Four

Edgar looked about to have an attack of apoplexy. Didn't want to drag Buggy into the situation, either, but he didn't give me much of a choice.
—from the journal of Sir Douglas Drury

A short time later, Juliette waited in the foyer of Lord Bromwell's town house. On the other side of the entrance hall, Lord Bromwell spoke with his obviously surprised butler, explaining what she was doing there. She would guess Millstone was about forty-five. He was also bald and as stiff as a soldier on parade. The liveried, bewigged footman who had opened the door to them stood nearby, staring at her with unabashed curiosity, while Sir Douglas Drury, grim and impatient, loitered near the porter's room.

Trying to ignore him, she turned her attention to her surroundings. She had never been in a Mayfair mansion, or any comparable house before. The entrance was immense, and richly decorated with columns of marble, with pier glass in the spaces in between. The floor was likewise marble, polished and smooth, and a large, round mahogany table dominated the center of the space, with a beautiful Oriental vase in the middle of it full of exotic blooms that scented the air. A hanging staircase led to the rooms above.

She tried not to feel like a beggar, even if her hair was a mess and her gown torn and soiled, her shoes thick and clumsy. After all, she reminded herself, she was in danger because of Lord Bromwell's friend. It wasn't as if she'd thrown herself on the genial nobleman's mercy for personal gain.

"Jim, is something wrong with your eyes that you are unable to stop staring?" Sir Douglas asked the footman in a voice loud enough that she could hear, but not Lord Bromwell and the butler.

The poor young man snapped to attention and blushed to the roots of his powdered tie wig.

She didn't want to be the cause of any trouble here, for anyone. However, she couldn't expect a man like Sir Douglas Drury to think about how anyone else might feel. He clearly cared for no one's feelings but his own—if he had any at all.

She could believe he did not, except for that kiss.

That must have been an aberration, a temporary change from his usual self, brought on by the blow to his head.

When Lord Bromwell and his butler finished their discussion, the butler called for the footman and said something to him. She hoped he wasn't chastising the poor lad, too!

"You're to have the blue bedroom, Miss Bergerine, which overlooks the garden," Lord Bromwell said, approaching her with a smile. "I hope you'll be comfortable. Ask Millstone or the housekeeper, Mrs. Tunbarrow, if you require anything. A maid will be sent to help you tonight."

A maid? She'd never had a maid in her life and wouldn't know what to do with one. "Oh, that will not be necessary. I don't need anyone's help to get undressed."

Sir Douglas made an odd sort of noise, although whether it was a snort of derision or a laugh, she couldn't say. And she didn't want to know.

"Very well, if that's what you'd prefer," Lord Bromwell said, as if he hadn't heard his friend. "If you'll be so good as to follow Millstone, he'll show you to your room."

"Thank you, my lord."

She started toward the butler, who waited at the foot of the stairs.

"We'd better have Jones drive quickly," she heard Lord Bromwell say to his friend, "although I'm sure Brix and Fanny won't be upset if we're late."

Juliette checked her steps. Fanny? Could that have been the name Sir Douglas murmured when he was injured? And she was the wife of a friend?

What did it matter to her if he had whispered the name of his friend's wife? What if they were even lovers?

Sir Douglas Drury could have love affairs with every lady in London, married or not, and it wouldn't make a bit of difference to her.

When Juliette awoke the next morning, she knew exactly where she was, and why. At least, she knew she was in Lord Bromwell's town house at his invitation, so she would be safe. It had been too dark to see much of the actual room to which she'd been led by the butler, who had used a candelabrum to light the way.

Once Millstone was gone, she'd taken off her worn, muddy shoes, thick, much-mended woolen stockings and her new dress that Lord Bromwell's money had made possible. Then she'd climbed into the soft bed made up with sheets that smelled of lavender.

If she hadn't been utterly exhausted, she would have lain awake for hours, worried about what had happened and what the future might hold. As it was, she'd fallen asleep the instant her head rested on the silk-covered pillow.

Now wide-awake, she surveyed the room and discovered she was in the most beautiful, feminine room she had ever seen or imagined.

The fireplace opposite the bed had pretty Dutch tiles around the opening. The walls were papered in blue and white. Blue velvet draperies covered the windows, matching the canopy and silk coverlet on the bed. The cherrywood bed and armoire standing in a corner gleamed from much polishing and wax. Armchairs upholstered in blue velvet as well as a round pedestal table, had been placed near the hearth. A tall cheval mirror, a dressing table with a smaller looking glass, and a washstand completed the furnishings.

Wondering how long she'd slept—for she could believe it had been several hours—Juliette stretched, then got up. Reveling in the feel of the thick, brightly patterned carpet beneath her feet, she went to one of the windows, drew the drape aside and peeked out, to see that the sun was indeed very high in the sky. Below, there was a small garden with a brick walk and a tree, and what looked like a little ornamental pond.

Wandering over to the dressing table, Juliette sat

and marveled at the silver-handled brush and comb. There was a silver receiver, too, and a delicate little enameled box of gold and blue. She gingerly lifted the lid. It was empty.

There was another box of carved ivory full of ribbons. Another, larger ivory box held an astonishing number of hairpins. She had never been able to afford more than a few at a time.

Like a child with a new toy, Juliette took the ribbons out of the ivory box one by one and spread them on the table. There seemed to be every color of the rainbow. Surely she could use one of the cheaper, plainer ones....

She picked up the brush and ran it through her hair. Doing so felt wonderful, and she spent several minutes brushing her hair before braiding it into one thick strand and binding it with an emerald-green ribbon. Then, using several pins, she wound the braid around her head.

She studied the effect, and her own face, in the mirror—a luxury she'd never had. At the farm she had only the pond for a looking glass and in London she had to be content with surreptitious glimpses of herself in the fitting-room mirrors.

She wasn't homely, but her eyes were too big, and her mouth too wide and full. Her chin was a little too pronounced, too. At least she had good skin. Excellent teeth, as well. And she was very glad to be wearing her new chemise, the linen purchased with the money Lord Bromwell had given her. It made her feel a little less out of place.

Nevertheless, she jumped up as if she'd been caught pilfering when a soft knock sounded on the door.

A young maid dressed in dark brown, with a white cap and apron, peeked into the room. "Oh, you're awake, miss!"

Without waiting for an answer, she nudged the door open and came inside carrying a large tray holding a white china teapot, a cup and some other dishes beneath linen napkins. There was also a little pitcher and three small pots covered with waxed cloth. Juliette could smell fresh bread, and her stomach growled ravenously.

The maid also had a silken dressing gown of brightly patterned greens and blues over her arm.

"Mrs. Tunbarrow thought you might like to eat here this morning, and she thought you'd need this, too. It's one of the viscount's mother's that she doesn't wear anymore," the maid explained as she set the tray on the pedestal table. "Lord Bromwell and Sir Douglas have already eaten. The master's gone off to one of his society meetings—the Linus Society or some such thing, where he can talk about his bugs. Nasty things, spiders, but he loves 'em the way some men love their dogs or horses. Sir Douglas is here, though. I heard him say he didn't have to be at the Old Bailey today. Lucky for him he can pick and choose, I must say."

Never having had a maid, and uncertain how to proceed, Juliette drew the dressing gown on over her chemise. It was soft, slippery and without doubt the most luxurious garment she'd ever worn. She stayed silent as the young woman plumped a cushion on one of the armchairs. "Sit ye here, miss, and have your breakfast while I tidy up a bit."

"Merci," she murmured, wondering if she should ask the maid her name, as she wanted to, or if the servant was to be treated as little more than a piece of furniture. The rare times she'd been summoned to the upper floors of Madame de Pomplona's establishment, the ladies' abigails had been like wraiths, sitting

silent and ignored in the corner on small, hard chairs kept for that purpose.

"I'm Polly, miss," the maid said, solving her dilemma, and apparently not at all disturbed that Juliette was French, although that could be because she was supposed to be Sir Douglas's cousin.

"I'm to be your maid while you're here," the lively young woman continued. "I can arrange your hair, too. I've been doing Lord Bromwell's mother's hair when she's in London, and she's right particular about it. Mrs. Tunbarrow thinks I have a gift."

"That will be lovely," Juliette replied, although she had never had anyone help her dress or do her hair, either.

Her mama had died when she was a baby and she'd never had a sister or a friend to assist her. Most of the time, Papa and Marcel forgot she was even there and even Georges could be neglectful. However, Polly was so obviously proud of her talents and keen to demonstrate them, why not let her?

"It's a terrible thing what happened to you," Polly said as she threw open the drapes covering the tall, narrow windows. "I can't even imagine!"

"It was not pleasant," Juliette agreed as she lifted the first napkin and discovered fresh scones. One of the jars contained strawberry jam, and her mouth began to water as she sat in the soft chair and picked up a knife.

"I tell you, nobody's safe these days. It's all them soldiers left to run amok after the war, isn't it? Still, you'd think a relative of a baronet'd be out of harm's way and not be robbed on the highway and left with only one dress to her name!"

Polly, busy straightening the bed, didn't see Juliette's sharp glance.

Sir Douglas and Lord Bromwell must have concocted this story of a robbery to explain why she had
arrived with no baggage. Thank goodness she had a
new chemise, or what would this maid be thinking?
"Yes, it was most unfortunate."

"And to have your own maid desert you just before
you sailed from France! I would have been too frightened to board, I would."

Clearly they had realized they would have to
explain her lack of companion or chaperone, too.

"I had no other choice. I had no lodgings and my
cousin was expecting me," Juliette lied as she bit into
the scone now spread with strawberry jam. It was so
good, she closed her eyes in ecstasy.

"And a generous cousin he is, too, I must say! It
looks like the Arabian nights in the morning room."

Juliette opened her eyes. "Arabian nights?"

"Lord, yes! There's all sorts of fabrics and caps and
shoes and ribbons. Sir Douglas went out early this
morning and came back with a modiste to make you
some new dresses, and a linen-draper and a silk
mercer, too."

A modiste? *Mon Dieu,* not…!

"Madame de Malanche dresses all the finest ladies,
including the Lady Patronesses of Almack's. And
Lady Abramarle, and Lady Sarah Chelton, who was
the belle of the Season six years ago. I remember Lord
Bromwell's mother thinking she was a bit forward.
And Viscountess Adderly, another good friend of Lord
Bromwell's.

"She writes *novels,*" Polly finished in a scandalized
whisper. "The kind with half-ruined castles and mysterious noblemen running around abducting women."

Relieved that Madame de Pomplona wasn't below,

and not really paying attention to what else Polly said, Juliette swallowed the last of the scone. She hadn't expected Sir Douglas to buy new clothes for her, but if she was to be Sir Douglas's cousin, she supposed she must dress the part. And if so, who else but Sir Douglas should pay, since she was in danger because of him?

"There's a shoemaker and a milliner, too," Polly continued as she made the bed. "It's as if he brought half of Bond Street back with him. I do wish I had a rich cousin like him, miss. Such fabrics and feathers and I don't know what all!"

Perhaps there really was an abundance of such items, Juliette mused, or perhaps the young maid was exaggerating in her excitement. After all, Sir Douglas would hardly spend a fortune on *her.*

Polly finished the bed and looked at the tray. "All finished? You haven't had a drop of tea."

"I do not drink tea."

Polly looked a little nonplussed. "Coffee then? Or hot chocolate? You're to have whatever you like."

"No, thank you." Juliette replied. She'd never had either beverage and was afraid she wouldn't like them. That would be difficult to explain if she'd requested one or the other.

"In that case, I'll fetch your new dress."

"I can get it," Juliette said, rising and heading toward the armoire, where she assumed her new muslin dress, likewise purchased with Lord Bromwell's money, must be hanging. It was no longer on the foot of the bed where she'd laid it last night.

"I don't know what they do in France these days, miss," Polly cried in horrified shock, "but you can't go wandering the house in your chemise!"

"What do you mean?" Juliette asked, confused, as she pulled open the armoire doors.

It was empty. "Where is my new dress?"

"Downstairs, miss."

They must have taken it to wash. "Is it dry already?"

Polly looked at her as if she'd lost her mind. "No, miss. There's a new gown for you. Madame de Melanche brought it. She made it for another customer, but when Sir Douglas told her about your troubles and that you had only an old traveling gown, she brought it along. I'll just run and fetch it—and tell Sir Douglas you're awake."

As the maid bustled out of the room, Juliette returned to the comfortable chair and sat heavily. Sir Douglas had described her new dress as an "old traveling gown"? It might not be of the best fabric, but it was well-made, by her own hands, and pretty and new.

She suddenly felt as she had when she'd first arrived in Calais, an ignorant country bumpkin. Except that she was not. Not anymore. And although she was poor, Sir Douglas had no right to insult her.

The door opened and Polly returned with a day gown of the prettiest sprigged muslin Juliette had ever seen. Delicate kid slippers dangled from her hand, and a pair of white silk stockings hung over her wrist.

These were all for *her?*

Juliette's dismay at Sir Douglas's description of her dress was quickly overcome by the beauty of the new one in Polly's arms. She let the maid help her into it, and the shoes and stockings, too. When she was finished, she went to study her reflection in the cheval glass.

She hardly recognized herself in the fashionable dress with short capped sleeves and high waist, the skirt full and flowing. "I feel like a princess," she murmured in French.

"It *is* pretty, isn't it?" Polly said, understanding the sentiment if not the words. "And you look like a picture, miss, although your hair's a little old-fashioned. Here."

She reached up and pulled a few wispy curls from the braid, so that they rested on Juliette's brow and cheeks. "Isn't that better?"

Juliette nodded in agreement. Perhaps she *could* pass as the cousin of a barrister, at least until Sir Douglas's enemies were captured.

Then she would go back to her old life—something she must remember. This was a dream, and dreams died with the morning.

"If you're finished eating, Sir Douglas said to tell you he's waiting for you in the morning room. I wouldn't keep him waiting much longer if you can help it, Miss Bergerine. He's, um, getting a bit impatient."

Sitting in Buggy's mother's morning room, surrounded by bolts of fabric brought by an anxious linen-draper with a droopy eye and an obsequious silk mercer whose waistcoat was so bright it almost hurt the eyes to look at it, Drury wasn't a bit impatient. He had already lost what patience he possessed, and if Miss Bergerine didn't come down in the next few moments, he'd simply order some dresses, a couple of bonnets and send these people away.

It wasn't just the men keen to sell fabric who were driving him to Boodle's for a stiff drink and some peace. In the north corner of the room decorated in the height of feminine taste, a shoemaker busily finished another pair of slippers, using one of Miss Bergerine's boots for size, the tapping of his hammer like the constant drip of water. A haberdasher kept bringing out more stockings for Drury's approval, and a milliner persisted in trying to cajole him into selecting feathers and laces and trim, bonnets and caps— when she could get a word in between the exuberant declarations of the modiste, who was dressed in the latest vogue, with frills and lace and ribbons galore, and more rouge on her cheeks than an actress on the stage.

Even the most riotous trial in the Old Bailey seemed as orderly as a lending library compared to this carnival. The commotion also roused memories better forgotten, of his mother's extravagance and endless demands, and the quarrels between his parents if his father was at home.

"Now take this taffeta," the linen-draper said, unrolling a length from a bolt as he tried to balance it on his skinny knee, quite obviously mistaking Drury's silence for permission to continue. "The very best quality, this is."

"Taffeta," the mercer sniffed. "Terrible, stiff stuff. This bee-you-tee-ful silk has come all the way from China!" He brought forth a smaller bolt of carmine fabric shot through with golden threads. "This would make the most marvelous gown for a ball, don't you agree, Sir Douglas?"

Despite his annoyance, Drury couldn't help wondering how a gown made of that silk would look on Miss Bergerine.

"And I have the latest patterns from Paris," Madame de Malanche interjected, the plume on her hat bobbing as if it had a life of its own. "I'm sure any cousin of

Sir Douglas Drury's will want to be dressed in the most stylish mode."

As if that plume had been some kind of antenna attuned to the arrival of young women with money to spend, Madame de Malanche abruptly turned to the door and clasped her hands as if beholding a heavenly vision. "Ah, this must be the young lady! *What* a charming girl!"

When Drury turned and looked at Miss Bergerine standing uncertainly in the doorway, he did have to admit that she looked very charming wearing a pretty gown of apple-green, with her hair up and a shy, bashful expression on her face. Indeed, she looked as sweet and innocent as Fanny Epping, now the wife of the Honorable Brixton Smythe-Medway.

That was ridiculous. There was surely no young woman, English or otherwise, less like Fanny than Juliette Bergerine.

Nevertheless, determined to play this role as he had so many others, he rose and went to her, kissing both her cheeks.

She stiffened as his lips brushed her warm, soft skin. No doubt she was surprised—as surprised as he had been by the difference in her attitude as well as her appearance.

"Good morning, cousin," he said, letting go of her.

"Is this all for me?" she asked, looking up at him questioningly, her full lips half-parted, as if seeking another kind of kiss.

Desire—hot, intense, lustful—hit him like a blow, while at the same time he experienced that haunting sense that there was something important about this woman hovering at the edge of his mind. Something…good.

He must be more distressed by this commotion than he'd assumed. Or perhaps he should ask Buggy about the possible aftereffects of a head injury.

In spite of his tumultuous feelings, his voice was cool and calm when he spoke. "After your ordeal, I thought it would be easier if Bond Street came to you."

"It is very kind of you, cousin," she murmured, looking down as coyly as any well-brought-up young lady, her dark lashes spread upon her cheeks.

He could keep cool when she was angry. He had plenty of experience with tantrums and volatile tempers, and had learned to act as if they didn't affect him in the slightest.

This affected him. *She* affected him.

He didn't want to be affected, by her or any other woman.

"Oh, it is *our* pleasure!" the modiste cried, pushing her way between them. "Allow me to introduce myself, my dear. I am Madame de Malanche, and it shall be my delight to oversee the making of your gowns. All the finest ladies in London are my customers. Lady Jersey, Lady Castlereagh, Princess Esterhazy, Countess Lieven, Lady Abramarle, and the beautiful Lady Chelton, to name only a few."

Drury wished the woman hadn't mentioned the beautiful Lady Chelton.

"I see that gown fits you to perfection—and looks perfect, too, I must say! I'm sure between the two of us you will be of the first stare in no time."

Miss Bergerine regarded her with dismay, a reaction the modiste's overly befrilled and beribboned gown alone might inspire. "I do not wish to be stared at."

Madame de Malanche laughed. "Oh, la, my dear! I mean all the young ladies will envy you!"

Not if she persuaded Juliette to wear gowns similar to her own, Drury thought.

"I believe you'll find my cousin has very definite ideas of what she'll wear, *madame,*" Drury said. "I trust you will defer to her requests, even if that means she may not be the most fashionably attired young lady in London."

"*Mais oui,* Sir Douglas," Madame said, recovering with the aplomb of a woman experienced in dealing with temperamental customers. "She will need morning dresses, of course, and dinner dresses. An ensemble or two for in the carriage, garden dresses, evening dresses, a riding outfit, a few walking dresses and some gowns for the theater." She gave Drury a simpering smile. "Everyone knows that Sir Douglas Drury enjoys the theater."

Her tone and coy look suggested it wasn't so much the plays that Sir Douglas enjoyed as the actresses.

"I do," he replied without any hint that he under-stood her implication. Or that she was quite wrong.

"I do not think I will be going to the theater," Juliette demurred. "Or riding, or out in a carriage. Or walking in gardens."

Madame de Malanche regarded her with alarm. "Are you ill?"

"*Non.*" Juliette glanced at Drury. "I simply will not need so many expensive clothes."

He could hardly believe it. A woman who wouldn't take advantage of the opportunity to run riot and order a bevy of new clothes whether she needed them or not? It wasn't as if she didn't require clothing, judging by the garments he'd already seen her wearing.

Or did she think he was ignorant of the cost? Or that he couldn't afford it? "Perhaps no riding clothes, since

I believe my cousin is no horsewoman. Otherwise, I give you carte blanche to get whatever you like, Juliette."

Madame de Malanche's eyes lit with happy avarice, but Juliette Bergerine's did not. "How can I ever repay you?"

She had obviously forgotten her role—and in the company of the sort of woman who could, and would, spread any interesting tidbit of gossip she heard.

He quickly drew Juliette into a brotherly embrace. "What is this talk of repayment? We are family!"

He dropped his voice to a whisper. "Remember who you are supposed to be."

He drew back and found Juliette regarding him with flushed cheeks. His own heartbeat quickened— because of her mistake, of course, and not from having her body pressed so close to his.

After all, why would that excite him? He'd had lovers, most recently the beautiful Lady Chelton. Yet he couldn't help thinking that most of them, including Sarah, would have taken advantage of this situation with a glee and greed that would have put the greatest thief in London to shame.

"My cousin is a modest, sensible young lady, as you can see," he said, addressing the room in general. "Having suffered so much during the war, she naturally feels compelled to be frugal. However, I have no such compulsion when it comes to my cousin's happiness, so please make sure she has everything she requires, and something more besides."

"I most certainly shall!" Madame de Malanche cried eagerly, while the linen-draper and silk mercer smiled, as did the shoemaker, still tapping away in the corner.

The overly excited haberdasher waved a pair of

stockings like a call to arms and the milliner came boldly forward with the most ridiculous hat Drury had ever seen, quite unlike the charming chapeau Juliette had worn when she'd left him in her room.

"Sir Douglas, the corsetier has arrived," Millstone intoned from the doorway.

That was too much.

"I believe that is my cue to depart," Drury said, hurrying to the door. "I leave it all to you, Juliette. *Adieu!*"

In spite of his desire to be gone, he paused on the threshold and glanced back at the young woman standing in the center of the colorful disarray. She looked like a worried general besieged by fabric and furbelows, and he felt a most uncharacteristic urge to grin as he beat a hasty retreat.

Only later, when Drury was in his chambers listening to James St. Claire ask for his help to defend a washerwoman unjustly accused of theft, did he realize that he had left a Frenchwoman to spend his money as she liked. Even more surprising, he was more anxious to see her in some pretty new clothes than worried about the expense.

At the same time, as the modiste and others pressed Juliette to select this or that or the other, she began to wonder if there wasn't another motive for Sir Douglas Drury's generosity.

Chapter Five

*Miss B. damned nuisance. Asks the most imper-
tinent questions. Might drive me to drink before
this is over.*
                    —from the journal of Sir Douglas Drury

Holding a sheaf of bills in her hands, Juliette paced
Lord Bromwell's drawing room as she waited for Sir
Douglas to return.

When the footman had first shown her into the
enormous room, she'd been too abashed to do anything except stand just over the threshold, staring at
the decor and furnishings as if she'd inadvertently
walked into a king's palace.

Or what she'd imagined a palace to be.

At least three rooms the size of her lodgings could
easily fit in this one chamber, and two more stacked one
atop the other, the ornate ceiling was so high. She
craned her neck to study the intricate plasterwork done
in flowers, leaves and bows, and in the center, a large
rondel with a painting of some kind of battle. The fireplace was of marble, also carved with vines and leaves.

The walls were covered in a gold paper, which matched the white-and-gold brocade fabric on the sofas and gilded chairs. The draperies were of gold velvet, fringed with more gold. A pianoforte stood in one corner, where light from the windows would shine on the music, and an ornate rosewood table sported a lacquered board, the pieces in place for a game of chess. Several portraits hung upon the walls, including one that must be of Lord Bromwell when he was a boy—a very serious boy, apparently.

The sight of that, a reminder of her kind host, assuaged some of her dismay, and she dared to sit, running her fingertips over the fine fabric of the sofa.

As time had passed, however, she'd become more anxious and impatient to present Sir Douglas with the bills. Although she'd vetoed the most expensive items and tried to spend Sir Douglas's money wisely, the total still amounted to a huge sum of money—nearly a hundred pounds.

If what she feared was true, Sir Douglas would expect something in return for his generosity, something she was not prepared to give. If that were so, she would have to leave this house and take her chances on her own. It was frightening to think his enemies might still try to harm her, but she would not be any man's plaything, bought and paid for—not even this one's. Not even if she couldn't deny that his kiss had been exciting and not entirely unwelcome.

At last, finally, she heard the bell ring and the familiar deep voice of the barrister talking to the footman. She hurried to the drawing-room door. Having divested himself of his long surtout, Sir Douglas strode across the foyer as if this house were his own. As before, his frock coat was made of fine black wool, the buttons large and plain, his trousers black as well. His shirt and cravat were brightly white, a contrast to the rest of his clothes and his wavy dark hair.

"Cousin!" she called out, causing him to pause and turn toward her. "I must speak with you!"

Raising a brow, he started forward while she backed into the drawing room. "Yes, Juliette? Are those today's bills?"

"*Oui,*" she replied. She waited until he was in the room, then closed the door behind him before handing him the bills. "I want to know what you expect from me in return for this generosity."

The barrister's eyes narrowed and a hard look came to his angular face as he shoved the bills into his coat without looking at them. "I told you before I don't expect to be repaid."

"Not with money, perhaps."

Sir Douglas's dark brows lowered as ominously as a line of thunderclouds on the horizon, while the planes of his cheeks seemed to grow sharper as he clasped his hands behind his back.

"It is not my habit, Miss Bergerine," he said in a voice colder than the north wind, "to purchase the affections of my lovers. Nor am I in the habit of taking poor seamstresses into my bed. This was not an attempt to seduce you, and the only thing I want from you in return for the garments and fripperies purchased today is that you make every effort to maintain this ruse for the sake of Lord Bromwell's reputation, as well as your own safety."

"Who *do* you take to your bed?"

The barrister's steely gaze grew even more aloof. "I don't see that it's any of your business."

"That man who attacked me thought I was your mistress. If I know about your women, I can refute his misconceptions if he tries to attack me again."

"Lord Bromwell and I are taking every precaution to ensure you aren't molested again. And I hardly think such a creature will care if he's made a mistake, at least if he has you in his power."

"So I am to be imprisoned here?"

Sir Douglas's lips jerked up into what might have been a smile, or a sneer. "You have never been in prison, have you, Miss Bergerine? If you had, you would know this is a far cry from those hellholes."

"Then I am free to go?"

An annoyingly smug expression came to his face. "Absolutely, if you wish."

No doubt he would like that, for he would then be free of his responsibility. He could claim she had refused his help and therefore he had no more duty toward her.

Perhaps he would even claim that by purchasing those clothes and other things, he had more than sufficiently compensated her, as if any number of gowns or shoes or bonnets could repay her for the terror she'd faced and might face again as long as he had enemies who believed she was his mistress.

Non, he could not abandon her so easily.

"Since you have put my life at risk, I believe I should stay." Then, determined to wipe that self-satisfied, superior look from his face, she asked, "So what sort of women *do* you take to your bed?"

Unfortunately, her question didn't seem to disturb him in the least. His lips curved up in what was definitely a smile, but one that, coupled with his dark hair and brows, made him look like the devil's minion.

"My lovers have all been married ladies whose husbands don't care if they stray or not."

"You like old women, then?"

His lascivious smile grew. "Experienced—but never a Frenchwoman."

"Oh? Why not?" she inquired, trying not to let her irritation get the better of her as she retreated behind one of the sofas.

"I believe their skills in the bedroom are vastly overrated."

"Believe?" she countered, brushing her hand along the rich brocade, her brows lifting. "You do not actually know?"

"I know enough to be certain that a Frenchwoman cannot be trusted, either in bed or out of it."

The arrogant English pig! "So now you will insult a whole country?"

"Why so indignant, Miss Bergerine? I merely gave you the information you claimed to seek."

She must be calm and control her anger. "Your friends who had the party… The woman's name is Fanny, I think? Is she your lover?"

He started as if somebody had fired a gun at his head. "Where did you get that outrageous idea?"

He was not so smug and arrogant now! "When you were hurt, you called her name, or else it was Annie. Perhaps you've had lovers with both names?"

In spite of his obvious shock, Sir Douglas recovered with astonishing speed. "I was unconscious, was I not?"

"Not all the time. Not when you whispered that name and kissed me."

He couldn't look more stunned if she'd told him they'd been secretly married. "I did *what?*"

"You put your arm around me and you whispered *'ma chérie'* and then you kissed me," she bluntly informed him. "Or as I suppose an English lover kisses," she added, as if his performance had been woefully inadequate.

Sir Douglas Drury blushed. Blushed like a schoolboy. Blushed like a child.

She wouldn't have considered that possible without seeing it for herself.

"I don't believe it," he snapped.

"I am not lying. Why would I?"

His hands still behind his back, he strode to the white marble hearth, then whirled around to face her. "How should I know what motives you may possess for wishing to say such a ridiculous thing? Or why you would pick Fanny, whom I most certainly do *not* desire. She is a friend, and so is her husband. I would never, ever think of coming between them even if I could—which I most certainly could not. They are very much in love. I realize that would be considered extremely gauche in Paris, but it's true."

"I am not telling lies."

He didn't believe her. She could see that in his eyes, read it in his face.

"What's the real reason for these questions, Miss Bergerine?" he demanded as he walked toward her like some large black-and-white cat. "Has somebody been telling you about my other reputation? Do you want to know if what they say about me outside the courtroom is true?"

She stood her ground, not retreating no matter how close he came. "I know all that I care to know about you, Sir Douglas."

"Oh?" His lips curved up in that dangerous,

devilish smile. "Perhaps you really want to find out what it's like to be kissed by Sir Douglas Drury when he's wide-awake."

That made her move.

"You pig! Dog! *Merde!*" she cried, backing away from him.

Not far enough. He reached out and grabbed her shoulders and pulled her to him. Before she could stop him—for of course she must—he took her in his arms and kissed her.

This was no tender kiss, like the one they'd shared before. This was hot and fierce, passionate and forceful. Seeking. Seducing. Tempting beyond anything.

His arms went around her and he held her tight against him, his starched shirt against her breasts. Her heart beat like a regiment's drum, sending the blood coursing through her body, heating her skin, her face, her lips. Arousing her, asking her to surrender to the desire and need surging through her.

A memory came, of the old farmer in the barn, stinking and sweaty, grabbing her and trying to kiss her, his movements fumbling.

This was not the same.

Or was it?

She was just a seamstress and there was only one way it could end if she gave in to the desire Sir Douglas Drury was arousing, the excitement she was feeling, the need.

She put her hands on his broad chest and shoved him away, prepared to tell him she was no loose woman, no harlot, no whore. Until she saw the look on his face...

He was as upset as she. Because he couldn't believe a woman like her would spurn his advances?

He was wrong. Very wrong! "You pig! *Cochon!* To take advantage of a poor woman who came to you for help!"

The door suddenly flew open and Lord Bromwell entered the room as if he'd heard her fierce epithets, except that he was smiling with his usual genial friendliness.

"Millstone said I'd find you both in here," he said. His smile died as he looked from one to the other. "Is something wrong?"

Sir Douglas turned to her, his dark eyes cold and angry as he raised a single brow.

She was not upset with Lord Bromwell. He was truly kind. But if she complained about his friend to him, what would he do?

She could not trust him completely, for she was French and he was English. She could not be certain he would not send her back to her lodgings.

She quickly came up with an excuse to explain why they had been arguing. "I spent too much on clothes. Nearly a hundred pounds."

Lord Bromwell gave Sir Douglas a puzzled look. "Why, that's nothing. I should think you could afford ten times that."

"I wasn't quarreling about the amount, which is trivial," Sir Douglas smoothly lied. "I was trying to make her see that she should have spent more. Madame de Malanche will be telling people I'm a miser."

Lord Bromwell sighed with relief, and he smiled at Juliette. "That may seem a large sum to you, Miss Bergerine, but truly, Drury would hardly have noticed if you'd spent twice that."

"One benefit of having a father with a head for business," the barrister noted.

"Oh, and I've brought company for dinner!" Lord Bromwell said, as if he'd just remembered.

Company? She was to have to act a well-to-do lady in company? How could he do such a thing?

A swift glance at Sir Douglas told her he was no more pleased than she, especially when a young couple came into the room.

The woman was no great beauty, but her clothes were fine and fashionable, in the very latest style, and her smile warm and pleasant. The gentleman was likewise well and fashionably attired. His hair, however, looked as if he'd just run his fingers through it to stand it on end, or else he'd been astride a galloping horse without his hat.

"Lady Francesca, may I present Miss Juliette Bergerine," Lord Bromwell said as Sir Douglas moved toward the window, his hands once more behind his back. "Miss Bergerine, this is Lady Francesca and her husband, the Honorable Brixton Smythe-Medway."

"Please, you must call me Fanny," the young woman said.

It took a mighty effort, but Juliette managed not to glance at Sir Douglas before she made a little curtsy.

"It is a pleasure to meet you, my lady," she lied.

Although the food was excellent and plentiful—including such delicacies as salmon, which she had never tasted before, and something called a tart syllabub, which was very rich and very good—the dinner was a nerve-racking experience for Juliette. Fortunately, she managed to get through it without making many mistakes by carefully watching and imitating the others, not touching a piece of cutlery or crystal glass until they did.

She also took care not to wolf down the excellent food as if she hadn't eaten in days, but was used to such cuisine.

And the wine! *Mon Dieu,* how the wine flowed! Yet she made sure she only sipped, and never finished a glass. She had to keep her wits about her.

The merry Mr. Smythe-Medway was very amusing, but she quickly realized there was a shrewd intelligence behind those green eyes. As for his wife, she *seemed* sweet and charming, but the test would be how she behaved when there were no men present. As Juliette had learned in the shop, women could be completely different then.

Juliette was so concerned with not making any mistakes, she took no part in the conversation. She doubted anyone noticed, for Mr. Smythe-Medway seemed quite capable and willing to entertain them.

His wife was just as quick-witted, if more subdued, and even Sir Douglas gave proof of a dry wit that made his friendship with the loquacious Smythe-Medway a little more understandable.

After what seemed an age, Lady Fanny rose and led Juliette to the drawing room, leaving the men to their brandy and, Juliette supposed, manly conversation. She couldn't help wondering what they would say about her and desperately hoped she hadn't done anything wrong.

"I must say I'm even more impressed with your courage now that I've seen you, my dear," Lady Fanny said as she sat on a sofa and gestured for Juliette to sit, too. The flowing Pomona green skirt of her high-waisted gown spread out beautifully, and the delicate pearl necklace she wore, although simple, looked lovely against her slender throat. "I was expecting quite an Amazon, not a petite woman like you."

What exactly had Sir Douglas and Lord Bromwell said about her and what had happened? Juliette wondered as she lowered herself onto the sofa opposite, her back straight, her hands in her lap, a part of her mind sorry Madame de Malanche hadn't had an evening gown ready for her to wear, too. Was Lady Fanny referring to the attack in the alley, or a robbery on the road?

"I was not so brave. It was very frightening," she prevaricated, thinking that answer would suit either situation.

"Drury and Buggy told us all about what you did for him. Potatoes! I would never have thought of that. Indeed, I think I would have been frozen stiff with fear."

The reality then. "I saw a man being attacked, and I went to his aid."

"And now we must come to yours. I'm very glad Buggy came up with this plan, and we shall do everything we can to help."

"Merci," Juliette murmured, wondering how this coddled English creature could be of assistance against evil men trying to harm her, or Sir Douglas. "I hope my presence here will not cause a scandal."

Lady Fanny laughed, and although her laugh was sweet and musical, Juliette still couldn't see what attracted Sir Douglas to Lady Fanny. To be sure, she was pretty, in a very English way, and seemed kind and good-natured, but she was so…bland. So boring.

Perhaps that was what he liked about her. She would never argue with him, or demand his attention, or likely question a single thing he did. She would be, Juliette supposed, a demure, obedient little wife.

"I wouldn't be too concerned about our reputations," Lady Fanny replied. "Buggy was considered quite eccentric until his book became a success, and as for Drury's reputation…"

Lady Fanny paused a moment before continuing, her cheeks a slightly deeper shade of pink. "I'm referring to his legal reputation. He's quite famous for his successes. He could have been a barrister of the King's Bench and possibly a judge by now, yet he remains at the Old Bailey. He prefers to represent the poor."

The arrogant, wealthy Sir Douglas Drury cared about the plight of the poor? Juliette found that difficult to believe.

"In some ways, Drury's had a very difficult life."

She found that hard to believe, too. "But he is titled and educated and rich."

"That doesn't mean he's never known pain, or heartache. His father spent most of his time on business ventures, and his mother—"

"Ah, ladies, here you are, and looking as lovely as a painting," Mr. Smythe-Medway declared as he sauntered into the room, followed by Lord Bromwell and a darkly inscrutable Sir Douglas.

Why did they have to interrupt *now?* Juliette thought with dismay.

"I hope Fanny hasn't been telling you she's made a terrible mistake marrying me," Mr. Smythe-Medway continued as he sat beside his wife on the sofa.

"Not likely." Lord Bromwell smiled as he settled in an armchair. "She's had years to learn all your bad traits, Brix, yet miraculously loves you just the same."

Apparently paying no attention to the conversation, Sir Douglas strolled over to the drapery-covered windows. He parted a panel and looked outside, as if he was more interested in the weather than the conversation.

Some inner demon prompted Juliette to call out, "Do you agree it is a miracle, Sir Douglas?"

He turned and regarded them impassively. "Not at all. I believe it was inevitable."

"Well, I say it *is* a miracle that Fanny fell in love with me," Mr. Smythe-Medway declared with a grin. "And one I'm thankful for every blessed day—but no more so than now, for gentlemen and Miss Bergerine, I have an announcement to make. Fanny's going to have a baby!"

Juliette cut her eyes to Sir Douglas. For a moment, it was as if he hadn't heard his friend, although Lord Bromwell rushed forward to kiss a blushing, smiling Lady Fanny on both cheeks and pump Smythe-Medway's hand while congratulating them both.

Yet when Sir Douglas finally turned and walked toward them, his smile appeared to be very genuine, and she could believe he was truly happy for his friends. It also made him seem years younger.

"I'm delighted for you both," he said, kissing Lady Fanny chastely on the cheek before shaking his friend's hand.

Maybe he meant what he had said. Perhaps he had never really loved her, after all, and was truly delighted for them.

Or perhaps, Juliette mused then, and as she lay awake later that night, he was an excellent liar.

Chapter Six

*I know full well Drury doesn't have any use for
the French, and why, but I don't understand his
increasing hostility toward Miss Bergerine.
He's treating her like a particularly annoying
species of flea.*

—From *The Collected Letters of
Lord Bromwell*

Drury sighed and leaned back against the seat of the
hired carriage two days later. God, he hoped they
found the louts who'd attacked them soon! It was
damned inconvenient having to live away from his
chambers and not being able to take long walks to
contemplate the tack he would take in the courtroom
and the questions he would ask.

Furthermore, he was no longer used to living surrounded by servants. For years now Mr. Edgar had
been both butler and valet, with a charwoman to clean
daily, and meals brought in from a nearby tavern when
he wasn't dining at a friend's or in his club.

Not only did Drury have to put up with the ubiquitous servants, he had to endure the presence of a very troublesome Frenchwoman who asked the most annoying questions.

Was it any wonder he couldn't sleep? Hopefully an hour or two of fencing would tire him out enough that he'd fall asleep at once tonight, and not waste time thinking about Juliette Bergerine's ridiculous questions.

Such as, was Fanny his mistress?

To be sure, there had been a time when he'd believed Fanny was the one woman among his acquaintance he could consider for a wife, given her sweet, quiet nature—until it had been made absolutely, abundantly clear that she loved Brix with all her heart. No other man stood a chance.

And whatever the sharp-eyed, inquisitive Miss Bergerine thought—for she'd watched him like a hawk after Brix had made his announcement—he was genuinely happy about his friend's marriage and their coming child. Brix and Fanny would be wonderful parents.

Unlike his own.

As for kissing the outrageous Miss Bergerine, he'd simply been overcome by lust—both times, whether he was awake or not.

At least the mystery of what he'd been trying to remember had been solved, for as soon as she'd spoken of the kiss, he'd remembered. It had been vague, like a dream, but he knew he'd put his arm around what had seemed like an angelic apparition, and kissed her.

Which just proved how hard he must have been hit on the head.

The carriage rolled to a stop and he quickly jumped out. He wouldn't even think about women—any women—for a while.

He dashed up the steps of Thompson's Fencing School. Entering the double doors, he breathed in the familiar scents of sawdust and sweat, leather and steel, and heard clashing foils coming from the large practice area. He'd spent hours here before the war, and then after, learning to hold a sword again, and use a dagger.

A few men sat on benches along the sides of the fencing arena. It was chilly, kept that way so the gentlemen wouldn't get overheated in their padded jackets. A few more fencers stood with a foot on a bench, or off to the side, and one or two nudged each other when they realized who had just walked in.

Drury ignored them and followed Thompson's voice. Jack Thompson had been a sergeant major and he shouted like one, his salt-and-pepper mustache quivering. He moved like it, too, his back ramrod straight as he prowled around the two men *en garde* in the practice area cordoned off from the rest of the room by a low wooden partition. Beneath their masks, sweat dripped off their chins, and their chests rose and fell with their panting breaths.

The first, thinner and obviously not so winded, made a feint, which was easily parried by his larger opponent.

"Move your feet, Buckthorne, damn you, or by God, I'll cut 'em off!" Thompson shouted at the bigger man, swinging his blunted blade at the young man's ankles. "Damn it, what the deuce d'you think you're about, my lord? This isn't a tea party. Lunge, man, lunge! Strike, by God, or go find a whore to play pat-a-cake with."

The earl, who must be the fourth Earl of Buckthorne, and who was already notorious for his gambling losses, made an effort, but his feint was no more than the brush of a fly to the young man opposite him. He easily twisted the blade away, then lunged, pressing the buttoned tip of the foil into the earl's padded chest.

"So now, my lord, you'd be dead," Thompson declared. "It's kill or be killed on the battlefield—and the victors get the spoils, the loot, the women and anything else they can find. Think about that, my lord, eh?"

The earl pushed away his opponent's foil with his gauntleted hand. "I am a gentleman, Thompson, not a common soldier," he sneered, the words slightly muffled beneath his mask. His head moved up and down as he surveyed his opponent from head to toe. "Or a merchant's son."

That was a mistake, as Drury and half a dozen of the other spectators could have told him.

Thompson had Buckthorne by the padding in an instant, lifting the thickset young man until his toes barely brushed the sawdust-covered floor. "Think your noble blood's gonna save you, do you? Your blood's the same as his, you dolt, or mine or any man's. You'd have done better to save your money and not buy your commission. Men like you have killed more English soldiers than the Frogs and Huns combined. Money and blood don't make Gerrard a better swordsman than you—practice does."

Pausing to draw breath, Thompson's glare swept around the room, until he spotted Drury.

With a shout of greeting and the agility of a man half his age, he dropped the earl and hurried over to the barrister.

"Good afternoon, Thompson," Drury said to his friend and former teacher as the earl staggered and tried to regain his balance. "I thought I'd come along and have a little fun."

"I beg your pardon," the earl's opponent said, removing his mask and revealing an eager, youthful face, curling fair hair, bright blue eyes and a mouth grinning with delight. "Are you Sir Douglas Drury, the barrister?"

"I am."

"By Jove, the Court Cat himself!" the young man exclaimed, his grin growing even wider. "I can't tell you what an honor it is to meet you!"

"Then don't."

Paying no more heed to the young man, who must be about twenty, Drury turned to Thompson. "Are you up to a challenge? I'm feeling the need for some martial exercise today."

Thompson barked a laugh. "Arrogant devil," he genially replied. "Giving me another chance to take you down a peg or two, eh?"

"We'll see about that." Drury cocked a brow at the fair young man, who continued to gaze at him with gaping fascination. "Have you never been informed that it's impolite to stare, Mr. Gerrard?"

"I'm sorry, s-sir," he stammered, blushing. "But you're Sir Douglas Drury!"

"I never cease to be amazed by the number of people who assume I don't know who I am. Perhaps I should wear a placard," Drury remarked as he started to unbutton his coat, a feat he could manage, albeit with some difficulty, thanks to the large buttons.

"Sergeant Thompson says you're the best swordsman he ever taught," Gerrard declared.

"Such flattery will make me blush," Drury replied before sliding a glance at Thompson. "The best you've ever taught, eh?"

The former soldier puffed out his broad chest. "You are. Not as good as me, mind, but good—for a gentleman."

"If I didn't know you better, Thompson, I'd say you were making a joke."

"No joke, Sir Douglas. You're good, but Gerrard here could probably give you a run for your money."

"Oh, no, I couldn't!" the merchant's son protested, even as a gleam of excitement lit his blue eyes. "Don't even suggest it, Sergeant."

"Too late," Drury said. "I'm willing if you are."

Gerrard shifted his weight and his gaze went to Drury's hands. He was so focused on those crooked fingers, he didn't see the slight narrowing of Drury's eyes before he spoke. "Have no fear that you'll be accused of taking advantage of a cripple, Mr. Gerrard. My hands may not be pretty, but they are fully functional."

As Miss Bergerine could attest.

Drury clenched his jaw, angry that he couldn't keep Juliette Bergerine out of his thoughts even here. Or at his club, or in his chambers.

"Go on, Gerrard," prompted the earl. He'd removed his mask and padded jacket, which obviously also operated as a corset for his bulging stomach, now more prominently displayed. He had the countenance of a man who would go to fat in a few more years, and likely already drank to excess. "See if you can beat him. I'll stand you drinks at White's if you can."

"I shall stand you drinks at Boodle's if I lose," Drury proposed.

"If we're going to wager," Gerrard said, "I'd rather it be for something better."

"Such as?" Drury inquired, expecting him to name a sum of money.

"An introduction to your cousin."

Drury went absolutely still. Those watching couldn't even be sure if he was breathing as he regarded Gerrard with that cold stare.

"I wasn't aware it had become common knowledge that my cousin is in London," he said in a tone that made some of the younger men think they were hearing the voice of doom itself.

"Is it supposed to be a secret?" Gerrard replied with an innocence that was either real or expertly feigned.

Give him a few minutes with the man in the witness box, Drury thought, and he'd know for sure.

"My sister heard it from her dressmaker," Gerrard explained.

Damn Madame de Malanche. He'd suspected she wouldn't be able to resist spreading that piece of news, but he'd hoped it would take more time before the lie became common gossip.

Despite his annoyance, Drury kept his feelings from his face as he peeled off his coat and tossed it onto a rack of buttoned foils nearby.

"It's no secret," he said, rolling back his cuffs as best he could with his stiff fingers. "I sometimes forget the speed with which gossip can travel in the city."

"Is it a wager then?" Gerrard challenged.

Drury undid his cravat and tossed it on top of his coat.

"Very well. And if you lose?"

"Whatever you like."

Cocky young bastard. "Very well. I may ask you for a favor someday. Nothing illegal or dangerous, but one never knows when one can use the assistance of a man of skill and intelligence capable of defending himself. Do we have a wager then, Mr. Gerrard?"

A very determined gleam came to the younger man's eyes. "Indeed." He pushed his mask over his face and saluted with his sword. "*En garde* as soon as you're ready, Sir Douglas."

"I'm ready now," Drury said, spinning on his heel and pulling one of the foils from the rack with surprising speed.

Gerrard stumbled back as Drury, unpadded and unprotected, saluted with the buttoned sword. He and Thompson had worked for hours to find a way for him to hold a sword after he'd come home, and while it looked strange, his grip was firm, and he had no need to worry that he would drop his weapon.

Gerrard recovered quickly and took his stance.

The merchant's son had probably never dueled, or fought for anything more important than drinks and bragging rights. Drury wondered if he realized he was facing a man who had killed without compunction or remorse. Who had pushed his blade into flesh and blood, and been glad to do it.

Of course, that had been under very different circumstances. This wasn't war, but a game, a cockfight, and nothing more—which did not mean Drury intended to lose.

He waited in invitation, letting the younger man make the first move. Gerrard opened with a fast advance, forcing Drury back while Gerrard's blade flashed, wielded with swiftness and skill. Drury countered with an *attaque au fer,* deflecting his opponent's foil with a series of beats, slashing down with his foil, or the sliding action of the *froissement,* pushing Gerrard's blade lower.

Then, while Gerrard was still on the attack, Drury countered with a *riposte.* Now on the offensive, he forced the man back, keeping up a compound attack with a series of beats, counterparries, a *croisé* and a cut.

By now, both men were breathing hard and they paused, by silent mutual consent, to catch their breath and, in Drury's case at least, reevaluate his opponent. The merchant's son was good—very good. One of the best swordsmen he'd ever encountered, in fact.

That didn't change the fact that Gerrard was going to lose. Drury would never surrender, not even in a game, not even after that foul, stinking lout in France had broken his fingers one by one.

He launched another attack. Gerrard parried, then answered with an energetic and direct *riposte*. No fancy flourishes or footwork for him, no actions intended to impress the excited onlookers; this fellow fought to win.

How refreshing, Drury thought, enjoying the competition. It was like fencing with a younger version of himself before the war. Before France. When a host of women had sought his bed, and more than one been welcomed. When he had still, deep down, dared to hope that he could find a woman to love with all the passionate devotion he had to give. Before he realized the best he could ever hope for was affection and a little peace. For Fanny, perhaps, if she would have him. If she hadn't loved another.

He lunged again, fast and hard, and it was a testament to Gerrard's reflexes that he wasn't hit before he dodged out of the way.

"Damn me, sir, you play for keeps," Gerrard cried, his shocked tone reminding Drury that this was not a fight to the death, or even a duel, and this young man had never done anything to harm him.

"Fortunately, so do I," the young man said in the next breath, making a running attack, trying to hit Drury as he passed.

The *flèche* wasn't successful, for Drury was just as quick to avoid the cut. But now the battle was on in earnest, neither man giving quarter, each using every bit of skill and cunning and experience he possessed until both were so winded and dripping with sweat, they could only stand and pull in great, rasping breaths.

"It's a draw, by God. As even a match as I've ever seen," Thompson declared, stepping between them. "Gentlemen, will you agree?"

Drury waited until Gerrard nodded and saluted with his foil. Then he, too, raised his foil in salute. "A tie, then."

He would have preferred to win, but at least he wouldn't have to introduce this clever young rascal to Juliette Bergerine.

"What of the wager?" Buckthorne called out. "Who has won the wager?"

"Neither, although I'll gladly stand Mr. Gerrard a drink or two at Boodle's," Drury replied, still panting.

"I'd be delighted, of course," Gerrard said, also breathing hard as he removed his mask and tucked it under his arm. "It would be a pleasure to talk to you about some of your trials, too, if I may. I intend to enter the legal profession myself, you see."

He paused, then continued with a mixture of deference and determination. "However, I'd also like to meet your cousin, if you'd be so kind."

Drury's eyes narrowed. Why was Gerrard so keen to meet Juliette? What had Madame de Malanche said about her? That she was pretty, which she was? That she was French, which she was? Or was there more to it?

What more could there be, if Madame de Malanche had been the source?

Would it look odd if he refused? Would it make Juliette more interesting to this young rogue and the other dandies of the ton if he kept her hidden away?

Yet who knew what Juliette might do or say to such a fellow? What if she lost her temper? What if she didn't?

"If you'd rather not…" the young fellow began, his brow furrowing.

That suspicious expression was enough to sway Drury's decision. Better to let him meet Juliette than make her a mystery. "Very well, Mr. Gerrard. As I'm sure you're also aware, we're staying with Lord Bromwell for the time being."

He gave him Buggy's address. "Present yourself tomorrow morning at nine o'clock and I will introduce you to my cousin."

Then Sir Douglas Drury's lips curved up in a way that had made hardened criminals cringe. "And might I suggest that if you're serious about pursuing a legal career, you refrain from making wagers with barristers."

Early that evening, Juliette bent over the napkin she was hemming in the elegant drawing room. The light would soon fade and she wanted to finish before it did.

All her life she had wondered what it would be like to be a lady—to have everything you needed, to never have to work or lift a hand, to have beautiful clothes and servants at your beck and call.

Well, she thought with a rueful smile, she'd discovered that while it was certainly delightful to be well fed and have pretty clothes, it was otherwise terribly boring. Now she could understand why the young ladies who'd come into the shop seemed so excited by the prospect of a new hat or the latest Paris fashion and bit of gossip. If she had nothing else to do with her time, her clothes might become vitally important, and gossip as necessary as food.

After spending hours by herself during the better part of two days, she'd finally gone to the housekeeper and asked if there was some sewing she could do. It would make her feel less beholden to Lord Bromwell for his kindness, and she was good at it, she'd explained, which was quite true.

"His lordship's guests don't work!" Mrs. Tunbarrow had cried, regarding her with horror, as if Juliette had proposed embalming her.

Undaunted and determined, Juliette had persisted, using her most persuasive manner—the same manner she'd used when asking questions about Georges in Calais, bargaining for passage on the ship to England, haggling for that small room in the lodging house and persuading Madame de Pomplona to give her work.

Mrs. Tunbarrow had reluctantly agreed at last and given Juliette napkins to hem, probably thinking she could have them resewn if Juliette proved incompetent.

"I'll wait in the drawing room."

"Merde!" Juliette whispered with dismay, for it wasn't Lord Bromwell come back from one of his many meetings trying to arrange his next expedition.

Sir Douglas Drury had returned.

Chapter Seven

*Didn't even see her until it was too late. Had no
idea she could be so quiet.*
    —from the journal of Sir Douglas Drury

Juliette didn't want to see Sir Douglas, and she especially didn't want to be alone with him in the drawing
room. She hadn't been alone with him since his friends
had come to dinner. She hadn't even spoken to him,
unless she hadn't been able to avoid it.

For an instant, she thought of fleeing, but her lap
was covered with her sewing and she would have to
pass him to get out of the room.

All she could do was shrink back into the wing
chair, grateful it was angled toward the hearth and not
the door, and pray he would not come in. Or if he did,
perhaps he wouldn't see her until Millstone came to
summon them to dinner, whenever that might be. The
meal would wait until Lord Bromwell returned from
his many meetings. Apparently planning a scientific
expedition required such efforts, even if one was rich.

Then the door opened and she heard Sir Douglas's

familiar tread upon the floor before he got to the carpet.

He stopped. Had he seen her? Had he realized they were alone? What was he thinking if he had?

Who could ever tell what he was thinking?

She was too nervous to sew, so she sat as still as a statue with the napkin on her lap, the sewing basket on the table beside her.

Sir Douglas still hadn't spoken, and she hadn't heard him come any closer. Perhaps he'd realized she was there and left the room. It would be rude, but not surprising, and she could only be grateful if he intended to ignore her the whole time she was Lord Bromwell's guest. Sir Douglas had been ignoring her very well lately—which was just what she wanted after his passionate, insolent kiss.

She got an itch in the middle of her back. A terrible, irritating itch. She was going to have to move, or squirm.

Was he there or not?

She couldn't wait. She had to scratch. Even so, she moved slowly and cautiously, until she reached the spot.

What was that little noise? It wasn't from her clothes as she scratched. Curious but wary, she peered around the side of the chair.

Sir Douglas stood at the mahogany table in the center of the room, idly flipping through the pages of an illustrated book about insects that Lord Bromwell had left there.

It was not an easy, simple thing for him. At meals it was obvious his fingers lacked flexibility, and they seemed even more stiff today. Nevertheless, he was smiling as she'd never seen him smile before.

There was no challenge in it, no mockery, no sense of superiority, no hint of seduction. He looked relaxed and amused, far different from the stern, arrogant, ungrateful barrister. Different, too, from the man who had kissed her so passionately.

Was this what he'd been like before the war that had changed so many people?

He glanced up and caught her watching him and his smile disappeared. "Good evening, Miss Bergerine. I didn't realize you were here. You should have said something."

"I didn't want to disturb you," she replied, attempting to betray nothing of her feelings, whatever they were. "You seemed so interested in Lord Bromwell's book."

He shut the tome abruptly, like a little boy caught with illicit sweets in his pockets.

Emboldened by that image, she said, "I didn't mean to disturb you. Do you like insects, too?"

"Not the way Buggy does," he replied.

He glanced at the chair opposite her, then picked up the book and started toward it.

The volume began to slip from his fingers. As he tightened his grip, he winced as if in pain, and it tumbled to the floor, hitting the carpet with a dull thud.

Forgetting the napkin, she hurried to pick it up and hand it back to him, only to find herself looking into a pair of cold, dark, angry eyes.

"Thank you," he growled, and she wondered if he hated being reminded of the limitations of his hands, or if it was because he didn't like *her.*

She didn't care what he thought of her. She was here because he had enemies who were also after her, not because she wished to be.

Picking up the napkin, she resumed her seat and once again began to sew, this time with steady hands. "Have you any news of the men who attacked us?"

"No," he replied as he sat across from her and opened the book. "What are you doing?"

She glanced up at him, surprised because it was obvious. "Hemming napkins."

"Surely Buggy didn't ask you to do that."

"*Non,*" she answered, intent on her work even though she was well aware he was watching her instead of looking at his book. "I am not used to having nothing to do and find I do not like to be idle. So I went to the housekeeper and asked her if she had any sewing I could do. In a small way, it gives me a chance to repay Lord Bromwell for letting me stay here—although it is not my fault I must."

"I apologise for the inconvenience," Sir Douglas replied, annoyance in his deep voice.

If he was angry, she didn't care. "Lord Bromwell—why do you call him Buggy? It is not a nice nickname, I think."

"Because he's always been fascinated by spiders. When we were at school, he used to keep them in jars by his bed."

She shivered. She hated the eight-legged creatures. "How unpleasant."

"It was, rather."

He said nothing more, and neither did she, but sewed on in silence until she finished the last few stitches of the final napkin. As she reached for the small scissors to cut the thread, he closed the book with a snap.

"What are you doing in London, Miss Bergerine?" he demanded, his question just as loud and unexpected.

"Why should I not be in London?" she retorted. "Is it forbidden for a young woman to travel here if she is French?"

"It's damned unusual."

He sounded very angry, but she would stay calm. And why not tell him? She was not ashamed of her reason. "I came here looking for my brother, Georges."

There was a long moment of silence before Sir Douglas answered, and his intense gaze became a little less annoyed. "I assume you haven't been successful."

"Regrettably, *non.*"

Another long pause followed, during which she refused to look away from his now inscrutable face.

Eventually he spoke again, slowly, as if weighing every word. "I have certain resources, Miss Bergerine, the same ones I'm using to try to find the men who attacked us. I shall ask them to include locating your brother in their efforts, as a further expression of my gratitude for saving my life."

She could only stare at him, not willing to believe he would be so generous. "You would do that for me?"

He inclined his head.

Despite her reservations about accepting a gift from such a man, relief filled her. She had been so long alone in her search.

And then came renewed hope, vibrant and bright, like a torch suddenly kindled in the darkness.

Overwhelmed by her feelings, she threw herself on her knees in front of him, and reached for his hand and pressed her lips upon the back of it. *"Merci! Merci beaucoup!"*

He tugged his hand away as if her lips were poison and got to his feet. "There is no need for such a melo-dramatic demonstration."

It was like a slap to her face. Abashed, but resolved not to show how he had hurt her, she rose with all the dignity she could muster. "I am sorry if my gratitude offends you, but you cannot know what this means to me."

Sir Douglas strode to the hearth, then turned back, his hands clasped behind him, his expression unreadable. "No doubt I do not. Now please describe your brother so that I may tell my associates."

It was to be a business transaction then. Very well. "He does not much resemble me," she began. "He is taller than I, about six feet, with brown hair that is straight, like a poker. His eyes are blue, and he is thin."

"Do you have any idea in what part of London they should begin their search?"

"No. The last news I had of him was from Calais. He wrote that he was coming to London, but he didn't mention any particular part, or if he was meeting anyone."

"He hasn't written to you from here?"

"No." She looked away, for what she had to tell Sir Douglas next was difficult to say, and it would be easier without his dark eyes watching at her. "His last letter was forwarded by a priest in Calais to Father Simon in our village."

She took a moment to gather her strength, to be calm, before continuing. "This priest wrote to Father Simon saying that Georges had been killed, found stabbed to death in an alley. A letter to me was in his pocket."

She looked up at the barrister, whose expression had not changed. "You are probably wondering why I do not believe that my brother is dead. A part of me thinks I should, that I must accept that Georges is gone, like Papa and Marcel. But I didn't see Georges's body and the priest who wrote the letter didn't describe it. He simply accepted that the letter found on the dead man belonged to him, so that man must be Georges. But what if he was wrong? Perhaps Georges was robbed of money and the letter, too, and it was the thief who was killed.

"So I went to Calais. The priest who wrote the letter had died of an illness before I got there, and nobody remembered much about the man in the alley, except that he had been robbed and stabbed."

"So you came to London hoping your brother was alive and somewhere in the city based on his last letter to you?"

"*Oui*. A fool's errand, perhaps," she said, voicing the doubts that sometimes assailed her, "but I must search and hope."

Or else I am alone.

"Your quest may prove to be futile," Sir Douglas replied, his voice low and unexpectedly gentle, "yet I cannot fault you for trying. No one should be all alone in the world."

"No one," she agreed in a whisper, regarding the man before her who, even with his friends, always seemed somehow alone.

"Sir Douglas, Miss Bergerine," Millstone intoned from the threshold of the drawing room, interrupting the rapprochement they'd achieved, "dinner is served."

Well after midnight, Drury stood by a tall window in his bedroom and raised his hands to examine them in the moonlight. Although he generally avoided looking at them, he knew every crooked bend, every poorly mended bit.

He remembered the breaking of each one, the pain, the agony, knowing that nothing would be done to set them and repair the damage. That when his tormentor was finished with him, he would be killed, his body either burned or thrown away like so much refuse.

He remembered the flickering flames casting light and shadows on the faces of the men surrounding him. The ones who held him down. The one who did the breaking.

He remembered their voices. The guttural Gascon of one, the whisper of the Parisian, the earthy seaman from Marseilles. The one who wielded the mallet, so calm. So deliberate. So cruel.

With a shuddering breath Drury lowered his hands, splaying them on the sill. Once, he had been proud of his hands. The slender length of his fingers. The strength of them.

He remembered the excitement of brushing their pads, oh, so lightly, over a woman's naked skin, and the woman's sighs as he caressed them.

Since his return, he had had lovers. More than one. He was, after all, still Drury, with his dark eyes and deep, seductive voice. He was still famous for his legal abilities, and for other abilities, too.

But never since he had returned to England had a woman deliberately touched his hands. Certainly no woman had kissed them.

Until today.

He was well aware that Juliette Bergerine had done so in the first flush of gratitude. No doubt if she'd had time to think, she wouldn't have done it.

But she had.

She had.

She believed him ungrateful, and he had been, that first day. She thought him arrogant, too.

She had no idea how that kiss had humbled him,

and the gratitude that had welled up within him at the touch of her lips on his naked flesh.

She would never know.

Yet he would reward her for a kiss that was worth more than gold to him. If her brother lived, he would do all he could to find him.

Starting at first light.

Juliette wanted to move, but she couldn't. It was dark, as if she were in a cave, and she was wrapped up like a mummy, her arms held to her sides. Turning her head from side to side, she realized she was caught in something—a spider's web, sticky and soft. Everything else around her was dark.

"You can't have him."

A woman's voice. Not kind and gentle. Harsh, triumphant, mocking.

"He's mine. I have only to say one word, and he will be mine forever."

Lady Fanny's voice, distorted. Ugly. "Did you think he could ever really care for you, you French trollop? Do you think I don't see how you secretly desire him, a man so far above you in rank, education and wealth? Do you think you could ever take *my* place in his heart?"

"Non!" Juliette protested, struggling to get free. Determined to get free. "He doesn't love you. He told me so."

The high-pitched laugh came out of the impenetrable dark. "And you believed him? You believe everything he says? Oh, my dear, he lies. He tells lies all the time, to you, to himself, to everyone."

"He does not love you!"

"He doesn't love you, either. He never will. He will

use you and cast you aside. He does the same to all his women. Why should you be different?"

Juliette twisted and turned, fighting harder to get free. "Then he would cast you aside, too."

"I wouldn't let him. I would kill him before I let him go."

Suddenly, light flared in the darkness and Juliette saw that she was not alone. His head bowed as if he was unconscious, like that first night, Sir Douglas hung on a cavern wall wet with moisture. He was encased in another web, the filaments spreading out like an angel's wings while that terrible, cruel feminine laugh filled her ears....

Juliette woke up, panting and sweating. It had been a nightmare. Another nightmare. Not of Gaston LaRoche in the barn this time, but of a demonic Lady Fanny who wanted Sir Douglas for herself. Who would kill him if she couldn't have him.

"Did I wake you, miss? I didn't mean to," Polly said as she crossed the room to open the drapes.

Trying to sit up, Juliette discovered the sheets and coverlet were wrapped tightly around her, just like the spider's web in the dream.

"I've lit a fire to take the chill off, and there's hot water to wash," Polly said, nodding at the jug and linen on the washstand. "It looks to be a lovely morning, miss."

The window Polly opened brought a breeze and the slight scent of damp earth and leaves.

Juliette lay still and closed her eyes, wishing she was in the country. How long had it been since she'd walked past open fields, with cows grazing, occasionally lifting their heads to look at her with their large, gentle eyes? What she would not give for a walk in the open air, far away from London and Sir Douglas

Drury, and the woman who sought to harm them both....

Woman? It had been men who had attacked them.

Men could be paid.

Paid by a woman who was angry with a former lover? Who might be spiteful and jealous? Who might be enraged enough to wish to kill the lover who'd left her, as well as a rival for his affection?

Had Juliette not seen and heard enough of women to know that their jealousy could be as strong and fierce as any man's? And that they were capable of great cruelty and malice?

She immediately got out of bed. "Is Sir Douglas at breakfast?"

"No, miss. He left at the crack o' dawn. Lord Bromwell's still in the dining room, though."

Disappointed that Sir Douglas was not there, Juliette decided she could still tell Lord Bromwell her idea, so she quickly washed and submitted to Polly's assistance with one of her new gowns. It was a very pretty day dress in bishop's blue.

"Do you know when Sir Douglas might return?" she asked as Polly hooked the back.

"No, miss. Depends how long he's at court, I suppose." The maid sighed and shook her head as her hands worked with swift, deft skill. "I wouldn't want to be questioned by Sir Douglas Drury in a courtroom, I can tell you—or anywhere else. A right terror in court, they say, although he never raises his voice or does anything theatrical like some of 'em do. He just stands there as calm as can be and asks his questions in that voice o' his until pretty soon, they wind up convictin' themselves. They call him the Court Cat, you know, because even if he isn't moving, it's like he's stalkin' 'em. Quiet, and then bang! They're caught."

Juliette had no trouble imagining this. "He wins most of the time?"

"He wins *all* of the time. The best there is at the Old Bailey."

Once Polly was finished, Juliette left her to tidy the bedroom and walked down the long corridor toward the staircase. As she descended, she passed a footman who dutifully paused and looked at the floor. While she might get used to having somebody dress her hair, she doubted she would ever get used to the way the servants turned away when she passed, as if they were not even worthy to be seen.

She arrived in the dining room and found Lord Bromwell seated at the long table, dressed in plain clothes, reading a book, and with a plate of half-eaten eggs quietly congealing in front of him. Two footmen stood at either end of the long sideboard, where a host of covered dishes rested.

Lord Bromwell glanced up, smiled and rose in greeting. "Good morning, Miss Bergerine!" He frowned. "You look tired."

"I had a bad dream."

"How unfortunate! Come, have some tea. It's just the thing to give you a little vitality. I'd steer clear of the kidneys, though."

No need to tell her that, Juliette thought, her stomach turning at the thought of that revolting English dish. "Just toast, please," she said, heading to the sideboard.

"Have a seat and I'll get it," the nobleman offered with his usual kindness.

As he set a plate with toasted bread before her,

Millstone appeared at the entrance to the paneled room, a silver salver in his hand and something akin to annoyance in his eyes. "I beg your pardon, my lord. There is a gentleman here who refuses to leave, even though I told him you are at breakfast and planning to depart in an hour."

Juliette hadn't heard about any journey. "You are leaving?" she asked the young nobleman.

"I have to go to Newcastle for a few days. Lord Dentonbarry may contribute to my expedition, if I can make it clear to him why he should."

Juliette couldn't help wondering that herself. After all, what good could spiders do anyone?

Lord Bromwell grinned, looking very youthful despite the wrinkles around his eyes which were neither completely blue nor gray, and the well-fitting morning coat that accentuated his broad shoulders.

"It seems odd to you, I'm sure," he said. "But all knowledge is useful in some way. And consider the spider's web, Miss Bergerine. Given its size and weight, the fibres are incredibly strong, yet very flexible. If we could figure out why, it would be very useful knowledge, don't you agree?"

She had never thought of a spider's web as useful before. They had always been nuisances, strung across a path, or cobwebs in corners. Or things to frighten her in her dreams.

Millstone cleared his throat. "The visitor, my lord?" he prompted.

"Oh, yes." Lord Bromwell studied the card. "Mr. Allan Gerrard. I've never met the man." He raised his eyes to Millstone. "What does he want?"

"He wouldn't say, although apparently, my lord, he was expecting Sir Douglas Drury to be here."

Lord Bromwell brightened. "Oh, he's probably come to see Drury," he said, as if that made everything all right. "Didn't you tell him Drury's gone to his chambers?"

Millstone cleared his throat with a delicacy that would have done credit to an elderly maiden aunt. "I did, my lord. He asked when Sir Douglas would be returning, and since I have no idea, I said I didn't know. Then he asked if your lordship and Miss Bergerine were here."

It was clear Millstone didn't approve of the young man, or having to interrupt Lord Bromwell at his breakfast.

Lord Bromwell didn't seem as concerned about that as confused by the man's request. "Miss Bergerine?" he repeated.

"Yes, my lord," the butler replied. "I told him I would inquire if you were at home."

A wild, hopeful notion burst into Juliette's head. Perhaps Sir Douglas had asked this man here because he could help find Georges.

She rose swiftly. "I will be happy to meet this Mr. Gerrard."

Lord Bromwell gave a good-natured shrug. "Very well, Miss Bergerine. Where have you put Mr. Gerrard, Millstone?"

"In the study, my lord."

"Excellent. Come along, Miss Bergerine. Oh, and Millstone, I still intend to leave within the hour."

Juliette had never been in the study of Lord Bromwell's town house. Unlike the other rooms, however, it was not a pleasant chamber. It was too dark and too much the English gentleman's, and it smelled strongly of tobacco.

A young man who'd been sitting in a heavy leather armchair got to his feet as she entered with Lord Bromwell. If this was Mr. Allan Gerrard, he was a nice-looking fellow, fair and with a pleasant smile.

"Mr. Gerrard, I presume?" Lord Bromwell said.

"Indeed, yes, I am," he answered. "I hope you'll forgive the intrusion. Sir Douglas agreed to meet me here—or so I thought."

Mr. Gerrard slid a shy glance at Juliette. "He offered to introduce me to his cousin yesterday. I suppose I shouldn't have stayed when your butler said he wasn't here, but I, um…" He shrugged his shoulders and gave them both a sheepish grin. "I was rather anxious to meet you, Miss Bergerine—and you, too, my lord."

"Might I ask why?" Lord Bromwell inquired, not quite as friendly as before.

Mr. Gerrard got a stubborn glint in his eyes of the sort Juliette had seen when a woman was told a certain fabric or shade wasn't right for her coloring, or the cut of a dress was less than flattering. "Surely it's no surprise I'd want to meet the celebrated author of *The Spider's Web*, or the beautiful cousin of Sir Douglas Drury. My sister's dressmaker spoke very highly of you, Miss Bergerine."

No doubt Madame de Malanche spoke highly of anybody who gave her a good deal of business. Nevertheless, Juliette smiled. "I'm flattered."

Apparently encouraged, Mr. Gerrard eagerly explained. "Sir Douglas and I decided to have a contest and we made a wager on the outcome. I proposed an introduction to you if I won."

"You're here because of a *wager?*" Lord Bromwell demanded incredulously.

Mr. Gerrard flushed and looked from one to the other. "Yes, well, it makes fencing more interesting if there's a wager."

"*Drury* made such a wager?" Lord Bromwell repeated, as if trying to convince himself that wasn't utterly impossible.

From what Juliette had heard of men of that class, they all gambled. Often. "He does not make wagers?" she asked.

"Not recently, or so I thought. Now if that's all, sir, I think you may leave," Lord Bromwell said with a curtness that was completely, and shockingly, unlike his usual manner.

Embarrassed for both herself and the blushing Mr. Gerrard, Juliette wasn't sure what to do or where to look.

Whatever he was feeling, however, Mr. Gerrard made a polite bow to her. "I'm delighted to have met you, Miss Bergerine. I hope you won't hold the circumstances of our introduction against me, and that we shall meet again."

Then he took her hand and lightly kissed the back of it.

No one had ever kissed her hand before. She discovered she didn't like it and quickly drew it back.

"Good day, Miss Bergerine. I'm sorry to have intruded, Lord Bromwell. I enjoyed your book very much, especially the part about scorpions. It's not pleasant to be stung, is it?"

With that, he touched his hand to his forehead in a jaunty little salute and marched from the room.

When he was gone, Lord Bromwell's long, slender hands balled into fists. "I'm sorry, Miss Bergerine. Drury shouldn't have used an introduction to you as the prize in a wager. It was in extremely poor taste, and he, of all men, should know better."

Her host started to the door before she could ask him what he meant. "If you'll excuse me, I'd best be on my way. Good day to you, Miss Bergerine. Although I hope the villains who attacked you and Drury will soon be caught, I look forward to seeing you when I return."

Then he was gone, leaving her to wonder why he'd been so upset about a bet. Didn't noblemen bet all the time? She'd heard several examples of wagers being written in the betting book at White's that seemed more outrageous than whether or not a young man could be introduced to a woman.

Why, then, was Lord Bromwell so upset? Or was this just another example of the difference between her world and theirs?

Chapter Eight

Nearly had a row with Buggy. Damned uncomfortable. Not as strange as what happened after, though.

          —from the journal of Sir Douglas Drury

Shifting from foot to foot as if he had an itch, Mr. Edgar stood in the doorway of the inner sanctum, the small chamber where Drury kept his law books and briefs from solicitors.

"Is something the matter?" Drury asked, one brow raised in query.

"Lord Bromwell's here to see you, sir. He's, um…he wouldn't let me take his hat."

"No doubt he's in a hurry to get as far from London as possible on the first day of travel," Drury replied as he got up from his desk and entered the main room.

Buggy was standing by the hearth, dressed in a greatcoat, hat and boots. And he was glowering, an expression rarely seen on his face.

"What the deuce were you thinking? Or did you

even *think* at all?" he demanded, his whole body quivering with righteous indignation.

Drury couldn't be more stunned if Buggy had slapped him.

"How you could even *think* to do such a thing after you nearly ruined Brix and Fanny's happiness over a bet?" he charged. "How could you involve Miss Bergerine in a wager? Haven't you already caused her enough trouble?"

Drury suddenly understood what Buggy was upset about, and wanted to smack himself on the forehead. "Gerrard. I forgot about Gerrard."

"I daresay you did, but he didn't forget your bet. He arrived this morning determined to have his introduction."

Another emotion swamped Drury, but he kept it in check as he went to pour himself a brandy. "I assume he got it?"

"He did!"

"And was he quite charmed by Miss Bergerine? She can be charming if she exerts herself."

"How dare you?" Buggy cried indignantly. "How can you insult her after what *you've* done? It's not her fault he came to meet her." Buggy jabbed a finger at him. "It's yours! And if she were charming, would you have preferred your supposed cousin be rude? Maybe you would. You're rude when it suits you."

Friend or not, Drury didn't appreciate being berated. He'd endured too much of that in his childhood. "I forgot about the damned wager."

"That's no excuse! I thought you'd seen the damage such seemingly silly things can do after you exposed Brix's bet about never marrying Fanny. It nearly drove them apart forever."

"This is hardly the same. Gerrard heard of Miss Bergerine from his sister, who had it from the dressmaker I employed. If I'd acted as if the introduction was not to be thought of, what do you think Gerrard, and every other young buck at Thompson's, would have thought? They would have been even more curious about her. I sought to avoid arousing any further speculation by agreeing to the wager."

"Did you lose for that reason, too?"

"I did *not* lose. It was a draw." Drury held out his hands. "Need I remind you I'm not the man I was? And it so happens, Mr. Gerrard is very good."

Buggy flushed and finally took off his hat, twisting the brim in his hands.

"I forgot about the wager because last evening," Drury continued, "before you returned from the Linnean Society, I learned that Miss Bergerine came to London seeking her brother. She's been told he was murdered in Calais before embarking for London as he'd planned. She hopes that was a terrible mistake and, although it's probably pointless, she came to London hoping to find him.

"As you know, I have certain associates who can be useful in such matters and, having decided to assist Miss Bergerine in her quest as a further expression of my gratitude, I was anxious to get the search started without delay. Gerrard and the wager completely slipped my mind."

Buggy tossed his hat onto a table and sat heavily in the nearest chair. "That's good of you, Drury. I know that sort of search doesn't come cheaply. I'm sorry I was so angry, but I was completely caught off guard by Gerrard's visit. And then to think you'd made such a bet… I don't want to go through anything like that again with you. It was bad enough when it was Brix."

"I point out that Brix was really in love with Fanny despite his denials, so that wager had more serious consequences. However, I have no such feelings for Miss Bergerine."

As for how Juliette felt about him... He preferred not to think about it. Instead, he poured his friend a brandy. Buggy took the proffered glass and downed it in a gulp. He had once said that brandy seemed like slightly flavored water compared to some of the brews he'd imbibed on his travels, and occasionally proved that must be true.

Drury would have preferred to let the matter drop without any more comment, but there was one question he felt compelled to ask. "Was Miss Bergerine upset?"

Buggy undid the top buttons of his coat. "She was a little surprised, although quite polite to Mr. Gerrard."

"She wasn't angry? I can easily imagine her flying into a temper. Heaven only knows what rumors would race about Almack's or White's about her then."

He wondered what rumors might already be spreading about her.

"Actually, she was very friendly."

Drury was sorry he hadn't used that nasty little maneuver Thompson had taught him when he had the chance. Then Gerrard wouldn't be intruding and demanding introductions.

"I should be on my way," Buggy said, rising. "I've kept my carriage waiting long enough."

Drury nodded a farewell. "Have a safe journey and I hope Lord Dentonbarry is generous."

Buggy inclined his head in return. "Try to be kind

to Miss Bergerine, Cicero. She's a remarkably intelligent, resilient young woman."

"I appreciate Miss Bergerine's merits," Drury
replied, although perhaps not quite the same way Buggy
did.

Unless she had kissed him, too.

"Then act like it. You can start by telling her you're
sorry," Buggy said, leaving that parting shot to bother
Drury until he could no longer concentrate on the case
he would soon be defending.

Because Buggy had a point.

Later that afternoon, Drury walked into the small
conservatory at the back of Buggy's town house. The
large windows allowed in plenty of light and a host of
plants, several of which had come back to England
with the young naturalist, thrived there even in winter.

Although he'd never asked, he'd often wondered if
Buggy had brought back exotic species of spiders to
go with the plants. Today, however, seeing Juliette
sitting on a little wrought-iron chair near some huge,
palmlike monstrosity of a fern, he forgot all about
Buggy's plants and his area of expertise.

In a gown of soft blue fabric, her thick, shining hair
with a blue ribbon running through it coiled about her
head, Juliette looked like a nymph or dryad sitting
quietly among the vegetation—until it occurred to
him, from the way she held her head in her hand, one
elbow on the chair's arm, that she also looked sad and
lonely.

As he had felt so many times, before the war and
after.

For her sake, he hoped she was right and her brother
was alive. He also hoped that he could help her find him.

There could never be anything lasting between them—their worlds were far too different—but he would feel finding her brother as excellent an accomplishment as saving an innocent from hanging or transportation.

Although he'd been quiet, Juliette must have heard him. She lifted her head and regarded him with those bright, questioning brown eyes.

He, who could so often predict what a man or woman might say in the witness box, who could read volumes in the movement of a hand or blink of an eye, had no idea what she was thinking. She was as inscrutable as he always tried to be.

He decided to waste no time, so got directly to the point.

"I'm sorry about the wager, Miss Bergerine, and I regret causing you any discomfort. I assure you, it will not be repeated."

"Lord Bromwell was very upset with you," she said.

Why had she mentioned Buggy? Drury still couldn't decipher anything from her expression or her tone of voice. "Yes, I know. He came to see me in my chambers before he left for Newcastle and made that very clear."

"So now you apologize."

He couldn't really claim that he would have apologized to her anyway. "So I have." *In for a penny, in for a pound.* "I'm also sorry I wasn't here to make the introduction. It wasn't my intention to leave that to Buggy. I went to see a man who's going to Calais for us. I worked with Sam Clark during the war. He's from Cornwall, and his family have been involved with smugglers for years, so he has a lot of friends on the docks there. If anyone can find out if that really was your brother in that alley, or if he boarded a boat for England, Sam can."

She rose and came closer, and as she did, he wondered why he had failed to notice how graceful she was.

"In that case, all is forgiven," she said. "Besides, Monsieur Gerrard is a nice young man. I did not mind being introduced to him."

Allan Gerrard was a forward, overreaching young man, and Drury didn't care to discuss him.

Juliette lifted a spade-shaped leaf belonging to a plant he couldn't identify, although Buggy surely could. Buggy, who obviously liked her a great deal.

She ran her fingertip along the leaf's spine, then its edges. "The men who attacked us—they still have not been found?"

Drury tore his gaze from her lovely fingers and clasped his hands behind his back. "London is a large city, with many places to hide. Such a search can take time, even for MacDougal and his men, and the Runners, too."

She strolled past him, her hand brushing another plant. "So we shall have to enjoy Lord Bromwell's hospitality a little longer."

"Yes."

She turned to face him. Women were often intimidated by him, or intrigued; rarely did they regard him as if they had something serious to discuss. "Have you ever thought, Sir Douglas, that the people who attacked us might have been hired by a woman? One of your former lovers, perhaps?"

No, he had not, because it was ridiculous. "I highly doubt that. My lovers have all been noblewomen— married noblewomen who have already provided their husbands with an heir, and who have had other affairs.

I've not ruined any happy homes, imposed my child in place of a true heir of the blood, or seduced innocent girls. And all the women whose beds I've shared have understood that ours was a temporary pairing, nothing more. I can't think of one who would be jealous enough or foolish enough to hire ruffians to attack us."

Juliette continued to regard him those shrewd, unnerving brown eyes. "You sound very certain."

"I am."

"Perhaps you are right, but such women also have great pride, and a woman's pride can be wounded just like any man's. I can easily believe such a one could be so mad with jealousy she would want to hurt you. That she would be so angry you ended your liaison with her, she wouldn't hesitate to do you harm, or hire a man to do so. And she would despise the woman she believes took her place in your bed."

"They all understand the way of the world," he argued. "Ladies do not commission murder, and certainly not over the end of a love affair."

Juliette's eyes widened with genuine surprise. "You believe that because they are rich and noble they are not capable of jealousy, or anger when an affair is ended? That they are finer, more noble creatures than men? If so, you should work for a Bond Street modiste. You would soon see that these ladies, for all their birth and finery and good manners, are capable of great spite and maliciousness. Some take huge delight in doing harm."

"With words, which is a far different thing from planning murder."

And far, far different from delivering the fatal blow oneself, as he had.

He forced those memories back into the past where they belonged, to focus on the present and Juliette, who was shaking her head as if he were pathetically stupid.

"A jealous or neglected or thwarted woman may be capable of anything, whether to try to win back her beloved, or to punish him. If you think otherwise, you are truly naive."

Nobody had ever called Sir Douglas Drury naive, and after what he'd seen of human nature in his youth and childhood, during the war and at the bench, he truly didn't think he was, whether about women or anything else. "None of *my* lovers would do such a thing."

"Then you are to be commended for choosing wisely. Or else they didn't love you enough to be jealous."

He had to laugh at that. "I know they did not, as I did not love them."

Juliette's brows drew together, making a wrinkle between them, as she tilted her head and asked, "Has anybody *ever* loved you?"

Her question hit him hard, and there was no way in hell he was going to answer it. She was too insolent, too prying, and it made no difference to the situation.

"Have *you* ever loved anyone?" she persisted, undaunted by his scowling silence. "Have you never been jealous?"

Up until a few days ago, he would have answered unequivocally no to both questions—until he'd been saved by an infuriating, prying, frustrating, arousing, exciting Frenchwoman with a basket of potatoes.

Nevertheless, he wasn't about to answer her question. "Whether or not my love has been given or received is none of your business, Miss Bergerine."

"If I had not been attacked because of you, I would agree that your affairs are none of mine," she agreed. "But I was, and if you are an expert in the courtroom, you are obviously not an expert on love. Nor can you see into a person's heart.

"I find it easy to believe that whatever you may have thought of your affair or her feelings, at least one of your *amours* has loved you passionately, certainly enough to be fiercely jealous and wish to do you harm. If she thinks I have taken her place, she would want me dead, too. And a rich woman usually gets what she wants."

This was ludicrous. He would know if any of his lovers bore him such animosity. "Fortunately, I *can* see into a person's heart, Miss Bergerine, or as good as. That's why I'm so adept at my profession. That's why I always win. So I am quite confident none of my former lovers is involved in these attacks."

"If you are so good at reading the human heart, *monsieur le barrister,* what am I thinking now?"

Damn stupid question.

Except…what *was* she thinking? And was it about him, or another man? Buggy? Allan Gerrard? Gad, she might be thinking about Millstone for all Drury could tell. He'd never met anyone more obtuse.

Yet there were other times when her emotions were written on her face as plainly as words on a page. Was it any wonder she was the most infuriating, fascinating woman he'd ever met?

"Well, Sir Douglas? What am I thinking?" she repeated.

He guessed. He was good at guessing—making assumptions on the merest shred of evidence and pressing until the full truth was revealed, even if it wasn't always exactly what he thought it would be. "I think you're very pleased with yourself, because you think you understand women better than I."

He remembered the way she'd stroked that leaf and noted the little flush coloring her soft cheeks. And because she seemed to want to tear his secrets from him, he would not hold back. "I think you're feeling desire, too—a desire you don't want to acknowledge."

Juliette laughed. Juliette Bergerine, a French-woman in England with hardly a penny to her name, laughed in Sir Douglas Drury's face.

"You are only guessing, *monsieur le barrister*," she chided, "and you are wrong. While I cannot deny you have a certain appeal, you are not the sort of man who arouses my passion."

He had felt the sting of rejection before. He knew it well and intimately. When he was a child, and even during her fatal illness, his mother had often sent him away. Although his late father had inherited a considerable fortune, he always claimed to have business to attend to. Drury had suspected that had often been an excuse to avoid both his wife and his son, whom he seemed to consider no more than an additional nuisance. Neither one of his parents had possessed the devotion or temperament for parenthood. Over time, Drury had come to believe he was immune to such barbs, only to discover here and now that he was not.

"So you see, you could be just as wrong about your lovers," she continued, speaking with decisive confidence, oblivious to the pain she'd caused. "Therefore, Sir Douglas, I believe we must not hide and wait and hope our enemy will show herself. We must force her to take action. I should not remain cloistered here. I must go out and about—and you must tell everyone we are to be married. For if there is one thing that will drive a rejected lover to distraction, it will be the notion that her usurper has achieved the greatest prize of all, a wedding ring."

Drury could think of a thousand things wrong with that idea—well, two, but they were vital. "People have been told you're my cousin."

"So? Do cousins not marry in this country?"

Gad. "And if this does tempt our enemy to act—provided the same person is responsible for both attacks—you will be in danger."

"These men you hire, this MacDougal person—could they not protect us and capture our enemy if we are attacked again?"

"It's too risky."

"But we must do *something.* The search does not progress, and I do not want to impose upon Lord Bromwell for much longer."

She was worried about imposing on Buggy? "He can afford it."

"Then you wish to continue this charade? What if it is weeks, or months?"

Weeks or months of returning to a comfortable house with Juliette waiting, sitting by the hearth with her bright eyes and busy fingers, her vibrant presence like a flame to warm him.

He must be losing his mind. Too many hours alone in that cell, waiting to be killed. Or perhaps he'd caught some tropical disease from one of the plants or specimens Buggy was always showing him. Or that blow to the head had been worse than he'd thought, because the vivacious Juliette, with her outrageous ideas, would never bring him the serenity he sought.

Indeed, life with her would never be placid.

She regarded him steadily, her mind quite clearly

made up. "I have no wish to live forever in a gilded cage. I have always had work to occupy my time, even if it was not always pleasant. My room was terrible— that I know. But it was *mine*. Here, I am like one of Lord Bromwell's spiders, trapped in a jar. The jar may be clean, it may be safer than the jungle, but the spider soon dies for want of fresh air."

So she should go. Be free and leave him. "If you wish to go, I'll arrange for your protection for as long as you feel it necessary."

"I am not so ungrateful as that!" she exclaimed. At last her steadfast gaze faltered and her voice became a little less assured. "I could not depart thinking you were still in danger when I can help you flush out your enemy."

Was he supposed to believe she cared about him? After everything she'd said to him? "Proclaiming we are to be married is a foolish, dangerous idea. It's also useless, because no former lover of mine is out to kill us. However, if you chafe at this life, you are free to go as soon as I've arranged protection for you."

Her expression unmistakably stubborn, Juliette threw herself onto another wrought-iron chair. *"Non,"* she said, crossing her arms. "I am not *your* guest. I am Lord Bromwell's, and he has told me I may stay. So *voilà,* I stay."

"The hell you will!" Gad, she was infuriating! "As for saying we're engaged—"

The sound of a throat being cleared interrupted him. Millstone stood at the door of the conservatory, his face scarlet. "If you please, Sir Douglas, the dress-maker has arrived with the garments for Miss Berge-rine. She's waiting in the morning room."

"Oh, how delightful!" Juliette cried, jumping up

as if everything was wonderful. "And now you will be able to take me to the theater, and Vauxhall, and all the other places in London I have heard about. Is it any wonder I agreed to marry you, my darling, despite your terrible temper?"

Millstone's eyes looked about to drop right out of his head.

"You weren't supposed to say anything," Drury growled through clenched teeth, as furious and frustrated as he'd ever been in his life.

"Oh!" she gasped, her remorse patently false as she covered her mouth her fingertips. "Forgive me! But I am so happy!"

And then she gave him a hearty smack full on the lips before taking his hand and pulling him toward the door.

The little minx!

"Not a word to anyone about this, Millstone," Drury commanded as she dragged him away.

"Until we give you leave," Juliette said with a joyous giggle, as if their secret engagement would soon be common knowledge.

She might feel like a spider in a jar, but he was the one caught in her web.

"Oh, Madame de Malanche, how happy I am to see you!" Juliette cried as they entered the morning room, a very pretty chamber used by the Countess of Granshire, Buggy's mother, when she wished to write her correspondence or entertain her friends. The walls were papered with a bucolic scene, and the furniture was slender and delicate. Even the writing desk in the corner looked as if it would shatter if someone leaned on it.

Right now, there were piles of boxes on the light blue damask sofa, the chairs and every side table.

"Miss Bergerine!" the modiste replied. "You look radiant today."

"Because I am so happy!" Juliette slid the captive Drury a coy, delighted smile.

He wanted nothing more than to escape, but he didn't dare leave Juliette alone with this gossipy woman wearing a dress of the most startling, eye-popping shade of yellow he'd ever seen. Looking at her was like staring at the sun, and just as likely to give him a headache.

"My cousin is delighted with her new wardrobe," he said, cutting off the voluble modiste before she could say a word. "Juliette, ring the bell for your maid while I pay *madame*."

"Of course, my love. But first, *madame,* I would like to ask you to make my wedding dress."

Madame de Malanche's hazel eyes grew nearly as bright as her dress. "You're getting married? You and Sir Douglas?"

"Juliette, ring the bell!" Drury ordered, glowering.

"Oh, he is such a shy fellow!" she cried, clapping her hands as if amused and charmed. "That is why I love him so!"

"Juliette," he warned.

Instead of going to ring the bell, however, she ran up to him and threw her arms around his neck. "Am I not the luckiest woman in England?"

Damn her! Did she think she could control this situation? Control *him?* He'd show her how wrong she was.

"As I am the most fortunate of men," he said in a low, husky whisper reserved for his lovers alone.

Then he took her in his arms and kissed her as if they were already married and this was their wedding night.

Chapter Nine

*So now the ton is under the impression I'm en-
gaged to be married. What a mess. Or I suppose Buggy would liken it to a tangled web.
And I'm a fly.*
                —from the journal of Sir Douglas Drury

Drury felt Juliette stiffen in his arms and told himself
that was good—until she began to kiss him back with
even more fervor.

Did she think she was going to win this duel? Did
she believe he was a slave to any of his emotions?

Determined to prove otherwise, he shifted and used
his tongue to gently part her lips.

As their kiss deepened, she ran her hands up his
back and entwined her fingers in his hair.

Oh, God help him, she was the most arousing—

"Ahem!"

He'd forgotten the damned dressmaker. Just as well
she was there and interfering; otherwise…

He was determined not to contemplate *otherwise*
as he drew back.

Juliette looked a little…dazed. As for how he felt…
He would ignore that, too.

"Call the maid, my love," he said huskily, "and go
with her to put these things away, or I fear we may
upset Madame de Malanche with another unseemly
demonstration of our mutual affection."

He fixed his steadfast, steely gaze on the modiste.
"I hope we can count on you to keep this information
to yourself, madame, until we've made a formal announcement. If you cannot be discreet, Miss Bergerine may have to take her business elsewhere."

"You may count on my discretion, absolutely!"
Madame de Malanche exclaimed. "Although you must
allow me to wish you joy."

"Thank you," Drury replied. Despite her assurance,
he feared the dressmaker would never be able to keep
what she had seen and heard a secret. Nevertheless,
he had to try.

"Ring for the maid, Juliette," he repeated, and this
time she finally did.

As soon as Drury could get away, he headed for
Boodle's. He needed a drink and he needed to get
away from women, as well as his own tumultuous
thoughts, for a while.

He should have told Madame de Malanche he was
not engaged to Juliette, and he *really* never should
have kissed her.

Especially like *that*.

What the devil was the matter with him? he wondered
as he entered the bastion of country squires come
to Town. Unlike White's or Brooks's, Boodle's was
favored by men more down-to-earth than most of the
aristocrats who frequented the other gentlemen's clubs.

That was why Drury preferred it. He'd also avoided White's ever since he'd written down the infamous wager between Brix and Fanny in the betting book there. Brix, however, never seemed troubled by the association and claimed Boodle's appealed to the duller members of the gentry.

Therefore Drury was duly surprised to find his friend lounging on a leather sofa in the main salon, long legs stretched out, drink in hand. Unlike most of the patrons of the club, he wasn't gambling. Neither was he foxed.

Brix held up a glass nearly full of red wine and gave his friend a wry grin. "Greetings, Cicero! I've been hoping you'd appear."

Mystified by his friend's presence, Drury feared the worst. "Have you quarreled with Fanny?"

"Good God, no!" he cried, straightening. "We don't quarrel anymore…well, not often, and usually about completely unimportant matters until we forget why we're quarreling, and kiss and make up. It's quite stimulating, actually. You should marry and try it."

"I am not the domestic sort," Drury said, wondering how he was going to explain Juliette's harebrained plan to his friends, and even more disturbed about what the ton would make of it, provided anyone other than Madame de Malanche would believe it.

Likely they wouldn't, he realized with…relief. Of course relief. What else should he feel?

"Really, why are you here?" he asked his friend again.

"My esteemed father and elder brother are in Town and they requested a convivial meeting to celebrate my happy news," Brix replied with another grin. "They're delighted I've not only done my duty and married at last—to a damn fine gel, as Father so charmingly puts it—but have already proved capable of carrying on the family name."

Brix's relationship with his father and brother had never been the best, so Drury didn't begrudge his friend the slightly sarcastic tone. Then Brix, being Brix, winked. "I can think of much more onerous duties, I assure you. And since I was here anyway, I thought I'd wait a while and see if you put in an appearance—and here you are!"

"Yes, here I am."

Brix wasn't completely insensitive to the subtleties of his friend's tone and he sobered at once. "More trouble? Not another attack, I hope?"

"No, although I believe Miss Bergerine is of the opinion that another attack would be a beneficial occurrence."

Brix looked justifiably confused. "Beneficial? How?"

"She's decided the attacks are the work of a jealous former lover of mine, a jilted *amour* paying to have us killed. She believes we should attempt to flush out my enemy by claiming to be engaged and going about together in public."

For a moment, Brix sat in stunned silence—but only for a moment. "Gad, I never thought of that, but I damn well should have. I would gladly have run you through when I saw you kissing Fanny."

Drury had hoped Brix had forgotten about that. "That was intended only to encourage you to finally voice your feelings," he said. He hurried on to the more important point. "My lovers all knew the terms of our relationship. I seriously doubt any of them would ever go so far as to—"

"*I* can believe it," Brix interrupted. "I think it's a brilliant explanation, especially for the attack on Miss

Bergerine. The question is, which of your lovers would be capable of such a thing? There've been…how many?"

It was not Drury's practice to discuss his liaisons, not even with his closest friends. "A few" was the only answer he would give.

Nor was he willing to concede that Juliette could be right. "I highly doubt that any one of them would be so malicious or have any idea how to find men to do the deed if she were inclined to have me killed."

"I think you underestimate the fairer sex," Brix replied, "as much as you underestimate your appeal to women."

"I'm a barrister, Brix. I know all about crimes of passion."

"Then why do you find it so difficult to credit Miss Bergerine's idea?" Brix demanded. "Is it because it's hers?"

"Don't be ridiculous. If I'm not willing to entertain the notion, it's because I know the women with whom I've been intimate. She does not."

"All right. Let's say it's not a former lover, but another person who wants you—and Miss Berge-rine—dead. After all your triumphs in court, you surely have scores of enemies, any one of whom might hire a gang of ruffians to kill you. They might even decide to harm you through a woman they believe is your mistress. It's still a good idea to flush them out. Otherwise, how long are you willing to wait for them to make the next move? I think you should do as Miss Bergerine suggests and bring them to you. You'll be ready, and MacDougal's got men you can hire to guard you and catch them if they strike.

"And what about Miss Bergerine?" he continued. "How long before you decide the danger's past and she can safely return to her home? She can't live with Buggy indefinitely. I don't think he'd mind, but it *is* a bit of an imposition, and he hopes to sail next spring."

"She's not 'living with Buggy.' She's a guest."

"Call it what you will, the Runners aren't having any luck finding out who attacked you, and neither are those other men you've hired. What else can you do? Or am I wrong, and you're quite content with the situation?"

Drury sighed, defeated. "No, I am not. So congratulate me, Brix, and wish me every happiness with my lively French bride."

Brix did, and not only that, he stood a round of drinks for the entire club, merrily announcing the reason for his generosity.

After Drury had accepted good wishes from several half-foxed patrons, Brix drew him aside, grinning like a jester. "Fanny and I are going to see *Macbeth* in Covent Garden tonight. You and Miss Bergerine should join us. That would really set the cat among the pigeons of the ton."

As disgruntled as he was, Drury had started out on the path, so he was resolved to see it through to the end. "Very well, we shall. And thank you, although I daresay this news will be all over Town before we even get to the theater."

Brix laughed. "I daresay you're right."

And he was.

"So then the little rascal says to me, as solemn as can be…" Mrs. Tunbarrow paused in her reminiscing, nodding her lace-capped, white-haired head at Juliette. "'There's things a lot more frightening than spiders, Mrs. T.' That's what he called me—Mrs. T. He couldn't say Tunbarrow when he was a mite."

Juliette smiled at the story about Lord Bromwell as she sewed the hem of an apron.

Impressed with her stitching and, Juliette suspected, happy to have an audience, Mrs. Tunbarrow had invited her to come sew with her in the housekeeper's sitting room. The whitewashed walls and simple furnishings certainly made this room more comfortable and cozy than Lord Bromwell's formal drawing room. It was almost like the farmhouse back home.

At first, she had thought Mrs. Tunbarrow might say something about the supposed engagement, but it seemed Millstone had followed Sir Douglas's orders and kept quiet. She had been tempted to mention it, but had not, wary of pushing Sir Douglas too far, and in spite of that tempestuous kiss. Better she be patient and cajole him into seeing the merit of her plan than do anything more to force him to accept it.

As for Mrs. Tunbarrow, she seemed to have accepted her presence with good grace. Or perhaps the woman had such a high opinion of Lord Bromwell, she believed any guest of his was worthy of respect and approval. Yet Juliette couldn't help wondering if Mrs. Tunbarrow, plump and motherly though she was, would treat her differently if she knew this particular guest was a poor French seamstress and not the cousin of Lord Bromwell's friend.

In spite of that worry, she felt safer here. Sir Douglas surely wouldn't think of looking for her in the housekeeper's sitting room. If he did come looking for her.

If he returned at all. He'd been so angry after what she'd done. She'd felt it in his kiss, at least at first. After a few moments, though…

She was being ridiculous. He'd been furious and had departed as soon as he could, announcing he was going to his club.

Yet he hadn't denied their engagement, as she'd feared he might. If anything, that kiss would serve to confirm it, which must mean he was going along with her plan. For now. She hoped. Because *something* had to change.

A prickling sensation began at the back of her neck, as if she was being watched. She half turned and discovered Sir Douglas in the doorway.

How long had he been standing there with his hands behind his back, observing them?

"Good day, Sir Douglas," she said warily.

Mrs. Tunbarrow hastily grabbed the apron from Juliette's lap, regardless of the needle and thread trailing from it. "We were just having a bit of a visit," she said, as if she feared Sir Douglas would complain.

"I don't mind if Juliette wants to sew," he replied. "Indeed, you make a very pretty tableau."

He had called her Juliette, and in front to the housekeeper. Well, why not? Were they not supposed to be cousins?

He came into the room and smiled at Juliette, a warm, tender, incredibly attractive smile that seemed genuinely sincere.

"I've decided you're quite right, my dear," he said, his voice also warm and tender. "There's no need to keep our engagement a secret."

He had seen the wisdom of her plan?

Sir Douglas held out a box covered in dark blue velvet. "Brix and Fanny have invited us to the theater tonight. I'd like you to wear this."

Juliette took the box and opened it with trembling

fingers. A necklace was inside, made of sparkling diamonds bright as stars in the night sky. It was the most exquisite thing she'd ever seen—and the most expensive.

Her gaze darted to his face. "You wish me to wear this?"

"I insist," he said, taking her hand in his and kissing it lightly. Delicately. Yet it sent what seemed like bolts of lightning through her.

As Mrs. Tunbarrow stared speechlessly, Juliette swallowed hard and forced herself to look at the necklace while he continued to hold her hand. "It is so lovely."

"Let me put it on you," he murmured, taking the box and setting it on the table. He removed the necklace and stepped behind her, laying it around her neck.

Feeling as if she was in an even more amazing dream, she lightly brushed it with her fingers as he worked the clasp.

Then he gave a sigh of frustration, his breath warm on the nape of her neck. "Mrs. Tunbarrow, will you fasten this for me?"

The housekeeper started, as if suddenly waking up. "Engaged! The two of you—engaged! Does Justy know?"

Justy? Did she mean Lord Bromwell?

"I intend to tell Lord Bromwell when he returns," Sir Douglas calmly replied. "I had hoped to keep our betrothal quiet until a formal announcement."

"Well!" Mrs. Tunbarrow cried indignantly, hoisting herself to her feet and letting the aprons tumble from her lap. "*Well!* This is a pretty business, I must say! Keeping secrets like that! From everybody!"

She marched to the door as Juliette set the beautiful necklace back in its box, suspecting she would never be invited to the housekeeper's room again.

Mrs. Tunbarrow whirled around on the threshold and, hands on her ample hips, glared at them. "A fine friend *you* are, I must say, Sir Douglas Drury, breaking that poor boy's heart!"

Then, with a huff, she marched away, her footsteps loud on the tiles.

"She obviously believes Buggy has an interest in you that has been thwarted," Sir Douglas observed with that aggravating calm, while Juliette felt as if she'd stepped into something she shouldn't.

"I hope with all my heart that she's wrong," she said quietly.

"You do? He *is* a peer of the realm," Sir Douglas replied as he shoved his hands into the pockets of his black riding coat. "There would be many women who would envy you."

"I do not want a lover," she said, moving to stand behind the chair. That seemed necessary…somehow. "He would never marry a woman like me."

Sir Douglas neither frowned nor smiled. His expression was completely noncommittal. "Buggy's not the sort of man to pay much heed to public opinion, or his parents', either. If he wants to marry, I'm sure he won't let anyone stand in his way."

"If he loved me, neither would I," she replied, "but he would have to love me with all his heart. I am not ignorant of the world, Sir Douglas. I know he would be shunned by his friends, his family and all of society. It would be the two of us alone, and only the deepest, most devoted and passionate love would ensure that he didn't come to regret marrying a girl like me."

"You don't think Buggy could love you that much?"

She thought of Lord Bromwell's friendly manner— but it was just that. Friendly. There was no hint of yearning, no hidden passion in his eyes when he looked at her. "*Non*. He is kind and affectionate, but he does not desire me. I'm sure he thinks of me as a friend, and no more."

Sir Douglas turned away and strolled toward the side of the room and a shelf holding some small papier-mâché dogs. "Perhaps you should enlighten Mrs. Tunbarrow on that point," he remarked as he studied them.

"I shall. And you must tell Lord Bromwell of our plan to pretend that we are engaged."

He continued to examine the rather garish knick-knacks. "Easily done. It won't be easy for you, though, returning to your old life when this situation is resolved."

"I think I shall not."

He slowly turned on his heel to regard her. "No?"

She saw no reason not to tell him of the plans she'd been making while she sewed. "The clothes you purchased for me—they are mine to do with as I please, are they not?"

"Yes."

"Then I shall sell them, and take the money and go back to France. I shall become a modiste."

He picked up the apron she had been working on and put it on the chair. "I am no expert on such matters, but I believe you sew very well and your taste is exquisite—certainly better than Madame de Malanche's. I'm sure you would be a great success."

She was flattered and pleased, but disappointed, too, although there was no reason she should be.

"How much money would it require to set up a shop?"

"I don't know," she answered honestly, glancing at the velvet box. Probably a fraction of what that necklace was worth. "I could work from my lodgings at first, until I have a clientele and enough money to rent a separate establishment."

"That could take years."

She didn't disagree.

"I believe it would be a sound investment to loan you the funds to set up your shop in Paris, or anywhere else you choose."

He spoke calmly, dispassionately, as if his offer was nothing—but it was everything to her. The only thing that could make her happier would be if Georges were alive.

Yet she tried not to react with too much emotion, since that disturbed him so. "Thank you. I will repay you every penny."

"I don't doubt it, or I wouldn't make the offer." His lips turned down slightly. "There's no more obligation to me than if I loaned my money to any other friend."

"I thought so," she said. This time, it hadn't even entered her head that he would make immoral demands of her.

"You don't seem very pleased."

He sounded disappointed.

"I am so happy, I cannot find the words!" she exclaimed, abandoning her attempts to subdue the excitement his offer inspired. "You cannot think what this means to me!"

His lips jerked up in a smile that even reached his eyes. "I believe I can make a fairly accurate guess."

"Oh, no, you cannot—not unless you grew up poor, with a father who didn't know how to raise a daughter.

Who went off to war when he found himself deep in debt, taking his oldest son with him, and leaving the younger to manage as best he could. But it was too much responsibility for Georges, who wanted excitement and adventure.

"So he mortgaged the farm for as much money as he could get and left me to be the prey of Gaston LaRoche, who was supposed to take care of me. Georges didn't know Gaston was a terrible man, but I soon found out.

"Thank God I can sew, and now, thanks to you, I can ply my needle for myself, and for Georges if he is found. If I work hard—and I promise you, I will!— I shall be free and independent." She shook her head, her eyes shining. "Oh, no, Sir Douglas, you cannot possibly know what this means to me!"

Just as she could not possibly know what her happiness meant to him, he realized, and that he liked her better when she wasn't trying to hide her feelings. He didn't enjoy it when she was…like him.

Shaken by that revelation, he picked up the velvet box and started toward the door. "Brix and Fanny will be coming to take us to the theater at six o'clock. Until then, Miss Bergerine."

"*Adieu,* Sir Douglas."

He checked his steps and looked back over his shoulder. "If we are to be engaged, you should call me Drury."

"Not Douglas?"

"No, not Douglas. Only my parents ever called me that."

When he was gone, Juliette sank down onto the chair. With Sir Douglas's help, she would be free to live in France, or anywhere she wished.

Except London.

She must not live where Sir Douglas would be, with his dark eyes and deep voice and the way he looked at her. And the way he kissed her. Not unless she wanted to risk her heart to a man who would never marry a woman like her.

Chapter Ten

Sat through Macbeth *last night. Didn't see much of it—too busy watching the audience. Whatever J thinks, didn't see anyone looking daggers at me. Saw plenty of men ogling J. Wished them all at the bottom of the ocean and that bitch Burrell with them.*

—from the journal of Sir Douglas Drury

"This is the most beautiful gown I've ever seen," Polly sighed as she hooked the back of Juliette's theatre dress. "And it fits you *perfectly*."

Juliette couldn't deny either observation as she looked at her reflection. It was indeed a beautiful gown of carmine silk shot through with gold, made in the latest style. The waistline was not near her waist at all, but just beneath her bosom, and the neckline was cut low, exposing the curve of her breasts. The sleeves were small caps, and the skirt was as fluid as water. Beneath, she wore so little in the way of undergarments, it was like being attired for bed.

The fabric had been very expensive and she had

tried to refuse it, until the mercer told her Sir Douglas thought it would suit her. Even the mercer's apparent archenemy, the linen-draper, had agreed, so Juliette had reluctantly acquiesced.

She did not regret it now.

"No wonder Sir Douglas is in love with you! You look as pretty as a picture."

Juliette blushed as a brisk knock sounded at the door.

"Aren't you ready?" Drury demanded when Polly opened it. "Brix and Fanny are—"

He fell silent as Juliette turned toward him.

"Yes, I am ready," she said, breaking the suddenly awkward silence, yet inwardly thrilled by the approval in his dark eyes. She didn't want him to be ashamed of his supposed fiancée.

Just as she could be proud to be seen with such a striking, well-dressed man. His black evening clothes fit to perfection, and his ruffled shirt and starched cravat were whiter than summer clouds. His hair, combed back, looked rather more severe than usual, yet that served to make his angular features even more attractive.

She would surely be the envy of any unmarried women in the theater, and more than a few married ones, too, no doubt.

Sir Douglas nodded at last and gruffly said, "Brix and Fanny are waiting."

He also seemed to recall that he had something in his hands. "Help Miss Bergerine put this on, please," he added, holding the blue velvet box out to Polly.

"Oh, Sir Douglas, it's lovely!" the maid breathed when she did as he asked.

"It was my mother's."

Juliette's hand went instinctively to the necklace. His mother's? A family heirloom?

"Come along then, Miss Bergerine," he said, putting out his arm to escort her. "We don't want to miss the curtain."

Polly followed with Juliette's cashmere shawl as they left the bedchamber and walked down the curving stairs. In the drawing room, Brixton Smythe-Medway stood by the mahogany table, his arms wrapped loosely about his wife. He was whispering something in her ear that made her smile, until they realized they weren't alone and quickly moved apart. Lady Fanny blushed, although her husband seemed not at all embarrassed.

He really was a brazen fellow, yet when he smiled with that mischievous look in his eyes, Juliette could only smile in return.

"What a handsome couple you make!" Lady Fanny exclaimed as she hurried toward them.

She was dressed in a very lovely gown of pale blue, with an ostrich feather dyed to match in her hair. Sapphires sparkled at her ears and around her throat, and she had a diamond-and-sapphire bracelet over her gloved wrist. She, too, had a light cashmere shawl to protect against a chill. "That gown is perfect! And your necklace…"

She glanced inquisitively at Drury.

"I thought she should have something of that sort to go with her gown."

"Very thoughtful, I'm sure," Lady Fanny said.

"Very expensive, too," Mr. Smythe-Medway noted. "Gad, man, you *do* want to cause a stir."

"If I'm going to do this, I intend to do it well."

"As you do everything," his friend replied in an

offhand way, suggesting to Juliette this was not a new observation, and that Mr. Smythe-Medway didn't begrudge Drury his talents or skills.

"Have you ever seen *Macbeth?*" Lady Fanny asked as she took Juliette's arm while Drury put on his hat.

"*Non.* I have never been to the theater, here or in France."

"Then it's sure to be absolutely thrilling. Lady MacBeth's scenes simply curdle my blood!"

The way Lady Fanny spoke, it was clear she didn't mind having her blood curdled on occasion.

Meanwhile, Juliette hoped she wouldn't lose the necklace or come face-to-face with her supposed fiancé's enemies.

When they reached the theater through progressively more crowded streets, Drury was the first to disembark. Still inside the town coach with the coat of arms of Lord Bromwell's father, the Earl of Granshire, on its door, Juliette could hear the voices of many people grow louder and more excited as he stepped to the ground.

"It's always like that," Lady Fanny said with a sympathetic pat on Juliette's arm. "Drury's famous, you see. You should hear it when we're with Buggy, or our friends who've also written books, Edmond and Diana. Sometimes we miss the curtain because people crowd around them so."

Mr. Smythe-Medway winked. "While we lesser satellites risk getting trampled underfoot."

He put his hand on the frame of the door and struck a martyr's pose. "I go to clear a path for you, fair damsels! If I'm not back by the stroke of midnight—"

"We'll go home without you," his wife interrupted,

her voice stern but her eyes laughing. "Enough nonsense, good sir knight, or we'll miss the start of the play and then you *will* face a dragon."

Making a comically horrified face, Mr. Smythe-Medway got out, then reached up to help his wife.

Juliette took a moment to summon her courage. There was nothing to fear, really. She would be with Drury and Mr. Smythe-Medway, and Drury would have his men watching over them, should anybody be so foolish as to attack them in a crowded, public place.

"Juliette?"

Sir Douglas was in the door, looking up at her expectantly.

"The men you hired…?" she asked in a whisper, as worried about the necklace as her own safety.

"Are here, in the crowd," he assured her.

She put her hand in his, noting how his gloves served to hide his damaged fingers. With her other hand on the precious necklace, she climbed out of the carriage. Immediately, the excited whispers grew louder and seemed closer, and she realized many of the finely dressed people nearby were watching them intently.

Not paying them the slightest heed, Mr. Smythe-Medway and Lady Fanny sailed into the theater. Her hand on Sir Douglas's powerful forearm, Juliette and the barrister hurried along behind them.

Entering through the pillared portico, Juliette momentarily paused in the vestibule, facing the staircase flanked by large columns. The space was full of people, several of whom broke off conversations to look at them. Clustered at the foot of the stairs like a flock of exotic birds was a group of women attired in colorful gowns that were cut so low and clinging, they left very little to the imagination. Several of them stared at Sir Douglas unabashedly, their gazes measuring, and more than one attempted to get his attention.

Could one of those women…?

Sir Douglas leaned close. "No," he whispered, his breath warm. "Those women are Cyprians, and I have never paid for my pleasure."

Courtesans. That explained their dresses and their bold manner.

There were several other women in the vestibule who appeared equally and boldly curious. Were all of them whores of varying status, too?

As their party continued forward, Sir Douglas and his friends nodded greetings to several people they passed. Eventually they reached the top of the stairs, where there was a little chamber with a statue inside.

"Well, isn't this a delight?" a woman declared. "It's been an age since you've attended the theater, Sir Douglas."

They all turned toward the woman who had spoken. She was about Sir Douglas's age, Juliette thought, and very beautiful, dressed in an elaborate silk gown of Clarence blue, with a turban on her head, the folds of fabric held in place by a sparkling ruby broach.

"Lady Dennis, a pleasure, as always," Sir Douglas replied. "May I present my fiancée, Miss Bergerine. I believe you already know Mr. Smythe-Medway and his bride."

Lady Dennis smiled as she ran a measuring eye over Juliette. "What a beauty," she said without enthusiasm. She tapped Juliette on the shoulder with her delicate ivory fan. "Brava, my dear. I never thought any woman would catch him—or want to."

Juliette tightened her grip on Sir Douglas's arm. "I thought he was considered a great prize."

"In one way, of course," Lady Dennis replied, brushing her fan across the tops of her breasts as she surveyed the barrister from crown to toe. "Still, I wish you the best of luck, Miss Bergerine," she continued, quite clearly implying that no amount of luck would be enough to save her from a sorry fate.

Lady Dennis must be a very bitter woman—just the sort to exact revenge for a love affair gone wrong. As she swept away to join her party, Juliette leaned closer to Sir Douglas and whispered, "Was she…?"

"No," he replied as they moved on, putting an end to that particular speculation. "I've also made it a point to stay away from vindictive women."

He nodded at another young woman, not as beautiful, but just as well attired. She smiled back warmly. "That is Lady Elizabeth Delamoute. And, yes."

Juliette said nothing, not then or when Sir Douglas quietly nodded a greeting at five other women and murmured yes about each one.

At last they arrived at Mr. Smythe-Medway's box, and before Juliette had even sat down in a chair upholstered in light blue cloth, Sir Douglas had acknowledged three more former lovers, including a beautiful woman in the loveliest of dresses, with the finest figure, in a box on the opposite side of the theater. At present she was surrounded by several obviously admiring men.

"Lady Sarah Chelton—my last," Sir Douglas quietly noted. "The pompous fellow on her left is her husband."

"She does not seem to miss you," Juliette replied, the slightly tart observation spoken without thought. Although how Lady Sarah Chelton could accept the attentions of those other men—including her husband's—after having been with Sir Douglas, mystified her.

Instead of looking annoyed, he smiled as if amused. "I daresay the sheets were barely cool before I was replaced."

"Then she is a fool!"

Suddenly realizing what she had said and, more importantly, what she had implied, Juliette snapped her mouth shut.

Sir Douglas raised her gloved hand and lightly kissed the back of it. "My dear, I'm flattered."

She should pull her hand away—gently, of course, as they were supposed to be engaged. Or at least, she should want to.

She should not be thinking that there were areas in this box no one could see from the pit or the stage, where they would be as good as alone.

"Much as I'm enjoying *your* performance," Mr. Smythe-Medway said quietly, "the play's about to begin, so I suggest you restrain yourself, Drury, or the actors may stage a riot because you're stealing all the attention."

Juliette immediately looked around the theater and the three levels of boxes decorated with gold and realized he was right. Meanwhile, Sir Douglas took his seat behind her.

She should be impressed and amazed by the architecture, the audience and the play about to begin.

She should not be wondering how many more women currently in this building had shared Sir Douglas Drury's bed.

Regardless of what anyone else in the audience thought of Edmund Kean's performance as Macbeth that night—and most of them thought it wonderful, judging by the applause—Drury was relieved when the final curtain came down.

How was it possible that so many of his former lovers had contrived to be at Covent Garden tonight? Even Lady Abramarle, whom he hadn't seen in months, was there. The only ones who were missing were Lady Tinsdale, who'd run off with the steward of her husband's estate and now resided, happily, in Upper Canada, and the unfortunate Lady Marjorie, who had drowned when her ship went down on a voyage to Italy.

Perhaps the rest had heard the news of his engagement and come to see his future bride.

As Kean appeared to make a curtain call, the audience rose as one, clapping and cheering. After a moment's hesitation Drury, too, stood up, dutifully applauding. Brix whistled through his fingers like some uncouth postboy, and Fanny wiped at the tears running down her cheeks.

Juliette, obviously confused, slowly got to her feet. "Is it time to go?" she asked.

"It's a compliment to the actor," Drury explained as he caught sight of Allan Gerrard and the Earl of Buckthorne in the pit among several other dandies of the Town and women of less than sterling repute.

The earl's fleshy mouth hung open as he stared, so that he resembled nothing so much as a giant fish. Gerrard, on the other hand, merely looked at Juliette with admiring approval. Several other men who were also supposedly applauding the accomplished actor were likewise staring at Juliette.

Drury put his arm possessively around her waist. "Just in case anyone's wondering if we are really engaged," he whispered into her shapely ear, telling himself that was the only reason he had to touch her.

If it felt pleasant, too…well, why should it not? She was a young, pretty, shapely woman, which no doubt explained why he'd also had to fight the urge to kiss the nape of her exposed neck, as well as wish every other man in the theater—except the happily married Brix—far, far away, including the actors.

Drury raised his voice over the cheers and applause. "I think we've accomplished all that we need to here."

He dropped his arm from her slender waist as the applause began to die down.

"Have you had many more lovers?" Juliette asked.

She didn't say it like a condemnation, but he found himself embarrassed nonetheless.

Gad, he was becoming as unreasonable and emotional as his mother. "No. One is in Canada, and another is dead."

He lifted Juliette's hand and placed it on his arm. "Now let's see if we can get to the street before the vestibule becomes another mob scene."

Fanny didn't protest, and since she and Brix were closer to the corridor, they led the way out of the box. They were starting toward the stairs, when Brix muttered a curse under his breath and halted, whispering to Drury and Juliette over his shoulder, "Ye gods, beware! Lady Jersey and her cabal approacheth."

Drury didn't bother to hide a scowl. He had little use for the ladies who chose who could enter the socially sacred confines of Almack's. Lady Sefton was considered kind and pleasant, as was Lady Cowper, but the same could not be said of the others, who were as haughty and arrogant as any woman— or man—could be.

He obviously didn't have to tell Juliette who they

were or why Brix spoke as he did, for her grip tightened on his arm and he saw a hint of dismay in her face.

"Don't worry," he said quietly. "They've never given me a voucher before, so I wouldn't expect them to start now, whoever I was engaged to."

She looked up at him not with relief or surprise, but indignant amazement. "They have not? Not ever?"

He blinked before he answered. He hadn't expected that she would care. "Not ever," he replied, as Brix and Fanny retreated to stand against the wall.

Juliette stayed right where she was, regardless of who was coming toward them. "Are you not the best barrister in London, and noble, too?" she demanded. Her smooth brow furrowed as if she was genuinely trying to find a suitable reason for the snub. "Or is it because of all these lovers you've had?"

"Good God, that's not it," Brix answered from behind them. "Countess Lieven surpasses him on that score. It's because he persists in remaining at the Old Bailey. If he would only go to the King's Bench and become a judge, I daresay they'd relent."

"As if I wanted to go to Almack's," Drury muttered. He hated everything Almack's and those supposedly fine ladies stood for. "Brix and Fanny haven't been given a voucher since they announced their engagement there. Buggy won't go even if they do provide a voucher, and neither will I."

"Down, Drury, down," Brix said. "Calm yourself."

"I am calm," he snapped. He mentally shook himself and reminded himself that the grande dames of London society were less important than his most poverty-stricken client. "If I'm bothered at all by those women, it's because of their treatment of my friends."

"As if we care, either," Fanny said with a smile.

With the insouciance of an imp, Brix suddenly stepped forward and clapped a hand on his friend's broad shoulder. "What do you say, Cicero? Shall we give 'em more reason to deny us?"

Without waiting for Drury's answer, Brix moved to block the party of ladies and gentlemen.

"Princess Esterhazy, aren't you looking charming this evening," he said to the plump woman leading the way.

Her lip curled as she drew to a halt. "Mr. Smythe-Medway, have the goodness to get out of the way," she ordered, her Austrian accent making it difficult to understand her words, if not her opinion of Brix.

"Of course! But first, you must permit me to introduce a young lady sure to be an ornament to London society." He literally pulled Juliette forward, making her let go of Drury's arm. "Princess Esterhazy, may I present Miss Juliette Bergerine, the fiancée of the most brilliant barrister of the Old Bailey, Sir Douglas Drury. Done rather well for himself, hasn't he?"

Princess Esterhazy's response was a sniff, and she clearly intended to pass by without another word.

Drury didn't care what they thought about him, but he wasn't about to let the old cat give his friends, or Juliette, the cut direct.

"Allow me the honor of continuing," he said, coming to stand on the other side of Juliette. "Lady Jersey, may I present Miss Bergerine?" He continued to introduce the entire party to her.

Ladies Cowper and Sefton smiled and nodded. Lady Jersey and Countess Lieven frowned, Lady Castlereagh scowled and Mrs. Drummond Burrell's nose couldn't have been raised any higher unless it levitated from her face.

After Juliette made a proper little curtsy, Drury thought that would be the end of it. The Frenchwoman, however, smiled with every appearance of courtesy, all the while regarding Lady Jersey as she might a stain upon her gown.

"Lady Jersey...I have heard of that little island," she said. "It's famous for producing excellent *cows,* is it not?"

Lady Jersey's eyes narrowed.

"No doubt you've been sharing much of the milk with Princess Esterhazy," Juliette continued as if making pleasant and harmless conversation. "Perhaps you should indulge a little less, Your Highness, and then you will be slimmer. Lady Castlereagh, I had heard you were eccentric in your dress, and I see that was not a lie. Speaking of such oddity, Mrs. Drummond Burrell, how brave you are to wear puce with your complexion. And, Countess, I am so happy that you can spare time from your many other interests to come to the theater so that I could meet you here."

The kindhearted Lady Patronesses who had been spared Juliette's apparently innocent, yet snide remarks, looked away. Lady Jersey's lips, however, had thinned until they disappeared; Princess Esterhazy turned as red as a beet; Lady Castlereagh looked as if she'd like to slap the insolent girl; and Mrs. Drummond Burrell's complexion became most unfortunately mottled. As for the countess, she glared at both Juliette and Drury as if her activities had been a state secret and Juliette had just revealed them to the enemy.

"Come, ladies!" Lady Jersey commanded as she all but shoved Drury out of the way.

"I wish you joy in your French wife, sir," Mrs. Drummond Burrell sneered. "I hope she won't be prone to such raging fits of temper as your unfortunate mother. It always struck me as a wonder she wasn't committed to Bedlam."

That damned bitch.

He felt Juliette's hand on his arm. "I'm sorry," she said softly, a look of grave concern in her brown eyes. "Perhaps I should not have—"

"Think no more about it," he brusquely replied, laying his hand over hers. "My mother was most assuredly sane, and Mrs. Burrell knows it."

He thought of the ladies' stunned surprise at Juliette's remarks and not only felt better, but wanted to laugh out loud. "Besides, it was worth the insult to see the looks on their faces."

"Worth it? I should say so!" Mr. Smythe-Medway cried with barely suppressed glee. "You were marvelous, Miss Bergerine! I don't think they've had a setdown like that in years—if ever."

"Sir Douglas! Mr. Smythe-Medway!"

Drury was not happy to see Allan Gerrard making his way toward them, especially with the Earl of Buckthorne at his heels.

"Who's that?" Brix asked out of the corner of his mouth.

"They fence at Thompson's. I had the pleasure of a fencing contest with the tall one. The other one's an earl from Surrey."

Mr. Gerrard and his companion came to a panting halt in front of them. "Ladies, gentlemen, good evening!" Mr. Gerrard exclaimed. "Sir Douglas, Miss Bergerine, what a pleasure to meet you here!"

Despite his annoyance, Drury did as etiquette demanded and made the introductions.

"Gerrard said you were beautiful and damme, he

was right!" the earl declared, taking Juliette's hand in his fat paw and bending down to slobber on the back of it before raising his eyes to stare at her breasts.

Mr. Gerrard looked as displeased as Drury felt, but it was not to the noxious earl he spoke. "You should have told me you were engaged. I would never had made that wager if I'd known."

"Please, do not worry," Juliette said, tugging her hand from the earl's grasp. "I found it rather amusing that my dear Drury would do something so high-spirited. He is not normally so." She slid him a wry glance. "It must be love, I think."

"He's a very lucky man," Mr. Gerrard said, giving her a wistful smile.

"Damn lucky," the earl cried.

Drury glared at the hapless nobleman. "Will you have the goodness to remember that you are not in a gaming hell? Your language is offensive."

The earl blushed. "Oh, yes, well, I was over-come…by her beauty."

"Then I suggest you find somewhere to lie down until you are more in control of your tongue."

The earl nodded and, still blushing, drifted away.

"Is there anything else you care to say to Miss Bergerine?" Drury asked the wealthy merchant's son.

"Only that I wish her every happiness," Gerrard replied with an aplomb that would have done credit to Drury himself.

"Thank you, Mr. Gerrard," she replied, giving him a smile that seemed to rip Drury's heart from top to bottom.

"Now, Gerrard, if you'll excuse us," he said, "it's getting rather late and I have a busy day in court tomorrow."

"I was just saying to Buckthorne that I was going to go to the Old Bailey to watch you. Do you have any idea when your case will come before the judge?"

"No," Drury lied.

"Can anybody watch a trial?" Juliette asked, her expression all innocent curiosity.

Mr. Gerrard lit up like a bonfire. "Yes, they can. Will you be there?"

She leaned a little closer to Drury, her breasts brushing his arm, causing his body to warm against his will. "I should very much like to see my Drury at his work."

My Drury. Why did she have to call him that? Why did he have to like the sound of it so much?

"You might have to sit in the courtroom all day," he warned, hoping that would dissuade her.

He should have known better.

"I will not mind." She slid a glance to Brix, who was grinning as if this were some kind of comedy enacted for his amusement, while Fanny looked a little worried—as well she should.

"The Old Bailey courtroom is not a theater, my dear," Drury said to Juliette. "It is for the business of law, not entertainment."

She pouted as prettily as he'd ever seen a woman pout, and regarded him with pleading eyes. "I want to see why you are so famous."

She was hard to resist when she looked at him like that, but truly, he didn't think the courtroom of the Old Bailey was appropriate…especially if Gerrard, and perhaps the leering earl, would be there, too.

"It's been a while since I've seen you work your magic," Brix remarked. He turned to his wife. "What do you say, Fanny? Would you care to watch Drury skewer his latest victim?"

Did he have to put it that way? "I think, considering your wife's delicate condition, it would be better if you all stayed at home."

Fanny looked at Juliette—Juliette!—before she answered her husband, as if her opinion mattered more than anyone else's. "I've never seen him cross-examine anybody before, and I'm not so delicate that sitting will hurt me. We can always leave if I start to feel unwell."

Juliette smiled as if she'd been given her heart's desire and gripped his arm again. "Please, my sweet, my dearest, won't you let me go?"

He'd likely have a bruise.

And what could he do? He was just as trapped as he'd been in the morning room with the dressmaker. "I'm helpless to say no."

"Oh, thank you! I am so happy!"

He most certainly was not. He had enough to think about during a trial, and the last thing he needed was Juliette and that impudent whelp Gerrard in the gallery.

"If you don't mind, I think I need some fresh air," Fanny said quietly.

Brix took one look at his wife, who had turned a little pale, and whisked her off her feet. Despite her protests, he continued to carry her to the stairs.

"Farewell, Mr. Gerrard, until tomorrow," he called out. "Come along, Drury, Miss Bergerine. No, Fanny, I won't put you down. Yes, I'm sure you're fine, but I'll not risk having you faint on the steps."

"*Adieu,* Monsieur Gerrard!" Juliette called with a wave of her hand as Drury hurried her along behind them.

"He is a nice young man, is he not?" she said lightly as they started down the stairs.

Drury did not answer.

Chapter Eleven

Sir Douglas Drury conducted the sort of cross-examination that, while lacking the emotional fireworks of some of his colleagues, more than achieved its aim.
—the *London Morning Herald*

The next morning, the Honorable Brixton Smythe-Medway led his wife and Juliette through the large gate in the semicircular brick wall outside the Old Bailey. The building was as imposing as a fortress, and Juliette could easily imagine how frightening it would be to be brought here as a prisoner.

Mr. Smythe-Medway, perhaps subdued by the architecture and nature of the edifice, paid the entrance fee without comment and they began to make their way through the narrow entrance to the spectators' gallery.

They were not the only people coming to watch the day's events, and Juliette caught excited whispers of Sir Douglas's name from several small groups as they continued toward the gallery. To think she knew such a famous person—and he knew her.

To think he had even kissed her.

"We seem to have left it a bit late," Mr. Smythe-Medway muttered, craning his neck to see if there might be a space for three people to sit together.

"Mr. Smythe-Medway!"

Waving his arm and smiling, not the least nonplussed by his surroundings, Mr. Gerrard stood well inside the gallery beside one of the pillars, his feet planted wide apart, as if he were trying to take up as much room as possible. Happily, the Earl of Buckthorne wasn't with him.

"Ah, bravo, Mr. Gerrard," Mr. Smythe-Medway said with satisfaction to his companions and an answering wave to Mr. Gerrard. "Between the two of us, we should be able to have enough room. Stay behind me, Fanny, and you, too, Miss Bergerine. I'll get you there." He paused and looked at his wife worriedly. "It is devilishly crowded, though. Maybe you ought to go home, Fanny."

Lady Fanny shook her head and her eyes revealed unexpected determination as she held a perfumed handkerchief over her nose.

"I should know by now it's pointless to try to get you to change your mind," Mr. Smythe-Medway said, exasperated. Even so, love shone in his eyes, as it did every time he looked at his wife. "Very well. Stay close behind me, then. Charge!"

He started through the crowd, most of whom were chatting as if they were at the theater. The smell of so many unwashed bodies in layers of clothing wasn't pleasant, but Juliette was used to far worse, so her handkerchief remained in her reticule.

Getting to Mr. Gerrard wasn't as difficult as she had feared, either. The crowd parted for the well-dressed gentleman and the two women behind him.

"Good morning, Miss Bergerine, Lady Francesca, Mr. Smythe-Medway," Mr. Gerrard said, speaking in a subdued tone, even though he was almost dancing with suppressed excitement. "We're in for a treat! I've even heard wagers are being made on the outcome of Sir Douglas's case—yet there he sits, cool as can be. I can only hope to be half so composed if I'm called upon to represent a prisoner in the dock!"

"Where is Sir Douglas?" Juliette asked, looking down into the courtroom, which was almost as crowded as the gallery.

"There's our Drury," Mr. Smythe-Medway said, pointing to the men in short white wigs and black gowns seated around a semicircular table covered in green baize.

She should have spotted him at once. He was the only one who didn't have piles of paper before him. Instead, he sat as he might at a dinner party, one arm across the table in front of him, the other in his lap, leaning back against the paneling that formed the front of the raised area where men in longer wigs and red robes sat.

"All the barristers sit at that table," Mr. Gerrard explained. "Some come with briefs, others hope to get them from the clerks." He nodded to one side. "And those fellows over there with the ink-stained fingers are the court stenographers. They use a special kind of writing called shorthand."

"Why is that mirror over that man's head?" she asked, indicating the figure standing across from the judges, separated from the rest of the room by a waist-high barrier.

"He's the accused," Mr. Gerrard explained. "He's in what's called the dock, and the mirror is supposed to reflect light from the windows onto his face so that the jury—those fellows right below us—can see him better and watch how he reacts when the witnesses speak."

"Where are the witnesses?"

"That's one speaking now in the witness box. The rest are waiting in another room."

Juliette didn't understand why it was called a witness box when it was round, and said so.

Mr. Gerrard shrugged. "No idea," he ruefully admitted.

She looked at the large windows, then back to the witness. "Is the wooden canopy over his head for shade?"

Mr. Gerrard smiled indulgently. "No, it's a sounding board, to amplify witnesses' voices so the judge and jury can hear them better."

"It does not seem to work very well. I cannot hear him."

"He's speaking rather quietly."

As if the white-wigged, middle-aged judge had heard them, he suddenly turned toward the gallery with a sharp, stern expression. "Order in the court! Silence, or I shall have the gallery cleared."

Juliette flushed guiltily, while Drury calmly raised his eyes and gave a small nod of recognition. She could read nothing from his expression—whether he was pleased to see them, or would rather they hadn't come.

The witness seemed a little flustered by the interruption, but he recovered after a moment and eventually continued stammering through his testimony regarding the character of the young man in the dock, who was accused of breaking a shopkeeper's window while drunk.

"Gentlemen of the jury," the judge began when the witness had finished.

"That's the charge to the jury," Mr. Gerrard told her in a confidential whisper, leaning closer to Juliette in a way that made her uncomfortable. If she'd been wearing a more low-cut gown and no shawl or bonnet, she would have suspected he was trying to peer down her dress.

Fortunately, she was not, but she felt uneasy nonetheless and inched closer to Lady Fanny.

After the judge finished, the men in the jury below huddled together for no more than a minute or two before one of them rose. "Guilty as charged, m'lud."

The judge nodded and the prisoner's shoulders slumped. He brightened considerably when the judge decreed that he only need pay a fine.

"Are trials always so fast?" Juliette asked wonderingly.

"Murders generally take longer," Mr. Gerrard replied, as an old woman was led into the dock. She wore a motley collection of skirts and shawls, and an old bonnet of rusty black covered her gray hair. Obviously frightened and nervous, she looked around as if she'd somehow washed ashore in a foreign land.

Although Sir Douglas hadn't moved when the new prisoner arrived, Juliette noticed a new and subtle tension in his shoulders as he sat at the barristers' table.

The old woman must be the reason he was there.

A man seated at a small table rose. "Harriet Windham, you are charged by your employer, Mr. John Graves, with larceny, for the theft of fifty pounds."

"I didn't do it!" she cried.

The judge hit something that made a sharp bang

and Juliette jumped. "You will get your turn to speak at the appropriate time," he said sternly. "Who represents the prosecutor?"

A stout barrister with quivering jowls got to his feet. "I represent Mr. Graves."

"Well, get on with it then, Mr. Franklin," the judge commanded.

"Yes, m'lud."

Gripping the sides of the opening of his black gown, Mr. Franklin turned toward the jury and thus the gallery, too. "Gentlemen of the jury, as you will soon discover, this is a simple case. On the afternoon of September second, Harriet Windham, then in the employ of Mr. Graves as a laundress, stole fifty pounds from his bedroom while supposedly fetching the bed linens to be washed. However, there was no need for her to fetch the linens, as they had, as always, been delivered to that area of the house where the washing was done.

"Furthermore, gentlemen, it can be proven that Harriet Windham was in dire need of funds, having gotten into debt in the amount of thirty-nine pounds, ten shillings, which she borrowed from a moneylender. On the afternoon of September fourth she paid the moneylender the full amount of the debt without any explanation as to how she had come by the means to do so.

"Also, as you shall hear, Mrs. Windham was observed sneaking down the stairs from the upper floor of the house on the second of September, and she was seen putting something in her petticoat pocket as she did so.

"Mr. Graves, who had discovered the theft upon his return in the evening of September second, heard of her strange behavior as well as her astonishing turn of good fortune, and immediately sought out Mrs.

Windham for an explanation. She refused to give one, leading him to conclude, as you must, that the coincidence of Mr. Graves's loss and his laundress's unusual activities are proof that Mrs. Windham is guilty of the theft of Mr. Graves's fifty pounds."

He glanced at Sir Douglas. "I should also point out, gentlemen of the jury, that one can only wonder what happened to the rest of the fifty pounds and how a woman like Mrs. Windham can afford such legal representation as solicitor James St. Claire and my esteemed colleague Sir Douglas Drury if she did *not* steal it."

There was a general babble of excitement from the people in the gallery, and the old woman gripped the wooden partition in front of her as if it were a lifeboat in a stormy sea.

"She can afford Drury because he represents her pro bono," Lady Fanny whispered to Juliette, who didn't know what that meant.

Seeing her confusion, Lady Fanny explained so that only she could hear. "For nothing, although he keeps that a secret, except to a very few."

That was wise, Juliette thought, or he would surely be pestered by all sorts of thieves and murderers. It was also unexpectedly kind.

Mr. Graves was called to the witness box and swore to tell the truth.

The moment Juliette saw him, however, she didn't like him, and as he began to recount his version of events, she liked him even less. He acted humble, twisting the rim of his tall beaver hat in his slender hands, his shoulders a little rounded as if he was overburdened by what had happened. His manner implied that he really didn't want to accuse Mrs. Windham, but he had no choice. She had stolen his money, and after he had trusted her, too.

Juliette was not fooled. He was exactly like the clients who came to Madame de Pomplona's salon and acted as if they were the most agreeable women in England when ordering a gown, only to continually request changes, or hint that the work should be done for less, or they would—oh, so regrettably—have to take their custom elsewhere, even if the gowns were nearly finished.

"Is something the matter?" Lady Fanny asked her. "You look as if you've seen Mr. Graves before."

Mr. Smythe-Medway moved closer. "He's not the fellow who attacked you?"

"No," she quickly answered, seeing Mr. Gerrard's avid curiosity. "That is not the voice, and he is too thin. But I believe he is lying."

"If he is, Drury will expose him," Mr. Smythe-Medway assured her. "Just watch."

Mr. Graves was still in the witness box when Sir Douglas got to his feet. He regarded Mr. Graves silently for a long moment, then began in a conversational manner, as if they were two men talking over drinks. "We have heard, Mr. Graves, that Mrs. Windham was in debt."

He paused.

"Here it comes," Mr. Gerrard whispered excitedly in Juliette's ear, as unwelcome as a buzzing fly.

"Are *you?*"

Mr. Graves looked taken aback—as did Mr. Franklin—and his face darkened with a blush before he answered. "I'm a man of business, and all businessmen have debts of one kind or another."

"Just so. Exactly what kind of debts have you incurred, Mr. Graves?"

"I told you—business debts. You can't buy and sell merchandise without borrowing from time to time."

"If you say so, Mr. Graves. Not being a merchant, I am woefully ignorant of the finer details of such enterprises. However, have you garnered any debts that are *not* tied to your business dealings? From, perhaps, gambling, to the tune of approximately eight hundred pounds?"

Graves gasped. "Who told you that?"

"I am not the one being examined, Mr. Graves. Do you have gambling debts in the amount of eight hundred pounds, twelve shillings and sixpence?"

"No! That's a lie! And whoever told you that is a damned liar!"

The judge banged that wooden thing again. "Such language will not be permitted in this courtroom. Restrain yourself, Mr. Graves."

The man seemed to shrink a little. "Yes, m'lud. But it's not true."

"Very well, then, Mr. Graves," Sir Douglas calmly continued. "How long have you known Mrs. Windham?"

"Ten years."

"You did not know her before you hired her as a laundress?"

Graves took a moment longer than necessary to answer. "No."

"And you did not *give* Mrs. Windham the fifty pounds you now claim she stole?"

"No!" Graves wiped his brow with the back of his hand. "Why would I do that?"

"Precisely what I hope to reveal. You did not give her the money and then threaten her, telling her that if she dared to speak of this to anyone, and especially your wife, she would be sorry?"

"No!"

Sir Douglas raised his brows as if surprised by that answer, but said no more as he returned to his seat at the green baize table. Mr. Graves, released from his testimony, quickly left the box.

Whatever answers the man had given, Juliette was sure he was lying, and Sir Douglas had discovered the truth. Mr. Graves had given the money to Mrs. Windham and later falsely accused her of theft.

And Juliette had no doubt the jury would think as she did, too.

Mr. Franklin next called on the moneylender who had been repaid by Mrs. Windham. He confirmed she had arrived at his place of business on the morning of September the fourth and paid her debt. He had the receipt with him, as a matter of fact.

Sir Douglas then approached the witness box. "Did Mrs. Windham tell you how she got the money to repay you?"

"No," the wiry, wary man replied. "Ain't none o' my business, long as I gets what's owed."

"How did she appear?"

"Just like she is now."

"Oh? Nervous and afraid?"

"Wearing them exact same clothes," the money-lender clarified, to the amusement of many in the gallery, including Mr. Gerrard.

Not Juliette. She could easily imagine being in that poor woman's place, falsely accused and confounded by what was happening. She also noticed that neither Lady Fanny nor Mr. Smythe-Medway seemed to find his answer funny.

"I apologize for not being more clear," Sir Douglas said, ignoring the reaction of the spectators. "Was she agitated, or otherwise upset?"

"A little bit, but then, most of my customers are."

"She was not furtive, or wary of being seen in your company?"

"No, can't say she was."

"Thank you, Mr. Levy."

The middle-aged, careworn Mrs. Graves was the next to be called. She swore her oath and repeated a story similar to her husband's—that the money had gone missing from their bedroom and no one else had been in that room except for Mrs. Windham.

When Mr. Franklin had finished his questions, Sir Douglas rose once more, his manner quite different from when he'd questioned Mr. Graves. Although his expression didn't alter much, Juliette felt—and she was sure everyone else did, too—that he wished to be gentle with the anxious woman toying with her bonnet strings.

"Now then, Mrs. Graves, we understand that Mrs. Windham has been in your employ for ten years."

"Yes."

"Your husband never said he had any acquaintance with her before he engaged her services?"

"No."

"In all the time you've known her, has Mrs. Windham ever stolen anything?"

"Not that I know of."

"Yet she has always been as poor as she is now?"

"I—I suppose so."

"What can you tell us of her family and her responsibilities?"

"Well, her husband's been dead a long time," Mrs. Graves said slowly. "And her boy, Peter, was killed at Waterloo. After that her daughter-in-law and grandson came to live with her. Mary—that's her daughter-in-law—has been sickly since she had the baby. I know Harriet worried about her and little Arthur—that's her grandson—terribly. They've had to call the doctor more than once, and he told her that Mary needed special foods and fresh air, so Harriet sent Mary and the boy to Brighton for the sea air."

Juliette wondered why Sir Douglas had sought that information. These problems would explain why the poor washerwoman needed money and why she would steal it.

"Did she know about your husband's debts?"

Mrs. Graves shook her head. "I never talked about my husband's business."

"Those are not the debts to which I am referring, Mrs. Graves. Did you not confide to Harriet Windham that your husband had started to gamble and you feared he would lead your family to ruin? Did you not tell her you had found promissory notes in his study in the amounts of seven hundred pounds and fifty pounds, and you feared he might owe even more?"

"I—I might have told her something like that," Mrs. Graves replied, "but Martin explained it all to me after the money went missing. Those weren't gambling debts. A shipment of olive oil got lost at sea. He hasn't been gambling at all. I was just being silly and worried for nothing."

"I see," Sir Douglas said, his tone implying that while he might not wish to question her further about that, he certainly didn't believe her husband's explanation. "What reason did he give for having fifty pounds in cash in your bedroom?"

"He didn't give me any. I didn't even know it was there until it went missing."

"In the past, when your husband has encountered

financial difficulties such as the loss of a shipment of goods, where has he gone to borrow money? A bank, perhaps, or a moneylender?"

"He goes to my father."

"Must he repay the money he gets from your father?"

Mrs. Graves looked around and licked her lips before replying. "No. It's a gift."

"A most generous parent, indeed! To your knowledge, when was the last time your husband received such a gift?"

"Last month, when the olive oil shipment was lost."

Sir Douglas had no more questions for Mrs. Graves, so she returned to the adjoining room as the next witness came into the courtroom.

The new witness was a pretty young woman dressed in a manner designed to flaunt her physical charms, like those Cyprians at the theater. Juliette also suspected her lips and cheeks got their color as much from cosmetics as nature, and she brazenly swayed her hips as she strolled toward the box.

Watching from above, Juliette caught the look that passed between the two women, one coming in, the other going out. Mrs. Graves obviously disliked the younger woman, while the younger woman regarded Mrs. Graves as if she were a poor, pathetic fool.

Chapter Twelve

Drury was in fine form, I must say. Of course, I suspect he had an added incentive. Normally he doesn't pay any attention to the gallery at all, but he certainly did this time.
—A letter from the Honorable Brixton Smythe-Medway to Lord Bromwell, *The Collected Letters of Lord Bromwell*

Once in the box, the young woman, who was identified as Millicent Davis, the Graveses' housemaid, surveyed the courtroom. Her bold gaze lingered longest on the barristers, and Sir Douglas in particular.

He, however, barely glanced at her and listened impassively as Mr. Franklin began his questions. "Miss Davis, please tell the court what you witnessed on the afternoon of September second."

"Well, Mr. Franklin, it was like this," Miss Davis eagerly replied. "I was dusting in the parlor and I seen Mrs. Windham sneaking down the front stairs and she was putting something in her petticoat pocket. Right strange it was, since she had no business to be on the stairs at all."

"Just so we are clear," Mr. Franklin said, "Mrs. Windham had no reason to be on the front stairs that day?"

"No, nor any other day. She's only a washerwoman."

"Thank you, Miss Davis," Mr. Franklin said as he returned to his seat.

Sir Douglas rose and even from where she sat, Juliette could tell that the brazen young woman should be wary. "So, you were dusting in the parlor, Miss Davis?"

"Yes, I was," she replied with a pert smile.

"You are diligent in your tasks, are you?"

"As much as most, I'm sure. I could see the stairs from where I was working."

"You told Mr. Graves about this strange behavior?"

"Yes, o' course I did!"

"When?"

The single word was like a gunshot, startling everyone, including the judge.

While Miss Davis flushed and balked, Sir Douglas said, "When exactly did you tell your employers what you had seen?"

"The n-next day," she stammered. "I…I forgot in all the hubbub."

"The hubbub that occurred the same day money went missing and you spied Mrs. Windham acting furtively on the stairs?"

Miss Davis looked around the courtroom as if expecting somebody to come to her aid or answer for her. "Yes," she muttered when no one did.

Sir Douglas raised a coolly querying brow. "Had *you* been in the master's bedroom that day?"

Miss Davis suddenly looked a little ill.

"You are under an oath, Miss Davis," Sir Douglas reminded her.

"I was there," she defiantly replied, "but I didn't know the money was there. Mr. Graves told me he didn't have any."

"You had some cause to be speaking of Mr. Graves's financial situation and he revealed that to you?"

"He…he'd promised to buy me a new dress and then he said he didn't have any money."

"Was there a particular reason he promised you a new dress?"

Miss Davis looked around the courtroom before she turned to the judge. "Do I have to answer that?"

"I presume her response will have a bearing on this case, Sir Douglas?" the judge asked the barrister.

"I believe so, yes, my lord."

"Answer the question, Miss Davis," the judge ordered.

"He was supposed to buy me a new dress because…because I'd earned it!"

"Indeed?" Sir Douglas replied as if fascinated. "How?"

She pressed her lips together, then tossed back her head and declared, "By getting into bed with him—but whatever I done, I still seen her—" she pointed at Mrs. Windham "—sneaking down the stairs!"

Many of the spectators burst out into excited whispers, until a stern look from the judge silenced them.

Juliette, however, was too worried to speak. She knew she wasn't the only one concerned with this apparently damning testimony when Lady Fanny grasped her hand.

Yet Sir Douglas seemed completely at ease as he

returned to his seat, reassuring Juliette without a word and reminding her that the trial wasn't over.

Mr. Franklin summoned a few more witnesses, all of whom bore testimony to Mr. Graves's sterling character and heartily denied he gambled or did anything remotely immoral. Coming after Miss Davis's answers, however, these testimonials fell rather flat.

"M'lud, that concludes the case on the part of the prosecution," Mr. Franklin said as the last of these men stepped down.

"Now Drury will speak, will he not?" Juliette asked Lady Fanny, sure he would make a speech that would leave Mr. Franklin's opening remarks in the dust.

"No, the barrister for the accused doesn't do that," Mr. Gerrard replied, although she hadn't asked him. "Mrs. Windham must speak for herself."

"That does not seem fair," Juliette said, frowning.

Mr. Gerrard looked taken aback, clearly shocked that anyone would question British legal procedure. "If a person is innocent, why would he need a barrister, except to question witnesses?"

"Is it not obvious?" Juliette retorted. "Look at poor Mrs. Windham! She is like a person lost in the wilderness. How is she to face all these men in their wigs and their gowns and not be afraid? And if she is afraid, she may become confused and make mistakes."

"She has a good solicitor, and Sir Douglas, too."

"What if she could not afford such counsel?"

Mr. Gerrard flushed and shrugged his shoulders.

What *could* he say? she supposed. It was not just.

Mrs. Windham cleared her throat, glanced anxiously at Sir Douglas and then began in a high, wavering voice that said more about her fear than her age. "I'm a good, honest, God-fearing woman. I've worked all my life, first as a scullery maid, then a washerwomen after my poor husband died. I've been working for the Graveses for nigh on ten years, with never a bit o' trouble between the mistress and me—nor Mr. Graves, neither.

"The day the money went missing, Mr. Graves come to me and told me his wife hadn't been feeling well, so I'd have to go up and fetch the bedding from their bedroom myself. I was worried about the missus and asked what was the matter, and he said nothing serious. Still, she ain't had time to get the linen changed.

"No trouble, says I, and I goes up to the bedroom. But there weren't no linen there, so I comes downstairs again. Three days later, there's the Runners at my door, sayin' Mr. Graves had accused me o' stealing and to come along with them.

"I was gobsmacked, and no mistake. I ain't never stole nothin' in my life, but they wouldn't listen. And then I gets to Bow Street and there's Mr. Graves, stern as a judge—beggin' your pardon, m'lud—and sayin' I stole fifty pounds out of his bedroom. But on my poor son's life, I didn't steal any money! I'm a good woman, I am!"

She began to weep, sniffling and swiping at her eyes.

"Thank you, Mrs. Windham," the judge said. "Sir Douglas, you may call your first witness."

"I have only one witness. Please summon Mary Windham."

Harriet Windham started and looked about to protest, but one glance from Sir Douglas and she covered her face with her hands as a pale, thin girl who didn't look more than sixteen went to the witness box. Her dress was shabby, but clean, her bonnet cheap and plain. She bit her lip and entwined her fingers as she stood waiting to be questioned.

"You are the daughter-in-law of Harriet Windham, are you not?" Sir Douglas asked, his voice calm and matter-of-fact. Indeed, it was almost soothing.

"Yes."

"Your mother-in-law, Mrs. Windham, offered no explanation to the moneylender for the payment he received. Did she tell *you* where she got the money?"

"Yes, but she made me promise not to tell."

That caused another flutter of excitement in the gallery, and Juliette, too, leaned forward anxiously to hear.

"You have sworn an oath in court to speak the truth," Sir Douglas reminded Mary Windham. "It seems you must break your oath to Mrs. Windham in order to be truthful to the court. Will you do it?"

Although she looked utterly miserable, the young woman nodded her head. "Yes."

Harriet Windham let out a cry of dismay.

Her daughter-in-law regarded her with anguish. "Better the truth and shame for what isn't a crime than be found guilty of stealing when you're innocent."

"Mrs. Windham, where did your mother-in-law say she got the money?" Sir Douglas repeated.

"From Mr. Graves."

"The same man who accused her of the theft?"

"Yes, sir."

"Did she tell you *why* he gave her the money?"

With baleful eyes, Mary Windham again looked at her mother-in-law. Then her demeanor changed to one of grim determination. "Because he owed her, she said, because of what he done to her twenty years ago.

She was a scullery maid in his mother's house and he got her pregnant. My husband was his son."

Juliette had suspected the man was not to be trusted; even so, she hadn't expected this, and neither had the other spectators. Even the court stenographers looked up from their work, mouths agape.

"So when the moneylender threatened to send us all to debtor's prison if she couldn't pay him back, she went to Mr. Graves and asked him to lend her the money instead. He wouldn't. He said he'd done enough for her giving her work now, although he was the reason she'd lost her place all those years before.

"So Harriet told him that she knew he hadn't changed his ways—that he'd been doing it with the housemaid, and if he didn't help her, she'd tell his wife. That put the fear o' God into him, because it's her father keeps his business going.

"So Mr. Graves, he said, come to the bedroom and I'll give you fifty pounds. So she did and he did, but he warns her that if she tells his wife about the money or what's been going on with him and Davis, she'll be sorry. He says he knows men that'll kill for a shilling and she'll wind up floatin' in the Thames—and me and Arthur, too. That's why she hasn't said where she got the money—she's afraid he'll do it. She'd rather be hanged or transported than risk our lives."

As the chatter in the gallery grew louder, Juliette began to wonder if Graves was an even worse villain than she suspected. Perhaps he'd heard that Sir Douglas would be acting for Mrs. Windham; surely he would be aware of his reputation. Perhaps he'd been so determined to keep his secrets, he had tried to have the man representing Mrs. Windham in court—a man known for ferreting out the truth—killed.

But why would he have Juliette attacked, too?

"Oh, Mary, Mary!" Harriet Windham cried. "Oh, my poor wee Arthur!"

"Quiet! Quiet in the courtroom!" the judge called out. "Sir Douglas, have you any more questions for this witness?"

"No, my lord," he replied, once more returning to the semicircular table and resuming his seat.

In spite of his apparent nonchalance, Juliette saw the tension in his body and the look of compassion he gave Mary Windham as the young woman left the witness box.

"Gentlemen of the jury," the judge said after she had departed from the courtroom, "you have heard the charge against the accused, and testimony as to what transpired during the afternoon of September second. Mr. Graves, the prosecutor, has given his version of events, as have his witnesses. The witness for the accused has given hers. I note that there is no evidence other than that of the witnesses, Mr. Graves and the accused. You must, therefore, render judgment based solely upon that testimony."

After he had spoken, the jury once again huddled in their seats, whispering.

Juliette clasped her hands with worry, while Sir Douglas likewise waited, sitting too still, his shoulders too straight, his gaze not on the jury or Mrs. Windham or the gallery. Instead, he stared out the window.

The jury soon returned to their seats and the man on the end rose. "My lord, we find Harriet Windham not guilty."

Juliette let out a shriek of relief and joy.

Drury's head shot up and he looked directly at her. Instantly embarrassed, she clapped her hand over her mouth and shrank behind the pillar. As she did, she realized that Mr. Smythe-Medway and his wife were apparently too busy smiling at each other to have noticed her faux pas.

"I knew it!" Mr. Smythe-Medway said gleefully after a moment, while Lady Fanny squeezed Juliette's hand. "Come on, let's get out of here. Fanny, you need fresh air."

Juliette didn't wish to stay in the courtroom either, now that Sir Douglas's case was over. Unfortunately, Mr. Gerrard had also decided to leave, and he followed them as they slowly worked their way back toward the narrow entrance. Several other people also made their exit, more than a few commenting on the character of Mr. Graves, or lack thereof.

Juliette immediately foresaw a downturn to the man's business, and while she didn't feel sorry for him, she pitied his wife. Hopefully Mrs. Graves's father would ensure that she didn't suffer because of her husband's behavior.

Once on the street, Mr. Smythe-Medway walked a short distance ahead of them to find a hackney.

"How long will Sir Douglas be at court?" Juliette asked his wife, trying not to notice Mr. Gerrard lingering nearby.

"I don't know," Lady Fanny replied. "Oh, there he is, with that poor woman and her daughter-in-law."

Juliette followed her gaze to where Sir Douglas, now without his wig and gown, stood talking to the two women. They were obviously thanking him profusely. Another man she recognized from the courtroom stood with them. He was not handsome, but not homely, either, and there was something pleasant about his smile.

"We might as well wait for Brix there as here," Lady Fanny said. "You can meet Jamie St. Claire. He's a solicitor who often calls upon Drury to present his briefs. He's a very clever young man, Drury says."

Juliette saw no reason not to cross the street, and the fact that it would take them a little farther from Mr. Gerrard made her even more keen to follow Lady Fanny's suggestion.

After nodding a somber greeting, Sir Douglas made the introductions and the two women shyly dipped curtsies. Jamie St. Claire seemed only slightly more at ease, and almost immediately excused himself. "I've got another client to see in Newgate," he said, touching his hat. "Good day, Sir Douglas, ladies."

"I was so happy that you were acquitted," Lady Fanny said to the Windhams after he had gone.

"We owe it all to Sir Douglas," Mary replied.

"I think not," Sir Douglas demurred. "Harriet owes it all to you, for revealing what she would not. And I assure you, you need not fear Mr. Graves. He won't lay a hand on you now that everyone's heard what he threatened to do."

The two women nodded, and for the first time, Harriet Windham smiled with genuine relief.

Sir Douglas turned to Juliette. "Well, Miss Bergerine? What do you think of British jurisprudence?"

"I have never seen a French trial, so I cannot compare," she answered honestly. "But I think you are a very good barrister."

The older woman gasped, then backed away as if Juliette had cursed. The younger woman's brows lowered and her eyes filled with hate.

For a moment, Juliette was stunned by the sudden

change…until she remembered what she'd heard in court. Their son and husband had died at Waterloo.

For a little while she had been able to forget the way most English people felt about the French.

The arrival of a hackney fortunately prevented any more conversation, especially when Mr. Smythe-Medway opened the door and cheerfully called out, "My lady, Miss Bergerine, Sir Douglas, your chariot awaits!"

"Get in," Sir Douglas ordered.

Juliette did, without question or delay.

As the carriage rolled toward Buggy's house, Drury paid no attention to Brix's excited postmortem of the trial or Fanny's measured responses. He was too aware of Juliette's subdued silence as she looked out the window beside her.

He had forgotten. He, who had vowed to hate the French for as long as he lived, had lost that hatred without even realizing it. He had forgotten, too, that he had not been alone in his prejudice, and that even good-hearted women like the two Mrs. Windhams could share it.

Yet they would have been even more upset if they knew the truth—that Peter Windham had not died at Waterloo. He'd been killed somewhere else in France, by cruel men who took their time to do it. He'd been deceived by the same duplicitous Frenchman who'd betrayed Drury. And broken all his fingers.

"I know!" Brix cried, drawing him from his unhappy memories. "We should all go to Vauxhall to celebrate Drury's latest triumph!"

He didn't feel like celebrating. Not now. Not even when Juliette turned from the window, her face alight with interest, and said, "I have never been there, and I would like to go—very much."

"Then it's settled," Brix declared, taking his wife's hand.

"Are you sure?" she asked Juliette. Fanny had always been a little more perceptive than her husband.

"Oh, yes."

Perhaps she really did want to go. And her next words told him why.

"It is a public place, is it not? Perhaps our enemies will finally take the bait."

Chapter Thirteen

The activities of young men in Vauxhall Gardens are nothing short of a disgrace and an affront to all decent people. I strongly urge the mayor to consider more effective safeguards, or the Gardens shall cease to be anything but a place of lewd and unacceptable activity.

—from a letter to the editor of the
London Morning Herald

"**V**auxhall Gardens?" Polly repeated as she dressed Juliette's hair in preparation for the evening of celebration.

"*Oui,*" Juliette replied, trying to sound excited.

She did want to see the famous Gardens, but those two women had reminded her that she could never really belong in England. The past few days had been a dream. A pleasant dream, but still a dream.

"Oh, it's something, miss, it is!" Polly exclaimed. "The walks and the fountain, and there's fireworks sometimes, too. It's a good thing you'll be with the gentlemen, though, miss. There's always scoundrels lurking in the Dark Walks. They lie in wait for young women and grab them and…well, I've heard they get up to all sorts of mischief."

It sounded like a suitable place for an ambush, Juliette realized.

She should be pleased, she supposed. Was it not her plan to encourage their enemies to make a move? Should she not be eagerly anticipating an end to this strange life, especially when she had the promise of her own shop to look forward to?

She *did* want this situation to be over and done with. Sir Douglas had promised her a future for which she was suited and that would surely make her happy, even if Georges were dead. The sooner she was free to pursue it, the better.

"Aren't you feeling well?" Polly asked worriedly as she shoved in the last pin to hold Juliette's hair into a simple style *à la grec*. She wore a pretty, and warm, gown of deep blue velvet, made without embellishment. It was simple, yet flattering, and didn't call attention to itself.

Not like the gowns those women at the theater wore.

"No, I am fine," Juliette said, rising. "I was just trying to imagine the Gardens. This will be my first time visiting them."

"You'll have a wonderful time, I'm sure!"

Juliette smiled with more hope than certainty as she picked up her cashmere shawl and hurried to the drawing room where Sir Douglas awaited her.

"Close the door, if you please," he said after she had entered, his manner somber and subdued.

Suddenly terrified, fearful that something bad had happened, she did as he asked.

"Is it Georges?" she asked in a whisper, her throat as dry as an empty cup.

"Oh, God, no!" he cried. He took a hesitant step forward. "Sam hasn't returned from Calais, and I haven't had any more news from MacDougal's men. It's not that at all."

Even as relief took away her terror, she wondered what had happened to his arrogance, his supreme confidence.

He came a little closer, still unexpectedly hesitant, almost…humble?

"I wanted to apologize, Juliette," he said, his voice deferential. "I was very unkind to you the day we met, worse even than the women today. Since I came home from the war, I've harbored a hatred of the French because of what happened to me there. I blamed your entire nation for the cruel, painful deeds of a few. I should have known better, behaved better. I'm truly sorry, and ashamed. I owed you my life, and I reacted like a spoiled, ignorant child. I hope you can forgive me."

She stared at him with amazement, not sure what to say.

He frowned. "Is it so hard to believe that I can admit when I've been wrong?"

He was again the Drury she knew—to her relief. That humble, tentative demeanor had made him seem like a stranger. An interesting stranger, but she preferred the confident man in control of himself and his world. That man made her feel safe and confident, too.

"You simply caught me unaware," she explained. "I was not expecting an apology."

"Do you forgive me?"

It was not exactly a demand, but he was not

pleading, either. He was acting as she would expect a proud man to act.

"Since you have apologized, yes, I forgive you," she answered honestly.

He took another step closer, his head tilting slightly sidewise, as a slow, seductive smile grew upon his darkly handsome face. "I'm very glad to hear that, Miss Bergerine. And you look very beautiful tonight."

This change was…not so welcome. She suddenly felt *less* confident, more the poor woman indebted to a rich man.

She backed away from him and that seductive smile. "Why do you say that?"

"I'm paying you a compliment. I think you're a beautiful woman."

"My mirror tells me I am not."

He was close now. Much too close. "Your mirror, Miss Bergerine, is a liar."

She should run away from him before he touched her and while she was still mistress of her rapidly beating heart. While she could ignore the desire coursing through her body like the strongest wine.

Yet her feet would not cooperate.

"You are more than beautiful, Miss Bergerine," he said softly. "You're also one of the most courageous women I've ever met."

"You—you flatter me," she stammered, unable to meet his intensely searching gaze.

What question was he really asking? What answer did he expect?

What answer did she want to give?

"Sir Douglas, the Honorable Brixton Smythe-Medway and his wife are here," Millstone announced from behind the closed drawing-room door.

Juliette gasped as if she'd been drowning, while Sir Douglas scowled as if he detested the Honorable Brixton Smythe-Medway and his wife.

"We're coming," he called out. Then he raised a coolly inquisitive brow. "Shall we, Miss Bergerine?"

"Yes," she said, taking his arm.

Although what she really wanted to do—God help her!—was kiss him.

As they rode in the Smythe-Medways' town coach to the Gardens, Juliette couldn't stop imagining what might have happened if Millstone hadn't interrupted. Kissing would have been the least of it, she suspected, and as she sat in the coach with Drury beside her, his thigh touching hers, his arm against hers, she opened the fan carved from sandalwood that dangled from her wrist and desperately tried to cool her heated blood.

"Too warm?" Mr. Smythe-Medway asked solicitously.

"Just a little," she murmured.

"Drury, you're looking a little flushed, too," his friend noted. "I hope you haven't caught gaol fever."

"I feel fine," he replied.

Regardless of his brusque response, Mr. Smythe-Medway reached over and pulled down the coach window a little. "Better?"

"I told you, I'm fine," Drury repeated more forcefully. "I wouldn't want Fanny or Miss Bergerine to catch a chill."

"I am quite comfortable," Juliette lied.

"This new shawl is very warm," Lady Fanny assured her husband with a smile. "Diana sent it."

For the rest of the journey, Drury and his friends discussed Viscount Adderley, his wife and their infant son, as well as somebody in the navy named Charlie. Juliette couldn't help feeling left out, but then, why should she be included? She didn't know these people and soon enough, she would be gone from their lives and they from hers.

When they arrived at the Gardens, they quickly disembarked. The gentlemen paid the fee and they entered.

It was like stepping into a fairy tale.

"Oh, this is lovely!" Juliette cried at the sight of the tree-lined avenue lit by hanging lamps.

"Five thousand lanterns are certainly impressive," Drury remarked as he took her arm to lead her down the Grand Walk bordered by elms. Mr. Smythe-Medway and his wife followed at a leisurely pace and soon were several paces behind them.

To any casual observer, she and Sir Douglas would look like another of the many couples in the Gardens that night, Juliette thought. There were larger clusters of people, too, and more than one obviously tense chaperone, as well as groups of young men who boldly eyed the young women. A few such men looked their way but, to her relief, a mere glance from Drury was enough to make them turn their insolent attention elsewhere.

She wondered if any of the men lounging about belonged to MacDougal. Some of them must. She hoped.

"I fear I'm too jaded to properly appreciate the glories of Vauxhall," Sir Douglas observed after a moment. "It takes fresh eyes and youthful enthusiasm to make one value it."

"You speak as if you are a hundred years old."

"I turned thirty last year."

"Oh, yes, very ancient," she replied, thinking how much more attractive a mature man was than a younger one, like Mr. Gerrard. "Soon you will no doubt require a cane."

"How old are you, Miss Bergerine?"

"Twenty."

"A mere infant."

"I am old enough to look after myself—and you, too. Remember?"

"How could I forget?" he replied with a hint of sarcasm.

"How can *I?*" she countered. "But I am no child."

"I can't forget that, either," he said quietly, his voice low and a little husky.

Her pulse quickened. Plan or no plan, perhaps she should not have come here with him.

"I fear we're both older than our years in some ways," he said after another silence. "Our experiences have made it so, whether we wished it or not."

She heard the acceptance, and the hint of despair. "Yet we survive, and you do good work, I think."

He gave her a little smile at that. "And you can make a woman happy with a pretty, well-made gown. Sometimes it's the little things that can make the most difference on an otherwise unhappy day."

She had not thought of her work in that way, yet when he said it, she felt as if she had received a wonderful compliment. To be sure, she would never save anyone's life by sewing, but it was still pleasant to think that she could make a small difference in a woman's life, if only with a dress.

They walked a little farther in silence, although it was becoming obvious that more than one person recognized Sir Douglas here, too. It was, she supposed, to be expected. "I see you are well-known everywhere in London."

"Unfortunately, yes."

"You do not enjoy being well-known?"

"It has its drawbacks." He slid her a pointed glance. "Have you forgotten?"

She turned away so he wouldn't see her face. She *had* forgotten. For a little while, she had forgotten this was just a ruse, and she was not really with him, not in that way.

Not in the way she wished she could be.

There. She had admitted it, at least to herself. But it must not be. She had too much to lose, including her pride and self-respect, if she succumbed to the urges of her body.

Trying to turn her thoughts from the impossible, she pointed to a structure on their left with a high curved dome. "What is that?"

"The Temple of Comus."

"Who?"

"Comus, the god of festivities, parties and…"

"And?" she prompted when his voice trailed off.

Because of his reluctance, she had an inkling what the "and" referred to, but that didn't prevent her from wanting to hear him describe it.

"Certain activities that tend to take place at night."

"Oh?" she murmured with mock innocence. "What kind of activities?"

"Between a man and a woman."

"Conversation? Music? A little supper?"

He stopped walking to look down at her with a quizzical expression. "Are you teasing me, Miss Bergerine?" His voice lowered. "Or do you really not know the sort of intimate activities to which I am alluding?"

The amusement that had been lurking in his eyes altered to something else, something deeper and more powerful, something that demanded a similar response from her in this magical place that seemed apart from the real world. Here, anything might happen, if she wanted it to, and if ever a man could lure her into forgetting her morals, she was looking at him now. If ever she had wanted to do improper things, she was tempted to do them here, with him.

"I have an idea." She might be a virgin, but she had heard things in the shop when the women talked among themselves, and she *had* grown up on a farm.

"Just an idea?"

"*Oui.* Did you think otherwise?"

"Your state, virginal or otherwise, is no concern of mine."

She came back to reality with a hard thump. What else had she expected? That he would be pleased? Relieved? That he would care?

He glanced back over his shoulder. "I see we've outstripped Brix and Fanny. Fine chaperones they are. Well, which way would you like to go, Miss Bergerine? The South Walk with its pretty ruins and fountain, or the Hermit's Walk with the charming representation of a religious fanatic?"

"If we wish to provoke your enemy, should we not go into the Dark Walks?"

He looked a little startled. "The Lovers' Walk?"

"We are here to entice your enemies into action, aren't we?" she challenged. "How better than by going to a suitable place for an ambush? You have men here to protect us even if I cannot see them, don't you?"

"I do, but I don't think walking into an ambush is

ever a good idea." Suddenly a scowl darkened his face. "Here comes that odious Buckthorne."

The earl was indeed staggering in their direction, his arms around two buxom beauties, much rouged and powdered. There was another fellow with them, likewise half walking, half leaning on two women who were dressed in a way that suggested they were paid companions. Juliette was relieved to see that the second fellow wasn't Mr. Gerrard. He had distressed her in the courtroom, but she didn't want to think he was a drunkard like the earl.

The earl and his female associates came to a halt, as did the other couple behind, the man nearly slipping to the ground.

"Make way there, can't you? You're blocking the bloody path," Buckthorne slurred. His eyes narrowed, then widened. "Oh, I say, is it…it is! G'evening, Sir Douglas."

He smiled at Juliette and tried to bow without falling over. "Miss Brid…Bertin…Bergine?"

"Good evening, Buckthorne," Drury growled, taking Juliette's arm and all but pulling her past them. "If you'll excuse us."

"I say!" the earl cried indignantly.

Drury ignored him.

"Bad breeding always shows, as my father used to say," the earl sneered behind them. "After all, his mother was a whore."

Drury hesitated, and Juliette wondered if he was going to challenge the inebriated nobleman to a duel after such an insult. Instead, Sir Douglas's lips tightened, and he continued to escort her to the Dark Walks.

"That man is a toad," she declared, indignant for Sir Douglas's sake.

"I'd consider that a rather generous assessment," he muttered before halting again and demanding, "What do you know about my mother?"

"Very little, except that I do not think she was a loving parent."

"Not loving to me, and not to my father," he replied, starting to walk again. "To other men, often. So the odious Earl of Buckthorne was unfortunately correct. She was also given to fits of temper and rages. She could be kind one moment, terrible the next. I never knew what to expect, so I quickly learned to avoid her if I could."

Juliette could imagine that. She could picture a wide-eyed, dark-haired, frightened little boy hiding from his parents, wanting to be loved, but afraid of them, too.

"My mother died shortly after I was born, so I had only Papa and my brothers," she said quietly. "Papa did not know what to do with a daughter. I did not fear him, but much of the time, it was as if I was not even there.

"I think he was relieved to go to war, to get away from the farm and his responsibilities and…and me," she whispered, the pain of that belief undiminished despite the years that had passed since he had gone.

"Nobody cared what might happen to me—except for Georges," she added, telling herself that was true in spite of the excitement in his eyes when he'd bade her farewell. "Georges promised to come back for me."

"Yet for whatever reason, he did not," Drury said, "and now you're as alone in the world as I am."

They had that, at least, in common. That, and one other thing she didn't want to think about, lest she act on that desire. "*Oui,* I am alone."

They had reached what must be the Dark Walks, for this way was much less brightly lit. She could see how certain…things could happen here.

Then she heard voices coming toward them from nearby—at least three men, a little the worse for drink, and one of them sounded like Mr. Gerrard.

She didn't want to meet him here any more than she had wanted to meet the earl. Neither, it seemed, did Sir Douglas, for he swore under his breath and ducked into the walk, pulling her with him.

"The last thing we need is to be accosted by a gang of drunken louts," he muttered under his breath.

She wasn't thinking of louts, drunken or otherwise. She was too aware of his hand around hers, and that they were as good as alone. Together. In the dark.

This way *was* dangerous, although not because of anyone else.

"I think one of them is Mr. Gerrard," she whispered, forcing herself to think of something other than Drury's proximity.

"If he's foxed, all the more reason to avoid him. Men can be stupid when they're drunk."

She remembered Gaston LaRoche, and his breath, which always reeked of stale wine. "We are better off here," she agreed, even if Sir Douglas's body was so close to hers, she could feel him breathing. His chest was rising and falling as rapidly as her own.

The group of men—and indeed, Mr. Gerrard was one of them, although he seemed the most sober of the lot—came stumbling closer. One of his companions started to sing a very coarse song, and soon they all joined in the chorus as they passed by. Fortunately, they didn't see the couple watching them from the shadows of the tall shrubs.

After they were gone, Juliette let out a sigh of relief. "That was…what do you English call it? A close call," she said, not eager to go back to the walk, even if Sir Douglas had moved nearer and his arm touched hers.

"Very close," he seconded. Then he said, sounding slightly puzzled, "I thought you liked Gerrard."

"He is a little too forward for my taste."

"You'll get no argument from me."

"Perhaps we should go back to the other path."

"Yes, we should."

"Right away."

"Without delay," Drury concurred.

Still, neither of them moved. It was as if the desire they'd been trying to ignore had enveloped them in the shadows. Here, in the dark, he was not Sir Douglas Drury, baronet, barrister, far above her in rank and wealth and power. She was not a poor seamstress from a country he despised.

They were simply a man and a woman, alone in the dark. A man and a woman who shared a passionate longing that here, alone in the dark, could no longer be denied.

They moved together as if pulled by invisible wire. Their lips met and their arms clasped and their bodies pressed close, chest to breast, thigh to thigh. Tongues tangled and hands explored. Breathing quickened. Limbs relaxed, yet there was tension, too, deep within.

Juliette shifted and felt his hard arousal, which excited her even more. His hand came around to cup her firm breast, kneading it gently until she moaned. Panting, she arched her neck, while his lips trailed lower. And lower still, to lick and suckle her breasts through the fabric of her gown and chemise, while her shawl fell unheeded to the ground. She clutched his thick dark hair. He grasped her buttocks and pulled her closer still, grinding against her with a low growl of need deep in his throat.

"Oh, please!" she gasped, encouraging him. "Oh, please!"

"Drury! Where the devil are you?" Mr. Smythe-Medway demanded, exasperated, from somewhere close by.

Mon Dieu, what were they doing? What was *she?*

Drury backed away while she quickly straightened her bonnet and bent down to retrieve her shawl. "Drury!" Mr. Smythe-Medway called out again. "I tell you, Fanny, this is too much. It's dangerous here, and he ought to know that."

"I'm sure he can protect her, and he's got MacDougal's men to watch them," Lady Fanny soothed.

"They'd better! Damn it, where are they? Drury!"

Silently cursing himself for being a weak, lascivious fool, Drury stepped onto the path. He never should have given in to the temptation to kiss Juliette. He should have kept his desire under control and not submitted to the primitive, primal urges pulsing through him, not even when they were alone in the dark.

"There's no need to shout like a fishwife," he said, addressing his friend, who was a few yards down the path. "We're right here. We spied the Earl of Buckthorne with some ladies of dubious virtue and took refuge in the shrubbery."

As Drury turned back, ready to give his arm to Juliette again, he hoped she'd composed herself and that she wouldn't be angry. After all, she had returned his passion measure for measure, and if he was guilty of lust, so was she.

She wasn't there.

"Juliette!" he gasped as a fear unlike anything he'd ever felt, even during his darkest days in France, broke over him like a river in flood. "Juliette!"

Forgetting Brix and Fanny and anything except Juliette, he shoved his way through the shrubs where she'd been standing.

He found himself on another path, dark and empty, deep in shadows. He struggled to subdue the building panic, the rising fear, and *think*.

Juliette wouldn't faint. She would struggle. She would make noise, if she could. If she was conscious. If she was alive.

She must be alive. He could think nothing else, accept nothing else. Drury closed his eyes and listened, listened hard, as he had all those days in that dark cell. He'd listened then for any sound that would tell him what might happen to him, or where he was, or the time of day.

Now he listened even harder for any little noise that would help him find the woman whose life now meant more to him than his own.

Chapter Fourteen

How could I have been so stupid?
  —from the journal of Sir Douglas Drury

Juliette struggled and tried to scream as someone—someone strong—dragged her farther back into the shrubs. Away from the walk. Away from Drury and the others. Away from help.

She kicked and twisted, the taste of a leather glove foul in her mouth. Where were the men who were supposed to protect them?

Then came the prick of something sharp at her throat.

"Make another sound and I'll kill ya," a deep male voice rasped.

Mon Dieu, Mon Dieu! That man again, only this time, he had a knife.

What could she do? She was alone, as always. Always, forever, alone, to fend for herself once more.

She was sure that this time he would kill her, whether she screamed or not. This time, it was truly life or death, so she must, and would, fight. Determined to do that, and regardless of the knife blade at her throat, she stomped on the man's boot with all her might.

He grunted and she felt the warm trickle of blood on her neck, but her actions were enough to make him loosen his hold. She plunged forward, charging against his encircling arm.

"Oh, no, you don't! Not this time," he growled, pushing her to the ground.

She landed hard on her hands and knees. He put his foot on her back and shoved her into the leaf-covered dirt. "You stinking French whore, spreading your legs for Drury."

Then, suddenly, his foot was gone. She heard panting, a scuffle. Turning her head, scarcely daring to breathe, she could see two men struggling in the dark, a knife blade flashing in the few spots of light from the moon.

The man with the knife was surely her attacker. And the other?

Drury! It was Drury, trying to wrest the knife from him with stiff, crooked fingers.

She scrambled to her feet. Her hand encountered a branch—not very thick, but it was better than nothing. She stumbled toward the men, who were turning as if doing some kind of bizarre dance.

With all the strength she could muster, she swung the branch at her attacker. Not letting go of the knife, he shoved Drury to the ground, then whirled around.

"Get back!" Drury shouted as the man came closer, an evil grimace on his face like something from a nightmare.

"I think they must be this way!" a voice called out.

Mr. Smythe-Medway. Oh, thank God, Mr. Smythe-Medway was coming.

With a curse, their assailant ran past her, down the dark path, disappearing like a phantom, while she rushed to help Drury to his feet.

"Did he hurt you?" he demanded, taking her by the shoulders.

He was no civilized barrister now; he was a warrior, hard and ruthless, ready and able to kill. She knew it. Felt it. Believed it.

"Not badly," she said, both exulting, and afraid the man would get away. "Did he hurt *you?* Your ribs—"

"Are fine."

"Then we must go after him! This is the chance we've been waiting for!"

"Not you."

Carrying a lantern, Mr. Smythe-Medway appeared on the path, his panting wife behind him. "There's Drury. And Miss Bergerine, too, thank God! Are you all right? You're bleeding!"

"A little cut. It is nothing," she said dismissively. "But the man who did it is getting away!"

She turned aside to look at Drury—and found him gone.

He had disappeared without making a sound. "Where—"

"He's after the lout who attacked you, no doubt," Mr. Smythe-Medway said as Lady Fanny pulled a small, delicate handkerchief from her reticule. "I wouldn't want to be in that man's boots when he catches him."

Lady Fanny reached up and wiped away the blood on Juliette's neck. "Can you walk?" she asked.

"*Oui,*" Juliette replied, anxious to get out of this place, yet even more anxious to find Drury and see him safe. He had no weapon, no knife with which to protect himself, and his hands… "Should we not go after Sir Douglas?"

"I think it would be better to take you back to Lord Bromwell's," Mr. Smythe-Medway said.

Shocked by that suggestion, Juliette vehemently shook her head. "*Non.* I will not leave this place without him."

"There's no use trying to follow Drury," Lady Fanny said with gentle sympathy. "We might only get ourselves lost, or waste time. He'll be quite all right, I'm sure. We can wait for him closer to the entrance, where there are seats and we can get you something to drink."

Juliette remembered Lady Fanny's condition. "You should not have—"

"I'm perfectly fine, although I wouldn't mind sitting myself," she said with a smile. "Come, we'll walk slowly."

"I have ruined your handkerchief."

"Think nothing of it. I have plenty."

Mr. Smythe-Medway and his wife tried to be helpful and comforting as they waited in one of the little booths where food and drinks were served, but Juliette knew she would not feel better until she saw Drury again.

She certainly did not want to see Mr. Gerrard, who came rushing toward them as if he'd been called upon to defend the country single-handedly. "Miss Bergerine, I've just heard what happened! How terrible!"

He had apparently gotten more sober since she had seen him last. "I am quite all right, Mr. Gerrard."

"Is there anything I can do?"

Other than go away? "No, thank you. We are

waiting for Sir Douglas to return, and then my friends will take me home."

"Are you sure?"

"Quite sure," she replied as Mr. Smythe-Medway got to his feet. He didn't look threatening, or even angry, yet there was something about his action that made it clear Mr. Gerrard should seriously consider leaving.

Before he did, however, the Earl of Buckthorne and his female companions appeared, stumbling toward the table where Juliette and Lady Fanny sat.

The earl came to an unbalanced halt and made a drunken bow. "Good evening again. Had a bit of excitement, I hear. That's what happens when you venture into Lovers' Walk. Too bad you were interrupted, eh? I know Sir Douglas Drury's quite the swordsman."

"Good God, is that little Billy Buckthorne?" Mr. Smythe-Medway cried before the indignant Juliette could respond. "Gad, last time I saw you, you were weeping at White's because you lost a game of whist. Of course, you were much younger and thinner then. How kind of you to be so concerned. And here I always thought you were a selfish little beast. Fortunately, as you can see, Miss Bergerine is in good hands."

"So I've heard," the earl sneered.

"That's a disgusting insinuation!" Mr. Gerrard charged, red-faced with rage. "I demand you retract it."

Juliette wanted them both to go away. They were like squabbling children, while all she wanted was Drury's safe return, whether he caught their attacker or not.

The earl drew himself up as much as his besotted state would allow. "Why should I? Everybody's saying the same thing. What's the matter, Gerrard? Upset because she won't spread her lovely legs for you?"

"I demand satisfaction!"

Before Juliette could tell them to stop acting like children, Mr. Smythe-Medway stepped between them. "Gentlemen, you are both in no condition to discuss such a matter, and as it happens, I believe Sir Douglas will not take it kindly if either of you duel over his fiancée. It would be exposing Miss Bergerine to the worst sort of notoriety and he would be forced to challenge you both. I realize young men are eager to prove their skill and valor by such means, but I also suspect neither one of you has seen Drury fight when something important is at stake."

Mr. Smythe-Medway woefully shook his head. "I don't recommend it, gentlemen. And I'm sure Miss Bergerine, sweet woman that she is, wouldn't wish to be the cause of anyone's premature death."

"No, I would not!" she most emphatically agreed.

Demonstrating how little he understood her, Mr. Gerrard remained righteously indignant. "I will only agree if the earl takes back what he implied about Miss Bergerine."

Mr. Smythe-Medway turned to the flushed earl. "No doubt you're the worse for wine, my lord. No shame to admit it and retract your statements." He nodded past the earl. "And I think it would be wise to do so before Sir Douglas reaches us and hears about it, or he might fight you here and now."

Buckthorne glanced nervously over his shoulder. Juliette didn't see anyone approaching, but apparently the threat was enough to make the earl reconsider. "I—I didn't mean it!" he stammered.

He grabbed the arms of the two women who'd been waiting nearby, whispering, giggling and eyeing both Mr. Gerrard and Mr. Smythe-Medway, regardless of the latter's wife, and scurried away.

"I suggest you likewise retire, Mr. Gerrard," Mr. Smythe-Medway said. "However well-meaning your offer to fight the sodden earl, I rather think Drury will not be feeling very grateful when he hears about it. Having seen him in a temper once or twice, I can tell you it's something to be avoided."

"What about Miss Bergerine?" the young man defiantly demanded. "I hope he won't be angry with her."

"Oh, she'll be fine. He would never take his anger out on a woman, let alone one he loves. He'll be consideration itself. Good evening, Mr. Gerrard."

The man finally took his leave, but not before bidding Juliette a subdued, and on her part, very welcome, farewell.

"Buckthorne is a disgrace to the English aristocracy," Mr. Smythe-Medway remarked as Juliette again wished Drury would return, and wondered what had happened to the men who were supposed to be protecting them.

"Perhaps we should take Miss Bergerine home," Lady Fanny proposed. "It's getting late and we have no idea how long Drury might be. I'm sure he'll realize where we've gone."

Fortunately, at that very moment, Juliette spotted him striding toward them. "Here he comes!" she cried, her fear and fatigue forgotten as she rushed toward him.

"I'm sorry, Juliette, he got away," he said, his voice full of regret, although traces of that primitive, wrathful warrior lingered in his eyes.

Having seen that part of him—the raw, vibrant emotion—she would never again believe he was as unfeeling as he pretended to be.

"Are you sure you are not hurt?" she asked, running an anxious gaze over him.

He shook his head. "No." He studied her neck. "You weren't badly cut?"

"It is a scratch."

"Where's Brix?"

She pointed back to the alcove where Mr. Smythe-Medway and his wife waited.

"What about the men who were supposed to be protecting us?" she asked as they went to join his friends. "Where were they?"

"Not as close by as they should have been. I've spoken to MacDougal's men, and rest assured, they won't make that mistake again."

She thought not, if he had been this angry when he talked to them.

"No luck finding the culprit?" Mr. Smythe-Medway asked when they reached them.

"No. Fanny, you're all right?" Drury asked.

"Other than distressed for your sake, and Miss Bergerine's, I'm quite well."

"Then let's get out of this place," he said, turning toward Juliette.

Instead of holding out his arm for her to take, and without a word of warning, he swept her up into his arms. She let out a little squeak of alarm and was about to protest until she caught sight of his determined profile and rigidly set jaw.

Mr. Smythe-Medway had refused to set his wife down at the theater, and his features had held only a portion of Drury's grim resolve, so Juliette was quite sure Drury would carry her to the carriage whether she wanted him to or not.

She surrendered to the inevitable and laid her head against his shoulder, letting him bear her from Vauxhall like a gallant knight who'd rescued his lady from a dragon.

When they arrived at Lord Bromwell's town house, Millstone appeared in the foyer.

"We had a slight mishap," Drury said, forestalling any questions from the butler. "Miss Bergerine should rest, and she's not to be disturbed in the morning until she rings the bell."

"Very well, Sir Douglas."

Juliette bid Drury a quiet *adieu* and started toward the stairs. All the emotions she'd experienced that night—excitement, fear, desire—seemed to come rushing at her now that she was safely in Lord Bromwell's house.

Reaching for the banister, she stumbled a little, and before she could regain her balance, Drury was once more picking her up in his strong, protective arms.

"Do not tell me to put you down," he warned under his breath.

She was too tired and too glad of his help to argue. "Thank you," she murmured, once more laying her head against his shoulder, grateful and weary. "Thank you for saving my life tonight."

She felt his chest rise and fall with a sigh as he carried her up the stairs.

When I am with him, I am safe, she thought.

And when she was not with him?

She would not think about that. She must not think about it, or she would burst into tears.

He set her down outside her bedroom door. She slowly, reluctantly, lowered her arms from around his neck, looking up into his inscrutable face, where that unemotional mask was once again fixed firmly in place.

"Merci," she whispered.

He nodded, then turned on his heel and marched back down the stairs.

He needed a drink—a good, strong drink to calm his shattered nerves.

If that man had hurt Juliette…if he'd killed her…

God help them both, for Drury would have hunted that man down and killed him with the swift ruthlessness he'd used once before, when he'd found the bastard who'd betrayed him and his colleagues during the war.

He reached the bottom of the steps and turned toward Buggy's study, where the stronger whiskey would be.

"Cicero?"

Drury slowly swiveled on his heel.

Clad in stained and muddy traveling clothes, his hair tousled and dark circles under his eyes, Buggy stood in the drawing-room door, his expression more stern and angry than Drury had ever seen it. "What's this I hear about an engagement?"

Chapter Fifteen

*Buggy looked all in. He says it's not a relapse, but
I'm worried. Wish he'd reconsider his expedition,
but he's too stubborn. Am glad J. hates spiders.*
    —The journal of Sir Douglas Drury

Buggy must have returned at breakneck speed—and
at no small cost to his health, judging by his appearance. Why had he hurried back? Because he had heard
about their alleged engagement and harbored tender
feelings for Miss Bergerine?

"It's part of a plan Miss Bergerine concocted," he explained even as he wondered what he would do if Mrs.
Tunbarrow was right and this hasty return meant Buggy
was in love with Juliette. "She thought that since both
MacDougal's men and the Runners haven't been successful, we should try to lure our enemy into the open
by claiming we're engaged. She has the idea that the
person behind the attacks must be a former lover of
mine. I wasn't convinced, but things couldn't go on as
they were, so I agreed. I should have asked Brix to write
you and explain."

Because he couldn't hold a quill well enough to write anymore.

"I see…." His friend turned to enter the drawing room and gestured for Drury to join him. Thankfully he sounded a little less angry. "Mrs. Tunbarrow wrote. I got her letter at Lord Dentonbarry's. She wanted me to know there were, as she put it, disgraceful doings afoot under my father's roof. She suggested I come home right away to deal with them."

And so he had—as if he didn't trust his old friend.

Deep in his heart, Drury knew that mistrust had some basis in truth. He'd been in the Dark Walks before, with other women, but never had he experienced the incredible excitement, the passionate arousal, he'd felt with Juliette. If Brix and Fanny hadn't come along the path when they did…

Leaning back against the mantel, Buggy asked, "Does this plan also require you to carry Miss Bergerine up the stairs?"

"I thought she needed my assistance."

As humiliating as it was, Drury would have to confess his failure. "I didn't protect her as I should have in Vauxhall Gardens tonight. I dropped my guard and she was dragged off."

"Dragged off?" Buggy repeated, aghast—as well he might be.

"Yes. Fortunately, she managed to get away."

"Did you catch the blackguard who did it?"

"No," Drury admitted. "I had some of MacDougal's men on watch, but they missed him, too. They're going to keep searching."

He drew in a ragged breath and glanced at his hands. He had fought the rogue as best he could, but not well enough. He couldn't get a decent grip on him, or make a fist to throw a punch.

Buggy abruptly got to his feet and left the room. To check on Juliette? Because he was angry? Was there more to his feelings for her than sympathy and concern?

Did he love her?

How could he? He barely knew her. It had only been a little while since that first night....

Only a little while, but it seemed an age, during which so much had changed.

Buggy came back into the room carrying two glasses. "I think we could both use this," he said, handing him a whiskey.

Drury gratefully downed it in a gulp and closed his eyes, savoring the taste and warmth. He was bone tired. Nevertheless, he wasn't going to leave until he had a better idea of Buggy's feelings, if that was possible. If his friend didn't retire first.

"I suppose you're going to hate me for putting her in danger or risking a scandal," he said. "But Brix agreed with the plan, and he and Fanny were with us tonight until we got separated."

Buggy sat on a sofa and regarded him gravely. "It's not a bad plan to draw the spider from its hiding place by putting a fly in the web, but it's obviously a risky one."

"Believe me, I was aware of that even before tonight, but Miss Bergerine insisted—and I agreed," he justly added. "Perhaps I shouldn't have, but unfortunately, I couldn't think of anything better to do. I'm sorry you came rushing home—at some risk to yourself, it seems. I'd hate to think this has caused a relapse."

Buggy was only recently returned from a long voyage, during which he'd contracted an illness. He had recovered, or so everyone had thought.

"Oh, I'm not sick. Just tired—and I would have left anyway." Buggy's expression grew disgusted. "Lord

Dentonbarry made it very clear that he wouldn't give a ha'penny to my expedition unless I agreed to marry one of his four daughters. After that, I couldn't get out of there fast enough. As if I'd take a wife when I'm about to sail off for three years, or would be so conceited as to expect a woman to wait for me to return."

"So you don't have any other bridal prospects in mind?" Drury asked with deceptive calm, although it felt as if he'd never asked a more important question in his life.

"Gad, no. I'm not going to marry anybody unless I'm in love, like Brix or Edmond. And I may never find a woman with the ability to overlook my interest in spiders and fall in love with me."

"Then I take it none of the daughters appealed to you?" Drury gravely inquired, while subduing the most inconvenient urge to grin.

"Not in the least, although I suppose it's not their fault they're ignorant and silly. As Mary Wollstonecraft put it so well, how can we fail to educate women and then condemn them for being ignorant? Then I got Mrs. Tunbarrow's letter and wondered... Well, Miss Bergerine is a remarkable woman, so I could see that perhaps..." He blushed. "I'm sorry if I wasn't as trusting as I should have been."

"It was only natural," Drury said. After all, how could he fault Buggy when he'd behaved as he had?

"Perhaps I did push myself a little bit to get home quickly, but I had to find out what was going on before Father hears anything and comes charging into Town. He questions my judgment enough as it is."

Drury felt another pang of guilt, except that the earl should know by now his son was no fool. "Surely not anymore. Not after your book was such a success."

"He still thinks everything I do a folly," Buggy said with a sigh. "Still, he's not here yet, so here's hoping he remains in blissful ignorance a while longer."

"And that this situation is resolved soon. After all, Miss Bergerine and I can't live with you forever."

Soon enough, she would have to go her way, as Drury must go his. He would never see her again, or hear her voice.

"It seems a pity Miss Bergerine has to go back to that sordid existence," his friend mused aloud.

"I agree, and I've made her an offer—a *business* offer," he hastened to add.

Briefly, he described what he'd proposed to Juliette, and that she had accepted it.

"I should have thought of that," Buggy said, clearly pleased. "I'll be happy to contribute if I have any funds to spare."

Drury didn't like that idea. "You've got your expedition to pay for."

"That's true," he agreed. "Well, I'm sure she'll be successful. She's really quite a remarkable young woman."

"Even if she hates spiders?"

Buggy laughed as he got to his feet. "A serious failing, although I seem to recall you recoiling more than once at the sight of one."

Drury couldn't refute that. He'd been afraid of the things, until he'd been caught by those French soldiers and learned what real fear was.

"Still, she's brave enough otherwise," Buggy said. "Now if you'll excuse me, old friend, I'm tired, so I think it's time I went to bed."

Drury likewise rose and followed him up the stairs, where he bade Buggy good-night before entering the finely appointed bedroom that was his for the time being. Spacious and elegant, it was a far cry from the much smaller room where he slept in his chambers, although that was quite comfortable enough for him. This room, with its huge canopied bed and gleaming oak furniture inlaid with walnut, the Aubusson carpet and tall looking glass, was too much like his father's bedroom at their country house.

Sometimes, when he was little, he would sneak into his father's room and sit in the armoire, inhaling the scents of tobacco and bay rum, and wondering why his father didn't like him. He must not, he'd believed, if he could stay away so much.

Drury strolled to the window and looked out at the street below. Buggy's family life wasn't the best, either. Yet although the Earl of Granshire constantly expressed his disappointment in his son, Buggy's mother adored him.

His mother had been even less of a parent than his father.

Would it have been better, Drury wondered, to be like Juliette, never knowing your mother, or to be like him, all too aware of his mother's faults and never feeling loved?

He turned away. The past was the past. He must look forward. He always tried to look forward.

Except that now, for the first time, the future looked even more lonely and bleak than his past.

Because Juliette Bergerine would have no place in it.

Later that night, Juliette sat by her window looking out at the garden illuminated by a full moon. It was as lovely as anything she had ever imagined, and she was warm and dry, wearing a nightgown of fine linen covered by a soft silk robe that Drury had purchased for her, asking nothing in return.

How, then, could she be anything but grateful to him, despite what had happened tonight? And she wasn't thinking about the attack.

She was remembering his kiss, his passionate embraces. The way he made her feel. The desire. The need.

She couldn't sleep, because every time she lay down on that soft bed and closed her eyes, all she could think about was being with him. Imagining how it would be to share his bed, his heart, his life.

That could never, ever be. He would marry a woman of his own country and class. If *she* came to his bed, it could only be as a mistress. But no matter how much her desire urged her to that life, she also remembered too well how it was to be abandoned and the prey of lustful men. She must not become any man's toy, to be discarded when he was finished with her.

Feeling a chill, she rose from her seat by the window and wrapped her soft robe more tightly around herself for warmth, then walked toward the looking glass and surveyed herself critically. Despite what some men said, she wasn't a beauty. She was too thin, too small, with eyes too big, mouth too wide, and she was too outspoken.

Probably no man would ever marry her. She would have her business, though, and that was something. And there was still a slim hope that Georges—

A sound broke the silence. It wasn't loud, and if she'd been asleep, she never would have heard it.

She went to the door and eased it open, straining to hear.

There it was again. She had no candle, but there

was a window at the end of the corridor and the moon shone brightly through it.

No other door was open; no one else appeared. Perhaps she'd imagined that sound…except there it was again. A low moan as if a man was in pain, coming from a room a few doors down. Not Lord Bromwell's, or that of his father or mother when they were in Town.

Drury's. Perhaps he was being attacked!

She ran down the hall, then hesitated before entering his bedroom. Other things could sound like that. Perhaps he had a woman with him. A servant, or some other female he'd brought secretly into the house.

But if it was an assassin…

Grabbing a candlestick from a nearby table to use as a weapon if necessary, she swiftly opened the door—and saw Drury alone, half-naked in the bed. The sheets were twisted around his torso, the covers bunched in his hands as he thrashed and moaned.

He must be having a nightmare.

A terrible one, it seemed, for his voice was rough and harsh, muttering in French. "Please, stop. Please, no more. Don't. For the love of God, don't!"

Then she realized he was sobbing.

She closed the door softly and hurried forward. Setting the candlestick on the bedside table, she sat beside him and, ignoring the sight of the naked arms and legs, took hold of his hand.

"Wake up!" she pleaded softly in French, gently stroking it. "You are safe now. Wake up!"

She pressed her lips to his stiff, crooked fingers. "You are safe now," she repeated. "Safe. Nobody will hurt you."

Tears of sympathy started in her eyes as she put

her other hand to his sweaty forehead and brushed back his damp hair.

At last he stilled, and the sobbing slowly ebbed. His eyes opened. There was anguish and dismay in their dark depths, until he focused on her face. "Juliette?"

"*Oui.*"

He sat up abruptly, yanking his hand from hers. His gaze flew around the room, then back to her, and his own unclothed state. Grabbing the sheet and wrapping it around him like a toga, he got out of bed on the other side. "What do you want?"

Did he think she had come here for some other reason than to help him? Was he truly so vain, or so proud, or so used to women making fools of themselves over him?

"You were having a bad dream," she said as she, too, rose. "I heard you and came to wake you."

"Get out," he ordered, pointing at the door. "Never come into this room again!"

Any sympathy she'd felt for him withered as she glared at him. "I came to your aid, *monsieur*—again. I had no other purpose. I am not some lonely, desperate noblewoman trying to find excitement in your bed."

He reached for his trousers and, letting the sheet drop, tugged them on. She did not turn away, lest she give him the satisfaction of thinking he could intimidate her with his nakedness. She had grown up on a farm with her father and brothers; she had seen naked men before, though none so well proportioned.

"No matter what you heard, you shouldn't be in my room," he muttered.

She crossed her arms and regarded him with cold annoyance. "Even if there was an assassin come to kill you?"

"Nobody could get in this room without being

caught," he declared, buttoning his trousers and grabbing a shirt.

"*I* got in," she retorted, paying no attention to his muscular chest. "Someone could sneak into this house during the day, and hide and lie in wait. There are tradesmen coming all the time, and servants."

"Be that as it may," he said, striding to the door, his feet still bare, "*you* should not be here."

He stood with his hand on the latch, waiting to open it for her.

Lifting her chin, she marched forward. "*Bonsoir, monsieur.* And next time, if it is an assassin, I shall simply let him kill you."

She was about to pass, until he put his hand on her arm. She paused and raised an imperious brow, expecting another aggravating remark.

Instead, he looked...remorseful. "Forgive me. I have nightmares sometimes. It isn't necessary for you to wake me, or try to help. I am used to them."

With a heavy sigh, he moved away from the door to another table, where she saw a crystal carafe of brandy and a small glass. But he didn't pour a drink. Instead, he leaned forward, his hands splayed on the wooden surface, and sighed as he stared at them. "My nightmares can be very bad."

She heard the pain in his voice and approached him slowly, cautiously. "I have nightmares, too," she admitted, "of the old farmer who tended our farm after my brothers and father left me. He was always trying to have his way with me in the barn. He never succeeded, but in my dreams, I cannot fight and get away. I am trapped and cannot move."

Still not looking at her, Drury pushed himself away from the table and walked to the window. He stood silhouetted in the moonlight, his broad back to her, his body slumped as if in defeat.

Like a god who finds he has been made mortal.

"Sometimes I dream I'm a prisoner again, chained to a wall," he said quietly. "And my fingers are being broken again, one by one. It took days for my captors to break them all as they tried to make me betray my fellow Englishmen."

"Did you?" she asked gently, wondering if guilt was also responsible for his nightmares.

"No. Someone else did, and so they were caught anyway. Most of them died a terrible death, as I was days tied to that chair, the pain beyond imagining, my fingers left as they were after they were broken."

"Yet you escaped," she said, marveling at the strength of will that must have made that possible, or he would surely have died, too.

"I was taken out of that cellar and thrown off a bridge into a river to drown. My captors were sure I was half dead already and wouldn't be able to swim to the banks. Fortunately, I did and was able to make my way to a safe place, where friends could help me get back to England."

"It is no wonder you hated the French after what they did to you. If an Englishman had done that to me, I would probably hate all of you, too," she admitted.

Drury drew in a ragged breath. "But tonight, I wasn't dreaming about that. I dreamed it was *your* fingers they were breaking, and I couldn't stop them. I had to watch and I couldn't make them stop."

He was so upset because, in his dream, he'd been unable to help *her?*

To be sure, it was only a dream, but to see him so distressed… To know he must feel something for her.

"It was just a dream," Juliette whispered, slowly approaching him. "I am here, and nobody is hurting me."

"But they could have tonight. If I hadn't found you in time, that man might have killed you and it would have been my fault."

"No!" she protested, taking hold of his broad shoulders to turn him so that he must look at her. "It was not you who attacked me, you who tried to hurt me. And if anyone has been mistaken, perhaps it was me, to come up with such a plan and to not have stayed closer to you."

"Your plan worked," he replied. "It drew out the enemy just as you thought, and it would have succeeded if I—and the men I'd hired—hadn't failed. I should have been paying more attention, been more aware of the surroundings. I shouldn't…"

He didn't finish, but turned away, so that his grim face was in profile.

"You shouldn't have kissed me?" Her voice was soft and without condemnation. "Perhaps I should not have kissed you back."

"We were both wrong."

"Do you really think that?"

In her heart, she knew *her* answer to that question. She didn't regret kissing him. Not anymore.

"I should have been stronger. It…it wasn't right."

"Because it was wrong to kiss a woman you cannot marry, or because of what happened afterward?"

"Does it matter?" he retorted, turning to face her. "It was wrong, and I shouldn't have done it—any more than you should still be here."

In his eyes she saw yearning, a need that matched her own, although his arms remained stiff at his sides. "Go now, Juliette, please. It's taking every ounce of my resolve to keep from kissing you again. From taking you in my arms and carrying you to that bed. From trying to seduce you and make love with you."

He wanted her so much?

She should leave. She could go, as he asked. She was sure that even if she did, he would still do all that he had offered. He would help her start her business. He would not hold her refusal against her.

The power, the choice, was hers. He would give her that, too.

She wanted to give him something precious, as well. The only thing of value she had—herself.

"And if I do not wish to go?" she asked softly. "If I wish to stay here and kiss you? If I want you to take me in your arms and to your bed, and make love with me?"

He drew back, astonished. Uncertain. Then wistful. Hopeful. "You can't mean that."

She gave him a pert little smile to show him that she most certainly did. Her decision was made, and she would not regret it. "Will you again try to tell me what I am thinking? You are not very good at it, you know."

He took hold of her shoulders, his anxious, yearning gaze searching her face. "You mean this?"

Her smile melted away. "With all my heart," she said as she raised herself on her toes and kissed him.

Chapter Sixteen

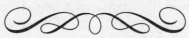

I never dared to think I could be so happy.
Should have known it wouldn't last.
　　　—from the journal of Sir Douglas Drury

Drury's response was tentative, but only for a moment. Then his arms encircled her and he clasped her to him, fervently returning her kiss.

Even now, even after what she'd said, she felt him holding back. Asking of her, not demanding. Seeking, not taking. Enticing, not commanding. But there was passion, too. Lurking. Restrained. Waiting for her answer.

Which she gave with that same tenderness at first, sliding her mouth over his, welcoming his kiss as desire burst into vibrant life, called forth by their shared and growing need.

He could be a hard man, cold and distant. He had been the enemy of her country—and for that, he had paid a high price. Just as she had paid a high price because men would make wars, and other men would fight them. Drury had suffered, as she had suffered.

He had lost what must have been beautiful hands—
strong slender fingers now stiff and bent, weak and
painful. Hands that nevertheless moved over her in a
way that made her forget he was anything less than
perfect. Or that she was nothing more than a poor
French girl who'd done him a service and who'd been
put in harm's way because of it.

She knew only the longing between them, the excitement and need building, heating her skin, her
blood, as his mouth slid with slow purpose over hers.

She held him tightly, on her tiptoes, her willing
body melding to his. It didn't matter what she was or
why she was there, or who he was or what he'd done.
They were together, and he was lonely, as lonely as
she. He felt the same need she did. He wanted her, as
she wanted him.

She felt it as surely as she'd felt the attraction
between them that had kept her kissing him that first
time, instead of drawing back immediately.

A low moan of pleasure escaped her throat when
he reached through her parted robe and delicately
cupped her breast. He seemed almost shy now, not as
he had been in Vauxhall Gardens.

Was it because of his fingers? Did he think she
would not welcome his touch?

She would prove him wrong. She didn't care that
his fingers were not perfect, that other people might
think the less of him because of them.

She reached for his hand and brought it to her lips.
His eyes opened, and their gazes met as she sucked
first one finger, than the others in turn, into the moist
warmth of her mouth. Broken or whole, they were his,
and she loved his hands.

She loved him. All of him, even his dark moods and

temper. She loved him, and she would be his tonight. She would not think of the future, or the past. This night was just for him, and for her.

With a look of wonder, he ran his hand through her hair, then cupped her head and pulled her close, taking her lips with fiercer passion. Letting his desire free. Giving himself to her, totally and completely, holding nothing back.

He angled himself between her legs, and she felt him hard and ready, just before he put his hand where she was damp, her flesh throbbing like a primitive call to pleasure and fulfillment.

His fingers did not seem crippled then, as he caressed and teased, through the fabric of her nightgown.

"Please, oh, please," she whispered as the tension grew. She gripped his shoulders lest she slip to the floor, her limbs too weak with desire to support her.

He swept her into his arms and carried her to his bed. He laid her upon it, and as she reached for him, he joined her there, his powerful body covering hers.

They kissed and caressed, tongues touching, entwining, dancing as their hands explored. There was no shyness, no timidity now. He was a man perfect in her eyes, and she was a woman perfect in his.

With his knees between her legs, his weight on his elbows, he pulled the drawstring from the neck of her gown and tugged it low so that he could pleasure her breasts. And pleasure it was, as his tongue and lips and mouth aroused her beyond anything she had ever imagined. She writhed beneath him, feeling his hard arousal, and worked his buttons until he was free.

She couldn't wait, but pulled her nightdress up and clasped him with her knees. "Please," she whispered.

"Not yet. Not quite yet," he murmured, his mouth

moving up her neck, along the throbbing path, to take hers again. Then he broke away to get rid of his trousers.

"Drury!" she pleaded as he tossed them on the floor.

"Are you sure, Juliette?" he whispered in French, his voice low and rough, but questioning, truly asking if this was what she wanted.

"Yes!"

He murmured more endearments in her native tongue as he settled between her legs and pushed inside. There was pain, a brief tearing, but she ignored it. He stilled a moment and stroked her hair as the pain subsided.

She had been a virgin, and now she was not. She was her own woman, free as few were, yet here and now, she was his. And he was hers. Together.

She looked up into his dark eyes and smiled. He smiled, too, as he lowered his head to kiss her again, tenderly. And then he was pushing more, filling her more, arousing her more.

Their passionate fervor exploded. She wrapped her legs around him and moved up to meet him, her body instinctively responding as he thrust, the rocking exciting her beyond anything. With her eyes closed, she arched her back, drawing in short, ragged breaths.

She was on a knife's edge. She was on the brink. She had never felt anything like…*this!* Wave after wave of pleasure and release overwhelmed her. She half rose, wanting to scream with the sheer joy of it, but pressing her lips together so nobody else would hear.

At nearly the same moment, a low growl burst from Drury's throat as he, too, reached the ecstatic moment of release.

* * *

Afterward, as he lay beside her, Drury knew he should be sorry. He should be upset that he had made love with this woman he wasn't going to wed.

She was the most amazing woman he'd ever met and the most incredible lover, but they shouldn't marry. She should have the independence she craved and the life she wanted to lead. There was so much she hadn't had, and he wouldn't take her ambitions away from her, to replace them with—what? The dull life of a barrister's wife in a land that was foreign and unwelcoming?

He pulled away and got out of bed. He washed, and when he turned back, she was sitting up, watching him.

He knew she really ought to go. She couldn't stay the whole night with him. Her reputation would be ruined, and what would Buggy say? He would surely see this as a betrayal, even if he didn't love Juliette himself.

In spite of that, Drury didn't want her to leave. He didn't want to be alone in the dark again. Not yet. Surely there was a little time to share.

"Will you stay with me a while?" he asked in French as he drew on his trousers and buttoned them.

"I would like that," she said, giving him a glorious smile that warmed his lonely heart, yet filled him with sorrow, too.

He sat beside her on the bed and took her hand in his, blessedly sure she would not recoil from that grasp.

"Is there nothing a doctor could do for your poor hands?" she asked, lifting the one holding hers and brushing a kiss along his knuckles.

"The only thing they could suggest was to break them again and hope they healed better." He couldn't suppress a shudder. "I couldn't face that, so they are as they are."

Not wanting to revisit that terrible time any longer, he brushed a wisp of hair from her forehead. "I haven't told you how lovely your hair is."

She reached up and ran her fingers through his. "I like yours, too, especially when it is like this. You look like a little boy."

He laughed quietly, feeling younger than he had since…well, since he was young. "Not in every way, I hope."

"Oh, no," she replied, her eyes dancing with charming vitality. "In other ways, you are very much a man."

His heartbeat quickened. "You're making me want to prove that."

"You're making me want you to."

They came together for a long, lingering kiss, and soon enough, he was.

The sky had lightened only a little when Juliette awoke, stretching her naked limbs with luxurious leisure.

"My God, you're beautiful."

She started, suddenly aware of where she was, that she was completely naked and that Drury was not beside her anymore.

He stood beside the bed, smiling down at her, and she realized it had been a light kiss on her forehead that had brought her out of a very pleasant dream. He was also holding her robe and nightdress in his hands. "I really hate to wake you, you look so sweet, but I don't think you should be here when the household stirs."

"No, I should not," she agreed, climbing out of bed and reaching for her nightgown.

With the most roguish grin on his angular face, he held it just out of reach.

"You devil, give that to me!"

"In a moment. First, I want to admire your exquisite body."

"Cretin. I shall go back to my room naked!" she declared, starting for the door as if she meant to do it.

He caught her hand and pulled her close. "You would, too, wouldn't you? If there's a devil here, I don't think it's me."

"Then give me my clothes."

"In exchange for a kiss."

"You see? A devil—an arrogant one, too."

"All right. No kiss. I like you naked."

"Beast!"

"Beauty!"

She could not resist smiling. He was so happy and merry, so different from the grim, grave barrister.

"Aha! Now I know how to make you concede," he said, pressing her closer and kissing her neck. "Flatter you."

She playfully pushed him back. "And I know how to handle you, *monsieur le barrister.* Strip naked."

"You'll get no argument from me there."

"You are impossible!"

"You are wonderful!" he countered, before glancing at the brightening sky beyond the window. Then he sighed and held out her garments. "Unfortunately, I have to leave. Sam Clark should be back from Calais."

With word of Georges, perhaps, she realized as she drew on her nightdress, her hands suddenly trembling.

"I hope he has good news for you, Juliette," Drury said softly. "I really do."

Juliette wanted Georges to be alive, although now the idea of living with her adventure-seeking, reckless brother wasn't quite as attractive as it had been before.

"You mustn't look so sad, Juliette. Sam could have good news."

Good news for Drury, if he didn't want her to stay with him.

She forced a smile onto her face.

"Oh, and I almost forgot—Buggy came home last night. He knows about the ruse. He thought your idea a good one, too—and it would have worked if I'd been paying attention."

She quickly embraced Drury. "It was not your fault my attacker got away, and we will find the man who wants to hurt us."

And then?

She would not think about *and then*. She would be Sir Douglas Drury's mistress while she could. "I must go, but I will come to you tonight," she promised, for the sky was brighter still and she shouldn't linger here.

She went to the door and eased it open before he could speak, then she slipped away and was gone.

Drury waited a few minutes, then went quietly out of the room, along the corridor and down the back stairs, all the while hoping Sam Clark would have good news.

Although if her brother lived, it was more likely Juliette would leave London. And Drury would be alone as he had never been before.

Sam Clark slid onto the bench by the table in a dim corner of a tavern in Southwark, on the banks of the Thames. The place was clouded with tobacco smoke from a host of patrons puffing on clay pipes, and the odor of roast beef and gravy hung in the air.

"MacDougal," he said in greeting to the figure barely visible in the shadows waiting for him there.

The man faced the door, with his back to the wall. His left eye was covered by a black leather patch held on with a thin leather thong, and his empty left sleeve was tucked into the old, worn woolen coat of the sort favored by seamen. He hunched a little forward, and the hand that held his mug of grog looked like a hawk's talon.

"Wha' news from Calais?" MacDougal asked, sounding very much the Scot.

"Surprisin' news," the Cornish Clark replied. "Seems Sir Douglas might not know his fiancée's family very well."

MacDougal's dark brows furrowed. "Why d'ye say tha'?"

"She's Georges Bergerine's sister, isn't she?"

"Aye. Get to the point, man!"

"All right," Clark said, his expression hardening. "Seems we both knew Georges Bergerine during the war."

"I wasna ever in Calais."

"Not there, and not by that name. We knew him as Henri Desmaries."

It was like a blow to the pit of Drury's stomach. Desmaries. Desmaries was Georges Bergerine? He couldn't believe it. He didn't want to believe it. "Are ye sure?"

"No doubt about it. Had it from two different blokes I can trust."

Neither man spoke as the barmaid set a mug of ale before Clark. After she had returned to the bar to tap another keg, Sam leaned conspiratorially closer to his companion. "Serves him right, getting done in an alley like that, the traitorous dog. I only wish I'd been there to lend a hand."

"Do they know who killed him?"

"No, and they don't much care. Just another poor sod who got robbed and stuck like a pig in an alley." Clark's eyes narrowed as he raised his mug. "Do *you* know?"

"Nay," Drury lied, even as he remembered the surprise on the younger man's face, the protestations that he'd done what he had for his country. Then his anguished expression as Drury shoved the blade up and under his ribs.

He had killed Juliette's brother. His damaged hand had held the special dagger with the thick handle he'd had made especially for that very purpose—to mete out justice for his dead friends, and for his broken fingers. He himself had driven the dagger home. He had taken away the last of her family.

But Desmaries had betrayed him, and so many others, including Harriet Windham's son. Henri—Georges—had helped the French soldiers capture him, and it had been Georges who, with grinning cruelty, had broken his fingers one by one.

"What do you reckon Sir Douglas'll do when he finds out that fiancée of his is the sister of a man who betrayed so many Englishmen? A man who'd sell his own mother for money?"

And perhaps—damn him!—a sister?

"I dinna ken," he said, getting to his feet. Needing to get out of here. Away from Clark, the smoke and the stench.

Needing to walk to clear his head and decide what to do. Should he tell Juliette that her brother was dead, or leave her in ignorance?

If he told her part of the tale, should he tell her all? That even after breaking his fingers, Georges had come to him in the night and offered to help him escape in exchange for money and the names of ten of his friends. Then five. Then even one. For a thousand pounds. Five hundred. Fifty.

Her brother was the worst villain Drury had ever encountered, in France or anywhere. A greedy, duplicitous scoundrel.

Whose sister he loved. Still loved, in spite of everything.

Oh, would to God he'd never sent Sam to Calais! "I'll tell Drury now."

"Aye, you'd better. I know what *I'd* do if the bitch I was pokin' turned out to be that man's sister," Clark muttered as Drury went to the door.

But Drury didn't hear him.

Chapter Seventeen

*I thought Drury looked bad when he got back
from France, but it was nothing compared to the
way he looked then.*

—from *The Collected Letters of
Lord Bromwell*

Try as she might, Juliette simply couldn't keep her
mind on her sewing. Drury had been gone so long! He
had left before breakfast and it would soon be time for
dinner.

Lord Bromwell seemed quite composed as he sat
reading in the drawing room with her, while she
kept looking out the window, trying to judge if it
was as late in the day as she thought. She had gone
to check the street more than once. Although that
must have been distracting, Lord Bromwell never
complained.

Eventually she gave up sewing and began to put
away the needle, thread and scissors. As she folded the
linen she'd been hemming, Lord Bromwell looked up
at her with surprise. "Finished?"

"It is getting a bit hard to see," she said, which was true.

"I'll have a servant light the candles."

She smiled as if that was good news. "Thank you."

He closed his book, tugged on the bellpull, and when the footman arrived, gave the order.

"Did you enjoy the theater the other night?" he asked as he returned to his seat and picked up the thick tome he'd been perusing. "Edmond Kean is a wonderful actor."

"It was very exciting, yes," she said, once more drawn to the windows to see if a hackney or hired carriage was coming down the street.

"Miss Bergerine?" Lord Bromwell said softly, and she realized with a start that he'd come up behind her.

"Oui?" she replied, her grip on the velvet draperies tightening a little.

"Has Drury done anything…untoward?"

She didn't know what to say. Had her host somehow found out about last night?

"Miss Bergerine," Lord Bromwell repeated a little more insistently, "please be honest with me. Drury is my friend, but you're a woman and my guest. I am, in a way, responsible for you."

She finally turned to face him. "No, he has not done anything wrong," she replied. After all, she had been more than willing.

Lord Bromwell relaxed. "Thank God. Although I trust him, I confess when I saw him carrying you up the stairs last night, I was worried." He gave her another smile. "You're a very lovely and interesting woman, after all, and I think he likes you very much."

"I like him, too."

Regretting revealing even that much, she hurried on. "He is a very excellent barrister and of course, I am grateful he has offered to help me start a new life in France."

"Yes, he told me about that."

"So as soon as these evil men who seek to harm us are caught, I shall be free to go back home and do so." She spoke as if that was the dearest wish of her heart. Once, it would have been.

"I shall miss you, Miss Bergerine," Lord Bromwell said with a kind smile, "and in spite of everything, I think Drury will, too."

As she would miss Lord Bromwell a little, and Drury much more.

"Juliette."

They both started and looked at the door. Drury stood there, leaning against the frame as if he were ill, or exhausted.

"What has happened?" she cried as she ran to him. "Are you hurt? Were you attacked?"

"No." He looked past her to Lord Bromwell. "Leave us alone, will you, Buggy? I have something to tell Jul…Miss Bergerine."

His sorrowful, leaden voice terrified her and dread clutched her heart. "Is it…is it about…about Georges?" she whispered, grabbing his arms.

He didn't answer. Instead, he looked at Lord Bromwell, who silently left them.

In that moment, Juliette knew. Without doubt. With absolute certainty.

Her brother was dead.

She let out a cry as if she'd been stabbed and threw herself on the sofa. She sobbed as she never had before, more wretched than when Father Simon had given her his news. She had not truly believed it then. She had hoped that the letter was wrong, the man in the alley someone else. She had believed she could still find Georges in this foreign city, and he would be alive and well.

That hope had been vain. Georges was dead and she was alone.

But not completely. Drury knelt beside her and gently stroked her hair. He did not speak. He did not have to. She felt his sympathy, knew that he cared. His touch was enough.

Sometime later, as her sorrow began to ebb a little, she heard hushed voices in the foyer—Lord Bromwell and the butler, she thought, before they drifted away.

How long had she given in to her sorrow?

She sat up, wiping her face with a handkerchief Drury wordlessly handed her. Then he pressed a drink into her hand. Where it had come from, or who had brought it or when, she didn't know. She'd been too wrapped in her grief to notice. She drank, the liquid burning her throat.

She choked a little as she handed the crystal glass back to him, and he set it on the table nearby.

"I thought I would be prepared," she said softly, wiping at the next tear that slipped from her eye.

He looked at her as if his own heart was breaking. "I don't think we can ever be truly prepared for the death of someone we love, as long as there's a chance for hope."

She nodded and twisted the damp handkerchief in her hands. "Your associate, this Sam Clark, he is completely certain?"

"He's sure, so we have to believe it."

She heard something in Drury's voice, something more than sadness. He sat beside her and took her hands in his. "Juliette, I'm so sorry," he whispered, his deep voice full of regret.

"I do not blame you for bringing me this news. I'm grateful—"

"Oh, God, don't say that!" he cried, jumping to his feet. "Of all things, don't say *that.*"

He strode toward the windows.

"What have I done?" she asked, following him, the tears beginning again.

He whirled around, his eyes frantic, as dismayed and disturbed as any man could be. "You've done nothing. Nothing! It's what *I've* done. *Me!*"

He held out his trembling hands. "Oh, Juliette, I did it. *I* killed your brother. With these hands, I held the knife and I killed him."

He covered his face with his crooked fingers. "Heaven help me, I was *glad* to do it."

She stood stock-still, too stunned even to breathe.

This man she loved, this man she had given herself to in every way a woman could, this man she had despaired of leaving, *he* had murdered her brother?

Drury drew in a deep, shuddering breath and lowered his hands, spreading his arms as if in surrender. "He betrayed me. To the French army. He told them I was a spy and sent others to find my friends. They killed them all."

For an instant, Drury's gaze hardened and she knew what he said was the truth. He had killed her brother. "It was your brother who broke my fingers."

She backed away, staring. "*Non. Non.* He could not do such a thing."

"It's true, Juliette. That's why I searched for him and why I killed him. Justice for my friends, and because of what he did to me."

"Justice?" she cried, appalled. "You who represent the law in your black robe and white wig—you speak of justice? To stab a man in an alley like a common thief? *That* is justice? That is *murder.* Whatever Georges did to you, you *murdered* him!"

"You can't possibly understand—"

She held out her hand to silence him. "Stop! Do not try to explain! Do not use your legal skills on me! Now hear *me,* Sir Douglas. Whatever my brother did, you did not give *him* justice. You passed judgment on him and you found him guilty, and you alone executed him. *You.* In a French court, he might have been exonerated. As a Frenchman in a time of war, he could justify his actions, too, just as you no doubt did. But when you killed him, the war was *over.*"

She could not stay in the same room with him. Not now. Not ever. She went to leave, but he ran after her and took hold of her arm. "Juliette—"

"Non!" she shouted, wrenching free. "I never want to see you again! I am leaving this place. I would rather risk attack than stay another moment in your presence. And if *you* are attacked, consider it *justice* for what you have done!"

This time, he let her go.

When she had left the room, when she had fled from him and run up the stairs, he left Buggy's house without a word.

Dawn had come. A cool, gray dawn, with a light rain falling.

Juliette had cried until she could cry no more. Now she sat on the side of the bed, looking out the window at the bleak, cold world, a world that only yesterday had seemed full of life and love and promise.

Until Drury had come back and told her the awful truth.

The terrible, shocking truth.

But after she had left him, after she had run here to hide and weep and curse God and the Fates, she had cried for another reason.

In spite of what Drury had done, she loved him still. When she thought of his ruined hands and the pain he must have endured, as well as his dead friends, she could understand how keen he'd been for vengeance. How necessary it must have seemed.

And Georges? Georges had left her behind. He had gone off to seek his fortune, and she had hoped he would send for her. In the still, dark hours of the night, after Lord Bromwell had again softly knocked on the door and asked if there was anything he could do and she had sent him away with thanks, Juliette had admitted to herself that she had never been sure her brother really would send for her, no matter what he said. Like her father and Marcel, Georges always thought of himself first. His promise to summon her could have been no more than a bid to make her stop crying. She could still see the excited gleam in his eyes, the delight, before he'd left her on the farm, with Gaston LaRoche.

She rose wearily and went to the window. The garden was soggy and gray, too.

What was she going to do? She couldn't take Drury's money to start her business now, even if he still offered it to her.

He must hate her, not just because she was Georges's sister—although that would surely be enough—but because she'd forced him to see what he'd done as something other than justice.

She wasn't wrong to condemn his action; in her heart, she believed in the rule of law. But so did he, and she had charged him with breaking the rules he represented every day. How could he forgive her for that?

"Miss Bergerine?"

Lord Bromwell had returned and was again outside the bedroom door. Had he been awake all night, too?

This time, she must speak to him. This time, she must tell him she couldn't stay here another day. She couldn't accept his hospitality any longer. She must go back to France.

Not home. France was not home anymore. The only place she had felt at home in a very long time was last night, here, in Drury's arms. When he'd held her after they made love, and then fallen into blissful sleep.

A jest of God, to give her that peace and happiness for not even one full day.

"Come in, my lord," she said, rising.

His kind, good-looking face was, as she had expected, full of worry and concern.

He was not alone. Lady Fanny was with him, regarding her with pity and sympathy. "Miss Bergerine, is there anything we can do?" she asked softly. "Please, you have only to ask."

She did not want to see Lady Fanny, who could have had Drury's heart so easily, and instead had loved another. "I think I should go back to France."

"Soon?"

"*Oui*. As soon as I can have my clothing packed."

"Drury will need a little while to get you the necessary funds."

"I want nothing from him. He owes me nothing, and I will take only the clothes I have worn."

After all, she needed something to sell, or she would have to beg in the streets, or sell herself.

The thought of letting another man touch her, as Drury had, proved too much for her to bear. She turned away to hide her face, the tears that threatened to fall.

Lady Fanny was beside her in an instant and put her arm around her waist. "Sit down, my dear, please. Buggy told us about your brother. I'm so very, very sorry."

Was that all they knew? That Georges was dead? Had Drury not told them what her brother had done? Did they not know how Georges had died, and why?

She would not ask, because if Drury had not, she might have to tell them herself.

"Buggy, would you mind leaving us?" Lady Fanny asked.

He immediately did as she requested, closing the door softly behind him while Lady Fanny wordlessly went to the washstand. She dampened a square of linen and returned. Sitting on the bed, she began to wipe Juliette's flushed cheeks.

Juliette wasn't a little girl, but she willingly submitted to the tender ministrations. It was pleasant, if one could call it that, to have such care.

This woman could have been a good friend, if only things had been different.

Lady Fanny took hold of Juliette's hands and held them firmly. "I'm sorry you won't accept Drury's offer. He meant well, I'm sure, although he might not have put it in the most diplomatic way."

How could Juliette tell her the truth? "It was not the offer that was wrong, or the way he made it," she said, unable to meet Lady Fanny's steadfast gaze. "I think he will want nothing to do with me after…after—"

She could not say it. The words lodged in her throat like blocks of wood.

Lady Fanny's grip tightened. "Don't you know that he cares about you?"

Juliette tugged her hands away and got up, too agitated to sit. "You do not understand!"

"Perhaps I understand more than you think. You've fallen in love with him, haven't you?"

She did not answer. Could not. Dared not.

"I hope so, because he's in love with you."

Juliette shook her head, unwilling to believe her. How could *she* know what was in his heart?

Lady Fanny rose and came toward her, and spoke with conviction. "I think that once, he may have believed he loved me. Or rather, he may have wanted to believe it, and hoped that I could fall in love with him. But he never truly loved me—not the way he loves you. That night at the theater, when I suppose you thought I was paying attention only to the actors, I watched Drury, too. I saw the way he gazed at you, and believe me, Juliette, he never looked at me that way.

"If he ever felt anything for me, it was affection, and perhaps he thought I could give him a quiet, peaceful home. But there would have been no passion. He did kiss me once, and I think he realized then that something would always be lacking between us. Even if I didn't already love Brix, I could never have loved Drury. Not the way you do—as he loves you, Juliette. If he's said or done something to make you believe otherwise, it's because he's never been in love before."

Her lips turned up in a rueful smile. "I daresay the power and depth of his devotion is quite startling to a man like him, who's so used to having his feelings under control."

Juliette shook her head. "No, you do not understand."

"You think a marriage between you won't work because he's a baronet and you're a French seamstress? I assure you, he won't let that stand in his way."

Juliette's hands balled into fists. Would this woman never be quiet and leave her alone?

"Do you really underestimate him that much? He's a famous man, my dear, and famous men can overcome many an obstacle."

She didn't understand. She never would.

"I'm sure that whatever's come between you—"

"No!" Juliette shouted, unable to restrain herself any longer. "He killed Georges. He killed my brother—the man who tortured him!"

Finally Lady Fanny was silent, too shocked and stunned to speak.

"My own brother betrayed him. Led his enemies to him. Helped to kill his friends. Georges himself broke his fingers. So Drury hunted him down and stabbed him."

Lady Fanny felt for the nearest chair and sat heavily. It was only then Juliette remembered she was with child.

Instantly, Juliette berated herself. She should have kept quiet. Kept her pain and anguish private. This woman had only been trying to help.

Juliette ran to the door and shouted for Polly, who was hovering anxiously at the top of the back stairs. "Water—quick! Lady Fanny is ill!"

"No, no, I'm all right," Lady Fanny protested from behind her. "Just…a little dizzy,"

Footsteps pounded on the stairs, and Lord Bromwell appeared at the door.

"Fanny! What's happened?" he demanded as he rushed past Juliette and knelt beside her.

"I'm all right. Really. I just had a bit of a shock. Juliette told me…"

She glanced up uncertainly, as if she would keep what she'd been told a secret, if Juliette wanted it that way.

She didn't. Not now. Let them know. Let them all understand why Drury hated her. "I told her how my brother died, and why."

And then she repeated her shame to Lord Bromwell.

As he stared in equally stunned disbelief, a horse's hooves clattered on the cobblestones outside, and the downstairs door banged open. "Fanny! Buggy!"

Had Mr. Smythe-Medway spoken with Drury? Was Juliette going to be sent from this house at once?

Lord Bromwell strode to the door. "Up here, Brix," he called out.

Fanny's husband took the stairs two at a time, and when he arrived, his hair was disheveled, his coat open, his boots splattered with mud, and he was sweating as if he'd run for miles.

"Good God, man, what's happened?" Lord Bromwell cried.

Mr. Smythe-Medway's tormented gaze went to Juliette first. "Drury's disappeared."

Chapter Eighteen

Mademoiselle—*If you wish to see your lover again, you will bring that necklace you wore to the theater to Clink Street, closest you can get to the river. If you involve the Runners or anyone else, Drury will die.*

A sharp slap brought Drury back to consciousness. With his cheek smarting from the blow, he opened his eyes, to find Sam Clark's smirking face not three inches from his own. "Had a nice little nap, did ya, *MacDougal?*"

Drury didn't struggle. He barely moved at all—just enough to know he was bound and, as he fought the panic, that he was tied to a chair. Just like he'd been bound before the mallet had come down on his fingers.

He *mustn't* panic. He mustn't be afraid. He had to be calm. He had to be strong.

He managed to keep his voice level as he raised a brow. "Have you gone quite mad?"

Clark sniffed, his breath foul and reeking of ale, adding to other odors. They were in a large room full of crates that stunk of…tar. And hemp. The floor wasn't rocking, so they weren't on a ship—but near one, perhaps. On the docks. A warehouse, no doubt.

Light came in from a row of windows, through shutters that were old and cracked. So it was day. Not a bright day, and it was raining. He could hear the drops hitting the wood.

"Oh, I'm not mad," Clark said as he straightened. "No, Sir Douglas, not mad at all. I've known you were MacDougal for months. And if you wanted a French whore, well, why not? But then I found out who she was. So I told ya, and what do ya do? Walk for miles, till I nearly wear out my boots watching ya. When you finally go back to Lord Bromwell's, I'm thinking here it comes. Now Pete and the others'll rest easier.

"But you didn't do nothing. Didn't kill her. Didn't hurt her. Didn't even have her arrested. I'm sure a clever fellow like you could have come up with something to get her thrown in Newgate and hanged or transported. No, you just go in and come out and walk some more.

"And this time, as I'm followin' ya, I start to get wise. You had that French bitch before, in France, during the war, didn't ya? Maybe that's how you met her brother. Never did know where you got him.

"How much did you get for informin' on us? It had to be more than her in your bed. Or were you that desperate?"

"I met Henri—Georges—through a mutual friend. You remember Alberto LaCosta? He introduced us."

"And then he got shot. Pull the other one."

"Whether you believe me or not, it's true. Now I suggest you let me go, or—"

"Or what? You'll have me arrested? Charged with something and hanged? Transported, maybe? Same if

I kill you, isn't it? But if you're dead, Pete Windham and the others'll be able to rest in peace, knowing they got some justice."

Justice? Drury opened his mouth, then closed it. What difference was there between what Clark was doing and what he'd done? Except that Drury was innocent of betrayal. "Sam, I did not betray you, or Windham, or anyone. I give you my word."

"As if that's worth anything!" Clark jeered. "Frogs killed him because you told 'em where he was, just like you told 'em about the others."

Drury fought to subdue his fear. "If I was in league with the French, would they have broken my fingers and thrown me into the river to drown? I suffered because I wasn't."

Clark smirked again. "So maybe Desmaries sold you out, too. Maybe they hurt you some—but you led 'em right to Pete. And they did worse than break his hands before they killed him—or didn't you know that?"

"Yes, I know how he, and the rest of them, were killed. But whatever you believe, whatever you've been told, I didn't reveal anything to the French."

Drury turned the full force of his stare onto Clark. "It was Desmaries himself who tortured me, Sam, and I killed him for it."

"You expect me to believe Georges Bergerine tortured you, and you killed him, and now you've got his sister for your mistress? She's in bed with ya because you killed her brother?" Clark laughed scornfully. "You must think I'm a right fool, too stupid to see through your disguises and lies. It was you and him and his sister in it together all along."

"Why the devil would I have sent you to Calais if

I knew the truth about Desmaries?" Drury asked. "It makes no sense!"

"To find out if he was really dead."

"I know he's dead. I told you, I killed him."

"Like I'd believe anything that comes out o' that lyin' gob o' yours."

"If you're so sure I'm guilty," Drury said, grasping at straws, "why haven't you killed me?"

"Because killin' you quick wouldn't be enough. Windham didn't die quick, so neither will you. And neither will she."

Clark's smile was malevolence itself when he saw the look of horror Drury could not hide. "A certain lady come to see me a while ago. Heard I could do a special kind o' job, and would, if the money was right. You think you're so clever, but you ain't the only one I work for. The lady's husband needs a few jobs done from time to time.

"So she comes to me and offers a lot o' money— enough to make it worth my while to kill you. She wants your mistress dead, too. Fine, says I. Let me do it in me own time, though. Fine, says she.

"And then I find out who that whore is. Sweet, I calls it. Desmaries ain't alive to pay, so his sister can do it for him. Come now, Sir Douglas, why look like that? She's French, ain't she? And everybody knows how you hate the French—or claim to, unless you can get under their petticoats, I suppose."

"Where *is* the whore?" a woman's voice demanded.

Drury started. "Sarah?"

Lady Sarah Chelton, as out of place here as a ruby brooch on a beggar's coat, picked her way toward them across the dusty warehouse floor, a lace handkerchief held over her shapely, disdainful nose.

Lady Chelton lowered her handkerchief, her nose wrinkling with obvious disgust. "Sir Douglas! How delightful to see you again."

"Sarah, what are you doing here?"

"Watching you suffer, as I have suffered for being with you."

God help him, Drury thought, Juliette had been right! He really hadn't believed it until now.

"We both knew the terms of our relationship," he replied, fighting to sound calm. "You would have ended it eventually if I hadn't. I'm sorry if I hurt your feelings—"

"Hurt my *feelings?*" she cried. She splayed her hands on his forearms and leaned forward, her face twisted with rage and hate. "You put me in prison, you selfish scum! My husband found out about us. He wouldn't have minded, except that you're only a baronet and an Old Bailey barrister besides. I miscalculated, you see, just as you have. If you'd been somebody like that idiot viscount friend of yours with the mania for spiders, he wouldn't have cared a whit. But you aren't.

"Now he won't come near me and if I take another lover, he's threatened to tell all the world I have a disease—the sort of disease no lady should have. And of course, divorce is out of the question—the scandal, you see. So I have no husband, no lover, no *life*— while you don't suffer at all, you whoring, stinking bastard!"

"I'm sorry for what's happened to you," he replied, shocked by her husband's reaction. He'd had no idea.

"That's not all, you cur! After beating me until I could hardly stand, my brute of a husband gave me to the servants. He called all the men into the drawing room one night and told them they could do whatever they liked with me. He would not press charges, and if *I* tried to, he would tell the court that I had done it before, many times, and that I liked it. He let them have me—even the stable boy! And there was nothing I could do. Nothing but submit!

"So now I'm going to be compensated for my humiliation after you watch Clark and his men take your French whore. They're going to let you watch them kill her, too. Wasn't it good of him to come to me and suggest this little plan? He thought I'd like to be in on the fun."

She whirled around, her silk skirts swishing, and looked at Clark, who was leaning against a pile of crates. "So where is the whore?"

"Not here yet," he replied, pushing himself off the crate.

"I can see that. Why not?"

Sam grinned. "Rafe's bringin' her. We had a bit of business to do first. He's worth something, Drury is. Might as well get paid before I kill him—the same way he got paid for killing my mates."

"You didn't tell me you were doing this for *money*," Lady Chelton charged.

"Oh, I'm going to kill him for pleasure, too," he replied. "But why not get some money while I'm at it? He's got it, I need it."

"Have you forgotten the money I've already paid you to capture him and his whore, despite your numerous failures?"

Sam laughed. "You mean the makin' 'em sweat part? I thought you'd appreciate that. Look at 'im sweat when he knows his French whore's goin' to die."

Lady Chelton smiled as she walked around Drury,

bound in the chair. He could smell her perfume as he cursed himself for ever being with her.

"How do you like it, my love? Being held against your will, bound and doomed? Now you know how it is for me, tied to my disgusting husband forever."

"I went to his chambers this morning to talk to him about...well, about you," Mr. Smythe-Medway explained to Juliette and the others. "But he wasn't there. Mr. Edgar said he hasn't seen him since the trial. He was frantic. Wanted to go for the Runners, but I told him to stay there in case Drury returns. I tried to assure him that Drury might have gone to Boodle's, but he wasn't there, either. So I came straight here."

"Perhaps he went walking," Juliette suggested, her own voice sounding odd and distant, like that of a little child lost in the dark.

She thought she'd known fear before. It had been nothing compared to this cold, terrifying dread.

"Maybe he did go walking, but he should have been at his chambers by the time I got there. Mr. Edgar says he has an appointment with Jamie St. Claire today, and he never misses his appointments. Didn't Drury take a carriage or hackney when he left here yesterday?"

Juliette shook her head. She must be calm, composed, as he would be. "I do not know. I was too upset to notice."

Lady Fanny rose and put her arm around Juliette. "She'd just found out that her brother is dead."

"I'm sorry," Mr. Smythe-Medway said, his face reddening. "I...maybe we should all go downstairs, except you, Miss Bergerine."

Where, she didn't doubt, Lady Fanny would tell them everything.

Lord Bromwell made an attempt to smile reassuringly. "I'd wager you're right, though. He's just gone walking and went rather far. He walks for miles sometimes."

"If you please, my lord."

A rather pale Millstone stood in the doorway. "Mr. Gerrard is below and he insists upon seeing Miss Bergerine."

"Tell him she cannot possibly speak with him now," Lord Bromwell replied.

"He says it's most urgent, my lord," Millstone said, obviously agitated. "It's about Sir Douglas."

Juliette ran past the butler without another word.

"Where is Drury?" she demanded, rushing breathlessly into the drawing room.

"I don't know," Mr. Gerrard replied helplessly, as Lady Fanny and the two gentlemen also came into the room. "I was going into White's when a footman stopped me and handed me this sealed note to bring to you. He called me by name and said it concerned Sir Douglas Drury. I came here right away. Has something happened to Sir Douglas?"

Juliette snatched the folded paper from him and broke the seal. "It is in French," she said, and started to read.

The note told her that if she didn't bring the diamond necklace to a specific location, Drury would die.

Die. The word lay there, a threat on paper. Unless she traded his life for his mother's necklace.

"It is a ransom note," she said, her voice shaking like her hands. "Someone has kidnapped him and now they want the necklace he let me wear to the theater, or they'll kill him."

Lord Bromwell reached out. "Please, let me see the note."

Mr. Smythe-Medway and Lady Fanny moved in to read it, too.

"This footman, he just came up to you on the street?" Juliette asked Mr. Gerrard.

"Yes. I thought it odd, but wondered if some friend or acquaintance had changed their plans, or perhaps it was an invitation." He shook his head sorrowfully. "It was an odd request, but then I thought I'd get to see you again, so…"

Juliette was in no mood for a young man's lovelorn sighs. "You came right away?"

"At once."

"This is a woman's hand," Lady Fanny announced. She sniffed the paper. "There's still the scent of perfume, too."

"A *woman* abducted him for money?" Mr. Smythe-Medway asked in wonder.

"Not money," Juliette pointed out. "His mother's necklace. It is not the same."

"No, it's not," Lady Fanny agreed. "And if it was only for money, why send the note to Juliette, and not Buggy, or us? No, there's more to this than money."

"Just like Miss Bergerine thought," Lord Bromwell agreed. "The question is, what are we going to do?"

"We must get the necklace and I must take it there," Juliette replied, shocked they would think there was any alternative.

"We can't simply take the necklace and assume they'll let him go," Lady Fanny said. "We don't know if he's even…"

Juliette's heart lurched.

"He isn't dead," she insisted, determined to believe it, needing to. Yet even as she spoke, she remembered her hope about Georges and how wrong she'd been about that. About him.

"Of course he's not dead," Mr. Smythe-Medway said firmly. "The man's got more lives than a cat. And unless his abductors are incredibly stupid, they'll know we won't surrender the necklace without seeing him alive. So the first thing we should do is alert the Runners and MacDougal's men, and fetch the necklace."

"But I must go alone!" Juliette insisted. "The note says so, or they will kill him."

"You must *seem* to be alone," Lord Bromwell corrected. "I'll go with you—secretly, of course." His lips jerked up in a little smile. "I may seem an academic sort of fellow to you, Miss Bergerine, but I assure you, I can fight quite well, and I've been in tricky situations before. And we can have some of MacDougal's men nearby. They're used to subterfuge."

"I'll go with you," Mr. Smythe-Medway said.

"No," Lord Bromwell declared without hesitation. "I'm not having you take risks when Fanny's having a baby. Besides, you should go for the necklace. Mr. Edgar will trust you with it. Fanny should stay here with Juliette."

Juliette didn't like that idea at all. "We must wait?"

"I'll not have you trying to ride through London. Brix and I can. When we're back, and after we've done everything we can to ensure your safety, I'll go with you to Southwark. God help us if Drury thinks we didn't protect you."

Lady Fanny reached out to pat her arm. "He's right. They'll make faster progress without us. And besides, there's always a chance Drury will escape on his own and come back here."

"What can *I* do?" Mr. Gerrard asked. "Please, I want to help."

Juliette wanted to believe him trustworthy, but his delivery of the note disturbed her. "I think perhaps it is better if you don't."

She wondered if the others would agree, and to her relief, Lord Bromwell said, "I think you should remain here, Mr. Gerrard, while we deal with this."

"Can't risk this news getting out until we've got Drury back safe and sound," Mr. Smythe-Medway agreed.

"I can keep a confidence," the young man said, obviously offended. "However, I'll ignore your insult in the hopes that I may be of some assistance."

Paying no attention to the insulted Mr. Gerrard, Mr. Smythe-Medway turned to Lord Bromwell as Millstone appeared at the door with Lord Bromwell's greatcoat and tall hat. "Do you think you'll have any trouble finding MacDougal? You should speak to the fellow directly if you can. He's the best, I understand."

Lord Bromwell shrugged on his coat and set his hat on his head as he replied. "Unfortunately, Drury *is* MacDougal."

"What?" Juliette gasped, and the others were equally surprised.

"He started to play the part during the war and kept it up here afterward," Lord Bromwell explained. "He felt it would be easier for him to gather information in disguise. Even the men he employs as MacDougal have no idea who they're really working for."

"You mean to say he's been sneaking around London disguised as a Scot? How's that even possible?" Mr. Smythe-Medway demanded. "He's too well-known. And what about his fingers?"

Lord Bromwell started for the door. "If you saw

him as MacDougal, with an eye patch and one arm tied behind his back as if he'd lost it, you'd never think it was Drury. And you know he's good with accents."

"My God," Mr. Smythe-Medway muttered as he followed him.

"Wait!" Juliette cried, although time was of the essence. "What if this house is being watched?"

Lord Bromwell thought a moment. "We could go over the roofs like we used to do at Harrow—if you're up for it, Brix."

Mr. Smythe-Medway drew himself up, a spark of determination as well as challenge in his eyes. "I may be an old married man, my lord, but if you can do it, so can I."

Chapter Nineteen

Criminal elements continue to plague our great city, despite the efforts of our courts and the Bow Street Runners. Even our finest citizens are not safe from their evil deeds.

—from an editorial in the
London Morning Herald

Juliette was at the door before the footman had a chance to close it behind the returning Brixton Smythe-Medway. Lady Fanny came with her, while Millstone hovered nearby like an anxious mother on the night of her daughter's first ball.

"I've got it," Mr. Smythe-Medway said at once, giving Juliette a smile. "Wasn't where I expected it, and poor Mr. Edgar was quite beside himself thinking it'd been stolen. We found it at last under Drury's pillow. Buggy back yet?"

"No," his wife replied as they all headed into the drawing room. "Come, sit down and catch your breath. My heart was in my throat, thinking you both were going to plunge to your deaths from the roof."

"And leave my child without a father and you without a doting husband? Perish the thought!"

"As long as you're safe," Lady Fanny said, looking up at him with such adoration, Juliette's throat constricted. They were so happy together, sharing a love she had now tasted and knew she would miss for the rest of her days.

But she would gladly endure that as long as Drury lived!

There was another commotion at the door, and this time, Lord Bromwell entered, with a group of rather rough-looking men behind him. They had to be the Runners, and if Lord Bromwell thought they could be inconspicuous, he was wrong. They looked like a troop of soldiers, which was likely what they'd been at one time.

"All here?" Lord Bromwell asked. "Got the necklace, Brix?"

"Yes. It was under his pillow."

"Interesting. Obviously he wanted to keep it close by as he slept," Lord Bromwell replied. However, his surprise at that conclusion, like hers, was short-lived.

They had other, more important things to think about.

A short while later, Juliette stood in the shadows of a half-burned warehouse near the Thames, just as the note had instructed. Lord Bromwell was somewhere nearby, although exactly where, she had no idea. The Runners were supposedly hidden close by, too.

It had taken some convincing for the Runners to do as she and Drury's friends wanted rather than start a search of the area. Fortunately, while they might have been able to ignore her own wishes, the combined force of a very serious Lord Bromwell, as well as the Honorable Brixton Smythe-Medway, made it a different matter. In the end, they had capitulated, on the understanding that the two noblemen would take the blame if things didn't turn out as they hoped. If Drury...

She would not think about that. Instead, she thought about the small dagger in her bodice from Lord Bromwell's collection of foreign artifacts, and the one in her garter, and the two very long hatpins Lady Fanny had stuck through Juliette's hair and bonnet. She would be searched, she had no doubt, but she could hope that at least one weapon would go undetected by the men holding Drury hostage.

Lord Bromwell had also coated the bottom of the heel of her shoe with some kind of paint. It would leave a trail for them to follow, he said.

Lady Fanny had asked what they would do if Juliette was put into a carriage, but her husband had assured her that the streets and alleys were so narrow and winding in this part of London, any conveyance would make very slow progress.

Whatever the objections, Juliette was not going to be deterred. She would do as the author of this note asked because Drury's life was at stake.

A man stepped out of the nearest alley. "All alone, eh? Just like we said."

She recognized his voice instantly, remembered the feel of his hand over her mouth, his arm around his waist. The way he smelled. *"Oui,"* she said, trying to subdue her fear. "Take me to Sir Douglas."

Another large, rough-looking man appeared behind the ruffian, who made a mockery of a bow. "This way, if you please—but first, give me that bag, and we got to cover them pretty eyes o' yours."

She held out her reticule without hesitation. The necklace wasn't there, but rather sewn into the seam of her chemise. "Of course," she replied. "Although if you think I have the necklace in there, you are a fool. I will not give it to you until I see for myself that Sir Douglas is alive and unharmed."

"Hidden it, have ya? We might just have to strip you naked right here, then."

She would not panic. She would be calm, like Drury. "I did not say I have it hidden in my clothes."

Although she did.

The man's eyes narrowed beneath the brim of his hat. "No necklace, no Drury."

"No Drury, no necklace."

"I ain't givin' him up without it."

"And I will not give you the necklace until I see him alive and well."

"Come on, Sam," his associate said, licking his lips and looking around anxiously. "We can't stand here all day."

"All right," the man named Sam growled. "We'll take her, and if she ain't got the necklace, we'll just have to kill her."

He leered at Juliette, who felt perspiration trickling down her sides and back. "But afore we do that, we'll have a little fun. Got to make it worth our while, after all. Take off that bonnet and cover her head, Rafe, and mind you be gentle. Don't want her all bruised up. Not yet, anyway."

Rafe yanked off her bonnet and the pins with it, nearly ripping the hair from her scalp. Then a heavy black hood went over her head, and her hands were bound tightly and painfully behind her.

Her cleavage nearly in Drury's face, Lady Sarah worked his gag lower. Sam Clark had gone to meet Juliette, and now they were alone except for one guard who stood silently near the door, able to see them but too far away to hear.

"Sarah, for God's sake, you have to realize this is wrong," Drury said hoarsely, while he surreptitiously worked his hands and wrists to loosen his bindings. If he kept her talking, if he kept her focus on his face, she might not see. The movement hurt like hell, but he'd felt worse pain before, and he had to get free.

"What, *now* you get religion?" she jeered as she drew back. "If you expect mercy from me, my love, you are sadly mistaken. And I won't listen to anything you have to say."

Her eyes gleaming with triumph, she smiled before she brushed her lips over his. "I only wanted to remember what I ever saw in you. I thought it was your kisses that made you memorable. It certainly wasn't your touch—not with those fingers."

"I'd like to touch you right now," he replied through clenched teeth. "Although I don't think you'd enjoy it nearly as much as you enjoyed making love with me."

She sniffed. "Even if you got me by the throat, you couldn't hurt me. Your hands are too weak—like the rest of you."

"I don't recall you ever complaining about that before, Sarah. And as it happens, my hands are getting stronger every day. I daresay you'd be surprised."

She slapped his face, the impact lessened by her kid leather glove. Besides, he'd been slapped and struck by stronger men and a more hysterical woman than she, many times. "Oh, Sarah, is that the best you can do? And after all we've been to each other?"

She hit him again as tears started in her eyes. "You and that little French whore are going to pay!"

"Juliette hasn't hurt you. If there is blame here, it is mine, not hers."

"Do you think I'm going to allow her to live after what you did to me? Oh, no, my sweet, sweet man, I'm going to let Sam kill her, and in front of you. First, though, he and his fellows are going to have her, just the way my husband's servants had me. I want to hear her cries of pain and anguish. I want her to suffer, and I want you to hear and see it all. And then Sam's going to kill you for me." A sob broke from her throat. "And then I'll have some peace."

"No, you won't, Sarah," he said, shaking his head and feeling sorry for her despite what she'd done and what she planned to do. "Believe me, I know. I've killed a man in vengeance. It brought no peace, only more pain."

Sarah drew herself up. "We shall see!" She pointed over his shoulder. "We shall see very soon, for here comes your little French whore."

With the black hood over her head, Juliette could barely breathe. Her shoulders ached. The man holding her—not the one called Sam, but Rafe—smelled of stale sweat and beer and dirty wool.

Holding her shoulder, he roughly pushed her forward. She nearly tripped over an uneven board, then twisted away from him. She'd rather fall than have him touch her again.

Her shoulder hit something that moved, and it fell.

Something wooden. The place smelled of damp, rotting wood. Tar. Wet stone or brick. They must be in one of the warehouses along the river.

At last, the man grabbed her shoulder to stop.

"I hope you weren't followed," a woman said.

She sounded like a well-educated, wealthy woman, the kind who came to Madame de Pomplona's shop.

"I'm not stupid," Sam grumbled from somewhere close by. "How come he's not gagged?"

"We were engaged in a delightful conversation," a man replied.

Drury! It was her beloved Drury! He was alive and talking as calmly as if they were in Lord Bromwell's drawing room!

Her despair lifted, although they were still in danger. But he was alive, and now she could truly have hope.

"It seems my lady doesn't think very highly of you, Clark," Drury noted.

"Liar!" the woman charged. "I never said any such thing."

"No honor among thieves, you know, Sam."

"Shut up!" the man growled. She heard him stomp across the floor. "There. That oughta keep ya quiet. And if that won't, look what we've got."

Somebody grabbed her arm and pulled her forward before the hood was torn from her head. She blinked in the sudden light, and then she saw Drury, tied to a chair and gagged with what looked like his cravat. His gaze met hers, steady, unwavering, strong.

Like himself. And as she must be, if they were to escape.

"Did she bring it?" the woman demanded.

Although she stood in the shadows, Juliette recognized her at once. She was the woman from the theater, the lady who had been Drury's last lover, Lady Sarah Chelton.

She wore an expensive pelisse that covered a gown of jonquil silk, a necklace of pearls, a large, ornately decorated hat and a veil covering her face. What need had she for Drury's mother's jewelry?

"Where is the necklace?" Lady Chelton nevertheless demanded. "If you wish your fiancé to survive, you'll give it to us."

"Since I see my beloved is alive, I will tell you—after you have removed his gag and untied him."

The lady came closer. "I think not." She glanced at the leader of the ruffians. "Mr. Clark, perhaps you should search her?"

The man chortled. "Just what I been thinking," he murmured as he pulled a long, wide knife from his belt. "Where to start, though, eh?"

Juliette didn't look at him. She gazed past him, to Drury. Drury, sitting bound and helpless, watching her. Willing her to be strong.

While his forearms stealthily twisted and turned, and his crooked fingers curled around the arm of the chair.

She still didn't look at Clark when he stood in front of her and slipped the tip of his blade down her cheek, along her neck and lower. "Maybe it's in here," he suggested as he shoved his other hand down her bodice.

Drury's expression was murderous. She stood perfectly still.

"God!" Sam cried, withdrawing his hand, the tip of his index finger bleeding. "She's got a knife in there!"

Angry now, he stuck his blade into her bodice, between her skin and chemise, and sliced her clothing open. The little knife Lord Bromwell had given her clattered to the floor. With a sneer, Sam kicked it away.

"That wasn't very clever. What else have you got in there, eh?"

She had to close her eyes as she willed herself to be strong for Drury's sake as well as her own as he roughly fondled her breasts.

"Or maybe you got it somewhere else, eh?" Clark sneered. "Under your skirt? Maybe your chemise. Let's find out."

He reached down, and as he bent, she brought up her knee, striking him hard in the face.

"Damn bitch!" Sam cried, the words muffled as he staggered back, his hands over his face, blood pouring between his fingers. "She broke my bloody nose!"

He lunged and struck her hard, making her stagger, the pain intense. "You'll be sorry, you French bitch. Rafe, strip her. Find the necklace. Then I'm really going to make her scream."

He didn't get the chance as, with a roar of primal rage, Drury tore the arms of the chair from its back. The seat and back splintered and fell to the ground as he shook like an enraged bear.

For an instant Juliette was as startled as the rest of them—but only for that instant. Because Rafe had let her go. She half turned and shoved him away hard with her shoulder. Falling to the floor, she worked her hands around so that she could reach for the other knife in her garter, even though they were still bound together at the wrists.

Drury charged Clark. The other man who'd been guarding Drury came running to join the fray, while Rafe lay groaning on the dusty floor. Two against Drury. Surely he would prevail.

Just as she got hold of the knife, Lady Chelton grabbed her hair, yanking her backward.

Juliette didn't let go of the blade, but pulled forward, landing on her knees. She didn't care if her hair got ripped from her head.

"Drury!" she cried, scrambling to her feet. He held the two men at bay with a broken arm of the chair now clutched in his hands like a club, the ropes dangling unheeded from his arms.

Still holding his nose, Sam ran forward, lifting his foot to kick her. Juliette fell on her stomach to avoid the blow and he missed. His arms flew out as he struggled to regain his balance and she got to her feet. She pushed him over and he fell hard on his back.

Clutching her knife, Juliette ran to stand back-to-back with Drury. Her wrists were still bound and she had no time to try to cut the ropes. As long as she held the knife, she could stab anyone who got too close. Surely Lord Bromwell and the Runners would be here soon. They would find them and help. They *must* find them.

Then she saw Lady Chelton pick up the small knife Clark had kicked away. Lady or not, Juliette thought, gritting her teeth, she would kill the woman if she had to.

Something dropped from the top of a crate beside the lady—the biggest black rat Juliette had ever seen. Lady Chelton screamed in terror and crashed into another pile of empty crates, sending them tumbling to the floor.

Distracted, the man facing Drury looked away. It was enough, and Drury swung the chair arm with all his might, striking the lout in the back of the head. The wood connected with a loud crack, knocking his opponent to the floor.

His face red with blood and rage, Sam Clark started toward them, his blade upraised.

"Take my knife!" Juliette called to Drury, but he

shook his head. "You keep it until this is over. I can't grip it anyway."

"That's right—he's a useless cripple who thinks he's gonna beat me with a rotten piece of wood," Clark sneered.

"You're the fool," Drury retorted. "I could beat you with my bare hands, damaged though they are. The wood's an additional benefit."

"I got away from you before," Clark scoffed.

"Because I thought Juliette might be hurt. You won't get away this time. I intend to stop you once and for all, and when you're taken, I shall greatly enjoy prosecuting you."

"You won't—"

Drury leaped, bringing the makeshift club down hard on Clark's arm. There was a sickening crack, worse than the chair breaking, and Sam staggered back, his knife falling from his hand. Drury swung again, and the man crumpled.

As he fell, Juliette spotted Lady Chelton making her way toward the door. Juliette ran at her and struck her with her shoulder, sending them both to the floor.

"I think not, my lady," she said, rolling over and getting to her feet, the knife still in her grasp.

But as the other woman slowly rose, her bonnet askew, her hair disheveled, her fine gown dusty and torn, Juliette saw the glint of the little knife in her gloved hands.

The woman looked past her, to Drury.

"I won't let you take me to prison," she warned, "and I won't go back to my husband. You can't know what…" She shook her head, her hands trembling as she gripped the knife. "I won't let you. I won't live like that. I won't live…"

As Juliette watched warily, Drury started to walk toward Lady Chelton slowly, cautiously, like the cat people compared him to.

"Sarah, please," he said softly. "Give me the knife. I'll speak to your husband. I'm sure something can be arranged."

"No! You don't know. You weren't there. He watched it all and laughed. He *laughed.* And he'll tell. He'll tell everyone."

"Sarah, please," Drury repeated.

She shook her head. "I did love you, you know. You didn't love me. I know that. But I can't. I won't."

And then she turned the knife and, with a look as determined as any Juliette had ever seen, drove it into her chest.

"Sarah!" Drury shouted, running to catch her as she fell.

He cradled the woman in his arms as they both slipped slowly to the floor.

"You," Lady Chelton whispered as she looked at Juliette, while a red stain spread over the bright yellow of her bodice.

"Oh, Sarah, you should have told me," Drury murmured as he held her. "I could have—"

"Helped?" she scoffed as a little trickle of blood slid down her chin.

Drury grasped her hand in his, but it was too late. He'd seen enough men die to know that there was no hope for her.

"Is there nothing we can do?" Juliette whispered.

Drury shook his bowed head and Lady Sarah Chelton, once the belle of the London Season, breathed her last.

Just as Lord Bromwell and the Runners arrived.

Chapter Twenty

Although I can't officially charge Chelton with anything yet, I've got Jamie searching any records he can find. I'm sure he'll find some sort of nefarious activity, and I'll take great pleasure in prosecuting the bastard, for Sarah's sake.

—from the journal of Sir Douglas Drury

"Well, at least that's something good to come out of the experience," Brix remarked as Mr. Edgar handed him a brandy and he regarded Drury's bandaged hands. "The doctor sounds quite hopeful. They'll never be perfect, of course, but ought to be better now that he's had a chance to reset them."

Drury nodded silently. Several of his fingers had been broken again when he'd destroyed the chair to which he'd been bound. Yet while they ached like the devil, that was nothing compared to the ache in his heart when he thought of living without Juliette, who was free now. Free to go wherever she liked. Away from him.

"And we can all be thankful Miss Bergerine wasn't

hurt," Buggy said from where he sat nearby, nursing his own drink. "Are you still intending to prosecute Chelton, as well as Clark and those other rogues?"

"Yes. No scandal can hurt Sarah now, and I want him to pay for what he's done. I'm sure Jamie will find something."

"Well, if anybody can do it, he can," Brix agreed. "I see the Runners have agreed to abide by our version of events."

They had decided to say that Sarah had also been abducted and had been killed attempting to escape. "It was the least I could do for her."

"What about Miss Bergerine?" Brix asked.

Yesterday, after Sarah had died and the Runners had taken custody of Clark and his men, Buggy had escorted Juliette back to his house. Drury had returned to his chambers, where Mr. Edgar had nearly collapsed with relief and joy. Then the valet had immediately gone for the doctor.

"She's going to go back to France, I suppose," Drury replied, masking his despair. "I still intend to lend her the money to start her own business. I daresay she's anxious to be on her way."

He hadn't actually asked her. He'd barely said a word to her after the Runners and Buggy had arrived at the warehouse. He'd been afraid to, certain she'd say she was leaving London. Leaving England. Leaving him.

"I've invited her to stay for as long as she likes," Buggy remarked.

Drury glanced at him sharply. "And?"

"She's packing her things."

She was going to go. Of course she would, and he would be alone again.

"Although Fanny's trying to talk her out of it even as we speak," Brix said lightly.

Drury wouldn't hope. Juliette was proud and stubborn and independent. If she wanted to leave, she would, and nothing anybody could say would stop her.

"I hope Fanny prevails," Buggy said. "Miss Bergerine does possess rather remarkable vitality, but this whole affair has surely been exhausting, and she's likely in no fit state for a journey, let alone finding a place to live."

"She probably doesn't want to be beholden to the friend of the man who killed her brother," Drury said.

"There is that, of course," Buggy grimly agreed.

"Do you intend to say goodbye to her?" Brix asked.

"No." Drury saw no reason to go through that ceremony. "I'm sure she has no wish to see me ever again."

Brix cleared his throat. "Fanny told me that if you said something like that, I was to remind you of a certain conversation you once had with her, on the subject of regrets. Apparently, Buggy," he explained to their friend, "he used the word *gnaw* to describe how they could affect a person."

Brix turned to Drury again. "It seems to me, my friend, that you're going to have a huge regret gnawing at you if you don't see Miss Bergerine again."

Drury got to his feet and strode to the window before he turned on his heel to face his friends. Who couldn't possibly understand what he was feeling—not even Brix, who'd nearly lost Fanny. "Even if I did want to see her, do you honestly think she would want to see *me?* I killed her brother, for God's sake. Juliette must *hate* me—but not nearly as much as I hate myself for what I've done."

There. He'd said it. Now they would understand, or at least have some notion of why he couldn't see Juliette again.

"Fanny thought you might say that," Brix noted, as serious as Drury had ever seen him.

"Oh? And did she also tell you what I ought to do?" he asked, sarcastic in his misery.

"She thinks you ought to tell Juliette that you love her."

Drury stared at him with wide-eyed disbelief. "I love her?"

"You do, don't you?"

"I agree with Fanny," Buggy said quietly. "Tell her how you feel, and if she still wants to leave, at least you've been honest with her."

"If you don't, you might regret it for the rest of your life," Brix added.

It was an odd sensation, hearing his two best friends tell him how he felt and what he ought to do. For most of his life, he'd gone his own way, not asking for help. Thinking he didn't need any. Believing he was destined to be always alone. "You both seem remarkably sure that I love her."

"You're not going to try to deny it—not to us," Buggy replied.

Brix went to his friend and took hold of his shoulders. "I have some idea of your dilemma, so I hope you'll listen to me. Go to her, Drury, and at least tell her that you love her. What's the worse that can happen?"

Drury pulled away. "She can tell me to my face that she hates me and never wants to see me again. That I ruined her life, and Sarah's, too. That I'm a terrible man and no one could ever love me."

A look of frustration kindled in Brix's blue eyes. "If she thought that, do you think she would have put her life in danger to rescue you?

"Fanny told me one other thing, if you insist on being a proud and stubborn ass. Juliette loves you. Fanny's quite certain of it and you'll be the worst sort of idiot if you let the woman go. Give her the chance to forgive you—and for you to forgive yourself. Now come, man, go to her. My phaeton is outside."

Drury hesitated. Even if Juliette had loved him once, could she still, after what he'd done? Would it be better to go to her and risk seeing hatred in her eyes, or stay safely here in his chambers? Never knowing. Always wondering what might have been…

Never in his life had he felt less confident, not even when he was a child and his mother shouted criticisms of everything he did.

Because never in his life had so much been at stake.

Yet he remembered what he'd told Fanny—how during his captivity, he'd thought about regrets. He'd been determined, then and afterward, to have as few as possible for as long as he lived, he'd said.

If he didn't go to Juliette now, if he didn't take that risk, what kind of regrets would he have for the rest of his life?

"I stand corrected," he said, at last sounding like the confident Drury they knew. "Mr. Edgar, my hat!"

"I do wish you'd reconsider and accept Buggy's offer to stay a little longer," Fanny said again, using her most persuasive tone of voice.

Juliette shook her head and continued to fold the thin chemise. Over by the bed, Polly sniffled and choked back sobs as she put the clothes Juliette had folded into the large trunk that Millstone had had brought down from the attic.

"Well, then, won't you come and stay with Brix and me for a few days?" Lady Fanny suggested. "We'd be happy to have you."

"Thank you, but, no," Juliette replied. The longer she remained in London, the worse it would be. Better to go away at once than to stay here in sorrow and perhaps meet Drury.

After Lady Chelton died and Lord Bromwell and the Runners arrived, she and Drury had hardly said a word. He had gone to his chambers and she had come back here with Lord Bromwell.

If Drury cared about her, would he not have spoken to her? No, it must be as she feared—that he could not bear to be near her. She was a reminder of betrayal and suffering.

A tear slid down her cheek and she turned quickly away, so Lady Fanny wouldn't see it.

"Polly, would you leave us, please?" the lady asked. "We'll ring the bell if we need you again."

Juliette wanted to tell her maid to stay. She didn't want to be alone with Lady Fanny, who had married the man she loved.

Polly sniffled, nodded and bobbed a curtsy before leaving the room.

Juliette wiped her eyes with the hem of her folded chemise before putting it in the trunk. She was going to get one of the lovely gowns out of the armoire when Lady Fanny laid her hand on her arm. "Juliette…if I may call you Juliette?"

She shrugged. Why not? She was just a seamstress, after all.

"Juliette, may we sit for a moment? We haven't had time to talk—really talk—since yesterday."

"What more is there to say?" she asked, though she left the gown in the armoire. "The villains have been discovered and taken by the Runners. In a fortnight, they will face trial and punishment."

"I meant we haven't talked about Drury."

Juliette tried to avoid what was really upsetting her. "His fingers—they will heal, will they not?"

"Better than before, his doctor hopes," Lady Fanny assured her as she sat on the edge of the bed. "It's not his fingers I'm worried about. I thought you loved him. If you do, how can you leave him like this?"

The accusing words hit Juliette like a slap. As if that was her first choice! As if she was eager to do so!

But she would not tell this English noblewoman how she suffered. She would not show this woman her pain. "Do you not know what he did? He killed my brother."

Who broke his fingers and killed his friends.

"Yes, I know that."

"Am I supposed to forget that?" *He never would.*

"If you loved him, I would hope you could understand why he did that and find it in your heart to forgive him. You didn't see him when he returned from France. He was a shadow of himself. They'd starved him, too. And wasn't it your brother who broke his fingers?"

Juliette glared at this woman who had had such an easy life, who could be with the man she loved, who understood nothing. "Yes! Do you think he wants to see *me* after that? That he can forgive *me?* My own brother did that to him! Whatever Drury felt for me, it surely cannot survive that!"

Lady Fanny didn't flush with anger or dismay. She simply continued to look at her steadily. "How do you know how he feels unless you ask him? If he loves you—and I believe he does—he won't hate you for what your brother did."

"He hated all of France for what Georges did!"

"It's easy to blame a country and a whole people for the actions of a few when you've been hurt and betrayed," Lady Fanny replied.

She rose and tilted her head as she studied Juliette's flushed face. "I think you're underestimating his capacity to love and to forgive. He loves you, Juliette. I'm sure of it. And if you leave like this, I think you'll be hurting him far more, and more profoundly, than your brother ever did."

Someone knocked on the door, and as Juliette tried to decide what to do, Lady Fanny went to answer it. Juliette heard voices urgently whispering, and when she turned to see who it was, Drury stood there. Alone.

Now that he was here, she didn't know what to do, what to say. She wanted to throw herself into his arms, but was afraid to move. She wanted to burst into tears, but didn't want his last image of her to be as a sobbing, hysterical woman.

His dark eyes were starkly pleading, his voice hoarse with suppressed emotion when he spoke. "I've been afraid to see you. Afraid to tell you how I feel, because of what I did to you. I'm so sorry for the misery I've caused you, Juliette. I could understand if you never wanted to see me again. But I had to see you, to ask you to forgive me." He held out his hands in a gesture of surrender. "And to tell you that I love you."

He loved her? In spite of everything?

She took a hesitant step toward him. "I can forgive you. I do forgive you. And I am so sorry for what my brother did to you."

There was still one thing left to say as wonder and hope replaced bleak despair in his dark eyes. "I love you," she whispered. "I love you with all my heart, no matter what you've done."

He looked as if he'd been reborn. All the fear and doubt and shame fell from him. All the misery and restraint disappeared, and in the next moment, she was in his arms.

How long they passionately, fervently kissed she didn't know, and didn't care. He loved her! Oh, thank God, he loved her as much as she loved him!

At last, however, he broke the kiss and drew back a little to regard her with happiness glowing in his dark, no longer mysterious eyes. "Since we love each other, I suppose we should do something about it."

There was one thing she wanted very much to do, one thing her body yearned for as much as her heart. Smiling, she glanced over her shoulder at the bed.

He laughed, a deep chuckle that rose from his broad chest like the laughter of Jove himself. "That, too. But I was thinking of something more permanent. Will you marry me, Juliette Bergerine?"

She gasped. "Marry?"

"People already think we're engaged," he reminded her.

"But I am not your cousin."

"Thank God. Buggy has some interesting theories about marriages between cousins that suggest it's something to be avoided. Still, even if that were true, it wouldn't be a legal impediment."

He brushed his lips across hers. "Will you marry me, Juliette?"

"I am French," she reminded him, even as her body responded to his touch.

"So I gather from your accent."

"The English do not like the French. It may make trouble for you."

"I don't care."

"But your profession—"

"Need I remind you I am Sir Douglas Drury, the Court Cat of the Old Bailey, the man who can look a criminal into confession? I hardly think my career will suffer because of whom I marry."

He sounded as arrogant as he had the first day, but then he smiled, and he seemed almost a boy in his happiness. She had to laugh as she slipped her arm around his neck, pressing her body closer to his.

"What about my shop?" she pertly inquired. "Am I to give up my independence?"

"I'd sooner try to stop a hurricane. Of course you must have your shop. And if I must give up the law and move to France, so be it. At least I speak the language."

He would do that for her? He would give up the law, his life's work, his fame, to go with her to the land he had so loathed? *Mon Dieu,* he must love her! And because she loved him, she saw another future for them both. A life that would not be quite so independent, perhaps, but that would have ample joys to compensate.

And even then, she was sure she would be more independent than many women. "I think perhaps if we are married, I will have plenty of sewing to do, for you and for our babies."

"Babies?"

She boldly caressed him. "Babies."

"I believe you're trying to seduce me, Juliette."

"*Oui, monsieur.* Shall I stop?"

His laugh was lower, deeper, more seductive. *"Non, ma chérie,"* he murmured as he bent his head to kiss her. *"Je t'aime."*

"Buggy, for the love of God, will you stop pacing and sit down? You're going to wear out the carpet," Brix said as he sat beside Fanny in the drawing room and stretched out his long, lean legs.

"Well, for the love of God, what's taking them so long?" Buggy demanded, halting, his arms akimbo. "They've been up there for hours. Surely they've managed to…"

He fell silent as Brix and his wife exchanged amused looks.

And then Buggy's face turned scarlet as understanding dawned. "I see."

"Rather slow for you," Brix observed with a grin. "I daresay all that remains is to be advised of the date of the wedding. Somehow I don't think they're discussing *that* at the moment."

"I certainly hope not," Buggy gravely replied.

"Drury?"

"Mmm?" he answered drowsily, one arm around Juliette as they lay together on her bed, the sheets a tangled mess, their hair disheveled, their discarded clothes lying on the floor where they'd fallen or been tossed in passionate haste.

Juliette traced the long, thin scar down his naked torso from his left shoulder to his belly button. "Is this from the war, too?"

He shifted as her hand continued its exploration. "That, my love, I owe to a certain naval officer currently at sea, Charlie Grendon."

She vaguely recalled the name from a conversation between Drury and the Smythe-Medways. Everything except Drury seemed a little hazy at the moment.

He lightly kissed her forehead. "It was a boyhood prank gone awry. I trust he's better with ropes now."

"You were all rascals, I think," she observed.

"Sometimes," he agreed. "How does it feel, loving a rascal?"

"I like it." She rolled so that she was atop him. "How does it feel to be in love with a seamstress?"

"Delightful. Especially when she has other skills."

Juliette lightly brushed her breasts across him, so that their nipples touched. "I am glad you think so."

"I was referring to your aim with potatoes."

She giggled, delightfully happy. "Perhaps if you make me angry, I will throw some at *you*."

"I look forward to it." He smiled up at her. "In fact, I can't wait, and I can't wait to be your husband."

She took one of his bandaged hands in hers and kissed it lightly. "Neither can I. When will these come off?"

"Not soon enough, I'm afraid." He stiffly waggled his fingers, wincing a little. "The doctor tells me they should be better than before. I believe I shall enjoy finding out just how much better they are. Until then, we'll just have to make do."

He raised his head and kissed the tip of her nose. "I love you, Juliette Bergerine, as I've never loved anyone in my life."

"I love you, Sir Douglas Drury, and I shall never stop loving you. Now make love with me with again— or are you too tired?"

"Not a bit, although Buggy and Brix and Fanny must be wondering what we're doing."

"I suspect, my love," she said with a throaty, seductive laugh as she leaned down to kiss him, "they can guess."

Wedding notice in the *London Morning Herald*:

Married, on Thursday, December second, at Lincoln's Inn Chapel, Sir Douglas Drury, Baronet, to Miss Juliette Bergerine. Also in attendance were the Right Honorable the Viscount Bromwell, noted author of *The Spider's Web,* the Right Honorable the Viscount Terrington and the Viscountess Terrington, the Honorable Brixton Smythe-Medway and Lady Francesca Smythe-Medway, Lt. Charles Grendon of His Majesty's Navy, Mr. James St. Claire, and a number of barristers and solicitors. The groom and his bride have recently taken a house in Mayfair, where they intend to reside while Sir Douglas continues his distinguished legal career.

* * * * *

Author's Note

Because the hero of this book is a barrister, I had to try to gain some understanding of the British legal system during the Regency Period. I confess that, for a legal layman, it wasn't easy.

Here are a few of the major elements that I think I should clarify, especially for North American readers more familiar with the American court system.

The British system had two types of legal representation, barristers and solicitors. I won't get into all the differences, but one of the basic distinctions is that solicitors deal directly with clients, while barristers represent clients at court.

For a long time, an accused person was not entitled to legal representation in British courts. It was felt that if individuals were innocent, they shouldn't need a lawyer to act for them, and the judge would look after their interests during a trial. It was also feared that having opposing counsel would make for long trials; the average length of a trial in the Old Bailey at that time was less than ten minutes. Cases came to trial much more quickly, too.

During the eighteenth century, accused persons were gradually allowed the services of a barrister, but barristers could only cross-examine witnesses. They could make no statements to the court, nor could they compel witnesses to appear.

Fortunately, the Prisoners' Counsel Act in 1836 changed this inequality.

Also, at this time the male-only jury didn't adjourn to a separate room to deliberate, and the same jury would try more than one case.

If you're interested in the legal background, you might look at *The Bar and the Old Bailey, 1750–1850*, by Allyson N. May (University of North Carolina Press), British History Online (http://www.british-history.ac.uk) and the Proceedings of the Old Bailey, also online (http://www.hrionline.ac.uk/oldbailey). The latter has transcripts of actual trials, including one regarding a duel that makes for fascinating reading.

I've tried to be accurate with the legal details, but the primary focus of my story is not trial and court-room procedure. Any mistakes should be laid at my door. *Mea culpa.*

The Viscount's Kiss

Margaret Moore

Chapter One

It has long been my dream to study these fascinating creatures in their natural habitat, to watch them as they spin their webs and go about the business of living, myself unnoticed save as another species of fauna inhabiting their world.
        —from *The Spider's Web,* by Lord Bromwell

England, 1820

That man does not belong here, Nell Springley thought as she surreptitiously studied the only other occupant in the mail coach headed to Bath. He'd been asleep when she'd boarded in London, and he was still asleep despite the rocking and jostling of the vehicle, his tall beaver hat tipped over his eyes and his arms crossed over his chest.

He was clearly well-to-do, for he wore a fine indigo frock coat of excellent wool and buff trousers that hugged his long legs. His blindingly white cravat, tied in an intricate and complicated knot, fairly shouted a valet's skillful expertise. His slender fingers were likewise encased in superbly fitting kid leather gloves and his Hessian boots were so brightly polished, she could see the reflection of her skirts.

Surely a man who could afford such clothes would have his own carriage.

Maybe he was a gamester who had gambled away his fortune. If he was the sort who frequented outdoor boxing matches, that might explain why what little of his jaw and cheeks she could see had been browned by the sun.

Perhaps he'd been in the Navy. She could easily imagine that figure in a uniform, his broad shoulders topped by an officer's braid, shouting commands and looking very dashing on the quarterdeck.

Or he could be a tosspot sleeping off a night of drunken merriment, having spent the rest of his money on wine. If that were so, she hoped he wouldn't wake up until they arrived in Bath. She had no desire to be engaged in conversation with a sot. Or anyone else.

The coach lurched over a particularly bone-jarring bump that rattled the baggage in the boot and made the guard riding outside the coach curse. Nell, meanwhile, grabbed the seat as her poke bonnet slipped over her eyes.

"Bit of a rough spot," a deep, genial male voice noted.

Shoving her bonnet back into place, Nell raised her eyes—and found herself staring at the most handsome young man she'd ever seen. Not only was he awake, his hat was now properly situated on his head, revealing amiable blue-gray eyes separated by a narrow nose bordered by angular cheekbones. He was young, and yet there were wrinkles at the corners of his eyes that suggested he'd had vastly more experience of the world than she.

But then, most people had more experience of the world than she.

Nell blushed as if she'd been caught eavesdropping and immediately clasped her hands in her lap and lowered her eyes.

As she did, out of the corner of her eye she spotted something moving on the fawn-colored, double crimson-striped seat beside her.

A spider! A big, horrible brown spider—and it was headed right for her!

Gasping, Nell lunged across the coach—and landed on the lap of the young man opposite, knocking his hat from his head.

"Steady!" he warned, his upper-class accent providing more proof he was from a well-to-do household.

Blushing even more, she immediately moved to sit beside him. "I—I beg your pardon," she stammered, feeling hopelessly foolish, while noting that one stray lock of brown hair had tumbled over his forehead, making him look rather boyish and far less intimidating.

"There's no need to be frightened," her companion said. "It's only a *Tegenaria parietina*. They're quite harmless, I assure you."

Now completely humiliated by her childish reaction, Nell didn't know what to say. Instead, she smoothed out her skirts and glanced at the seat she had so abruptly vacated.

The spider was gone.

"Where is it?" she cried, gripping the seat and half rising regardless of the swaying motion of the coach. "Where's the spider?"

The young man held up his hat. "In here."

He had it in his *hat?*

He gave her an apologetic smile. "Spiders are of particular interest to me."

However handsome he was, however gentlemanly, he was definitely eccentric and possibly deranged.

"Please keep it away from me," she said, inching as far away from him and his hat as she could get. "I hate spiders."

The young man heaved a heavy sigh, as if her common aversion was a very serious failing. "That's a pity."

Considering everything she'd done in the past few days, to be condemned for disliking spiders struck Nell as completely ridiculous.

"Most spiders are harmless," the young man continued, peering into his hat as if the spider were a cherished pet. "I'm aware that they aren't as beautiful as some insects can be, like butterflies, but they are as useful in their way as butterflies or bees."

He raised his eyes and smiled, and she was immediately sure he never lacked for partners at a ball. "However you feel about spiders, you must allow me to introduce myself. I'm—"

With a loud crack, the coach flew up as if it were alive before coming down with a thunderous thud that sent Nell tumbling from her seat. Her companion reached for her, pulling her against his body, as horses shrieked and the driver shouted and the coach began to tip sideways.

It fell over, landing with another thud, and Nell found herself sprawled on top of the young gentleman and hemmed in by the seats.

He studied her in a way that sent the blood throbbing through her body as even the tipping coach had not. "Are you all right?"

She didn't feel any pain, only an acute awareness of his

body beneath her and his protective arms around her. "I think so. And you?"

"I believe I am undamaged. I suspect something went wrong with a wheel or an axle."

"Yes, yes, of course," she murmured. She could feel his chest rising and falling with quick breaths, as rapid and ragged as her heartbeat, even though the immediate danger had passed.

"I should investigate and ascertain what has happened." She nodded.

"Right away," he added, his gaze locked onto hers and his handsome, sun-browned face so very close.

"At once," she whispered, telling herself to move yet making no effort to do so.

"I may be of assistance."

"Yes, of course."

"I wonder…?"

"Yes?"

"If I should attempt an experiment."

"Experiment?" she repeated quizzically, having some difficulty following his line of reasoning and, at that particular moment, not really sure what an experiment was.

With no further warning, without even knowing her name let alone being properly introduced, the young man raised his head.

And kissed her.

The pressure of his lips was as light and beguiling as the brush of a moth's wing, as delicious and welcome as warm bread and hot tea on a cold day, and more arousing than anything she'd ever experienced—completely different from that other unexpected kiss only a few short days ago that had ruined her life.

As he was different from the arrogant, domineering Lord Sturmpole.

This was what a kiss should be like—warm, welcome, exciting, delightful...as *he* was.

Until, with a gasp like a drowning man, he broke the kiss and scrambled backward as far as he could go, so that his back was against what had been the floor of the coach.

"Good God, forgive me!" he cried as if utterly horrified. "I can't think what came over me!"

She just as quickly scrambled backward between his legs, until her back was against the coach's roof.

"Nor I," she replied, flushing with embarrassment and shame, for she *did* know what had come over her—the most inconvenient, ill-timed lust.

This was hardly the way to travel unnoticed and unremarked!

"It must have been the shock of the accident," he offered as he got to his feet, hunching over in the small space and blushing as if sincerely mortified. "If you'll excuse me, I shall inquire as to our circumstances."

He reached for the handle, which was now over his head and without any further ado shoved the door open and hoisted himself up and out as if he were part monkey.

Crouching on the pocket of the door in the side of the coach, Nell straightened her bonnet and took stock of the situation. She was in an overturned coach. She was unhurt. Her clothes were disheveled but not torn or muddy. Her bonnet was mostly unscathed, while the young gentleman's hat had been crushed beneath them, along, no doubt, with the spider inside it.

She had also kissed a handsome stranger who seemed

to feel genuine, heartfelt remorse for that action, despite her obvious—and incredibly foolish—response.

She must be jinxed, born under some kind of ill omen. What else could explain the difficulties that had beset her recently? Her employment as companion to Lady Sturmpole had seemed a stroke of good fortune, then turned into an unmitigated disaster. She had been relieved to catch this coach at the last minute, only to have it overturn. She had been glad she would have to share the journey with only one other traveller, and he was asleep—but look how that had turned out.

As abruptly as he'd departed, the young man's head reappeared in the opening. "It seems the axle has broken. It will have to be fixed before the coach can be righted, so we shall have to find an alternate means of transportation. If you'll raise your hands, I'll pull you out."

She nodded and obeyed. "I'm afraid your hat is ruined and the spider dead."

"Ah," he sighed as he reached down for her. "Poor creature. Perhaps if I had left it alone, it would have survived."

Or perhaps not, she thought as she put her hands in his.

He pulled her up with unexpected ease, proving that he was stronger than he looked. It seemed his apparel, unlike many a fashionable young gentleman's, was not padded to give the appearance of muscles he didn't possess.

Once she was out of the coach, the soft light of the growing dawn illuminated the burly coachman, dressed in the customary coachman's attire of green coat and crimson shawl. He was lying on the verge, a bloody gash in his forehead and his broad-brimmed brown hat a short distance away. His red coat splattered with mud, the guard held the reins of the four nervous horses that had already been unharnessed from the coach. He also held a rather ancient blunderbuss. One of the horses had clearly broken a leg, for its left rear hoof dangled sickeningly. Thankfully, no passengers rode atop the mail coach; if they had been in a crowded stagecoach, people might have been seriously injured or killed.

The young man climbed off the coach painted maroon on the lower half, black above, with a red undercarriage, and the Royal cipher brightly visible on the side, then reached up to help her down.

She had no choice but to put her hands on his shoulders and jump. He placed his hands around her waist to hold her, and again she felt that unaccustomed warmth, that inconvenient lust, invade her body.

He quickly let go of her the moment she was on the ground, suggesting he was no lascivious cad and had been truly distressed by his kiss in the coach.

"Since you're not hurt, I should see to the driver," he said, giving her a short bow that wouldn't have been out of place at Almack's, before going to the driver and kneeling beside him.

After the young gentleman removed his soiled gloves, he brushed back the driver's gray hair and examined the wound in his scalp with a brisk, professional manner.

Perhaps he was a doctor.

"Am I dyin'?" the driver asked anxiously.

"I very much doubt it," the young man replied with calm confidence. "Scalp wounds tend to bleed profusely with very little provocation. Have you any other injuries?"

"Me shoulder. Just about twisted off when I was trying to hold the horses."

The young man nodded, then proceeded to test the area

around the coachman's shoulder, making him wince when he pressed one particular spot.

"Ah," the young man sighed, and the driver's eyes opened wide. "What?"

The young man smiled. "Nothing serious, Thompkins. You've strained it and shouldn't drive a team for a while, but I don't believe there's been any lasting damage."

"Thank God," the driver muttered with relief.

Then he frowned, anger replacing anxiety. "There was a damn dog in the road. I should have just run the bloody thing over, but I tried to turn the horses and hit a rock and—"

"Thompkins, there is a young lady present, so please refrain from profanity," the doctor gently chided as he got to his feet.

The driver glanced her way. "Sorry for my choice o' words, miss."

"Is there anything I can do to help?" she asked, not the least offended by his words, given the circumstances.

The young man untied his cravat and held it out to her. "You can use this to clean the wound, if you will— provided the sight of blood doesn't make you ill?"

"Not at all," she replied, taking the cravat, which smelled of some exotic scent she couldn't name.

"Then I'll see to the horses," the young man said as he absently unbuttoned the collar of his shirt, exposing his neck and some of his chest. Both were as tanned as his face.

Perhaps he was a doctor on a vessel.

The driver started to sit up. "Maybe I'd better—"

"No, you should rest," the young man ordered. "Enjoy having such a charming and pretty nurse, Thompkins, and leave the horses to me. Tell her about the time I tried to drive your team and we wound up in the ditch."

The driver grinned, then grimaced. "Aye, my lord."

My lord? A noble physician? That was very interesting… except that she should be thinking about how they were going to get to Bath and what she should do when they got there.

"First, I need a few words with your nurse," the nobleman said, taking her arm and drawing her a short distance away.

Concerned the driver was more seriously injured than he had implied, she ignored the impropriety of his action and tried to ignore the sensations it engendered, like little flames licking along her skin.

"Is the driver seriously hurt after all?" she asked anxiously.

"No, I don't believe Thompkins has a serious concussion," he said, to her relief. "However, I'm not a doctor."

"You're not?" she blurted in surprise. His examination had certainly looked like that of a medical man.

He gravely shook his head. "Unfortunately, no. I have a little medical training, so I know enough to be aware that he should be kept conscious, if at all possible, until we can fetch a physician. Can you do that while I see to the injured horse and ride to the next inn on one of the others?"

"Yes, I think I can keep him awake."

The young gentleman's lips flicked up into a pleased smile that again sent that unusual warmth thrumming through her body. As she returned to the driver and tried to soothe her nerves, he started toward the guard holding the horses.

She heard the nobleman ask the guard where the pistols were as she began wiping the blood that had slowed to a trickle.

"Under my seat," the man nervously replied, glancing

at the high backseat at the rear of the coach, for mail coach guards generally carried pistols as well as a blunderbuss, to fend off highwaymen.

"I'll hold the horses while you put that poor beast out of its misery," the young gentleman offered.

"What, you want *me* to shoot it? I couldn't!" the guard protested. "I can't be destroyin' government property! It'd be my job. Besides, I'm to look after the mail, not the animals."

"Surely an exception can be made if a horse has broken its leg," the young man replied.

"I tell ya, I'm supposed to guard the mail, not take care o' the horses!"

"I will not allow that poor animal to suffer."

"*You* won't? Who the devil are you?"

"Shut yer gob, Snicks," the driver called out. "Let the viscount do what has to be done."

He was a viscount? A *viscount* had kissed her?

"I'll pay for the horse if need be," the young nobleman said as he marched toward the overturned coach with such a fiercely determined look on his face, he hardly seemed like the same man.

The guard scowled but said no more as the viscount found the pistol which, like the blunderbuss, looked as if it had been made early in the previous century.

With the gun behind his back, murmuring something that sounded like an apology, the viscount approached the injured horse. Then, as the guard moved as far away as he could, the nobleman took his stance, aimed and shot the horse right between its big, brown, limpid eyes.

As the animal fell heavily to the ground, the viscount lowered his arm and bowed his head.

"Couldn't be helped," the driver muttered roughly. "Had to be done."

Yes, it had to be done, Nell thought as she returned to dabbing the driver's wound, but she felt sorry for the poor horse, as well as the man who had to shoot it.

The viscount tucked the pistol into the waist of his trousers before returning to Nell and the driver. Between the pistol, his sun-darkened skin, open shirt and disheveled hair, he looked like a very handsome, elegant pirate.

Pirate. The sea. A viscount who liked spiders who'd gone to sea…

Good heavens! He had to be Lord Bromwell, the naturalist whose book about his voyage around the world had made him the toast of London society and the subject of many articles in the popular press. Like so many others, Lady Sturmpole had bought his book and talked about his remarkable adventures, although she didn't bother to actually read *The Spider's Web*.

No wonder he could be calm in a crisis. Any man who'd survived a shipwreck and attacks by cannibals could surely take an overturned coach in stride. As for that kiss, he must often be the object of female attention and lust. He probably had women throwing themselves at him all the time and assumed she was another who was intrigued and infatuated by his looks and his fame.

And because he was famous, the press might take an even greater interest in a mail coach overturning, perhaps noting that Lord Bromwell had not been the only passenger and asking her name and her destination and why she was in the coach….

With a growing sense of impending doom, wishing she'd never caught the coach, never gone to London, never decided to go to Bath and, most of all, never met *him,* Nell watched as the handsome, renowned naturalist swung himself onto the back of one of the horses and galloped down the road.

Chapter Two

*Fortunately, I have been blessed with a practical na-
ture that allows me to take immediate action without the burden of emotion. Thus, I was quite calm as
the ship was sinking and my concern was to help as
many of my shipmates as possible. It was after the
ship had gone down and the storm had abated, after
we had managed to retrieve some items necessary to
life and found ourselves on that tiny slip of sand
seemingly lost in the vast ocean, that I laid my head
on my knees, and wept.*

—from *The Spider's Web,* by Lord Bromwell

As Lord Bromwell—known as Buggy to his closest
friends—had expected, the sight of a dishevelled, hatless,
cloakless man mounted on a sweat-slicked coach horse
charging into the yard of The Crown and Lion caused
quite a stir.

A male servant carrying a bag of flour over his shoulder
toward the kitchen stopped and stared, openmouthed. Two
slovenly attired men lounging by the door straightened.

The washerwoman, an enormous basket of wet linen in her arms, nearly dropped her burden, while a boy carrying boots paid no heed where he was going and nearly ran into one of the two idlers, earning the curious lad a cuff on the side of the head.

"There's been an accident," Bromwell called out to the hostler as the man ran out of the stables, followed by two grooms, a stable boy and a man in livery.

Bromwell slid off the exhausted horse and, after unwrapping the excess length of the reins from around his hands, gave them to the stable boy. Meanwhile, the grooms, liveried fellows, idlers, bootblack and washerwoman gathered around them. "The mail coach broke an axle about three miles back on the London road."

"No!" the hostler cried, as if such a thing were completely impossible.

"Yes," Bromwell replied as the inn's proprietor, alerted by the hubbub, appeared in the door of the taproom. He wiped his hands on the soiled apron that covered his ample belly and hurried forward at a brisk trot that was impressive for a man of his girth.

"Gad, is that you, Lord Bromwell?" Jenkins exclaimed. "You're not hurt, I hope!"

"I'm perfectly all right, Mr. Jenkins," the viscount replied, slapping the worst of the mud from his trousers. "Unfortunately, others are not. We need a physician and a carriage, as well as a horse for me, for I fear we won't all fit in one vehicle. Naturally I shall pay—"

"My lord!" Mr. Jenkins cried, his red face appalled, his hand to his heart as if mortally offended. "Never!"

Bromwell acknowledged the innkeeper's generosity with a smile and a nod. He'd always liked Mr. Jenkins, which made his father's disparaging treatment of him even more painful to witness.

"You there, Sam," Jenkins called to the hostler, "get my carriage ready and saddle Brown Bessie for his lordship— the good saddle, mind.

"Johnny, leave those at the door and run and fetch the doctor," he said to the bootblack. "Quick as you can, lad."

The boy immediately did as he was told, while the hostler and grooms returned to the stable, taking the coach horse with them. Adjusting her heavy basket on her hip, the washerwoman started back toward the washhouse and the two idlers returned to their places, where they had a good view of incoming riders and vehicles.

"Come in and have a drink o' something while they're getting the horse and carriage ready," Jenkins offered. "I expect you'll want to wash, too."

Bromwell reached up to touch his cheek and discovered he was rather muddy there, too. "Yes, indeed I would," he replied, following the innkeeper toward the main building, a two-storied, half-timbered edifice, with a public taproom and dining room on the lower level and bedrooms above.

Although Bromwell had lost what vanity he'd possessed years ago, believing his looks nothing to boast of especially compared to those of his friends, as he walked behind Jenkins through the muddy, straw-strewn yard, he couldn't help wondering what his female fellow passenger had made of his appearance.

More importantly, though, what the devil had possessed him to act like a degenerate cad? To be sure, she was pretty, with the most remarkable green eyes, and he'd noticed her trim figure clad in a plain gray pelisse when she'd briskly approached the coach before getting on in London. But he'd met pretty young women before. He'd even seen several completely naked during his sojourn in the South Seas. Indeed, while he'd found her pretty, he'd had no trouble at all pretending to be asleep to spare himself any conversation before he really had fallen asleep.

If he hadn't, he might have started to wonder sooner why a woman who spoke with such a refined accent and had such a manner was travelling unaccompanied.

She could be a governess or upper servant, he supposed, going on a visit.

Whoever she was, he should be thoroughly ashamed of himself for kissing her—and he would have been, had that kiss not been the most amazing, exciting kiss he'd ever experienced.

"Look here, Martha, here's Lord Bromwell nearly done to death," the innkeeper announced as he entered the taproom and addressed his wife, who was near the door to the kitchen. "The mail coach overturned."

Mrs. Jenkins, round of face and broad of beam, gasped and bustled forward as if about to examine him for injuries.

"No one has been killed or seriously hurt, as far as I can determine," Bromwell quickly informed her. "Your husband has already sent for the doctor and has offered replacement transportation."

"Well, thank God nobody was badly hurt—and ain't I been sayin' for years them coaches were gettin' too old to be safe?" Mrs. Jenkins declared, coming to an abrupt halt and resting her fists on her hips. She frowned at them as if *they* were personally responsible for the mishap and had the authority to correct everything and anything amiss with the delivery of the Royal Mail.

"Aye, Mother, you have," her husband mournfully agreed, agreement being the best way to react to Mrs. Jenkins's pronouncements, as Bromwell had also learned over the years. "Have Sarah bring some wine to the blue room while Lord Bromwell cleans up a bit—the best, o' course. He'll need it."

"There's clean water there already and fresh linen, my lord," Mrs. Jenkins said briskly as she turned and disappeared into the back of the inn.

"She's right, though," Jenkins said as he continued to lead the way, even though Bromwell was as familiar with this inn as he was with the ancestral hall. "Them coaches are a disgrace, that's what."

Bromwell remained silent as they passed through the taproom, although several customers turned to stare at him and excited whispers followed in his wake.

It was not just because of the accident or his dishevelled appearance, for he heard them uttering his name and, as was all too usual, the words *shipwreck* and *cannibals*.

He was never going to get used to this sort of curious scrutiny and the agitation occasioned by his mere arrival in a room, he thought with an inward sigh. Although he was glad his book was a success and increasing interest in the natural world, it was at times like these that he longed for his former anonymity.

Had the young lady in the coach known or guessed who he was? Did that account for her heart-stopping, passionate response?

And if so, what should he do when he saw her again? How should he behave?

Jenkins opened the door to the best bedchamber.

"There's clean water in the pitcher, although it's cold, and linen there," he said, nodding at the simple white china set and towels on the washing stand.

"Thank you, Jenkins."

"Sing out if you need anything, my lord."

"I shall," Bromwell promised as the innkeeper left the room and closed the door.

The inn's best bedroom was small compared to his room at his father's estate or the London town house, but comfortable and snug under the eaves, with inexpensive, clean blue-and-white cotton draperies, linen and basin set. A colorful rag rug lay on the wooden floor that creaked with every move he made, as would the bed ropes if he lay down.

His friend Drury had complained about that when he'd stopped here on his way to spend some time at Christmas a few years ago, Bromwell recalled as he stripped off his mud-spattered jacket and rolled up his sleeves.

He could just imagine the stunned expressions on his friends' faces if he told them what he'd done today. Not shooting the unfortunate horse—they would expect no less—but that he, good old shy, studious Buggy Bromwell, had kissed a woman whose name he didn't know and whom he'd only just met. They'd probably be even more shocked if he confided that he wanted very much to do it again.

Several times, in fact.

Of course he knew it was man's nature to seek sexual gratification and he was not abnormal in this regard (as certain very willing young women in the South Seas could attest), but he had always behaved with due decorum in England.

Until today.

His equilibrium must have been disturbed by the accident, he decided as he splashed cool water over his face, then picked up a towel and vigorously rubbed his face. Men could act very differently under duress, as he'd seen more than once on his last voyage. Some of the men who could be courageous on land had become whimpering and helpless during a storm at sea and the men he'd been sure would flee at the first sign of trouble had stayed and fought for their companions' safety.

"I've got yer wine, my lord," Mrs. Jenkins declared behind the door, taking him out of his brown study or, as his father would say, "another of your damn daydreams."

"Come in," he called as he rolled down his wrinkled sleeves.

The woman entered the chamber with the force of a strong wind, a wineglass held out to him.

"It's a miracle and a mercy nobody was killed," she declared, her buxom body quivering with indignation while Bromwell downed the excellent wine in a gulp. "I've been telling Jenkins for years some of them coaches weren't fit to be on the road. You ought to get your friend Drury to sue. He never loses, I hear."

"Drury only handles criminal cases," Bromwell replied as he set down the glass and picked up his jacket. "This was an accident, caused by a stray dog and Thompkins's decision not to run it over. I won't go to court over that."

He put on the soiled jacket that his former valet would have wept to see. Not knowing how long he would be at sea, or if he would even return, he'd given Albert a well-earned reference and paid him an extra six months' salary before dismissing him. Since his return, he hadn't bothered to hire another, much to the dismay of Millstone, the butler at his father's London town house, even though Millstone had to admit Bromwell had learned to tie his cravat like an expert, having spent several hours practicing when there was nothing else to do at sea.

What would Millstone make of this latest mishap? Probably he'd just sigh and shake his head and comment that some men led charmed lives, although his lordship really ought to buy a new carriage. He could certainly afford it.

So he could, if he wasn't planning another expedition.

If he told Millstone about kissing the young woman, the poor man would likely drop down in a faint, as shocked and surprised as his friends would be—as shocked and surprised as he had been when it finally dawned on him that he shouldn't be kissing a woman he'd only just met.

Perhaps, as his father complained, he'd been too long away from England.

"Are the horse and carriage ready?" he asked Mrs. Jenkins, who seemed rather keen to linger.

"They should be by now, my lord."

"Good." He looked out the window at the sky gray with thickening clouds. "If you'll excuse me, Mrs. Jenkins, I must be on my way."

She smiled. "Always the perfect gentleman, my lord!"

Not always, he thought as he hurried past her.

Not always.

Bunching the cravat tighter in her hand, Nell glanced up at the sky. The gray clouds were definitely thickening, and moving closer.

"Never fear, lass," the driver said, wincing as he shifted. "Lord Bromwell'll be back with help soon. That lad can ride like the wind."

She gave the driver a smile, but her eyes must have betrayed that she wasn't completely reassured, for he patted her hand as his eyes drifted closed. "I've known him since he was six years old. Might not look like it, but he's the finest horseman I've ever seen. Brave, too."

"But not, perhaps, a competent mail coach driver?" she suggested, trying to keep Thompkins awake.

To her relief, he opened his brown eyes again. "Well, to be sure, that wasn't his finest hour, but he was only fifteen at the time."

"Fifteen? He could have been seriously hurt, or even killed!"

The driver frowned. "Don't you think I knew that? O' course I refused the first time he asked, and lots o' times after that, but he wouldn't let up till I gave in. And he had his reasons all worked out, logical-like, beginning with his skill and how far he'd go—only a mile or so. But that wasn't why I finally gave in. I knew he wanted something to brag about when he got back to school, so his friends would think he was as good as they were—although he's worth the lot of them and always has been and I said so at the time. But he got this look in his eyes, and well, miss, I didn't have the heart to refuse him. We didn't have any passengers that day and if the road hadn't been so slick in that one place, it would have been all right.

"Should have seen him at the start," Thompkins continued, grinning at the memory. "Like one of them Roman charioteers, standing up and working the reins like an old hand until we hit that slick spot and went into the ditch. But no damage to the coach and we was only a little late. Not that it made a mite of difference to his father, though, when he found out what'd happened."

Thompkins sighed, then frowned. "You should have heard the way the earl carried on. Any other man might have been proud of the lad for wanting to try and getting that far, but not him. You'd think young Lord Bromwell'd lost the family estate or murdered somebody.

"The viscount, bless him, told his father he'd forced me to agree to it by saying he'd see I lost my job if I didn't. Well, that was a lie, but he was cool as you please, and damn—pardon me, miss—if his father didn't believe him. And then not another word did young Lord Bromwell say. He just stood there covered in mud from head to toe, and his lip bleeding, too, like the earl was giving a speech in the House of Lords that had nothing to do with him.

"Oh, he's a rum cove, all right, even if he's a nobleman. Have you read his book?"

"I'm sorry to say I haven't," she replied, wishing that she had.

"To be honest, I ain't read it, either, since I can't read at all," the driver admitted, "but I heard all about his narrow escape from them savages and the shipwreck, too. And the tattoo, o' course."

Nell paused in her ministrations. "Lord Bromwell has a tattoo?"

Thompkins grinned and lowered his voice. "Aye, but he ain't never told anybody what it is, or where. Just that he got one. Some of the nobs have made a bet on it and put it in that book at White's, but so far, nobody's collected."

Nell was aware of the famous betting book at that gentlemen's club, and that men who belonged would—and did—wager on almost anything.

Thompkins looked past her and pointed down the road. "Thanks be to God, here he comes."

Nell looked back over her shoulder. There was indeed a horse and rider coming toward them, and it was Lord

Bromwell. He still wore no hat, so his slightly long hair was ruffled by the ride, and his coat was as muddy as his formerly shining boots.

"Mr. Jenkins of The Crown and Lion is sending his carriage and a doctor. They should be here soon," Lord Bromwell said as he drew the brown saddle horse to a halt and dismounted.

Nell discovered she couldn't meet his steadfast gaze as he came toward them. The memory of those moments in his arms and especially of his kiss were too vivid, too fresh, too disturbing. Instead, she continued to wipe Thompkins's forehead, even though the bleeding had stopped.

Lord Bromwell's boots came into her line of sight. "I trust the patient is resting comfortably?"

"Aye, my lord," Thompkins replied, "although my head hurts like the devil."

"You're not dizzy or sleepy?"

"Not a bit, my lord. The young lady and I have been having a fine time."

The toe of Lord Bromwell's boot began to tap. "Have you indeed?"

"Aye. I told her about the time you drove the coach, and we talked about yer book."

She risked a glance upward, to discover that Lord Bromwell looked even more rakish and handsome with his hair windblown and his shirt still open and the hint of whiskers darkening his cheeks. However, his expression was grave, his blue-gray eyes enigmatic, and his full lips that could kiss with such devastating tenderness betrayed no hint of emotion.

She swallowed hard as she looked back to the driver.

"I wasn't aware you were the famous Lord Bromwell,"

she said, determined that he appreciate that, although what kissing him without the excuse of his fame might suggest about her, she didn't want to consider.

"Forgive me for being remiss and not introducing myself sooner. And you are?"

"Eleanor Springford, my lord," she lied, hoping he would mistake her blush for bashfulness and not shame.

The driver's eyes twinkled with mischief. "We were talking about yer tattoo, too."

"It's a common practice among the South Sea islanders," Lord Bromwell gravely replied, as if it was the polite thing to do, like taking tea. "Ah, here comes Jenkins's carriage."

With that, he strode off to meet it, leaving Nell to wonder what such a man would make of her if he ever learned the truth.

Chapter Three

I believe it is an intense curiosity and an unwillingness to simply accept the world without further explanation that separates the scientist from the general population. It is not enough to see a thing; the scientist seeks to find out the how and why it works, or in the case of the natural world, how and why a creature does what it does.
— from *The Spider's Web,* by Lord Bromwell

"The supper will be served in half an hour, my lord," Jenkins announced from the door of the slightly smaller, more cramped room Bromwell had taken when they returned from the scene of the accident so that Miss Springford could have the better one. "The wife's glad she killed that chicken this afternoon, or she'd be in some state now, I can tell you, what with you here and all."

"I've been here plenty of times before," Bromwell replied as he reached for his brush, determined not to look a complete mess when he went below. "She should know I like everything she makes, especially her tarts. When I was stranded on that strip of sand, I would have sold my soul for one."

"Tush, now, my lord, that's almost blasphemy, that is!" Jenkins cried, although he beamed as proudly as if he made the tarts. "I'll be telling the wife, though. She'll be pleased."

"As I am by her tarts," Bromwell said, bringing his hair into some semblance of order, although it occurred to him that it was in need of a trim.

"Ah, here's Johnny now with your baggage, my lord."

"Thank you," Bromwell said as the boy carried in his small valise.

With another nod, Jenkins left him to change, followed by the gaping Johnny, who paused on the threshold to look back and whisper, eyes wide. "Was you really nearly et by cannibals, my lord?"

"I might have been, if they had caught us," Bromwell replied gravely, and quite truthfully.

The lad's eyes grew even wider.

"If you'll excuse me," Bromwell said, starting to close the door.

The lad nodded and disappeared.

Bromwell shut the door with a sigh. He was seriously beginning to wish he'd left that part of his voyage out of his book. Everybody asked about it, to the exclusion of many other fascinating events and observations.

Well, in mixed company, at any rate, he thought as he took off his soiled shirt, trousers and stockings. When he was with men after suppers or in the clubs, they wanted to know about the women and sexual practices, waiting with avid and salacious curiosity.

They were inevitably disappointed when he began describing the flora and fauna of the islands, including spiders, instead. Sometimes, if they listened and were patient, he would describe a *heiva,* a celebration involving dancing, the *otea* done by men, the *upa upa* by couples, and the *hura,* called hula in Hawaii, danced exclusively by women.

Recalling some of those dances and the dancers who'd performed them, he donned a clean white shirt, woollen trousers and stockings. What would Eleanor Springford think of those dances?

What would she think if she knew he'd participated?

Between that, and his insolent kiss, she'd certainly think he was no gentleman, although her response hadn't been exactly ladylike, either.

He suddenly remembered that he'd heard her name before, and his heart began to pound as if he were again participating in an *otea. Lady* Eleanor Springford was the daughter of the Duke of Wymerton. She was also one of the many young ladies his mother had mentioned in hopes he would take a wife and stop chasing after spiders.

What the devil was a lady of her wealth and family doing dressed in such plain, inexpensive clothes and travelling alone in a mail coach headed to Bath?

He had no idea, but he doubted it was a pleasure trip.

If she was in some sort of trouble, it was his duty to help her; it would be his duty whether she was twenty and pretty, or sixty and the homeliest woman he had ever met.

Determined to speak with Lady Eleanor and offer her any assistance he could render without further delay, Bromwell hurried down to the dining room.

But when he entered, he found the room full of people he'd never seen before, and he couldn't see the duke's daughter anywhere.

Everyone fell silent when they realized he had arrived,

so he plastered a weak smile on his face and, as he continued to silently search for Lady Eleanor, again damned the fame he'd never wanted.

"Oh, my lord! What a tragedy!" cried an overdressed, middle-aged woman wearing a silk gown overburdened with ruffles and frills, in a shocking combination of orange and pink that wouldn't have looked out of place in a bordello.

She hurried toward him past a group of silent, brawny men. He suspected they were local farmers or tradesmen dragged here to meet the famous naturalist by their wives, many of whom were equally colorfully dressed in the latest styles.

"Indeed, it was a most unfortunate occurrence," he muttered, unable to look directly at that gown another moment.

"I've been after them to fix that road," a man growled as he ran a puzzled gaze over Bromwell, thinking, no doubt, that the viscount didn't look like a world-famous explorer.

Bromwell had long since given up trying to explain that he was a different sort of explorer, that his journey had been intended to find flora, fauna, insects and especially spiders, not lands to claim, people to conquer or resources to exploit. "May the local government take heed," he said politely.

"They will if you write a letter to the *Times* about it," the man declared as Jenkins appeared, dressed in what was surely his Sunday best.

Bromwell's discomfort increased as Jenkins introduced him to the local gentry like he was some prized possession Jenkins was eager to show off, beginning with the man who'd complained about the roads. Since Bromwell liked Jenkins, he submitted, but he also continued to look for Lady Eleanor, until he decided she must be dining in her room.

This was going to be a long evening, he thought as he stifled a sigh, taking one last survey of the room.

At last he spotted her, crammed into the corner as far as she could get and wearing a flowing gown of pale blue silk like something fairies had cut out of a summer's sky. Unlike the other women's gowns, the cut was simple, with a bodice high in the back, a modest neckline, tight sleeves and only one ruffle at the hem. Her dark brown hair, which had been covered by her simple straw bonnet, proved to be thick and lustrous in the candlelight. It had been done simply, yet elegantly, around her gracefully poised head. In spite of the simplicity of her gown and hair, she was easily the most elegant, best-dressed woman in the room.

Having been blessed with uncommonly good eyesight, however, he immediately noticed something odd. Unlike the clothing she'd been wearing earlier, her gown did not fit properly. It was too large in the bodice, gaping where it should be snug, and tight under the arms. The length wasn't quite right, either, as if it had been made for a slightly taller woman.

Excusing himself from the group surrounding him, he immediately made his way toward her.

"Good evening," he said with a bow when he reached her and kissed her gloved hand, keeping his attention on her solemn face.

It took every ounce of his self-control not to glance down at that gaping bodice.

He'd want to hit any man who did, even if it was one of his friends. *Especially* if it was one of his handsome, charming, interesting friends.

"Good evening, my lord," she said, her expression impassive, her eyes unreadable, as she inclined her head and he realized her gloves didn't fit properly, either.

"How is Thompkins?" she asked as she pulled her hand away.

"Well on the road to recovery," he replied. "He won't be able to drive for a few days, though."

"I'm glad to hear he'll suffer no permanent injuries. We shall require a different driver, though. Perhaps you, my lord?" she suggested, giving him a questioning look that both embarrassed and delighted him.

"I've given up my career as a driver. Much too risky."

Her beautiful eyes widened. "Unlike travelling around the world to all sorts of savage places looking for spiders?"

"Ah, but I don't attempt to captain the vessel. I'm merely a passenger."

She laughed, a lovely, musical sound that went straight to his heart.

For the first time, he understood how his friends had fallen so deeply in love with their wives, and so quickly. He had always found that baffling, for they had all been men of the world who'd had other liaisons with beautiful women before meeting the women they married. Or in Brixton Smythe-Medway's case, realizing the woman who would make him blissfully happy had been his acquaintance from boyhood.

Not that he was lacking similar worldy experience with women, but when Lady Eleanor laughed and her eyes sparkled as she looked at him, he felt as if she was the only woman he would ever want to be with for any length of time. Ever.

He immediately stepped back. She might be in trouble and he would help her if he could, but he had to be free of emotional entanglements.

"Ah, here's the supper!" Jenkins announced, giving him the opportunity to beat a hasty retreat.

"You sit at the head, my lord," the innkeeper invited, "since you're the guest of honor."

Bromwell acknowledged his request with an inclination of his head and took his place, relieved to see that Lady Eleanor was to be seated at the far end of the table covered with a long white cloth and sporting what was no doubt Mrs. Jenkins's best Wedgwood china. He was also asked to say the grace.

Once that was over, he turned his attention to the food.

Or at least he tried to, for despite his wish not to become involved with any woman at this point in his life, as the supper of potato soup, roasted beef, stuffed chicken, boiled vegetables and fresh bread progressed, with wine and ale and fruit, he couldn't ignore Lady Eleanor, even though he was pestered with questions.

They were the same ones he got asked every time he was in company, about the shipwreck and the cannibals. He tried to be patient and emphasize the various new species of plants, animals, insects and spiders they'd found, but nobody seemed very interested in that.

Except Lady Eleanor, whom he caught listening avidly as he described the spiders in Tahiti, although she blushed and looked away when she met his gaze.

He also noticed that Lady Eleanor ate the plain, wholesome, plentiful and delicious food with impeccable manners, as delicately and demurely as a nun, taking tiny bites. Every so often, however, she would lick her soft, full lips, a motion that was more alluring to him than the swaying of a naked Tahitian woman's hips during a *hura*.

What might have happened if they had met in London,

at Almack's, or a ball, or one of Brix and Fanny's parties? Would he have felt the same powerful attraction and found a way to be properly introduced, or would he have thought her simply another rich heiress of the sort his father was forever pestering him to marry, and avoided her completely?

Such speculation was pointless. They had met under very unusual circumstances and he had most insolently and inappropriately kissed her. She must surely think he was a rake, a lascivious libertine.

If he could help her, it might make her think more highly of him and erase the poor first impression he must have made.

Whatever the outcome, he would do all he could to discover if she required his assistance and render any aid he could before he went on to the family estate.

And then he would never see her again.

A few hours later, Nell waited anxiously as the full moon rose and shone in through the mullioned window. She was going to have to leave without paying her bill. She had very little money left in her purse and no idea how long it might be before she could earn more.

The bright moonlight would mean it would be easier for someone to notice her as she absconded, but it also meant she would be better able to see where she was going. Since the only mode of transportation she could afford was her feet, she didn't want to fall and injure herself.

What would her parents say if they knew what she'd done today, and yesterday and the day before that? They had tried to raise a good woman, sacrificing much to send her to an excellent school, to learn manners and deportment and etiquette, to be the equal of any well-born gentlewoman.

All for nothing. It was a mercy they were dead, so they would never know what had happened to her, and what she'd done.

Hoping everyone was asleep at last, she rose and, taking her valise in her hand, eased open the door and listened again. She heard nothing, save for the occasional creak of bed ropes from Lord Bromwell's room.

Perhaps he wasn't alone. It had sounded as if he'd come up the stairs by himself after she had retired; nevertheless, she wouldn't be surprised to learn that he had a woman with him—some comely serving maid or one of the women at supper who had been gawking at him. She could well believe women had vied for his favors even before he'd become famous, and he must practically have to beat them off with a stick since his book had been published.

If he had come to expect such a reaction, it was no wonder he'd kissed her and then sought her out before dinner, even though it should have been obvious she didn't want to have anything more to do with him. She couldn't.

Sighing, Nell crept cautiously into the hall and closed the door behind her. The hall was as dark as pitch. Putting her hand to the wall, she carefully made her way toward the stairs.

"The coach isn't due to depart for some hours yet."

There was no mistaking Lord Bromwell's voice.

Nell turned. Although she couldn't see his face clearly in the dark, his body was as close as it had been in the coach, and if she could only see the vague outline of his body, she could feel his warmth as if he were embracing her.

Fighting to calm her racing heart, she gave him the excuse she had prepared. "I couldn't sleep, so I thought I'd see if I could find some wine."

"You felt it necessary to wear your pelisse and bonnet, as well as take your baggage, to get a nocturnal beverage?"

"I was afraid I might be robbed if I left my valuables in my room."

He stepped closer and she could see him better now, although it was still dark. He wore only his boots, buff trousers and shirt open at the neck. "You must have a lot of valuables."

"No, but I can't afford to lose what little I have. I'm sorry if I disturbed you," she said, continuing toward the stairs.

He put his hand on the wall ahead of her, so that he blocked her way. "Something is wrong," he said, his voice gentle but firm. "I wish to be of service, if I can."

He wanted to help her? He sounded genuinely sincere, yet how could she trust him? How could she trust anyone?

Besides, she'd lied to him about who she was. "The only thing amiss, my lord, is that you won't let me pass. Let me go or I shall call for help."

His voice dropped even lower. "No, you won't."

Sweet heavens, had she completely misjudged him? Was he a man to be feared after all?

But she didn't dare rouse the innkeeper or other guests, either, so she kept her voice low as she commanded him again to let her pass.

A door opened below and heavy footfalls sounded on the wooden floor of the taproom, then started toward the stairs.

She mustn't be found here, especially with him, especially dressed as he was.

She turned and ran back to her room. He followed and before she could get the door shut, he was inside the room, closing it behind him.

Chapter Four

Someday, we may learn what forces move the salmon to make that dangerous journey upstream to spawn, or why a dog will sit for hours by the bed of its deceased master. Yet for now, there remain instincts and emotions, reactions and defensive intuitions, unknown and mysterious, that govern every living creature upon the earth.

> —from *The Spider's Web,* by Lord Bromwell

Panting, aghast, Nell's whole body shook as she faced him. Yet in spite of her distress, she stayed silent, for the footsteps came up the stairs, then past the room. Another door opened farther along the corridor. Mrs. Jenkins's voice mumbled a sleepy greeting to her husband, who muttered something about a sick horse before the door shut again.

"Get away from the door," Nell ordered with quiet ferocity, gripping the handle of her valise, prepared to swing it at Lord Bromwell's head. She had been trapped by a man before and fought her way free, and she would do it again if necessary.

Unlike Lord Sturmpole, however, the viscount addressed her not with arrogant outrage, but as calmly as if they were conversing in a park on a summer's day. "Are you planning to walk to Bath in the dead of night?"

His tone and his distance were a little reassuring, but she wasn't willing to trust him. "I've told you what I'm doing. Now let me pass!"

"There's no need to be frightened," he said, still not moving any closer. "I won't hurt you. I'm hoping I can be of service to you."

Service? What kind of service did he have in mind? Lord Sturmpole had claimed she would benefit from his attentions—and suffer if she refused.

Yet there was one important difference between her situation in Sturmpole's study and this. She had been horrified by Lord Sturmpole's advances; she had not been by Lord Bromwell's.

Nevertheless, she wasn't about to let him know that, or to have anything more to do with him. "Perhaps my impulsive reaction to your impertinent embrace has given you the wrong idea, my lord. I assure you that I do not go around kissing men to whom I've not been introduced. Or those to whom I *have* been introduced, either," she added.

"I'm delighted to hear it, but the service I wish to offer is not the sort you seem to be assuming. Despite my lapse of manners earlier today, I'm not a cad or scoundrel who seeks to take advantage of a woman. It's obvious something is amiss here, and my only intention is to find out what it is and help you if I can."

"By holding me prisoner?"

He ignored her question. "If all is quite well, why are

you travelling alone, wearing gowns that don't fit properly and neglecting to use your title? And why, my lady, are you attempting to leave this inn in the middle of the night?"

It felt as if the room had grown very cold. "I am not a lady."

"You're not Lady Eleanor Springford?"

Nell struggled to hide her growing panic. She wasn't Lady Eleanor, or any kind of lady. She'd heard that name in school, from one of her fellow students who was forever bragging about her lofty, if distant, relations. Nell had thought it wise to use a name similar to her own because it would be easy to remember.

That seemed the most ridiculous of reasons now.

But surely if he had met Lady Eleanor, he would have known at once that she was an impostor and said something before this, or summoned the law.

"No, I'm not and I never said I was," she replied, wary and determined to reply with more care. "Nor am I running away. I'm going to visit my uncle in Bath. As for my gown, I thought you were an expert on spiders, my lord, not ladies' fashions."

"It is my nature to be observant."

"My *modiste* had a terrible seamstress in her employ. Unfortunately, there was no time to find or hire a better one before my departure."

She crossed to the window and turned with an indignant huff, despite her trembling legs and the trickle of perspiration down her back. "There is the door, my lord. Now that I've explained, please use it."

He planted his feet and crossed his arms. "Not until I'm sure you're not in trouble."

Oh, God help her. She believed he meant that, and that he had no selfish, licentious motive—but why did she have to encounter a chivalrous gentleman here, and now? "Your aid is quite misguided, my lord. I am in no trouble."

"Then, unfortunately, I must assume you're attempting to renege on the payment of your night's accommodation."

She stared at him, aghast, her mind working quickly. He was right, after all, but of course she couldn't admit that.

She thought of one excuse he might accept. "There may be another explanation for my wish to leave this room, my lord."

He raised a querying brow.

"Has it not occurred to you that I might be afraid to be sleeping so near the man who so impertinently kissed me? Who can say what else you might be capable of, as your presence in this chamber attests?"

His eyes widened. "You fear I would *attack* you?"

"Why should I not believe you are capable of such an act? You did, after all, embrace me without my consent or invitation, accost me in the corridor, follow me into this bedroom and you refuse to leave."

"I'm a gentleman, as my friends and associates will tell you, or the Jenkinses."

"I don't call your behavior today very gentlemanly."

He ran his hand through his hair before he answered. "Nor can I," he admitted. "However, it is not unknown for people to behave under duress as they never would otherwise. I believe it was so in my case. I was not quite myself after the carriage overturned."

Neither was she.

Still, she wasn't going to let him think he could behave any way he would, and she would accept it. "The women on that island you were describing at supper—would they consider you a proper gentleman, if they knew what behavior was expected of one?"

"Yes, they would," he firmly replied. "I acted in complete accordance with their customs and beliefs."

"As *I* have done nothing wrong."

"Perhaps not," he replied, "but either you are some kind of cheat or criminal, or you're running from someone or something. If it is the former, I am duty-bound to hold you here. If it is the latter, I ask you again to allow me to be of assistance. But whatever your answer, I'm not going to allow you to go wandering about the countryside at night. It's too dangerous and I would never forgive myself if something happened to you."

Whether he was genuinely concerned for her safety or not, she could see his determined resolve and realized he wouldn't leave until she gave him an explanation that was both feasible and believable.

She would have to come up with one.

Remembering what the driver had told her about Lord Bromwell's father and the way he'd chastised his son, she put down her valise, which contained her clothes, her toilet articles and three of Lady Sturmpole's gowns.

Spreading her arms in a gesture of surrender, she spoke as if reluctantly revealing the truth. "Very well, my lord. You are quite right. I *am* Lady Eleanor Springford and I *am* running from someone—my parents and the Italian nobleman they're trying to force me to marry. The count is rich and has three castles, but he's old enough to be a grandfather and lecherous into the bargain. He has twice as many mistresses as manors and, despite his age, gives no sign of wishing to be loyal to a wife. That's why I ran away and have no maid or servant to accompany me."

"This is the nineteenth century, not the Dark Ages," Lord Bromwell said, his brow furrowed. "Surely you could simply refuse the betrothal rather than running away alone and putting yourself in danger."

She walked to the washstand and toyed with the end of a towel. "I suppose one can't expect a man who's been free to travel the world to understand the pressure than can be brought to bear upon a woman to marry, especially if the groom is a very wealthy aristocrat and her family not as rich as people believe."

"Actually, I can," Lord Bromwell said from where he still stood by the door. "My parents were far from pleased with my choice of career and my mother begged me not to go on my last expedition, so I do know something about parental expectations and coercion. Yet surely they would have relented in time. I daresay they're frantic with worry about you now."

"Perhaps. I'm unfortunately certain they're searching for me, although I hope they're still looking in Italy."

"You've come all the way from Italy *by yourself?*" he asked with undisguised awe.

She'd really come all the way from Yorkshire, but she couldn't admit that, either. "Yes, our family went there for my father's health."

That was what Letitia Applesmith had told them and Lady Sturmpole had confirmed during an afternoon of gossip with a friend that Nell had dutifully endured.

Lord Bromwell's frown deepened and she wondered if he knew something she didn't about the Duke of Wymerton or his family, until he said, "Yes, I believe my mother mentioned that."

"Travelling alone wasn't as difficult as I feared," Nell

said, relieved. "Most people were very kind, especially the women, who guessed, I think, that I was fleeing an unhappy domestic situation. Sometimes a man made an unwelcome remark, but no one touched me until…well, until you, my lord."

He blushed like a bashful boy, and she hurried on, not wishing to dwell on that encounter. "It must have been the shock of the accident that made me tell you my real name and I beg you not to reveal it. You're so famous, the press is bound to hear about the coach overturning, and perhaps learn who was with you. I'm hoping to get to the home of my godfather, Lord Ruttles, in Bath as quickly as possible. He will take my side and protect me, I'm sure."

"I see," the viscount said, regarding her with such genuine, kind sympathy, she felt like the worst, most degenerate criminal in the world. "Do you have any money? Or is the lack of it the reason that you're sneaking out?"

Trying to ignore his sympathetic expression, she said, "I have a little money left, but not enough to pay for this room."

"I shall gladly assume that cost."

She was sure he could afford it, so she didn't protest. "Thank you, my lord."

"Despite your success thus far, I am not comfortable allowing you to continue your journey alone and short of funds. Would you consider accepting an invitation to my family's estate? It's a few miles outside Bath. You'll be safe from pursuit there, and you can send a message to your godfather to come to you there."

His cheeks colored and his gaze drifted to the floor. "You need not fear that I shall attempt to take advantage of the situation, or of you."

Recognizing his generosity for the disinterested kindness it was, she was grateful, even if she couldn't accept his offer. "Thank you, but I couldn't impose and I think it would be better if I don't involve you or your family in my troubles, my lord."

"As you wish," he replied, his disappointment obvious, although his tone was still kind and concerned. "However, you must allow me to pay for your room tonight and provide you with sufficient funds for the rest of your journey."

He reached into his trouser pocket and produced a wallet of thin, soft leather. He opened it and drew out several ten-pound banknotes.

She didn't want to accept, but she needed the money. "Thank you, my lord," she said, taking the bills he held out to her and folding them in her hand. "I shall never forget your generosity."

Or your kiss.

"I shall repay you as soon as I can."

Whenever, if ever, that might be possible, and provided she wanted him to learn that she had deceived him.

He smiled, looking incredibly handsome and virile in the moonlight. "I must say I didn't expect to have such an exciting, eventful coach ride to Bath."

"Neither did I. I don't know what we would have done after the coach overturned if you hadn't been there."

"I'm sure you would have managed. You're obviously an intelligent, resourceful woman."

Coming from another man, that might not have seemed a compliment. Coming from him, however, she was sure it was. "As you are a most courageous, chivalrous man."

He began to walk closer. She waited, holding her breath, expecting—hoping for—another kiss.

Until he immediately halted a few feet away. "I had

best get back to my room before I'm discovered here and explanations are required. I wouldn't want our reputations to be ruined, although mine is already subject to some speculation."

Tucking the notes into her bodice, she followed him to the door, sorry for the lies, wanting him to know she was truly grateful, because she would never be able to repay him. After tomorrow, she would never see him again. "I really do appreciate your kindness and generosity, my lord."

A cock crowed in the yard below and he gave her a wry little smile as he eased open the door. "Good *day,* my lady."

"Wait!" she cried softly.

He turned back, his blue-gray eyes wide with query.

She couldn't help it. She had to do it.

She grabbed the front of his shirt, pulled him forward and kissed him. Not lightly and tenderly, as he had kissed her in the coach, but passionately, fervently, as her desire demanded.

Lord Bromwell stiffened, motionless with either shock or dismay. For a terrible instant, she thought he was going to push her away—but then his arms went around her and he held her close, deepening the kiss, his tongue probing until she parted her lips. She relaxed against him, her knees soft as pudding, her breasts pressed against his hard, muscular chest.

How he could kiss! Excitement ran along her veins, her flesh, setting it tingling with need. She had recoiled from her former employers' unwelcome embrace with all the force of her outrage, but she wanted nothing more than for Lord Bromwell to pick her up in his strong arms and carry her to the bed and lay her down and…

As if he could read her mind, Lord Bromwell moved farther into the room, taking her with him and shoving the door closed so that her back was against it. Still kissing her, he slid his hand around her side to cup her breast through her pelisse and gown.

Her breathing quickening, her body warming, she slipped her hand under his shirt, feeling his heated skin, the muscles bunching beneath. She had never been this intimate with a man, had never wanted to be, but every part of her mind urged her to tear off his shirt and press her lips to his naked skin.

She began to bunch the tail of his shirt in her hands and lift it until, with a gasp, he broke the kiss and stepped back, his eyes wide in the dawning light.

His chest heaving, his brow furrowed with scholarly concentration. "Once again, forgive me. Being a civilized human being, I should be able to overcome my primal urges."

His primal urges? This time, she had been the one to act upon hers.

He put his hand on the latch. "I wish you well, my lady."

"And I, you, my lord," she whispered as he slipped out of the room.

Nell moved away from the door toward the bed. She had never been more ashamed, not even when she was stealing from Lord Sturmpole.

What came over her when she was with Lord Bromwell? How could she behave with such wanton disregard for the risk she was taking, and that his fame engendered?

She had barely sat on the end of the bed before Mrs.

Jenkins blew into the room carrying a steaming pitcher of hot water.

"Good morning," she said as she set it on the washstand. "All ready for an early start, I see. It's a fine day for travelling, I must say. Breakfast will be ready shortly. I'll just make up the bed, if you don't mind."

Nell quickly went to wash.

"Quite a fine fellow, isn't he?" Mrs. Jenkins asked.

"Who?" Nell asked, although she was sure she knew to whom Mrs. Jenkins referred.

"Why, Lord Bromwell, o' course," the woman replied as she plumped the pillow. "You're a very lucky woman, my dear."

"We were fortunate he was with us with the coach overturned. We might have worsened Thompkins's injuries if he'd not been there to tell us not to move him."

"That's not what I meant. I wasn't born yesterday, my dear," the innkeeper's wife replied.

"He's never brought a woman here before, though, nor have any of his friends," she continued as she worked, "and a fine lot of scoundrels they can be, or so I've heard, all but the lawyer. He's as grim as a ghost, that one. Hard to believe he's married now, but then, I'd have said I'd never see the day Lord Bromwell would bring his—"

"I fear you're under a misapprehension, Mrs. Jenkins," Nell interjected, wondering why she'd let the woman go on for so long. "Lord Bromwell didn't *bring* me and I am not his anything. I was merely a passenger in the same coach."

Again, Mrs. Jenkins straightened, but this time she frowned. "Say what you like, my girl, but the floors creak something fierce. You weren't alone in this room."

"I was upset after the accident and couldn't sleep. You simply heard me moving about. By myself."

Mrs. Jenkins shook her head. "There's no point lying to me. I've never seen Lord Bromwell look at anything the way he looked at you last night, 'cept the time he caught the biggest spider I ever laid eyes on in the stable."

"I hardly think it's a compliment or a sign of affection if he regards me as he would a spider," Nell retorted in her best imitation of a haughty young lady. "If indeed, he does regard me with anything more than mild interest."

"You sound just like him, too, when he's going on about his spiders," Mrs. Jenkins said with a sigh, apparently not the least put off by Nell's imperious manner. "Can't follow the half of it. He's got a lovely voice, though, ain't he?"

He did, but Nell wasn't going to agree in case the woman took that for additional confirmation of her suspicions.

The innkeeper's wife fixed her with a worldly-wise eye. "And then, I saw him leaving your room."

That wasn't so easy to explain. Nevertheless, she tried. "He merely wished to ascertain if I had been able to sleep despite the accident."

"You're a smooth one, I must say," Mrs. Jenkins replied with a wry shake of her capped head as she wrestled the featherbed back into place. "But there's no need to lie to me. I don't blame you a bit, even if others might. Why, if I was twenty years younger and unmarried, I'd be the first to…"

She cleared her throat and her broad cheeks pinked. "Well, I'm not, so never mind. I just wanted to say this before you go. He's a good man, and a kind one, so I hope you won't break his heart."

"I am in no position to do so," Nell firmly assured her, "nor will I ever be and I say again that he came to my room only to ascertain if I was all right."

"Have it your own way then," Mrs. Jenkins replied, clearly still not believing her explanation.

This situation was getting worse and worse, Nell thought with dismay. She was a decent, respectable young woman—or had been until six days ago. Now she could be branded a thief and immoral into the bargain, especially if Lord Bromwell paid for her accommodation.

On the other hand, Lord Sturmpole would never suspect the woman he was chasing was the same woman others believed to be the mistress of the famous Lord Bromwell.

"Have you informed Lord Bromwell of your conclusion?" she asked.

"If it was anybody else," the innkeeper's wife replied, "I'd have thrown them out the minute I realized what was goin' on. Jenkins and I run a respectable inn, we do."

So she had kept her suspicions to herself, which was a relief. "Thank you for your kindness and discretion," Nell said. "Lord Bromwell and I are most grateful, especially if you'll continue to keep our secret."

"Worried about losing sponsors for his next expedition if word gets out, is he?" Mrs. Jenkins asked with triumphant satisfaction.

Nell hadn't known the viscount intended to sail again, but she hid her surprise and nodded, for a scandal would surely hamper such efforts despite his previous success.

"Well, my dear, you can count on me. But mind what I said about breaking his heart, or you'll have me to reckon with!"

"I shall," Nell promised, even as she noted the good

woman didn't seem to care about the state of *her* heart. Perhaps Mrs. Jenkins considered her simply mercenary, with no heart to break. "Do you know where Lord Bromwell is now?"

"In the stables, I think, probably looking for another spider."

Nell suppressed a shiver as she hurried from the room.

It didn't take her long to find Lord Bromwell. He was standing by the stables, talking to one of the grooms.

He still wore no hat, and his hair ruffled slightly in the breeze. He also had on dark trousers, white shirt, light green vest and the same shining boots and well-fitting gloves. He leaned his weight casually on one leg, and she could hear him laughing.

His laugh was as nice as the rest of him.

She hoped he never found out the truth about her. That way, he might remember her with affection, as she would certainly remember him.

Before she could catch his attention, a large black coach with an ornate coat of arms on the lacquered door came barrelling into the yard. The driver, dressed in scarlet and gold livery, shouted and pulled on the reins with all his might to stop the coach, while the footmen at the back held on for dear life as it came to a rocking halt.

No one in the inn's yard moved—not even the dogs— or spoke as one of the livered footmen leapt down, staggering a bit as he went to open the door of the coach and lower the step.

A tall, imposing gentleman appeared, wearing an indigo greatcoat with four capes and large brass buttons. As he stood on the step, his gaze swept over the yard until it came to rest upon Lord Bromwell.

As if announcing the end was nigh, the man threw out his arms and cried, "My son!"

Chapter Five

Of course Drury won the case, as expected. We're having a little dinner party to celebrate, but nothing that you should mourn to miss.

I trust you're handing your pater *and* mater *with your usual savoir faire when you're not taking refuge in your sanctuary, although how you can concentrate in such surroundings is beyond the limited powers of my comprehension.*

—from a letter to Lord Bromwell
from the Honorable Brixton Smythe-Medway

There had been many times in his life that Bromwell had craved his father's attention.

This was not one of them.

"My lord," he said, dreading what this sudden, unexpected advent signified as he walked quickly toward the Earl of Granshire, who actually deigned to alight in the yard in spite of the gawking servants, other travellers and the mud.

Normally his father only left his estate for the opening of Parliament, or if some important business matter made a visit to his banker or solicitor in Bath necessary. Even then, more often than not, such men came to him.

He hadn't even gone to Dover when his son had returned after two years at sea.

"I came to bring you home to your mother," the earl announced.

As if he were a child who'd run away after a fit of pique, Bromwell thought, his jaw clenching, very aware that Lady Eleanor was watching from the taproom door.

He'd noticed her at once, of course, drawn to her presence like a migrating swallow to Capistrano, feeling her proximity before he saw her. Like his ability to know what time it was without consulting a watch or clock, he couldn't explain the phenomenon; it simply was.

As she was simply lovely, and exciting, and the most desirable women he'd ever met.

"Your poor mother was beside herself when we received your message about the accident," his father declared, making Bromwell instantly wish he hadn't sent it, even if his delayed arrival might cause her to worry.

"Never fear, my dear, I said," his father continued, raising his hand as if calling upon supernatural powers, "I shall retrieve him!"

Bromwell doubted any actor currently appearing at the Theatre Royal could deliver those lines better. Indeed, at this precise moment, he could well believe his father had missed his true calling.

"I regret giving Mother any cause to worry," he said. "There really was no need for you to come. I'm quite all right."

"Perhaps, but it could have been otherwise. That's what comes of selling your carriage and travelling in a mail coach!"

"Plenty of people travel in mail coaches without mishaps," Bromwell said, although he suspected it was useless to try to make his father appreciate that such accidents weren't common.

"*Plenty of people* are not the heirs of the Earl of Granshire," his father retorted. "Fortunately, I have come to spare you any further indignities."

It took a mighty effort for Bromwell not to roll his eyes. "Naturally, I'm grateful. If you'll wait in the taproom, I'll settle the bill with Mrs. Jenkins and then we can be on our way."

The earl's lip curled at the corner, as if his son had suggested he wait in a cesspool. At nearly the same time, however, a cool breeze blew through the yard and the door of the kitchen opened, sending forth the aroma of fresh bread.

"Very well," the earl agreed. "Quickly, though, Bromwell. Your mother is prostrate with worry."

That was likely true, Bromwell thought as he followed his father across the yard. She was probably lying in her chaise longue with a maid hovering nearby.

The earl halted in mid-step at the sight of Lady Eleanor. "Who is that charming creature?" he asked, not bothering to subdue his stentorian voice.

God give me strength! Bromwell thought as he hurried forward to make the introductions, wondering if he should omit the mention of her title, as she had before.

She spoke first, saving him that decision. "I am Lady Eleanor Springford," she said with a bow of her head, "and I owe my life to your son."

Bromwell was torn between wanting to admit the situation hadn't been as dire as Lady Eleanor painted it and kneeling at her feet.

The earl drew himself up and placed one hand on his hip. "I would expect no less of my son."

"Her ladyship was quite an angel of mercy to the poor coachman," Mrs. Jenkins interjected, coming up behind her like a large and vibrant acolyte. "They make a lovely couple, don't you think?"

Bromwell's heart nearly stopped beating. What the devil had prompted Mrs. Jenkins to make such an observation— and to his father, of all people! It could only have been worse if she'd said it to his mother.

"Indeed," his father replied, running a measuring, arrogant gaze over Lady Eleanor, who endured his scrutiny with amazing aplomb.

"Perhaps we'd all be more comfortable inside," she suggested.

"Yes, of course," the earl agreed. "Justinian, you may attend to your business while I share some refreshments with Lady Eleanor. Come along, my lady."

With that, he swept her inside, calling for wine as he went, and left Bromwell standing in the yard.

Fearing what his father might say about him in his absence, Bromwell immediately followed them inside and paid Mrs. Jenkins what both he and the lady owed for their night's accommodation.

It struck him as a little odd that the innkeeper's wife didn't make any comment about his payment of both bills, but he was in too extreme a state of agitation to dwell upon it. No doubt she thought he was merely being a gentleman.

That done, he hurried to join his father and Lady Eleanor by the hearth, taking note that there were only two glasses of wine and his father had already finished his.

"Ah, Bromwell, here you are!" the earl exclaimed as if

his son had been miles away instead of across the room. "Were you aware that Lady Eleanor's father is the Duke of Wymerton? I went to school with him, you know."

No, he hadn't known that his father and the Duke of Wymerton had been at the same school, although perhaps he should have guessed. His father seemed to have gone to school with eighty percent of the nobility. That might explain why so many were, like his father, woefully ignorant of anything except the classics. Even then, their grasp of those subjects was often rudimentary at best.

"Did you indeed, Lord Granshire?" she asked. "He's never mentioned it."

That didn't please his father, but at least he didn't accuse her of lying. "What brings you to Bath at this time of year, my lady?"

"I'm going to visit my godfather, Lord Ruttles."

"I don't think so."

Lady Eleanor started, as well she might, at his father's firm response.

"He's hunting grouse in Scotland and won't be back for at least a month," his father continued.

Unfortunately for Lady Eleanor, that was probably true. His mother had a prodigious correspondence and kept abreast of all the nobility's comings and goings.

"Rutty always was absentminded," the earl remarked, then he smiled as if he'd just solved all the world's ills. "You must come and stay at Granshire Hall until he returns, Lady Eleanor. My wife and I would be delighted to have you."

Bromwell didn't quite know how to react. On the one hand, as he himself had said, that would be the safest place for Lady Eleanor. On the other hand, perhaps that wasn't the best idea after all.

Unfortunately, and despite his best efforts, he seemed incapable of maintaining a due sense of propriety and decorum in her presence. It was as if he imbibed some sort of potent brew that took away all restraint when she was nearby—and it seemed she had a similar reaction to his presence. How else to explain that second passionate kiss? That had certainly been at her instigation, not his, even if he'd been too thrilled and aroused to end it at once.

As he should have.

Lady Eleanor looked equally confused and hesitant. "Oh, my lord, I don't think I should impose—"

"Nonsense! It's no imposition at all," the earl interrupted. "Indeed, you would be doing us a great favor. My son has been too much among sailors and other savages. He needs to spend more time with civilized people and young ladies in particular, or I despair that he'll ever attract a suitable wife."

Bromwell nearly groaned out loud. His father had been told more than once that he wasn't ready to marry and wouldn't be for years. "Father, it may be that Lady Eleanor would prefer to arrange—"

"You see, my lady?" the earl cried. "His manners are distinctly wanting. You must come to Granshire Hall and stay for as long as you like. Summon your maid and have her bring your baggage. Bromwell, see to it, will you?"

As was usually the case, there was no room for discussion, not even for Lady Eleanor.

Giving in to the inevitable, Bromwell dutifully started to stand while the earl hoisted himself to his feet. "On second thought, if I want it done properly, I had better attend to it myself. We wouldn't want my coach to tip."

Bromwell did not point out to his father that he had had

no part in causing the accident, either through the improper storage of baggage or the mail, or by driving. Nor had he damaged the axel, put out the rock, or sent the dog running across the road.

"But I don't…have a maid," Lady Eleanor finished in a murmur as the Earl of Granshire marched out of the taproom like a soldier bound on an errand vital to the government of the realm.

Bromwell let out his breath in a sigh. "As you may have noticed, my father is the sort of fellow who won't take no for an answer. If you don't give in, he's liable to demand why not and attempt to persuade you for the better part of the day."

Lady Eleanor clasped her hands in her lap, looking pretty and vulnerable and uncertain all at once. "Since my godfather is gone from Bath, I'm grateful for his offer and gratefully accept."

She flushed. "I hope you don't think me a sinful wanton because of…because I… When you were leaving the room this morning, I thought we'd never see each other again."

"Of course I excuse you," he said. After all, how could he not, without condemning himself, too? "Just as I hope you don't consider me a rakish cad."

"No, and I'm sorry I said those things to you. Sadly, there are too many bad men in the world, and I was afraid to trust you."

"And now?"

"And now, I believe I can."

Feeling as if he was back on solid ground after being suspended and twisting in the wind, Bromwell smiled with relief. "Then let us assume our unusual behavior was due to the accident and begin anew."

When she smiled in return, his body's immediate and

powerful response made a mockery of his determination to maintain his emotional distance. But he must, so he would, no matter how stimulated he was by her presence.

Her smile drifted away and a vertical line of worry creased her brow. "Unfortunately, there is one other problem, my lord. I don't have a maid, or even proper clothes. Perhaps I should explain my circumstances to your father."

"I think not," Bromwell firmly replied even as he wondered what it would be like to try to kiss away that little wrinkle. "My father would no doubt say it's your duty to obey your parents and write to your father at once. And as it happens, a friend of mine faced a similar situation not long ago, when the lack of a maid could have led to awkward questions and explanations. We shall tell my father that your maid has run off and taken most of your clothes with her."

"You'd lie to your father?"

"In this instance, yes." *For your sake.*

She didn't seem quite convinced. "Won't your father expect the authorities to be summoned if he thinks there's been a robbery?"

"Not if I offer to take charge of the investigation. Even if he doubts my competence, he'll be happy not to be bothered with such matters."

She stared at him with wide-eyed surprise. "Surely he can't doubt your competence after all you've done, the places you've been, the dangers you've faced and survived?"

He was pleased that she was so surprised and thought so highly of him; even so, he answered honestly. "As you heard, he can and he does. However, the important thing is that you'll be safe at Granshire until your godfather returns."

Her green eyes sparkling like emeralds, Lady Eleanor

finally acquiesced. "Very well, my lord. I shall accept your father's generous invitation and—woe is me!—my abigail has run off with my clothes!"

Riding in the earl's fine coach should have been enjoyable, for the weather was fine, the vistas lovely, the coach well sprung and the seats upholstered in thick silk damask and cushioned with horsehair. Nell had a whole side to herself and, with Lord Bromwell across from her, the journey could even have been quite entertaining. She'd always liked to read histories of Britain, and she was sure a learned man like Lord Bromwell could tell her even more about this part of the country, and the Roman settlement and spa so close to Stonehenge.

Unfortunately, Lord Bromwell's father was also in the coach. Worse, he apparently felt silence in a coach some kind of sin, so he talked the whole way while they were forced to listen, trapped like flies in a web. He complained about the sorry state of the roads, the exorbitant cost of building supplies, the inefficiency of the mail, the generally terrible government and the difficulty in finding good servants.

Once she caught Lord Bromwell's eye and gave her companion-in-captivity a sympathetic smile, but that proved to be something of a mistake, for his eyes brightened and his full lips began to lift, instantly reminding her that he was a very attractive man who kissed with passionate, consummate skill.

Blushing yet again, ashamed yet again of her wayward, lascivious thoughts, she turned her attention back to the boastful earl, who had now moved on to the subject of the renovations to his estate and his hall.

"The very finest situation in the county since I've rebuilt

the house," the voluble earl noted, as if he'd personally laid every brick. "The gardens were designed by Humphrey Repton. Cost a fortune, but worth every penny, I think you'll agree.

"Nothing but the best for the earls of Granshire and their heirs, my lady. Yes, it'll be a lucky young woman who marries my son, provided he can be persuaded to stop gallivanting all over the world after those insects."

"As I've explained to you before, Father," Lord Bromwell said with an air of long-suffering patience, "spiders are not insects."

"All right, spiders," the earl said. "Disagreeable things they are, too."

Lord Bromwell opened his mouth, then closed it again and gazed silently out the window.

"While they can be a little unnerving up close," Nell said, coming to their defence for his sake, "I understand most of them are harmless—and I'd rather come upon a spider than a wasp."

She had her reward when Lord Bromwell looked at her as if she'd just announced she was Mother Nature and going to provide him with a sample of every spider in existence.

His father's expression was only slightly less impressed. "So, you like spiders, my lady?"

While she was happy to help Lord Bromwell, or at least defend his interest, there was a significance in his father's look and manner that was all too easy to understand, and that ought to be nipped in the bud.

"I can't say I like them as much as your son," she admitted with a bland smile, "but I suppose most people don't like them as much as your son."

"No, they do not," the earl replied, as if Lord Bromwell

wasn't there. "He'd spend hours staring at them spinning webs in the stable or outbuildings when he was a boy. His mother and I thought he'd ruin his eyes."

"Obviously he didn't," she said.

"And then he just about gets himself killed sailing off around the world looking for bu…spiders."

"As I've also explained, Father," Lord Bromwell said, and it was clear his patience was wearing thin, "there are things to be learned from nature and I want—"

His father waved his hand dismissively. "I'm not saying discovery isn't all well and good, but leave it to those better suited to such deprivations, I say."

Lord Bromwell's ears turned red. "Perhaps we can discuss this later, Father. In private."

The earl once more addressed Nell rather than his son. "He's no doubt going to try to convince me to give him more money for his next expedition. We'll just have to try to persuade him to stay in England, though, won't we, my dear?"

As if she could, she thought.

And now, having met his father, she could more easily understand why Lord Bromwell might want to sail to the far ends of the earth.

"Father, why don't you tell Lady Eleanor about the grotto?" Lord Bromwell suggested.

"Ah, yes, the grotto!" the earl exclaimed. "The latest thing, you see. Very charming and rustic. I've got a hermit, too. You'll have to go and see him. Plays the pipes. Infernal noise, really, but very picturesque."

Nell glanced at Lord Bromwell, who was looking out the window the way a prisoner in a dank cell might gaze at the sky through the bars, longing for freedom.

"I suppose, Lord Bromwell, that spiders like the grotto?"

With the suggestion of a smile on his face, he turned to address her. "As a matter of fact—"

"Spare us another lecture, my son," the earl said as the coach turned off the main road and down a long, sweeping drive. "We aren't the Royal Society—and soon you shall see something worth talking about, my lady."

Lord Bromwell wasn't the only occupant of the coach whose patience was wearing thin. "Many people are talking about your son's book, my lord."

Instead of looking proud or pleased, Lord Granshire frowned darkly. "Some parts of it anyway. Have you read it?"

"I'm sorry to say I have not."

"Nor should you. Why Bromwell put in that nonsense about those savages—"

"*Those savages* are in some ways more civilized and humane than many a supposed gentleman I could name," Lord Bromwell snapped, his tone so brusque and sharp, it was like a slap—something he seemed to realize at once. "Forgive me, my lady, but I fear too many ig—too many people have made similar comments, and I feel I must speak up for the maligned native peoples. Granted some of their customs may be difficult to understand, but many of ours are equally baffling to them. The handkerchief, for instance. They don't understand why one would wish to collect—"

"Bromwell, have the goodness not to discuss bodily functions in mixed company!" his father ordered.

"I only wished to point out that—"

"Never mind that now," his father dismissed. He gestured grandly toward his left and beamed at Nell. "Here is Granshire Hall."

Nell looked out the window to see the drive curve in front

of an imposing mansion of gray stone. It was indeed built in the latest style, with several tall windows and three stories. It had, she guessed, at least thirty bedchambers and who could say how many rooms on the main floor. There was also likely an army of servants to clean and maintain it.

"What do you think of it, my lady?" the earl asked proudly.

She wanted to tell him exactly what she thought of *him,* but instead answered his question. "It's very lovely. I don't think I've ever seen a more splendid home."

The earl fairly purred with satisfaction as the coach rolled to a stop and a footman jumped down to open the door. Lord Bromwell got out first and extended his hand to help her.

The earl got down beside her, then, brushing aside his son, took her arm and led her into the magnificent country house. She managed a quick glance over her shoulder, to see the viscount speaking to the coachman as if he wasn't a bit disturbed by his father's behavior.

He was, she supposed, used to such treatment.

Inside the hall, she discovered more evidence that the earl's boasts had not been empty bragging. The builders had used beautiful materials—Italian marble on the floors, and mahogany inlaid with lighter oak in the grand entrance hall and staircase. Ornate plasterwork on the ceiling surrounded an elaborate painting of a classical scene that quite took her breath away. She'd never seen so many half naked, fighting men depicted anywhere.

"The Battle of Thermopylae," Lord Bromwell explained as he came up behind her. "My father admires the Spartans, although you'd never know it from his hall."

"Fallingbrook!" the earl bellowed just as a stout man who had to be the butler came to stand almost at his elbow.

"Welcome home, my lord," the butler said, after nodding a greeting at Lord Bromwell and giving him a grin that disappeared the instant the earl turned to him.

"See to my son's baggage, Fallingbrook, and that of our guest, Lady Eleanor Springford, the daughter of the Duke of Wymerton. Tell Mrs. Fallingbrook her ladyship will be staying and requires the services of a maid, her own having absconded with most of her baggage."

The middle-aged butler's sandy brows rose. "Indeed, my lord?"

"Indeed. Servants are going to the dogs in this country, just like the government." Lord Granshire turned to Nell and was just as suddenly all sweetness and light. "Fallingbrook will show you to your room."

He turned back to the butler. "The green room for Lady Eleanor. Where's the countess?"

"In her sitting room, my lord. She asked that Lord Bromwell come up as soon as possible."

The younger man nodded and bowed to Nell and his father before trotting up the staircase and disappearing from view.

Nell tried not to feel abandoned, or afraid. After all, thanks to her education, she need have no fear she wouldn't know how to conduct herself in a stately home or among the nobility.

"If her ladyship will follow me," the butler said, "I'll take you to the green room."

"She'll need clothes, Fallingbrook," the earl called out as he hurried up the stairs ahead of her. "Tell your wife to find her something in my wife's dressing room. The countess has scads of gowns she never wears."

"As you wish, my lord. Please, follow me, my lady."

* * *

"Justinian, my boy!" the Countess of Granshire cried, holding out her arms as her son entered her sitting room.

It was a small chamber, well-appointed and comfortable, beside her bedroom on the main floor that opened onto the terrace and formal garden—or as Bromwell always thought of it, nature made unnatural.

As he'd expected, his mother was reclining on the chaise longue, with a gilt pedestal table close at hand bearing a lamp and what was clearly pages of correspondence.

Bromwell knew enough of medicine to realize his mother wasn't seriously ill. He'd tried to tell her so many times, until he realized that his mother used poor health as a means to get and keep his father's attention, as well as his own.

He embraced her and sat on a delicate harp-back chair beside the chaise. "You're looking rather better, Mother," he said, as he always did.

"A bit, perhaps. Dr. Heathfield has given me some marvelous new medicine."

"Oh? What is it?"

She waved her hand feebly. "I don't know. I didn't ask. But it doesn't taste bad."

Bromwell clenched his jaw and said no more about her medicine, although he would try to find out what it was as soon as possible. Dr. Heathfield wasn't a quack, but he wasn't the most learned man of medicine either, and his mother might be better off without his latest potion.

"It's so good to see you," his mother said with a sorrowful smile. "I was so worried when we got the message about the accident."

"Didn't Father tell you that I was quite all right? I said so in my note."

"Oh, yes, of course, but a mother always worries, even when her son's in the same county."

He understood exactly what she was *not* saying—that she worried even more when he was at sea. However, since she hadn't raised the subject of his next voyage directly, neither would he.

His father burst into the room and came to a halt, feet planted, arms akimbo, as if he were a military man, which he was not and never had been.

"So, has he told you?" he demanded of his wife. "He's been travelling with a *woman*."

Chapter Six

*In nature's kingdom, nurturing is primarily the re-
sponsibility of the female of the species. The male
may possess the finer plumage or coloring and may
be the larger, heavier and more muscular sex, but
over and over again I saw that it was the mothers
who were the fiercest when their offspring were
threatened. At such times, the fine plumage, size and
weight of the males counted for very little against the
determination of the protective females.*

　　　　　—from *The Spider's Web,* by Lord Bromwell

His father made it sound as if his association with Lady
Eleanor was illicit, not merely coincidental, and the earl
wasn't so much scandalized as shocked and, beneath
that, proud.

Bromwell wasn't overly surprised by his father's reaction.
He suspected his father was even rather relieved to think his
son had a mistress. It was no secret to Bromwell that his
father had doubted his inclinations when it came to his sexual

proclivities. Certain passages in his book should have reassured him in that regard, if his father had ever read it.

He doubted his father had done more than glance at the title page.

"She's Lady Eleanor Springford, the daughter of the Duke of Wymerton," he clarified, "and we aren't travelling together as you imply. We happened to be in the same coach, that's all. We are mere acquaintances."

The earl's eyes narrowed. "Mere acquaintances, eh?"

"Yes, Father, mere acquaintances," he confirmed, even if she was an acquaintance he'd kissed more than once, that activity arousing such a primal passion in him, he could still hardly believe it.

"What's a duke's daughter doing travelling in a mail coach?"

"I was in a mail coach."

"Because you sold your carriage. Her father has at least two coaches and twice as many carriages."

Trust his father to remember a detail like that about another nobleman. "Perhaps she prefers to travel with people of another class. One can have some very interesting discussions with people of different backgrounds."

His father looked at him as if he had just announced that he believed himself the king of Tahiti, while his mother murmured something about contagious diseases.

"Mail coaches are faster than a post chaise," he truthfully added, hoping his father would find that simple statement of fact enough of an explanation.

"If she'd been in one of the duke's coaches, her maid probably wouldn't have run off with her clothes," his father said.

"She has no clothes?" his mother asked, looking as if

she thought they meant Lady Eleanor was wandering about as naked as a newborn babe.

"A few," Bromwell quickly assured her.

He then repeated the lie he'd suggested to Lady Eleanor. His parents hadn't been staying at the London town house when that excuse had been used before.

"Oh, the poor woman, to have so many catastrophes at once!" his mother cried, moving as if she were going to get up, until his father threw himself into the nearest chair covered in emerald-green and gold brocade.

"That's why I invited her here," his father said. "Your son would have had her going to some hotel in Bath, despite the riffraff she might meet there. Besides, her father was one of my best friends at school."

"Really?" Bromwell said, not able to hide his skepticism. "I've never heard you speak of him."

"Maybe if you paid attention to dinner conversation once in a while, you would have," his father retorted.

Maybe if you conversed about something interesting, I would, Bromwell thought. Instead of voicing that thought aloud, however, he said, "I didn't realize we had a connection to the family. I've never met them, have I?"

That question didn't increase his father's opinion of his son's intelligence. "You probably had your nose in a book the last time they were here. They've been in Italy for the past five years. I thought they were still there."

Bromwell racked his brain, but for the life of him, he couldn't remember meeting Lady Eleanor.

"She must make free of my wardrobe, if my clothes will fit," his mother offered, "or they can be made over if they don't."

"Thank you," Bromwell said, pleased by her generosity.

"I've already directed Mrs. Fallingbrook to select some garments for our guest," her husband said. "I'm sure the duke will be grateful for any assistance we can render his daughter."

Bromwell was quite sure the duke's response would not be favorable if he ever learned they'd given sanctuary to his daughter as she fled a marriage they were keen to promote. Unlike his father, however, he didn't care what the Duke of Wymerton—or anyone else—thought of him for helping her.

All that mattered was that she was safe, and free.

"Her looks have improved considerably, I must say. She's grown into quite a beauty," his father noted with an unmistakable significance that made Bromwell want to roll his eyes with frustration. "I've told you, Father, that I've no intention of taking a wife anytime soon."

"Well, you should!" his father growled, glaring at him. "I'm not going to live forever, you know, and it's your duty to provide an heir, or this house, this estate—all that I and your ancestors have worked for—will go to that tosspot second cousin of mine in Jamaica. I won't stand for it, Bromwell!"

"Now Frederic, must you quarrel?" the countess pleaded. "Justinian's only just arrived and—"

"No, Mother, we shan't quarrel," Bromwell said as he got to his feet. No doubt this visit had been a colossal waste of time and effort, except that he'd made his mother happy, and met Lady Eleanor. "I'm well aware of Father's opinions, as he should be of mine. I know my duty, as you call it, but I also have a calling that I consider at least as important."

"You call studying bugs a *calling?*" his father demanded.

Bromwell ignored that question and addressed his mother as well as his father. "I'm not opposed to the idea of marriage, but I won't leave a wife behind in England while I'm on my expedition. Now if you'll excuse me, I'd like to rest before supper, provided you'll allow me to stay even though I have no interest in Lady Eleanor as a prospective bride."

His mother reached out and took hold of his hand, then looked beseechingly at her husband.

"Of course you can stay," his father muttered.

"Thank you, my lord," Bromwell said with formal politeness and a bow before he turned and left the room.

Nell looked out the window at the beautiful gardens laid out below and wondered how soon she could get away.

To be sure, this bedroom, with its lovely flowered wallpaper of roses and vines and delicate mahogany furnishings, was absolutely charming and more comfortable than she would have expected. Given the grand entrance hall, she'd been anticipating a vast, chilly chamber with a huge curtained bed from the Elizabethan age. Instead, because it faced south, the room was bright and warm and even cozy. Everything was spotless, from the linen on the washstand to the silk draperies. There wasn't a speck of dust, not even in the crevices of the ornately carved wardrobe, suggesting that the chamber was cleaned daily whether anyone was using it or not. A thick Aubusson carpet covered the floor and a gilded cheval glass stood near a screen painted with an oriental scene that hid the washstand.

A knock sounded on the door, and in the next moment, a tall, thin, middle-aged maid glided into the room with some gowns over her arm. "Mrs. Fallingbrook said you were to have these, my lady," the maid intoned, her voice as sepulchral as her manner.

"Thank you," Nell replied, thinking it was a relief that a lady didn't owe a servant any explanations for anything, whether it was her presence or apparently missing garments, while wondering how Lord Bromwell's meeting with his mother had gone.

Surely better than any encounter with his father, who clearly didn't appreciate his son's intelligence or accomplishments.

"I'm to be your maid while you're here. My name is Dena. Shall I help you change, my lady?" the woman asked as she laid the gowns on the bed.

There was a light green one of silk that was very pretty, a scarlet one of soft wool with gray trim that was more suitable for an older woman, and a pretty sprigged muslin with a square neckline she could hardly wait to try on. "The muslin, I think, please."

The maid didn't reply as she took Nell's pelisse, then helped her change her simple gown of light brown wool for the muslin.

Fortunately, Nell had no cause to be ashamed of her chemise or pantelettes. Although it had been an extravagance, she'd purchased new ones before she'd gone to the Sturmpole estate in Yorkshire, suspecting that life as a lady's companion was going to permit few luxuries.

She had not expected it to be dangerous.

Soon enough Nell was dressed in a gown that, if it didn't fit perfectly, fit as well as the blue silk she'd worn the night before. She had no jewellery, so she tied a ribbon she retrieved from her valise around her neck.

Looking at herself in the cheval glass, she was pleased

with the effect. She didn't study her reflection long; she knew she was a pretty girl thanks to the features she'd gotten from her mother—large, bright eyes and delicately arched brows over a slender nose. From her father she had inherited her chestnut hair, excellent teeth, full lips and a jaw that was a bit too strong, perhaps.

"How shall I do your hair, my lady?" Dena asked without any enthusiasm.

Nell fetched another ribbon and suggested a simple style, with the ribbon woven through it. "Do you think you can do that?"

"Yes," the maid said curtly, taking the ribbon as Nell, subduing a sigh, sat at the dressing table.

"I didn't mean to imply you were incapable," she said.

The maid didn't reply.

"Have you been with the family long?" Nell asked amicably, hoping to mend the apparent breach as the maid began to brush her hair with brisk, hard strokes.

"Twenty years, my lady."

"So you've known Lord Bromwell from boyhood."

The maid didn't respond.

Undeterred, Nell asked, "Was he an adventurous sort of child?"

"I can't say, my lady. I wasn't the nursery maid."

"Surely you would have heard if he was."

"He got into trouble now and then," Dena conceded. "But how he could be so thoughtless and sail off and worry his poor mother half to death after she spent all those sleepless nights nursing him when he was sick so often…"

Dena fell silent, her lips so compressed it was as if they were locked together to prohibit another word from escaping.

"I suppose all spirited boys get into mischief now and then."

When Dena didn't reply, Nell tried a different tack. "You must be proud to work for the family of such a famous naturalist."

Dena's dark brows drew even closer together.

"His book was very well received," Nell prompted.

The maid's expression grew yet more disapproving.

"I take it, Dena," Nell said, "that you aren't impressed by Lord Bromwell or his field of study?"

At last the woman spoke, and it was as if a dam had broken—or she finally felt she'd been given the opportunity to voice opinions too long held in check. "Spiders, of all things! Nasty, creeping creatures! I can't think what God was about creating them.

"As for the viscount, he used to be a fine young gentleman but then he went on that voyage and what he did when he was with those heathens, walking about nearly naked, dancing those disgusting dances and drinking their foul brews, and no doubt doing who knows what with the native women…well, it's enough to make a Christian woman sick!"

However Dena felt about his adventures, Nell's reaction was quite different. She immediately envisioned Lord Bromwell nearly naked, dancing with wild abandon in torchlit shadows under a palm tree, then slipping off into the bushes with an equally half naked woman.

Who looked a lot like her.

She shoved that disturbing yet exciting vision out of her mind and wished more than ever that she'd read Lady Sturmpole's copy when she'd had the chance. "You've read his book?"

"Mrs. Fallingbrook took it upon herself to read it aloud in the servant's hall during dinner, until I asked her to stop," Dena replied. "It ruined my appetite to hear about an English gentleman, the son of our employer, behaving like that. *I* think he ought to be ashamed of himself.

"It nearly killed his poor mother, him going off like that, despite her pleading for him to stay," Dena continued. "She took to her bed for weeks after he sailed and we were all afraid it would be the death of her and then there he is, acting like a heathen himself!"

"But he returned," Nell noted, "and his book is a great success. His mother must be pleased about that."

"She would be if he'd settle down and marry and not go sailing off again for who knows how long."

Nell was sure Lord Bromwell didn't plan his expeditions as a means to upset his mother; his zeal for his chosen field and his belief in the necessity of learning about the natural world made that quite clear.

And after all, he wasn't the only man who travelled far from home. Mothers, sisters and wives of whalers and other seamen must get used to their sons and brothers, fathers and husbands being gone for years at a time.

Or perhaps, she silently acknowledged, they had merely learned to hide their fears beneath a mask of stoic acceptance.

She couldn't fault the countess for being worried or Dena for her sympathy for her mistress, especially when she recalled how her own mother had cried before leaving her at school. She, on the other hand, had been too excited by the possibility of making friends to be sad, as Lord Bromwell was no doubt excited by the possibility of making new discoveries.

"He's advancing the cause of science and our understanding of the natural world," she pointed out in his defence.

The maid's only response was a loud and scornful sniff. Fortunately, Dena had also finished dressing her hair.

"I'll be here to help you when you retire, my lady," she said, stepping back.

That wasn't exactly cheerful news, but there was no way to refuse, Nell supposed. "Thank you," she said, rising and leaving the room, heading for the drawing room where, she assumed, the family would be assembled prior to proceeding to the dining room.

This must be how prisoners being taken to the Old Bailey must feel, she thought as she went down the stairs. Afraid, uncertain, worried that every past transgression was going to be used against you…

She hesitated on the threshold of the drawing room and slowly surveyed the grand chamber dominated by an ornate fireplace of marble, wide and with a mantel the height of a man's shoulders. Two figures of women in Greek garments were on either side of the opening, and a large pier glass hung above it. The walls were painted a pea-green, with white plasterwork of Grecian urns and vines around the ceiling. The furnishings were of various gleaming woods, and included several Hepplewhite chairs and a Grecian couch upholstered in green silk, with curving gilded arms and feet. The heavy velvet draperies were still pulled back to allow the last of the daylight to shine into the room, although candles in shining silver holders had also been lit, and a fire kindled in the fireplace. A painted screen stood near it, and there were more paintings on the walls, of men, women and children in sober family groups dressed in the fashions of years gone by. Huge oriental vases full of roses and hothouse flowers stood on side tables, their scent mingling with beeswax and burning coal from the fire.

It was a lavish, expensively decorated chamber, if not an overly pleasant one.

Nor was it unoccupied.

In evening dress and with his hands behind his back, Lord Bromwell stood by the window, looking rather like a beetle among the butterflies as he stared up at the moon as if contemplating its composition.

Chapter Seven

So much remains to be learned about the natural world, including human beings. Are we subject to the same needs and instincts as the lesser orders, or can our impulses be controlled by reason and rational discourse, as we would like to believe?
—from *The Spider's Web,* by Lord Bromwell

What a will of iron must be concealed beneath that handsome, studious, civilized exterior, Nell thought as she studied him, noting his well-cut and immaculate evening attire of dark cutaway coat, gray vest, white shirt and cravat, breeches and silk stockings that proved his calves were as muscular as the rest of him. How dedicated he must be to his chosen field to continue his studies despite his disapproving, critical father and his fearful, anxious mother. She doubted she would have the strength to do what he had done in the face of such resistance. Her parents had always been kind and loving, seeking the best for her, wanting her to be happy.

Which made her crime that much heavier to bear.

She went farther into the room, treading on a dark green carpet that must have cost hundreds of pounds. Looking at him now, in this room and in those clothes, she found it almost impossible to believe that he had danced with wild abandon among heathens.

She might have found it completely impossible to believe if she hadn't felt the unbridled passion in his kiss. Having experienced that primitive desire, feeling her own aroused by his touch, she knew there was a wild, untamed, virile male beneath those expensive, civilized clothes.

Lord Bromwell turned. That lock of hair had fallen over his forehead again, bringing a boyish charm to his otherwise elegant appearance.

He smiled, yet made no move to come any closer. She smiled, too, longing to tell him that, having met his parents, she admired him even more. That he looked breathtakingly handsome in his evening dress. That she wished with all her heart she really was a lady and his equal. That he would kiss her again, and not stop with kissing.

Instead, she seated herself on the edge of the Grecian couch and folded her hands in her lap. "I regret that I haven't yet had the pleasure of reading your book. I was wondering if I could borrow a copy from your father's library to read while I'm here."

Instead of looking pleased by her request, Lord Bromwell's expression grew decidedly uncomfortable. "Of course, if we can find one. He's probably given away all the ones I gave him."

Surely a man who could brag for hours about his house and grounds would keep a copy of his own son's bestselling work. "He must have one, at least. Where is the library?"

"This way," Lord Bromwell said, walking to the door, "but I fear you're going to be disappointed."

As he must be, if he was right.

Nevertheless, and hoping he was wrong, she followed him out of the drawing room to the library a short distance down the wide, marble-floored corridor with brisk, eager steps.

What if she was wrong, and there was no copy there? What should she do? Console Lord Bromwell? Vilify his father?

She put any thought of comforting him from her mind as they entered a large room with long, narrow windows on the south side and shelves of dark oak on the others. Lord Bromwell went to the hearth and got a brimstone match which he used to light an oil lamp on one of the side tables by the windows.

In the brighter light, she noted one was a chess table, the pieces lined up ready for a game. A picture of a bucolic country scene populated by people clothed in the fashions of the previous century hung over the black marble fireplace. Busts of long dead Romans and Greeks stood on top of the shelves, like so many spirits watching over them. The several volumes on the shelves were leather-covered, and all appeared of recent manufacture.

There was a large Pembroke table in the center of the room, with a single book upon it. Surely if any book deserved pride of place…

She went there at once and soon Lord Bromwell was beside her. He set the lamp on the table, illuminating the cover and title of the book: *Peerage of England, Scotland and Ireland*.

Nell didn't dare look at Lord Bromwell and didn't know what to say. *I'm sorry* seemed hardly adequate.

Instead, she set her mind to figuring out where a man as vain and proud as the earl would put his son's book.

"Perhaps it's over here," she said, heading toward the nearest shelf.

"We shouldn't waste our time," Lord Bromwell said with quiet resignation. "I'll have one sent to you via your godfather, with my compliments."

Which meant she would never receive it and he would find out that she'd been deceiving him. Yet what else could she say except, "Thank you."

"It's no trouble. I have several. Not that I go sending them out to everybody I meet..."

His voice trailed off into an embarrassed silence.

She risked a swift glance at his face, to see that he was blushing from his collar to his hairline and said, "I think you're a very remarkable man, Lord Bromwell."

"I think you're a rather remarkable woman, to have travelled so far by yourself," he replied, not meeting her gaze. "For a young woman to even decide to do such a thing, and in the face of parental disapproval, is astonishing."

"It seems we both have had to disappoint our parents in order to be free."

Except, in her case, her parents were dead, and she was all alone.

As he was, at least in one way. Even here in the family home, no one understood him or the forces that drove him. The desire to learn. The zeal to discover. The willingness to risk everything in the advancement of science. She didn't fully comprehend what compelled him, either, but she could easily admire him for his dedication and devotion.

As she stood beside him close enough to touch, the glow of the lamp surrounded them, a circle of enveloping light in the encompassing darkness, as if they were all alone in this vast mansion, this county, this country, the world. An island of sanctuary in a hostile world.

Only the two of them, separate, but not alone. Not anymore.

She could have no hope for any kind of future with him. She was a thief, a fugitive and a liar. She was here under the most false of pretences, taking advantage of his kindness and generosity, and her only hope should be that he never found out the truth.

She parted her lips, ready to say something, anything, to break the spell cast by the lamplight and her admiration and sympathy.

He leaned closer, as if to listen.

Or to kiss her.

"My lord, dinner is served," the butler announced from the doorway.

At Fallingbrook's announcement, Bromwell immediately moved away from the beautiful and far-too-tempting Lady Eleanor.

If she knew the thoughts and images that swirled in his head about her, she would think him the most lascivious libertine in England. She must never know, and he must and would master his desire. He must and would behave as he should, no matter how enticing she was.

She needed his help, not his unwelcome advances.

"Shall we?" he said, politely offering her his arm.

She duly laid her hand upon it and they dutifully and silently proceeded to the dining room.

"Ah, here you are!" his father cried as they entered and his triumphant smile was almost too much to bear in silence.

Almost, for what could he say to his parent that wouldn't alert Lady Eleanor to his father's persistent wishes regarding his future?

Surprisingly, his mother was there, too, looking more alert and healthy than she had in a long time. She had always enjoyed the company of younger women, and he had more than once suggested she have a companion, but that proposal had always been met with her own kind of stubborn resistance. She would say she wouldn't need a companion if her son would visit more often and stay longer.

Since the countess was already seated and made no effort to stand, her son brought Lady Eleanor to her. "Mother, this is Lady Eleanor Springford. Lady Eleanor, my mother, Lady Granshire."

"Delighted," his mother murmured as Lady Eleanor dropped her hand from his arm and dipped a curtsy.

His father, meanwhile, nodded at the liveried, bewigged footman, who pulled out a chair that would be to his right at the table.

"My lady," the earl said, nodding toward the chair.

Again demonstrating her admirable, amiable poise, Lady Eleanor gave her host a pleasant smile, then did as she was ordered and took her seat.

After the earl delivered a grandiose grace as if it were the Sermon on the Mount, supper was served.

Bromwell was well aware he need not be ashamed of any meal in his father's household; unfortunately, the price for such sumptuous fare as turtle soup, turbot with lobster, lamb cutlets, venison, beef, goose, peas, salad, meringues à la crème and chocolate cream was having to listen to his father, who had an opinion, however ignorant and ill formed, on everything.

Lady Eleanor ate as delicately as before and listened politely. She never ventured a remark unless the earl asked her a direct question, an opportunity that came precisely once, when he asked her about the condition of Italian roads compared to English ones. Even then, he didn't really listen to her response. He simply continued to assert his opinion that English roads were in a disastrous state and all those convicts being shipped off to Australia could be put to better use fixing the roads and verges in England.

Having witnessed the disembarkation of men, women and children from a convict ship in Australia, Bromwell didn't disagree. "It might mean more of them survive," he noted. "The conditions on those vessels—"

"I'm not saying we should keep them here to do them good," his father cried as if Bromwell had suggested putting them up in hotels, "but as a means of saving the government money."

"To make them slaves," Bromwell said. "You've never been to a sugar plantation, or you would realize that slavery—"

"Is not what we're discussing. We were talking about roads—the very roads that nearly got you killed."

"The accident wasn't that bad," Bromwell replied, trying to be patient. "We were not in danger of dying."

"If there had been passengers on top of the coach, though," Lady Eleanor ventured, "they might have been seriously injured or killed."

"Ah! There!" his father cried triumphantly. "Exactly my point!"

Bromwell tried not to feel betrayed. "I admit that's true, especially if we'd been going at a faster rate of speed. Nevertheless, I think there's a vast difference between saying that the roads should be kept in good repair and using slave labor to ensure it."

"This is what comes of an expensive education," his father complained to Lady Eleanor. "Theory over practicality every time. Maybe if my son stayed in England instead of haring off after bugs, he'd realize the state this country is in."

"When you have seen as much of the world as I have," Bromwell said quietly, thinking of certain images that would be forever burned into his brain, "you can appreciate how fortunate we are, although there is much that could be done to improve England, and the English."

His father's brows lowered. "Now you sound like one of those damned Frenchmen, spouting off about *liberté* and *equalité*. Look what happened there. Turned the country into a bloody mess."

Lady Eleanor shifted uneasily in her chair, and his mother looked equally uncomfortable.

"Perhaps we should refrain from political discussion until the ladies have retired to the drawing room," Bromwell suggested, hurrying on before his father took that as an indication that his son was admitting he was wrong. "Did I not see a new horse in the stables, a very fine black hunter?"

"Yes, you did," his father replied. "Got it for the new season. Wonderful animal."

His father proceeded to describe not just the qualities of his latest purchase, but every other horse and hound he possessed. Although changing the subject was precisely the goal Bromwell had hoped to achieve, he subdued yet another sigh as he wondered what Lady Eleanor made of his family.

At last the final course of fruit and chocolate crème had been served, and the ladies left him alone with his father. Instead of returning to politics, however, Bromwell was forced to endure another lecture on his duties as an Englishman, a nobleman and especially the heir of the Earl of Granshire.

Having been subjected to this harangue several times before, Bromwell allowed his mind to drift to Lady Eleanor, although that proved to be something of a mistake. His imagination immediately conjured the picture of her lithe, graceful body engaged in a *hura,* the dance done by the women of Tahiti, which was as different from a measured, genteel English ballroom dance as it was possible for a dance to be.

"Well, Bromwell? What do you intend to do?" his father demanded, tugging his mind back to cold reality.

"For now, join the ladies," his son replied as he rose and headed for the door.

Nell had thought the dinner at the inn had been like trying to make her way through a maze, but that was nothing compared to the tension she experienced in the Earl of Granshire's dining room. Thanks to her education—which the earl would likely consider a waste of money—she knew what glass to drink from and how to manage the fish bones; otherwise, she felt like the unwilling spectator at a trial, with Lord Bromwell as the defendant and his father both judge and jury. His mother, for all her apparent concern for her son, said nothing in his defence. Instead, she sat as silent as a spirit and picked at her food like a bird.

No, that wasn't right, she thought as she sat across from Lady Granshire, who was reclining on the Grecian couch in the drawing room while they waited for the tea. A ghost might have groaned or tipped over a chair to reveal its presence. Lady Granshire simply ate her food, sipped her wine and ignored the conversation around her.

Perhaps she was used to such conversations between her husband and son, which surely meant they weren't uncommon. Poor Lord Bromwell! How difficult it must be for him here!

"You're shivering," the countess said with maternal concern. "Shall I have a footman fetch you a shawl?"

"No, I'm quite all right, thank you," Nell replied. If anything, the room was rather too warm, for the fire had been built up while they'd been in the dining room, probably for Lady Granshire's benefit.

Lord Bromwell and his father would no doubt find the room almost unbearably warm. Of course, having been in such hot climes during his voyage, Lord Bromwell might not find such temperatures uncomfortable, although he might be tempted to remove his coat...

"I do hope you're not coming down with something. Perhaps I should have Dr. Heathfield see you when he comes for his weekly visit."

"No, I'm sure I'll all right. I must thank you for the loan of this gown and the others."

The countess gave her a shy smile that was very like her son's. "Think nothing of it. I have too many to wear." She leaned forward and took hold of Nell's hand with unexpected strength. "You mustn't mind my husband, Lady Eleanor. He is arrogant and stubborn and easily agitated, but he can be kind and generous, too."

"It's hardly for me to judge him," Nell protested, taken aback by her fervor.

Lady Granshire let go of her hand and lay back. "It's just that he had certain aspirations for his son and Justinian has ignored them and gone his own way."

"To great acclaim," Nell observed.

"Yes," the countess agreed, "but—"

She fell silent when Lord Bromwell appeared in the door. He nodded a greeting, then went to stand by the window in the same attitude as before, feet planted, hands behind his back, but this time, it looked as if he was preparing himself for a rigorous dressing down, not studying the moon or stars.

His father entered and posed by the hearth, his elbow on the mantel, shoulders back, chest out, in an attitude that, she suspected, he thought made him look imperial and impressive.

"What a charming picture!" the earl declared as he regarded them with a condescending smile. "To think I have two of the loveliest women in England in my drawing room!"

His wife blushed, while Nell gave the supercilious, boastful earl a meaningless smile. At least he wasn't criticizing his son.

"And of course, I wish to have two of the loveliest women in England at our hunt ball. You will stay for that, won't you, Lady Eleanor?"

She avoided looking at Lord Bromwell. She shouldn't care what he thought of that suggestion, because she didn't dare attend. Any such gathering might mean an introduction to someone who knew the real Lady Eleanor.

"When is it?" Lord Bromwell inquired.

"Gad, Justinian, you should know. It's always the first Saturday of November," his father replied.

"I was asking for Lady Eleanor's benefit," he calmly explained.

A month. She didn't dare to remain here a whole month.

"I suppose you've invited the usual set?" Lord Bromwell asked his mother.

"Of course."

"Will Lady Jemisina be attending?"

Whoever Lady Jemisina was, Nell hated her instantly.

His mother's eyes brightened and she darted a swift, thrilled look at her husband. "I've already had her acceptance."

"And her father?"

That question doused the happy light in Lady Granshire's eyes, while Nell felt as if she'd unfairly maligned the harmless Lady Jamesina. "Yes, but Justinian, you must promise me you won't—"

"Gad!" his father cried. "Do you hear *nothing* that I say to you? You will *not* pester our guests with requests for sponsoring another ridiculous expedition!"

Nell looked swiftly at Lord Bromwell, expecting him to flush or frown or even leave the room. Instead, he merely raised a brow as he replied, "How do you know that I don't have something of a more personal matter to discuss with Lady Jemisina's father?"

His mother clasped her hands as if she was about to receive her heart's desire. "You *do?*"

In spite of her rational realization that there could be nothing between Lord Bromwell and her, Nell suddenly felt disappointed and dismayed—until Lord Bromwell gave her a swift, inscrutable glance and said, "I may—or I may not. I was merely pointing out to my esteemed parent that since he cannot read my mind, he can only guess at my intentions.

"Now if I might make a suggestion, I think Lady Eleanor is rather fatigued. Perhaps, my lady, you'd like to retire?"

"Yes, I would," she quickly agreed, thinking it best to get away from them all, but especially from Lord Bromwell, before she did something really foolish.

Like fall in love with him.

Early the next morning, Nell slipped out onto the terrace and continued into the garden. Wrapping the cashmere shawl Lady Granshire had provided about her shoulders, she kept to the paved walks, for the dew was still sparkling on the grass.

The yew hedges, shrubs and edges of the walks were all neatly and precisely trimmed. The flower beds were pristine, the plants evenly spaced, the roses expertly pruned. Every portion was formal and clearly planned to the last detail.

Instead of being impressed, however, as the earl would no doubt expect, the formality and man-made arrangement made her yearn for wild, open country or a forest, where plants and trees grew untended and free.

Perhaps that was another reason Lord Bromwell had gone to sea, to get away from the constraining regulation of his family's estate.

She encountered a ha-ha at the far end of the garden. The sunken fence was in a shallow moat and beyond it she could see a path leading into a wood. Determined to reach that bit of natural nature, she stepped back a few paces, took a deep breath, ran and jumped.

She almost fell and spent a few frightening moments teetering on the brink of the opposite side before she got her balance. Once she did, she walked briskly along the path into the shadows of the oaks, beeches and alders, feeling triumphant and happy to be away from the stifling formality of Granshire Hall. Large royal ferns, browning with the season, lined the path and carpeted the wood floor, along with wild garlic and campion. Lichen clung to the tree trunks, and years of fallen leaves made her progress silent. She spotted two chaffinches on a branch overhead, their slightly red breasts a bright spot among the yellowing leaves.

The way was uneven and a little rocky, and she wasn't exactly dressed for a long walk, but after a little while, it was as if she'd left the Earl of Granshire's estate far behind and entered a mysterious, enchanted wood. She wouldn't have been surprised to come upon a fairy ring, or a centaur, or a unicorn.

Or a knight on horseback, clad in chain mail and looking like Lord Bromwell.

She supposed she was running away again, albeit in a less drastic manner. She probably ought to leave Granshire Hall and the viscount and his family—but where exactly was she going to go? Where would she be safe from the law and Lord Sturmpole?

The memory of that terrible night invaded the peace of the wood. She felt the same horror as she had when she realized Lord Sturmpole had no intention of paying her wages unless she submitted. The struggle that ensued. The locked door. Her escape and fear and flight...

She paused beneath a willow beside a babbling stream, the leaves a canopy made by Mother Nature, the grass a natural carpet. If only she could stay here forever...

Something that was most definitely not the stream, or a bird, or the call of an animal, broke the silence.

Somebody was singing. Or rather, chanting, followed by rhythmic clapping.

Keeping to the edge of the stream, she slowly followed the sound until she reached an opening where the stream formed a deep pool. There, at the edge, she could see the singer, who was also dancing, or so she supposed the rhythmic steps and arm movements must be.

It was Lord Bromwell, clad only in dark trousers and boots, chanting in a foreign language and moving his body as she'd never seen a body move, in a dance like no dance she'd ever seen and a very far cry from a quadrille or a waltz.

Chapter Eight

The process is both time-consuming and somewhat painful, as I can personally attest. I declined the full tattoo given to adult males, which caused much hilarity among the women, who clearly thought I was admitting I was but a child despite my years and certain other evidence that I was not.
　　　—from *The Spider's Web,* by Lord Bromwell

Nell stared in complete fascination, marvelling at the lithe ease and grace with which Lord Bromwell moved, the undulations of his body, the deep bends and the way he moved his knees back and forth like the wings of a butterfly. She had never seen anything like it, and likely never would again.

He turned, so that he was facing away from her, and she spotted something on his back, slightly visible above the waistband of his trousers. It was a dark mark, like a large birthmark…or a tattoo?

It had to be, she thought as she inched her way forward. What was it supposed to depict? She was too far away to tell and too much of it was covered by his trousers to guess what it was with any accuracy—and she really shouldn't linger here. Surely he would be mortified if he found her there, as she would be to have him know that she'd been watching him.

Nevertheless, she hesitated, then decided it was worth the risk to listen to his chant and watch him dance like some sort of warrior from long ago calling on his gods.

Until a dog bayed nearby. Loudly.

Lord Bromwell instantly stopped dancing while, with a gasp, Nell began a hasty retreat.

A huge black dog burst through the bushes nearby, growling and baring its teeth as if it was about to attack.

Nell stopped dead, too panicked to scream. The dog stood where it was and began to bark as if to summon an army.

"Quiet, Brutus! Sit!"

Relief flooded through Nell as the dog did as Lord Bromwell commanded, abruptly settling on its haunches, silent and panting, as Lord Bromwell appeared from the trees. He had hastily donned a white shirt that was still half undone and open nearly to his navel, as well as a blue frock coat.

"I'm sorry if he frightened you," he said, walking up to the huge, slavering dog and patting its head. "The game-keeper must be nearby. I suspect Brutus thought you were a poacher, but even so, he's all bark, which is why he's an excellent guard dog."

She sidled closer to the animal and put out a hand to pat him. The dog's tail began to thump as he looked up at her with mild brown eyes.

"See? Now he's a friend for life," Lord Bromwell assured her, while she tried not to glance at the opening in his shirt and that expanse of sun-browned naked chest. "What brings you this far from the house, and so early?"

Before she could answer, an elderly man in leather gaiters and a heavy black coat, with a felt hat pulled low on his forehead, stepped out of the trees. His face was nearly as brown as his hat, much wrinkled, and he had the widest mouth she'd ever seen. He also had a shotgun cradled in the crook of his arm.

Although he bobbed his head in greeting, his eyes, shaded by the hat, narrowed when he saw her.

"This is Billings, the gamekeeper, my lady," Lord Bromwell said before turning to address him. "I'm afraid poor Brutus gave Lady Eleanor quite a scare."

"He was only doin' his job, my lady," the gamekeeper said gruffly.

"He has a very loud bark."

"Aye, like his father—and a good thing Castor were loud, or his lordship here would be nothing but bones."

"There are some caves nearby and when I was about ten, I decided to go exploring," Lord Bromwell explained with a rueful grin, reminding her that he was not as old as his fame and accomplishments might lead one to believe. "I got stuck trying to squeeze into an opening and couldn't get out. Brutus's sire found me and the rescue party was able to follow the sound of his barking to get me out.

"It was not," Lord Bromwell added self-deprecatingly, "my finest hour."

"Oh, now, I dunno," Billings replied, tipping back his hat and revealing sparse gray hair. "Come out of it laughing, he did, like it was all just a lark to him."

"Because I had every faith you'd find me."

Billings shook his head. "After hours alone trapped in the dark? Enough to give grown men the willies."

"It wasn't dark the whole time," Lord Bromwell corrected, leaning his weight on one leg and speaking as if they were at a dinner party. "My candle lasted for most of it and there was a *Meta menardi* to keep me company."

"That'd be some kind of spider, I suppose," Billings said.

"The common name is the orb-weaving cave spider," Lord Bromwell replied.

Billings shook his head as if perturbed, but there was a glint of pride in his dark eyes and the hint of a smile at the corner of his wide mouth. "Most boys go for puppies or ponies. The viscount here goes for spiders. Has he shown you where he keeps 'em? It's not far."

Nell glanced at Lord Bromwell, who was swiftly buttoning up his shirt as if he'd suddenly realized he'd been exposing a rather vast amount of skin. "I don't think she'd be interested in my specimens, Billings."

"Oh? Scared of spiders, are you?"

"Not unless they're very close to me," she replied.

"They're all dead," Billings assured her.

"Except for the harmless sort who usually inhabit such buildings," Lord Bromwell amended.

"Not that we let folks know that," the gamekeeper said with a wink. "Haven't had a poacher on the place since his lordship come back because they think he might have brought some poisonous ones back with him and let 'em loose."

"I'd very much like to see Lord Bromwell's collection," Nell said honestly. After all, they would be dead.

"Well, then, since I've already seen 'em, Brutus and me'll be off," Billings said.

He slapped his hand against his thigh, and the dog rose

and trotted toward him. Then, giving the viscount a nod of farewell, and Nell a grin, the gamekeeper disappeared back into the trees with his dog.

"Do you really want to see my collection?" Lord Bromwell asked shyly when they were alone. "I won't be offended if you'd rather not."

Suddenly, the risk of being alone with him seemed far less important than learning about the subject that interested him so much that he would take such risks to collect specimens and bring them home. "Yes, I do."

He smiled with delight and the warmth of it seemed to heat her down to her toes before he turned and pointed at a brown stone building a little way in the distance. She hadn't seen it before because it was half-hidden by shrubs and ferns and surrounded by thick trees, and she had been too busy watching him dance.

"Billings started that rumor about poisonous spiders himself, to keep poachers away," the viscount said as he led the way. "He thought it would be more effective than laying traps."

"Apparently it works."

"Apparently," Lord Bromwell said, sliding her another boyish grin, and her heartbeat seemed to skip.

Reaching the small stone structure, he leaned forward and pushed down on the latch, then shoved open the rough wooden door before stepping back to let her enter ahead of him. "Welcome to my idea of heaven, Lady Eleanor."

She moved past Lord Bromwell into the dim building that was about twenty feet wide and thirty feet long. The only illumination came from two wide, square windows that were half-shuttered and a small fire in the hearth at the other end of the room. There were shelves to her right bearing several glass jars with objects floating in them and a large, cluttered table of scarred oak in the center. On the table were the remains of a candle in a simple pewter holder in addition to an oil lamp, as well as some papers and what might be a box of pencils of the sort artists used. Beside the rough stone fireplace was a wooden cabinet with wide, narrow drawers. Shelves above it held a few books. There was also an assortment of what looked like cooking utensils, a kettle, plates, cups and cutlery, along with some other things she couldn't begin to name, on an ancient sideboard on the other side of the hearth. A cabriole sofa with a sagging seat was along the wall to her left, with a pillow and rumpled blanket at one end.

Lord Bromwell squeezed past her and went to fold the blanket. "Forgive the disarray. Normally nobody comes here except me. The servants won't set foot in the place. Sometimes I sleep here when I'm working on a paper, as I was last night."

The blanket folded, he hurried to the hearth and took a brimstone match from a container on the unfinished wooden mantel. He put it into the fire, then used it to light the oil lamp. As it glowed into life, she could see what floated in the jars.

Spiders. Large ones, small ones and several sizes in between. Some were dark, some colourful, one or two were completely black.

No wonder the servants wouldn't come here, she thought as she wrapped her arms around herself. "I didn't realize they could get so big," she murmured, staring at one particularly enormous specimen.

"Oh, they can," Lord Bromwell replied. "I have other specimens, too, in the drawers."

He nodded at the cabinet. "It pains me to have to kill

them, but there is no other way to bring them home for further study."

He reached for one of the bottles. "This fellow is the same kind that gave you such a turn in the coach, *Tegenaria parietina,* also known as the cardinal spider because Cardinal Wolsey apparently shared your reaction to them."

"It's a common reaction to spiders, of course," he continued as he regarded his collection. "Even the daughter of one of the first men to write well of them seemed to have had a similar response. Her name was Patience."

He slid Nell a sidelong glance. "Perhaps you've heard of her? Her father was Dr. Thomas Moufet."

"Little Miss Muffet?" Nell cried. "She was a real person?"

"So it seems," he said, grinning, "although I don't know who came up with the rhyme."

He moved further down the shelf and pointed at another specimen. "And this beauty is a tarantula from Italy. Its poisonous bite is supposedly cured by music and wild dancing."

She thought of *his* wild dancing, the memory so vivid and exhilarating she doubted she would ever forget it. "You don't believe that?" she asked, for his expression was decidedly amused.

How would he look if he'd known she'd seen him when he thought he was alone?

"No," he replied with a shake of his head, "although it's an interesting notion. Inhabitants of the same regions where this spider dwells used to hold rites dedicated to Bacchus. I suspect the bite of the tarantula is merely an excuse to continue similar unbridled excess and all manner of…"

He cleared his throat and immediately went to the next species. "This is a spider that I found near Kealakekua Bay, in Hawaii, where Captain Cook was killed."

As he continued describing his collection, he became more enthused and entertaining, and less the serious scholar.

She'd never met a man so keen on his profession, so thrilled by his work, so excited by his studies. So handsome and charming, so modest and yet so heroic. So lean and yet so muscular....

"Am I boring you? I can get quite carried away, I know," Lord Bromwell asked, obviously misinterpreting the far-off look in her eyes.

"Not at all," she answered. What would he think or do if she confessed she'd just been imagining him without any clothes on?

"Would you like some tea? I have some, and there's water in the kettle. Unfortunately, I don't have any milk or sugar."

"A cup of tea would be lovely," she said, "if you think we can spare the time."

He stepped briskly toward the fireplace. "My mother never comes down to breakfast and my father's never been an early riser."

"Then please, let's have some tea."

Nodding, he hung the kettle from a pot crane and moved it over the flame. He fed more wood into the fire and got two cups and spoons and a tin from the sideboard. "I'm aware spiders aren't as attractive as butterflies or flowers, but they're still worthy of study. For instance, their webs are amazingly strong for their size and weight. Just think what we could do if we could figure out how to imitate the properties of spiders' silk! Unfortunately, not many share my opinion. Mostly they, like my father, consider my devotion to the study of spiders a waste of time."

"Which makes your dedication that much more impressive."

"Do you really think so?" he asked eagerly, turning so quickly toward her that the stray lock of hair fell over his forehead again.

"I do," she confirmed, moving closer to the table and leafing through some sketches there. They were very good, proving that Lord Bromwell was a man of many talents.

"My father has never understood me at all," Lord Bromwell said with a sigh. "I was a great disappointment to him as a child. I wasn't a particularly robust boy, and I preferred reading to riding and hunting.

"I became interested in spiders when I was recovering from scarlet fever. A cardinal spider inhabited a corner of my room across from my bed and when I had no new books to read, I would watch it.

"The maids kept destroying its web, but the spider always returned and built another. I was fascinated by both the web, and the creature's persistence."

She imagined him as a lonely little boy with only a spider for company. And yet…"Thompkins said you're an expert horseman."

"Practice, over many years, aided by the instruction of my friends who all ride better than I," Lord Bromwell replied.

"You seem to have outgrown any tendency to sickliness," she noted as she studied a particularly fine drawing of a plant she'd never seen before.

"Not completely," he said, coming closer as she picked up another picture, this one of a hairy-legged spider. "I became very ill during my last voyage. Measles, of all things. Fortunately, I didn't lose my eyesight."

"Or the world would have lost a talented artist as well as naturalist."

"I'm competent enough to draw from life, but I'm hardly an artist," he demurred.

Acutely aware of his proximity, she tried to focus her attention on the sketches of insects and plants. "These are very realistic."

She was nearly at the bottom of the pile when a very different picture caught her eye. She drew it out and found a charcoal sketch of herself, looking pensive and plaintively out of the window of the coach.

It was startling to see herself so accurately rendered with a few strokes of charcoal. "I thought you were asleep for most of the journey," she murmured. "The next time I share a coach with someone I think is sleeping, I might have to kick him to make sure."

His lips curved up in a rueful smile. "If I had known how much I would enjoy your company, I would have stayed awake."

The kettle began to whistle and she let out her breath as he went to make the tea, trying to calm her rushing heartbeat. "I don't blame you for preferring to spend time here, but it must get a little lonely sometimes, just you and the spiders."

"Billings and Brutus join me sometimes, and bring a rabbit to stew. Then we have quite a little party," he said, pouring boiling water through the tea strainer into a pot. "I did miss Granshire when I was at sea, more than I thought I would. I even missed Father, although there was a certain chieftain in Tahiti who reminded me of him a great deal. Obuamarea had a daughter he was particularly keen I marry. Of course I had to refuse."

"Was she pretty?" Nell asked.

"Very, once one got used to the tattoos."

She remembered the black mark on his back and wondered again what it depicted.

He handed her the cup, which she rested on her knees. "I probably shouldn't have gotten one myself, but I was curious about the process. I do wish, however, that I'd kept that particular experience out of my book."

She wrapped her hands around the warm cup. "Is there really a bet about it at White's?"

"Sadly, yes, there is. My friend Brix—the Honorable Brixton Smythe-Medway—made it. He called the wager repayment for a certain bet some friends and I made that caused him some grief—but if you knew Brix, you'd believe as I do that he would have done it anyway, just to make mischief."

"He doesn't sound like the sort of friend I'd like."

"Oh, he's really a fine fellow," Lord Bromwell said as he leaned back against the sideboard, holding a chipped teacup. "He's a bit of a comedian, that's all. We met at school and he was the first boy to speak to me. That's how I met Edmond and Charlie and Drury, and we've been friends ever since, although they can't quite understand my interest in spiders, either.

"But I could never be an attorney like Drury, or write poetry and novels like Edmond. Brix is helping to improve his father's estate and Charlie's in the navy, so I suppose I have the most in common with him." He gave her another rueful smile. "But listen to me going on about myself! Tell me about your interests, my lady."

"I—I don't have any," she admitted, feeling woefully ignorant and boring.

"Surely there must be something?" he prompted. "You can rest assured I shall be open-minded."

She truly believed he would be, even if she expressed an interest in something scandalous, like a career upon the stage.

There *was* one thing she wanted, one dream she'd always harboured that seemed safe enough to mention. "I've always wanted to have children."

And a home, and plenty of money, but she didn't add those things.

"So have I," he said as he put his empty teacup on the sideboard. "Someday, when I'm no longer able to go on expeditions, I hope to be so blessed. But until then, I won't ask a woman to marry me only to make her wait for me to return, always wondering if I'm safe or if the ship's gone down."

As his mother waited. As she would wait now, for word of him. "You could take her with you, couldn't you?"

"I would never subject a wife to the crowded conditions and deprivations of such a voyage."

"What if a woman were willing to wait for you?"

He spoke firmly and unequivocally. "I would tell her not to."

"Whoever you choose to marry, whenever you choose her, she will be a very lucky woman," Nell said as she got to her feet.

"I doubt that," he said, reaching out to take her cup and setting it beside his on the sideboard. "I am a titled man with a mania for spiders who happened to write a book that, for now, is popular. Next year, next month, someone else will be the toast of London, and I'll merely be an eccentric nobleman, the same as I was before."

"You are more than that," she protested, upset that he so obviously believed what he'd just said, no doubt the legacy of the censure and ignorance of others, especially his father. "You're a kind, generous, heroic man any woman would be proud to marry."

He tilted his head and studied her as if she were one of his specimens. "Would *you* marry me if I asked?"

He wasn't really proposing and even if he did, she could never be his wife. He deserved a rich, titled woman who could support his scientific endeavors as much as he deserved the respect and praise of his family and peers. She knew it as surely as she drew breath and he liked spiders, no matter how much she wished it could be otherwise.

Nevertheless, she answered honestly. "I believe any woman would be happy to be your wife."

"Any woman?" he asked quietly, moving closer.

"Any woman," she confirmed.

It was time to leave, before she said or did something she would regret. "We should go, my lord."

He nodded and didn't move.

She waited, scarcely breathing.

He took a step closer.

So did she.

For she could bear it no longer. Although it would be wrong and foolish and might lead to more trouble, she couldn't help it. She had to give in to her longing.

So she rose up on her toes, and kissed him.

Chapter Nine

Every culture and every species has its own unique mating rituals, but all lead to the same end: procreation. It is one of nature's strongest urges, as great as the need for food and water, shelter and warmth.
—from *The Spider's Web,* by Lord Bromwell

For a horrible moment, Nell feared that she'd made another terrible mistake, until Lord Bromwell put his arms around and responded with passionate fervor as if he'd been waiting for this since that other kiss. Angling himself closer, he pressed his tongue against her closed lips and it seemed the most natural thing in the world to part them.

Yet even that close contact was not enough. She wanted to be more intimate, to feel his skin beneath her hands, to let him feel hers.

Leaning into him, she pulled his shirt free of his trousers and slipped her hands beneath, revelling in the sensation of his hot flesh beneath her fingertips as she tentatively, gently, slid her hands upward. She laid a palm over his taut nipple while his own hands glided up her back. Her knees seemed soft as melting butter, and in one swift, fluid motion, he picked her up and carried her to the worn sofa where he laid her upon it as if she were Sleeping Beauty.

Then he stood back and looked at her. At that moment, he was no restrained Englishman, his actions ruled by man-made rules of etiquette. He was a hero, a warrior, a man who had been tested and proven by trials she could scarcely imagine.

Yet he was also a man of flesh and blood, whose storm-gray eyes bespoke the needs of that longing flesh, that heated blood.

His chest rose and fell rapidly as he tore off his jacket and tossed it aside before joining her on the sofa, covering her body with his.

She rejoiced in the weight of him, the length and strength of his body, as she hurried to undo his shirt. He kissed her cheek, her jaw, and then her neck, his mouth working its way lower and lower, until he reached the rounded softness of her breasts.

Here, for now, she no longer cared that he was a lord who thought she was a lady. That he was as far beyond her as the moon was from the earth. That he had seen and done so much, and she had done so little, and not all of it good.

When she had all the buttons undone, she pushed him back a little and he laughed deep in his throat as she shoved his shirt from his shoulders, revealing his chest completely. He was leanly muscular, more like a young farmhand than the half-naked prizefighter she had once seen at a fair.

Kneeling, he put his arms around her and pulled her so that she was sitting up, her breasts against his chest as he began to undo the hooks at the back of her gown.

Society would say she should be appalled and demand

that he stop. Her heart and her body said otherwise, and to them she listened, kissing his shoulder as her hands ventured to the waistband of his trousers.

The back of her gown opened and his hand slithered inside, loosening her bodice still more. "Let me," she murmured, lying back and tugging the sleeves down. Her bodice followed, until only her thin chemise covered her breasts.

"You're so beautiful," he murmured, gazing at her with desire-darkened eyes.

"So are you," she whispered, reaching for him again.

"I should stop now, before—"

She raised herself and silenced him with another passionate kiss. He said no more, but kissed with swift, fierce passion, as if his desire had finally escaped. Or been set free.

His hands moved over her, gliding, stroking, caressing, arousing. She reached for the buttons of his trousers, but he caught her hand. "Not yet," he whispered as he kissed her earlobe. "Not yet."

She gasped when he sucked her earlobe into his mouth and stroked it with his tongue. Where had he...in the South Seas...?

Soon she neither knew nor cared where he'd learned what he did as his lips and tongue moved elsewhere on her body. He teased her nipples, the pleasure unlike anything she'd ever known, and her desire bloomed like a flower after a drought, unfurling and yet there was a tightness, too, like a piece of yarn being stretched nearly to breaking.

She raised her knees and brought her hips closer to his. Her skirts were between them, but she could feel his hot arousal. She knew what that boded, and was eager, not afraid.

She reached for his buttons again, and this time, he didn't stop her. His breathing grew more erratic, more rushed, as she felt his hand on her leg, raising her skirt, feeling for the drawstring of her pantelettes, pulling it until the knot was undone and he could insinuate his hand inside.

She gasped when he touched the moist hair and moaned when he pressed the heel of his hand against her, while his fingers moved with delicate determination.

She had no idea that…that she…

She tugged down his trousers, freeing him, boldly running her hand over his smooth, hardened length.

"I want you," she whispered. "I want you to make love with me."

"I want you, too," he panted as his finger slid inside her.

That wasn't what she meant…but it felt so good….

She instinctively grasped him a little tighter and ran her hand over him. A low groan escaped his lips, encouraging her, exciting her.

He pressed the heel of his hand against her again and a second finger joined the first, making her gasp. And the tightness grew.

"Please…" she murmured, shifting, trying to make him see that she really did want to love him. That she was anxious to love him.

He pushed once more with his hand and the tension snapped. Crying out, she half rose with the strength of her release, gasping and grabbing his shoulders, her toes clenching.

As the powerful throbbing passed, she fell back and heard his hoarse breathing. She had had relief, but he had not. She raised her arms and pulled him down to kiss, sliding her body toward him, wanting to give him the only thing of value she possessed—her body.

"No," he gasped, abruptly pulling away and tucking himself back into his trousers. "As tempted as I am, I won't. No matter how I feel. I won't marry or ask for a promise of marriage before I sail, and there mustn't be a child."

His words were like a bucket of cold water on her head. And yet how could she blame him? He was both right and wise.

As he got off the sofa and reached for his jacket, she pulled her bodice back up and her skirts down. "I understand, my lord," she said, his title a fitting reminder that whatever their feelings, they could never share a future.

"I—I'm sorry," he stammered, walking across the room toward the shelves before he turned to face her. "I have not behaved like a gentleman."

"Nor I like a lady," she said quietly, reaching back to try to hook her gown.

"I was planning to go to London today and I believe it would be best if I stayed there until I must return for the ball. My self-control is not what I thought it was."

Neither was hers and no doubt he was right to stay away, for if she felt so dismayed by this parting, how much worse would she feel if they'd given in to their desire?

Perhaps it was time she left Granshire, too.

As if he'd read her mind, he said, "You should stay here until your godfather returns to Bath."

In response to the letter she hadn't written, and never would, although she'd say she had. "I don't want to impose upon your parents."

"Trust me, my lady, it would be no imposition. Indeed, you would be doing them a kindness. My father is happy to entertain the daughter of a duke, and my mother will be better for the company."

Since he put it that way, and because she had little money and would be safe from Lord Sturmpole here, she said, "Very well, my lord, and thank you."

"There's no need for thanks," he replied brusquely.

"If you don't mind, I require your assistance on another matter," she said, determined to be calm and composed.

He raised his brows.

She turned her back to him. "I cannot hook my gown."

"Ah."

He came behind her and she could hear his soft breathing as he did up the hooks he had so recently unclasped. She wouldn't think about his lean, deft fingers that had stroked and caressed her and aroused her, or the end of that act. She wouldn't imagine what it would be like to be with him without it being wrong and a mistake.

Because it was, and there was nothing that could change that.

"Now you had best return to the hall," he said when he was finished. "I'll follow in a little while."

A few minutes later, Bromwell watched as she hurried away along the path. Then he closed the door and leaned back against it, his eyes closed.

He had always sought knowledge, craved it as other men did wine or wagering, never minding hardship or difficulty if it was in service of that goal. But here, at last, he had found something that threatened, as nothing else ever had, the course he had been so determined to tread since he'd watched that single spider spin its web in the corner by his bed when he was six years old.

* * *

"Back so soon, my lord?" Mrs. Jenkins cried later that afternoon when Lord Bromwell strolled into the nearly empty taproom of The Crown and Lion.

The only other inhabitants at that hour of the day were two farmers quaffing some ale near the kitchen, and another traveller sitting on the settle near the hearth.

"I'm going back to London for a few days," Bromwell replied. "How's Thompkins? Doing well, I hope?"

"Well enough. He went to London the day after you left—the doctor thought he could and he wanted to rest in his own bed."

"As long as the doctor approved," Bromwell said, not worried if that was the case. The driver hadn't seemed that badly hurt to him, either. "He didn't try to drive, though, did he?"

"Lord love you, no! He went inside the coach."

Smiling at the mental image of Thompkins seated inside the coach instead of atop it, no doubt criticizing the other driver the whole way back to London, Bromwell rubbed his hands, which were still a little chilly from the ride. "Now that my mind is at ease about his health, I'll have one of your tarts while the hostler saddles a fresh horse for me."

"O' course! Moll, one of the apple tarts for his lordship! And tea. Be quick, girl!" Mrs. Jenkins called as she hurried off to the kitchen.

Meanwhile Bromwell sat at a table beside one of the windows overlooking the yard.

Although the interior of the inn was relatively calm and quiet, the yard was busy with grooms and stable boys and servants going about preparing to receive the next stage. It was due at any moment, Bromwell knew from his own particular interior timepiece, but whether it would actually arrive at the appointed hour was subject to conjecture. That was one reason he preferred the mail coach when he didn't ride.

A harried-looking female servant with cap askew appeared with a tray bearing the aforementioned tart, as well as a teapot, cup and saucer. Mrs. Jenkins took the tray from the woman's hands and carried it toward the viscount as if bearing a gift to Caesar.

"Here you are, my lord. Just baked this morning," Mrs. Jenkins said, placing the tray before him. "All by yourself, are ye, then?"

"Yes," he replied, distracted by the aroma of the sweet-smelling tart. When he'd been shipwrecked, he would have sold his soul to have one bite of a tart like this.

"The young lady's well, I hope? Not suffering any troubles after the accident?"

The tone with which Mrs. Jenkins asked her question and the sly inquisition in her friendly eyes caused Bromwell to leap to a conclusion he should have considered before, and for some reason had not.

"She was quite well the last time I saw her," he replied, making it sound as if that was days ago, before he finished the last of the excellent tart.

Wiping his mouth with the napkin, he got to his feet. "Good day to you, Mrs. Jenkins. Commend me to your husband, will you?"

"I will, my lord," she said, her brow furrowing as she picked up the tray and watched him stroll out again.

"Tell me, Mrs. Jenkins, who was that fine young fellow?" the stranger sitting on the settle asked, nodding at the door through which the viscount had exited.

"That's Lord Bromwell, the naturalist," Mrs. Jenkins replied.

"The one who was nearly eaten by cannibals?"

"Aye, that's him," she replied proudly. "He always stops here when he's going between his family's estate and London."

"But not always alone, eh?" the man asked with a knowing smile.

"He's a *gentleman,* the viscount is," Mrs. Jenkins huffed like an irate mother hen. "The young woman we was referring to came in the same coach as him the last time, that's all."

"The mail coach that overturned? I heard about that at the inn I stopped at last night. It was quite fortunate no one was injured. Who was the young woman? A friend of the viscount's?"

Mrs. Jenkins frowned. "She's a lovely, modest young lady, that's what," she snapped before she bustled off to the kitchen as if something of great import required her attention.

"Pardon me, I'm sure," the traveller muttered insincerely as he rose and went to the window, where he watched the famous Lord Bromwell ride out of the yard.

Chapter Ten

What could I say to him? That he should give her up and let her go? That if he loved her, he should try to win her heart, even if it meant forgoing his expedition?

What if he listened and then his decision proved to be a mistake? I nearly destroyed my own chance for happiness; I wouldn't wish to be responsible for destroying his.

—from the journal of Sir Douglas Drury

"Drury!"

Sir Douglas Drury, baronet and barrister, gowned and bewigged, came to a startled halt outside the Old Bailey. Spotting Bromwell's familiar face in a hackney cab, he smiled and, with his ruined hands clasped behind his back, made his way across the busy street.

"I must protest being accosted in that insolent manner, my lord," Drury said with mock severity as Bromwell pushed open the door for him to enter. "I am not a peddler."

"I most humbly beg your pardon," Bromwell replied with equally feigned remorse. "However, I feared a silent wave of my hand would fail to capture your notice. Deep in thought over a case, were you?"

"Actually, no," Drury admitted. "Juliette's been a little unwell."

"Nothing serious, I hope?" Bromwell asked, his own dilemma momentarily forgotten in his concern for his friend's wife.

"No, I don't believe so," Drury replied with an expression that assuaged Bromwell's dread. "What brings you back to London? Business, pleasure or spiders?"

"Spiders, mostly. I'm presenting a paper to the Linnean Society on the Brazilian wandering spider," Bromwell said. "However, I'd also like to ask your advice on a legal matter."

Drury regarded his friend with genuine surprise. "Don't tell me you've done something illegal?"

"It's nothing of a criminal nature."

"Thank God. But if it's not criminal, you would likely be better off consulting a solicitor. I'm sure Jamie St. Claire would be happy to help you," Drury said as he settled back against the squabs and hit the roof to signal the cabbie to drive on.

"If you think that best," Bromwell replied, "although I'd like to keep it as private as possible."

Drury's eyes flared with surprise, which he quickly and effectively masked. "If you tell me, I can present the facts to Jamie without involving you or mentioning any specific names."

"I'd prefer that," Bromwell said, thinking Lady Eleanor would probably prefer that, too.

"There was a woman in the mail coach with me on the way to Bath," he began as the cab lurched over a rut in the street, "and there was an accident. The coach overturned—

nobody was seriously injured," he hurried to assure his startled friend.

"Thank God," Drury muttered. "Continue."

"We were quite literally thrown together, and…"

This was likely not a good time to mention the kiss. If there ever would be a good time.

"Afterward, I discovered she's in some difficulty, so I invited her to stay at Granshire Hall. She's there now, enduring my parents. It's her situation that requires legal advice."

"Ah." Drury steepled his fingers that, while better than they'd been when he'd first returned from France, were still misshapen. "Was this woman an elderly grandmother or a middle-aged matron?"

"No. She's young."

"Pretty?"

"Very."

Drury raised a dark brow. "Does she like spiders?"

"Sadly, no. But at least she didn't run out of my laboratory when she saw my collection."

Drury's other brow rose. "You invited her into your laboratory?"

"She, um, was walking in the woods and I met her near it, so yes, I did."

Bromwell saw no need to explain that he'd spent the night in the lab so he wouldn't have to see her, or think about her sleeping a short distance down the corridor in Granshire Hall.

Drury held up his hand. "Perhaps this should wait until we're home. Otherwise, you'll just have to repeat these details to Juliette—or would you rather this was strictly between us?"

Bromwell thought a moment. It wasn't a situation he

was eager to share. On the other hand, Juliette was a kind, bold, clever woman who'd had her share of troubles, so she might have some valuable advice. And although he had every faith that Drury would keep this discussion private if he requested it, he wasn't keen to put secrets between a man and his wife. "No. I think Juliette's opinion might prove helpful, too. Brix and Fanny are still visiting with Edmond and Diana in Lincolnshire?"

"Yes. You'd want their advice, as well?"

He shook his head. "Gad, no!"

He could just imagine Brix's merry interrogation regarding the circumstances of his first encounter with Lady Eleanor and Diana would probably want to use it in the opening of a novel. Even worse, Edmond might take it into his head to compose a sentimental poem. He still hadn't gotten over Edmond's *Ode to an Arachnid*. "That is, I don't think the lady in question would care to have too many others know her troubles.

"How is your new house?" he asked, turning the conversation away from Lady Eleanor and to Drury's recent purchase.

On the edge of Mayfair, it wasn't the most prestigious location, but Drury had never cared about the trappings of success. Indeed, he hadn't even owned a town house until he'd gotten married. Until then, he'd lived in his chambers at the Inns of Court. He'd chosen this town house, he'd explained, because it was well built, with the latest in modern conveniences, and sure to increase in value over time.

"Fine, although Juliette is full of plans for painting and curtains and those sorts of things. I confess, old friend, that there are times I seek sanctuary in my study."

Bromwell shared a companionable smile. "As I flee to my laboratory when my parents try my patience to its limit."

That building could be a sanctuary for other reasons, too, as he'd recently discovered.

The cab rolled to a stop and as Bromwell looked at the white Georgian town house, he had to agree that Drury had spent his money wisely. Built across from a small park, it was in excellent condition with tall windows so clean they sparkled.

A young man in butler's attire opened the door as they got out of the cab and went up the steps.

"Good God, that's not Mr. Edgar, surely?" Bromwell cried, for the fellow was the spitting image of Drury's longtime servant, although at least twenty years younger.

"It's his son," Drury replied. "We call him Edgar Minor."

They had barely crossed the threshold and given Edgar Minor their hats when Drury's wife came rushing down the stairs right into her husband's arms.

"If you please, my dear," he chided even as he held her close, "we have company and the door to the street is still open."

Despite his frown, he wasn't fooling Bromwell or Edgar Minor or his wife, either. His eyes were too full of love and laughter.

"Oh, Buggy doesn't mind, do you, my lord?" Juliette asked after giving her husband a hearty kiss.

She left her husband's arms and hurried to Bromwell, kissing both his cheeks in the French manner. "Welcome! Of course you will stay for supper and tell us all about the plans for your expedition."

"Of course," Bromwell agreed with a smile. He had liked Juliette from the moment he'd met her. Although

Drury had never said so, Bromwell had guessed his friend had suspected him of harbouring a *tendre* for the French seamstress.

He hadn't. There hadn't been any woman who'd touched his heart until Lady Eleanor landed in his lap.

"Buggy has a friend with a legal dilemma," Drury said as they entered the comfortably appointed drawing room done in soothing tones of blue and cream. It was much smaller than the drawing room at Granshire Hall, but Bromwell would trade this for the other in a heartbeat.

"Oh? I hope it is not a serious one," Juliette said as she took a seat in a wing chair by the Dutch tiled hearth.

After her husband had joined her and Bromwell was sitting on a brocade-covered chair opposite, she picked up a small item from the sewing basket beside her, set it on her lap and threaded a needle.

Bromwell studied the fabric for a moment before he realized it was a small nightgown. A baby's nightgown.

"That looks a little small for Amelia," he said, referring to the recent addition to the family of the Honorable Brixton Smythe-Medway.

Juliette glanced at her husband and smiled, her brown eyes shining. "It is not for Amelia."

Bromwell followed her gaze to his friend, who was trying to appear nonchalant.

And failing miserably.

It didn't take a genius to realize what that, and Juliette's slight illness, must mean. His friend was going to be a father, too.

At once Bromwell envisioned this house as his, with Lady Eleanor seated by the hearth in the evening, sewing a little garment for their child.

Never before had he imagined a domestic future for himself. When he'd contemplated marriage, he had never thought beyond the ceremony and even that as some distant event, when he was too old to travel.

But now, here, this vision of a future with Eleanor struck him like a blow, a sudden, sharp, powerful pang of longing.

"I thought you would be happy for us," Juliette said, her brows knitting.

Bromwell came to himself with a start and smiled. "Oh, I am!" he said, hurrying to shake Drury's hand and kiss her cheek. "Delighted for you both. I envy you, that's all. That leaves only Charlie and me unmarried and childless."

Juliette resumed her sewing. "Someday, a woman will win your hearts and you will both be as happy as my Drury and me."

"I hope so," he answered, although the vision receded as he remembered his plans for his expedition. "In the present, however, I need your husband's help with my friend's dilemma."

He proceeded to describe Lady Eleanor's recent history and when he was finished, Juliette was wide-eyed with dismay. "Oh, the poor girl! To be forced to marry an old man!"

She looked at her husband, who was equally upset, although a stranger would probably have assumed he wasn't at all affected by what he'd heard. It took long acquaintance to see the subtle changes in the set of Drury's jaw and the glint in his dark eyes to realize he was disturbed.

"British law requires that both parties consent to any marriage," Drury said, "so it's a good thing she returned to England."

"And by herself, too!" Juliette exclaimed. "A brave girl, and clever, too, no doubt."

"Very," Bromwell confirmed.

"Unfortunately, as far as the law is concerned, she is her father's chattel until she's married, and then she becomes her husband's. However, if her parents are in Italy, we might be able to have her godfather declared *in loco parentis.* Jamie will know for sure, but even if that's unlikely to succeed, the legal suit might cause her parents to reconsider their position."

Bromwell felt better already.

"Perhaps if their daughter were to find her own husband, especially a wealthy and titled gentleman, they would relent even faster," Juliette suggested.

Bromwell flushed, but spoke just as firmly to her as he had to his father. "I have no intention of marrying anyone until I'm no longer able to travel, provided Lady Eleanor would even consider it."

"I did not necessarily mean she should marry you," Juliette returned, her hands as steady as her voice. "Maybe she will meet someone at your father's hunt ball. You wish her to be happy, do you not?"

He did—although the thought of her being happy with anyone else wasn't a welcome one.

"The first thing to do," Drury said in his usual logical, businesslike tone, "is to see what Jamie has to say about the law in such matters. Until then, everything is mere speculation, and I would much rather speculate on the subject of Edmond's new book. Apparently he's taken it into his head to write about something called a vampyre."

"Indeed, he has. He wrote to me about them, because they're not unlike spiders in some aspects," Bromwell replied, happy to leave the subject of Lady Eleanor for a while and speak of other things.

Even if she was never far from his thoughts.

The day after Lord Bromwell went to London, Mrs. Fallingbrook took Nell on a tour of Granshire Hall. It was indeed a magnificent house, although it was more like a museum than a home.

She spent another few days wandering about on her own and attempting to avoid the earl, who bored her nearly to death talking about his plans for the house and gardens. He was considering waterworks on a scale to rival Versailles, or so it seemed, and she had to wonder how the cost for such a venture would compare to the cost of his son's proposed expedition.

The countess kept mostly to her room, and the servants were busy and preoccupied preparing for the hunt ball, as well as the guests who would soon arrive in anticipation of that major event.

She walked in the garden and occasionally to the viscount's laboratory, where she dusted the jars and found herself studying the contents not with revulsion, as when she'd first seen them, but with increasing interest. She was surprised to discover how many kinds of spiders there were, and how different they could be from one another. Some of them were even rather beautiful.

Afraid she might disturb Lord Bromwell's work in some way, she hesitated to do more than dust the jars and wash the few dishes. She did open the narrow drawers of the wooden cabinet carefully and slowly, to find even more specimens of spiders, dried and mounted. They were like little jewels, lying so still in their trays.

This morning it was too damp to go to the wood and or the laboratory, so she decided to go to the library and find a book to read. It was one of the more comfortable rooms in the house, and as she strolled around the perimeter she remembered being here with Lord Bromwell, wondering if he was going to kiss her…hoping that he would….

Such thoughts would avail her nothing, she told herself, and she tried to concentrate on finding a book to read for education, if not amusement, since most of the volumes were histories of ancient Rome or Greece, Italy, England and France, or philosophy and religious sermons.

She gave up hope of finding anything appealing after she had gone around the entire room and found herself once again by the door. Sighing, she pushed it half closed and glanced at the shelves behind it.

The Castle of Count Korlovsky by Diana Westover was on the middle shelf, right at eye level. She'd heard of that book, and also the author, the wife of Viscount Adderley. Their marriage had been something of a sensation not so long ago. Indeed, Lady Sturmpole had been so fascinated by the gossip, one would think the author was one of her relatives, although she was not.

Nell pulled out the book and read a little of the first chapter. Then a little more. Taking the volume, she was about to head for a chair to spend the rest of the morning reading when another book, on the far end of the shelf almost completely hidden by the door, caught her eye:

The Spider's Web.

This must be how Lord Bromwell felt when he discovered a new kind of spider, she thought as she eagerly pulled it from the shelf, happy for another reason, as well. This meant his father had kept a copy, after all.

She hurried to one of the large chairs near the window and settled down to read. She would save Diana Westover's book for later; first, she must read Lord Bromwell's.

As she expected, the viscount's book was no dry, scientific report about spiders or the other various species of flora and fauna he encountered and collected.

In spite of the many scholastic elements of *The Spider's Web,* it was also a rousing adventure, full of exciting events and danger, as well as humor and wry observations not just about foreign cultures and habits, but about life aboard ship. Many times Nell could practically smell the salt air and hear the crew's colourful language.

Nor did Lord Bromwell leave out the less attractive facets of life in close quarters. Often she could almost smell the bilge water and taste the hard biscuits, see the rats and hear the snores.

It was no wonder he didn't want to take a wife on such a voyage.

Then there were the dangers, not just the hurricane that had wrecked their ship, killed some of the men and left the others stranded on an island little more than a spit of sand, but the unpredictable inhabitants of the exotic lands who might welcome visitors, or kill and eat them. Lord Bromwell, the captain and the rest of the crew had never been quite sure which sort of encounter it would be until they landed.

Some of their experiences with the natives were of a distinctly pleasant nature. He spoke of their food, their social customs, their tattoos and their dances, and she realized he'd been doing something called the *upa upa* by the pond. As for other, more intimate, activities between the native population and their visitors, Lord Bromwell was discreet and couched his language carefully, but she could read between the lines. She was fairly certain he hadn't kept aloof from the women.

And he had done more than dance.

Yet through it all, running like a thread of spider's silk, were two obvious themes—Lord Bromwell's passionate interest in his subject, and his modesty. And if he hadn't already proven to her that he was a capable, intelligent, admirable man, she would know it now.

A man cleared his throat loudly.

Startled, she looked up, half-expecting to see Lord Bromwell himself, as if reading his book had conjured him all the way from London like a magic spell.

It was not Lord Bromwell; it was his father, who stood with his chest out, his hands behind his back, rocking on his heels and regarding her gravely.

"I've been looking for you, Lady Eleanor," he announced. "There is something I wish to discuss with you."

For a horrible moment, she wondered if he'd discovered she was not who she claimed to be, until she realized he would surely be more angry and direct if he had.

No, it must be something else he wished to talk about, so Nell subdued a sigh and girded herself to hear more about fountains, or water pumps, or the difficulties of shipping Italian marble.

Instead—and what proved even more unnerving—the earl didn't say anything at first.

She shifted uncomfortably, but wasn't about to venture a remark.

"I presume you know that my son is the only living child of my wife and I?" the earl said at last.

"I had assumed so, since no one ever spoke of siblings," she replied.

"Which means that, in due course, he will be the Earl of Granshire, a most noble and ancient title."

Nell inclined her head in silent acknowledgment of that fact.

"He will be a very wealthy man. This estate and the house in London will be his, as well as a considerable fortune. His wife would, therefore, have every luxury and comfort."

"She would also have your son, a not inconsiderable reward," Nell pointed out.

"Provided she could get him to stay in England and not go haring off after more bugs!" the earl said with a frown, clapping his hands behind his back and starting to pace.

Nell didn't know what to say to that, so she didn't reply.

"He could have been anything," Lord Granshire grumbled as he marched back and forth. "A statesman—even Prime Minister. He was the cleverest boy at his school. All the masters said so. Instead he wastes his time and talent on bugs! They even called him Buggy Bromwell at school. My son, the heir of Granshire, a viscount, smartest lad at Harrow—Buggy! It's enough to make a man tear out his hair!"

"Surely you must be proud of him now," she protested, dismayed by his attitude and alarmed by his vehemence.

"How can I be proud of a son who studies bugs? Who dances with savages? Who won't do his duty and marry and get an heir?"

"I'm sure he'll marry some day and hopefully there will be children."

The earl stopped pacing to fix her with a searching gaze that, at the moment, reminded her of the son he seemed to hate. "If my son could be persuaded to marry and especially if he could be persuaded to give up this notion of another voyage, I would be very grateful. His bride could count on a very generous wedding gift from his grateful father."

His meaning was unmistakable. He was offering her a bribe to marry his son.

"And you need not think he'll be lacking in the bed-chamber," his father continued. "His book provides ample evidence that—"

She leapt to her feet before he went on. "By God, sir, you should be ashamed of yourself! What kind of a father are you? Are you truly that stupid, that blind to the merits of your son?

"You should be *proud* of him. He could have been a rakehell, a cad, a scoundrel. He could be a gambler or a sot. He could be getting into debt or spending his money on Cyprians. Instead, he's contributing to the sum of human knowledge. He's doing something good and hon-orable. I'm sure there are many other men who would envy you your son and not belittle his work or consider him lacking, as you so obviously do.

"As for his taking a wife, there will be no need to bribe a woman to seek his hand. He's not only intelligent and brave, capable and clever, he's kind and generous—and there can be no doubt that such a man would be wonder-ful in every way a woman desires."

The earl flushed as if he was on the verge of an apoplec-tic fit, but she didn't care. She didn't care if he demanded that she leave at once, or threw her out of Granshire Hall on her ear. At the moment, she didn't even care if he summoned the magistrate.

"How dare you?" he demanded. "How dare you stand there and berate me! I don't care if you are the Duke of Wymerton's daughter, you have no right to speak to the Earl of Granshire that way."

"Perhaps I don't, but *somebody* should," she retorted. She grabbed the two books on the table beside the chair and marched to the door. "If you'd like me to leave in the morning, I shall, and gladly!"

At the door she turned to face him one last time. "And if I am ever so fortunate as to have children, my lord, I hope I shall encourage them and not stifle them. That I shall love them as every child deserves to be loved, even if they like spiders. Or ants. Or snails. I wish—"

That I had any chance at all of being your son's wife.

Tears of rage and indignation and dismay choked her, so she said no more before she fled the library.

Chapter Eleven

The poison of the Phoneutria nigriventer, *while virulent, may not necessarily be deadly. However, if it is not, it may cause priapism, which turns what should be a pleasant state of arousal into an hourslong ordeal and can lead to permanent impotence.*
— from a presentation by Lord Bromwell
on the Brazilian wandering spider

At the sound of approaching servants, whom she most certainly didn't want to meet, Nell ran into the nearest room.

She found herself in the huge ballroom with pier glass on the walls, its inlaid, waxed wooden floor gleaming, and French doors leading onto the terrace. She hurried beneath chandeliers shrouded with cheesecloth so they looked like large white nests, then out the doors, across the terrace and into the garden.

Dashing away her tears with the back of her hand, she paid no heed to the threatening skies and chilly breeze; nor did her steps slow when she reached the ha-ha. She leapt across and kept going, heading for Lord Bromwell's laboratory where she would be alone and undisturbed, where she could gather her thoughts and make her plans.

And leave him a note of farewell.

After what she'd said to the earl, he would surely insist that she leave. At once.

She reached the laboratory and went inside. Her hands trembling, she set the books down on the sideboard, lit a fire in the hearth and slumped into one of the chairs. No wonder Lord Bromwell had his working space so far from the hall!

The door creaked open and she turned, expecting to see Billings or perhaps Brutus on the threshold.

Not Lord Bromwell.

His face full of concern, he rushed toward her. "My lady, are you all right? What's happened? I saw you running from the house."

Surprised, delighted, then worried about what he would say when he learned of her confrontation with his father, she immediately got to her feet.

She hesitated to answer, but decided there was no point dissembling. "I had an argument with your father."

"Ah," he sighed as if he wasn't at all surprised. "Please sit down and I'll make some tea."

She didn't want tea, but she couldn't think of a good reason to refuse.

"You mustn't be upset about that," he said as he filled the kettle from a pitcher of water near the hearth. "He's a stubborn, opinionated man, but whatever you quarrelled about, he'll be swift to forgive a duke's daughter."

Perhaps so, but she wasn't a duke's daughter.

And worse than that, she'd been far too tempted to accept the earl's bribe and try to win his son's hand in marriage without worrying about the consequences.

"What did you quarrel about?" Lord Bromwell asked as he sat opposite.

He might as well know, in case his father tried to bribe another young lady. "My lord, are you aware of how far your father is willing to go to see you married?"

"I'm aware that is one of the goals of his life and that he's willing to do a great deal to bring it about, with or without my cooperation," Lord Bromwell replied grimly. "How much is he selling me for these days? I believe my price was up to five thousand pounds before I sailed. I expect he's dropped it some, now that I'm famous. Or maybe he hopes for a quick sale so he could announce our engagement at the ball."

"How can he do such a thing?" she asked, relieved that he knew his father's schemes, but upset for him nonetheless. "How can he have so little grasp of his son's merits that he thinks he must pay a woman to marry you?"

"He's a man of fixed notions and I was a disappointment to him as a child. He still sees me as a weak, sickly lad with odd fascinations, likely to die at any moment."

"That doesn't excuse his treatment of you."

"No," Lord Bromwell replied without bitterness. "It does, however, explain it."

She flushed, more sorry than ever that she had lost her temper. Obviously, Lord Bromwell didn't feel the need for anyone to champion him. "I'm afraid I berated him quite thoroughly before I left the room without waiting to be excused."

Lord Bromwell's eyes widened and he ignored the steaming kettle. "You walked out on him?"

"Yes. I suppose now he'll demand that I leave."

Lord Bromwell's amazement turned to reflection. "Perhaps not. He tends to fly into a rage easily, then calm down just as swiftly. It means he doesn't brood and is rarely sullen, but that also makes it difficult to know what to expect from him sometimes. Fortunately, since you're a duke's daughter, I believe he'll be inclined to act as if nothing at all untoward has happened between you."

He gave her a companionable smile as he finally lifted the kettle from the crane and began to make the tea with the same deliberate care he likely brought to the studies that made him famous.

He paused when he saw the books on the sideboard, Diana Westover's on top.

"Have you read much of Diana's book? It's quite exciting," he said as he poured the water from the kettle into the teapot.

"I started it, but I found another I prefer," she said, rising and putting *The Castle of Count Korlovsky* to one side, revealing the book beneath.

He flushed and smiled and then busied himself with the tea.

"Your father kept a copy after all," she said, returning to her seat.

"So I see."

"You're a wonderful writer, my lord. I feel as if I'm there with you, through the good and the bad. And I had no idea spiders came in such variety until I met you."

His smile grew, although he still didn't look at her. "That is why I wrote my book—so more people could appreciate not just spiders, but all the wonderful plants, animals and insects of the world, as well as the different peoples. The variety is really quite astonishing."

Lord Bromwell handed her a teacup and, taking the chipped one again, settled back in his chair.

"I have good news for you," he said, not aware that

everything he did for her made her feel more like a criminal and less worthy of his good opinion. "I spoke to my friend the attorney, who described your case—without naming you specifically—to one of the best solicitors in London. There may be a way to either make your parents see reason, or be deprived of their control over you."

Feeling like the worst, most ungrateful sinner on earth, Nell gazed down at the cup in her lap.

What would happen if people learned he'd been tricked, duped into thinking that he was helping the daughter of the Duke of Wymerton instead of the poor offspring of a clerk and his wife?

What would he think of her then, and after she was gone, or if Lord Sturmpole found her and had her arrested?

"I thought you would be pleased," Lord Bromwell said with puzzlement. "Or are you still upset about my father? Don't be. I'm quite used to his machinations."

"It's not that," she said, raising despondent eyes. Whatever happened, she couldn't bear deceiving Lord Bromwell another moment. Every deed he did, every word he said, was like a sword in her side, or another step on the road to damnation. The time had come to be honest with this man who was so honorable, so good and so generous. "I'm not a duke's daughter. I'm not Lady Eleanor Springford. My name is Nell Springley, and I'm a thief."

Bromwell heard her words, comprehended their general meaning, and yet it was as if he'd been struck by a poison dart, one that rendered its victim inert.

She wasn't Lady Eleanor, daughter of the Duke of Wymerton? She was somebody else entirely—and a *thief?*

"I stole some gowns and money from Lord Sturmpole

of Staynesborough. I didn't do so out of greed, or because I'm a habitual thief," she hurriedly continued. "My father was the younger son of a knight, my mother a merchant's daughter. They raised me well and sent me to a good school, but when they died of a fever within two weeks of each other, I discovered my father had gambled and borrowed too much. I was left penniless. Through friends from school I found employment as a companion to Lady Sturmpole at their estate in Yorkshire.

"Lord Sturmpole was never there, though, and I never received a penny of my pay. When I complained to Lady Sturmpole, she told me to write to her husband. I did, but he only wrote back with excuses and promising to pay the entire amount when he arrived in person. Lady Sturmpole assured me her husband would make all right when he returned from London and since I had no one to turn to, very little money left and nowhere else to live, I stayed.

"Lord Sturmpole finally arrived some five months after I did. I was called into his study to receive my wages, or so I thought. I was also going to give him my notice.

"When I got to the study, he told me he would be glad to pay me all that he owed, and more, if I would…" She blushed and drew a deep, ragged breath. "If I would let him come to my bed."

Bromwell didn't speak. He couldn't. He had never been more outraged and furiously angry in his life, and not even the most colourful epithet seemed appropriate to describe a man who would treat her in such a manner, or make that obscene offer.

"Naturally I refused at once and demanded my wages. Instead of paying me, he…he tried to…"

As she fell silent, her eyes anguished, her throat working,

Bromwell set down his teacup before he shattered it. "There's no need for you to go into details. I can guess what he tried to do. He should thank God he didn't succeed."

Or I would hunt him down and kill him. Painfully.

"No, he didn't," she confirmed. "I fought back and when he tired, he locked me in the room. I called out to the servants to help me, but they wouldn't. He's the only employer for miles and they wouldn't risk his displeasure, I suppose. I finally managed to get the lock open with a letter opener. The house was quiet—no doubt Lord Sturmpole thought I'd see sense in the morning.

"So I got a few of my clothes and what money I had, and then I went to his wife's dressing room and took three gowns and the pin money she kept in a drawer. It wasn't much—not nearly enough to cover my wages. And then I ran. The stagecoach went by not far from the estate and I managed to meet it just in time."

By now, the worst of Bromwell's fury was subsiding, to be replaced by a cold anger and firm purpose. He would see that Lord Sturmpole regretted what he'd done, and what he'd tried to do.

However, all he said to the anguished woman before him was, "What you did seems perfectly justifiable to me."

"And to me, or I wouldn't have done it. Unfortunately, I'm sure he wouldn't hesitate to have me charged with theft if he finds me. That's why I was travelling alone and told you I was Lady Eleanor. Until the coach overturned, I was planning to take ship to Ireland, or America, where he couldn't find me."

The knuckles of her clasped hands whitened as she leaned forward and regarded Bromwell beseechingly, as if he were a judge at the Old Bailey with the power of life and death over her. "I promise you, my lord, I did *nothing* to encourage Lord Sturmpole or make him think I would welcome his advances. You must believe me in spite of what I've done. I've never broken the law before."

It wasn't difficult for him to answer her heartfelt plea. "I do believe you. The man cheated you, so you took goods in compensation. He did something far worse than robbery. He attempted to rape you."

She flinched when he said "rape," reminding him that while she was courageous and strong, she had been through a terrible ordeal.

"Forgive me if my choice of terms distresses you," he said in a gentler tone. "I'm trying to think in legal terms, because I believe his is by far the greater crime. He should be imprisoned, if not hanged."

"He is a powerful man," Nell noted warily.

"Who must and will be stopped," Bromwell said firmly as he got to his feet.

Although she was relieved that Lord Bromwell believed her, he was as angry and upset as if he were the one who'd been attacked.

"I doubt you're the first women in his employ he's treated in this manner and I fear you won't be the last unless he's imprisoned and convicted."

She had been so worried about her own fate, she hadn't stopped to consider if anyone else had been the victim of Lord Sturmpole's lust. "Yes, I see."

Lord Bromwell began to pace, just as his father had. "I'll speak to my friend Drury. He's the best barrister in England. He'll know how to proceed in a way that will lead to Sturmpole's conviction and your safety." He stopped and faced her squarely. "You must promise me that you'll stay here and continue to be Lady Eleanor until we've done so."

Lord Bromwell spoke softly, but there was resolve beneath his words and a sternly determined expression in his stormy eyes. Now she was looking not at a well-educated, civilized viscount, but the heir of Celt, Saxon, Norman, Viking, Roman—every warrior race that had ever set foot and fought in Britain.

"Leave my father to me," he continued. "I'll ensure that you're welcome to remain at Granshire Hall until I can return from London."

She nodded, sure he would. But his plan also meant he would be leaving her here again, without him.

His visage softened a little, making him more like the Lord Bromwell she knew. "I can appreciate why you felt driven to lie to me and I bear you no grudge or ill will. I only wish you had felt confident enough in my compassion to tell me sooner."

"I wanted to," she truthfully replied, regretting that she hadn't. "I was afraid to trust anyone."

"And now?" he prompted.

"Now I can."

She thought he might embrace her then, or kiss her, but he didn't. He held out his arm with as much formality as if he were about to present her to the Prince Regent. "We should return to the house. I'll find my father and smooth things over with him, then leave for London at once."

"But you've only just returned."

"The sooner I see Drury, the sooner Sturmpole can be stopped."

She could not argue with that, so she took his arm,

gathered up the books from the sideboard and together they went back to Granshire Hall.

Dena, her cap and apron white as snow, her serge dress clean as it could be and her expression grim as death, was dusting the bedroom when Nell returned, her lips pursed as if the presence of dust was a personal insult.

The dour maid was one of the last people she wanted to see after the events of the morning, or to have to speak to; however, she supposed she had no choice but to accept her presence.

"I found Lord Bromwell's book in the library," she said, setting the pair of volumes on the table by the bed. "And *The Castle of Count Korlovsky,* too. I hear it's very good."

Dena merely sniffed and continued to dust.

"I gather it's rather frightening."

Dena frowned. "I wouldn't know, my lady. I don't read novels."

She would have used just that tone if she'd said, *I don't like novels. Bunch of nonsense.*

Nell sat on the end of the bed. "Don't you ever feel you want a bit of nonsense?" she asked. "Something to distract you from the cares of the day?"

"Some of us don't have that kind of time, my lady, and would find better uses if we did."

Nell's nerves were already stretched taut, and the maid's disrespectful manner grated. "I don't know to whom you think you're speaking, Dena, but I suggest you address me with more respect."

Dena stopped dusting and her face grew red. "Respect?" she repeated. "You expect me to respect a woman trying to seduce Lady Granshire's son?"

Nell could scarcely believe she'd heard aright—except for the look on Dena's face. "I am not trying to seduce Lord Bromwell!"

If there was any seduction here, it was mutual—but she would not enlighten Dena on that point.

"Say what you like, Lord Bromwell will never marry you. He'll see through your snares," Dena retorted, shaking her dust rag at Nell with every word. "Lady Granshire's son may be odd, but he's no fool."

"I am *not* trying to trap Lord Bromwell into marriage, or into my bed!"

Dena's expression revealed exactly what she thought of Nell's protest. "You won't be the first who's tried and you won't be the last," she said firmly. "Batting your eyes and looking at him like that."

"I do not bat my eyes at him! I admire and respect him."

"I wasn't born yesterday, my lady."

"Neither was he," Nell shot back before she remembered she was supposed to be a lady, and therefore a servant's superior. "How dare you speak to me in this fashion? Who are you to say whom Lord Bromwell should or should not marry?"

The maid balled her dust rag in her work-worn hands. "I'm sorry, my lady, but I'm worried about the countess. She's always been good to me, and she's not strong. Even though the viscount doesn't think she's really sick, she's not really well, either. If Lord Bromwell makes a bad marriage, that'll be as bad as him going on another voyage. I fear either one'll be the death of her."

Dena might not be the most pleasant of women, but clearly, a fiercely loyal heart beat within that narrow chest.

"Then you may rest easy, Dena, and stay for another

twenty, for I assure you, I wouldn't marry Lord Bromwell even if he asked me."

The maid's eyes widened as if she couldn't believe a woman would ever refuse the viscount's hand. "Why not?"

"I have no desire to marry a man who will leave me for months and even years at a time to go chasing after spiders," Nell lied.

"But I thought—"

"What you thought was obviously wrong."

Her anger diminishing, Nell spoke sincerely. "Even if I wouldn't marry the viscount, I do like him, so there will be one more woman who'll be worried about him when he sails. We shall all have to pray for his safe return."

"Aye, my lady."

Nell took a few conciliatory steps toward her. "Perhaps if you don't have any pressing responsibilities, you could stay and help me alter the gown the countess gave me for the ball? I fear it's a bit too long."

Dena's thin lips twitched up in a smile for a fraction of a second. "I'll be happy to, my lady."

Then, to Nell's further surprise, her expression grew curious and conspiratorial. "Is it true what they're saying in the servants' hall? Did you really take Lord Granshire to task about his son?"

Nell nodded. "I did, so now I'm also worried he'll send me away."

"Oh, I wouldn't be concerned about that, my lady," Dena said with unexpected confidence as she went to the wardrobe and got out the Nile-green silk gown with rounded neck and puffed sleeves. "He may bluster and bellow, but if the countess wants you to stay, you'll stay."

* * *

Bromwell strode into his father's study, where Fallingbrook had said he could find the earl. It was a room that Bromwell always entered with trepidation even now, having been forced to endure parental cross-examinations and lectures in this chamber for as long as he could remember.

It didn't help that his father had had the room decorated like some sort of hunting lodge of the damned, with the heads of stags and boars, as well as swords, pikes and crossbows on the panelled walls. A portrait of his grandfather, stern and disapproving, or perhaps suffering from chronic indigestion, gazed down from above the limestone mantel. There were smaller, equally frowning faces of his other ancestors there, too, as if they sat in judgment of the heirs of Granshire and found them all lacking.

A similar expression was on his father's face as he stood by the windows surveying the gardens. Plans for the massive waterworks he was planning to build were spread out on the desk nearby.

"Father, I must speak with you," Bromwell announced, doing his best to control his tumultuous feelings.

The earl turned to face him, his expression strangely enigmatic. Normally his father's mood and emotions were as easy to read as a book produced with a very large font. "Ah, Justinian. I had heard you were come home. So, she has already complained to you, has she?"

"If you're referring to Lady Eleanor, she's told me what happened between you."

"Then you are aware that she dared to upbraid me. She

told me, and in no uncertain terms, that I do not sufficiently respect your work and your dedication to it."

Bromwell still couldn't decipher his father's mood, but his voice was oddly calm, considering what he was describing.

His father's next words took him completely by surprise, making Bromwell feel as disoriented as when the coach had overturned.

"She's right. I don't. I don't understand why a grown man of good breeding and fortune would want to spend his time on a cramped, stinking ship looking for bugs."

Bromwell subdued a sigh. He should never have entertained any hope that his father would ever appreciate his son's chosen life's work—but at least he'd kept a copy of his book.

It was better, too, that he was annoyed with his son, not Lady…Miss Springley. "I have long since given up expecting you to."

The earl cleared his throat. "However, she's wrong to think I don't believe you're a fine man and that I'm not pleased with you. I'm proud of your behavior in dire circumstances during your voyage. I respect the fame you've justly earned with your book. You've brought honor to our family's name, Justinian."

Bromwell hadn't felt this rattled in years, not since he'd realized the ship was going down, so it took a moment for him to be able to speak and he seemed to have developed a lump in his throat.

"Thank you, Father," he said at last. "That means a great deal to me."

His father walked toward the desk and began to roll up the plans. "I've always been proud of you," he said, without looking directly as his son, "and if you'd gone into politics or even the law like that friend of yours…"

He glanced sharply up at his son, then cleared his throat again and looked back at his plans. "Never mind. You didn't, and you could have done worse—and I didn't need Lady Eleanor to point that out."

Bromwell refrained from noting that apparently he did.

His father set the plans aside and sat behind his desk, gesturing for Bromwell to sit as well, in the sort of over-stuffed chair his father preferred.

When he had, the earl looked him straight in the eye. "Lady Eleanor's a remarkable young woman."

It didn't sound as if his father was angry at her or, he thought with relief, intending to ask her to leave. "Yes, she is."

"A bit high-spirited, but there's nothing wrong with that in a young woman, especially if she's pretty. She's clever, too, I think."

Bromwell suddenly realized where this train of thought was heading.

"A man could do a lot worse for a wife," his father noted, proving that Bromwell had guessed correctly, and it was not a welcome conclusion.

"Lady Eleanor told me about your offer regarding marriage," Bromwell replied. "I thought I had made it quite clear the last time we spoke on that subject that while I'm not averse to the notion of marriage, I won't take a wife until *I* decide the time has come. Besides, no woman of sense would wish to marry a man who was planning to leave home for several months, if not years."

Which was another example of Miss Springley's intelligence and good sense.

"Wives of soldiers and sailors put up with such separations all the time," his father countered.

"Yes, but at least they can expect to have letters and other news."

"Your voyage depends on getting the money you require. What if you can't?"

"I shall, just as I did before."

His father crossed his arms. "Since you are so set upon sailing, *I* will pay."

Bromwell couldn't have been more surprised if his father had declared a wish to accompany him.

"On one condition."

Chapter Twelve

*Creatures in the natural world have many ways of
hiding. Some keep to the shadows and dark places.
Others have developed hides or fur that make them
difficult to spot in foliage, such as the tiger or leop-
ard. Others resemble inanimate objects, so that although they are in plain view, they are as good as
invisible to their pursuer.*

        —from *The Spider's Web,* by Lord Bromwell

Bromwell realized he should have known the offer would
come with a catch.

"You must marry before you sail," his father declared.
"If you do, not only will I pay the expenses of your expedition, I'll provide your wife with an establishment in
London, or anywhere else she chooses, servants, a carriage
and an income of five thousand pounds per annum for the
rest of her life."

As shocked as Bromwell was by his father's proposal,
it hadn't escaped his notice that his father hadn't stipulated

whom he must marry. The earl would surely feel quite differently if he knew the truth about Miss Springley.

And yet to have such an offer…it was as tempting as Miss Springley. And if he married Miss Springley, that would solve her problems as well as his own.

Except that she had said she wouldn't want to be married to a man who then abandoned her for years, and he still believed it would be wrong to desert a wife so soon after marriage. "Do you have any particular bride in mind?"

His father looked as startled as he had been. "Why, Lady Eleanor, of course. If I am any judge of women, you have only to ask her. Her defence of you was most impressive and impassioned."

Bromwell got to his feet. "I regret to disappoint you yet again, Father, but in spite of your offer, I will not ask her, or any woman, to marry me before I sail."

That unfortunately familiar look of exasperation came to his father's features.

"What the devil is wrong with you, Justinian?" he demanded as he, too, rose, so they stood eye to eye. "You want your expedition. Very well. I give it to you—and all you have to do is marry a beautiful woman who cares for you, a woman who will be well taken care of while you're gone." His father spread his hands. "What more can you want?"

His father would never understand. Never. "I won't be bribed into marriage, Father, and neither will she. I managed to finance my previous expedition without your aid, and I will do so again. If and when I marry, it will be for love, not money, or even to further my work."

His father sat heavily in his chair. "God save me from foolish young men and their romantic notions!"

Bromwell tilted his head to regard the man who had

sired him and with whom he seemed to have so little in common, except for some physical features like hair and eye color. And yet… "If I am stubborn and romantic in my notions, it's probably because my father is both, as well."

Lord Granshire couldn't have looked more shocked if Bromwell had struck him. "Romantic? Are you mad?"

Seeing his father with new eyes, Bromwell smiled and gestured at the plans now curling at the edges. "The fountain you're having built—Venus and Adonis are in the center of it, are they not? Only a romantic would choose two lovers for such a centrepiece.

"I think there are other qualities I owe to my parents as well, such as my persistence. My mother continues to hope I can be dissuaded from sailing. And many another father would have thrown up his hands at my refusal to marry years ago. Mine, however, still tries to persuade me."

His father had apparently been struck speechless, so Bromwell continued without waiting for a response. "I'm going back to London today, Father, and I hope you'll allow Lady Eleanor to remain here until the ball."

The earl found his voice as he put his hands on his desk and hoisted himself to his feet. "Yes, of course she may stay. I had no intention of asking the daughter of the Duke of Wymerton to leave."

He regarded his son with a most unusual expression, as if he were still considering what Bromwell had said and attempting to decide if he agreed.

A decision apparently made, he cleared his throat and said, "I have to go into Bath later today. Why don't you join me for that part of your journey? You can tell me all about the paper you're presenting to the Linnean Society."

That was another surprise that took Bromwell aback. He

glanced at the portrait over the fireplace, half-expecting to see that the mouth of his grandfather's portrait had fallen open with equal shock. "You know about that?"

"I'm not completely in the dark about your activities, my son, even if I don't know the exact subject. Some spider, no doubt. I trust it's an exotic one."

"The most dangerous specimen yet discovered, the Brazilian wandering spider," Bromwell replied.

"That should keep 'em all awake. Now come along, Justinian," his father ordered as he started to the door. "We'd best take our leave of your mother and that young lady whose heart you're going to break."

Bromwell came to a dead halt. "Do you really think I could do that?"

His father raised a brow. "If I am any judge of women," he said before continuing out the door.

As Bromwell dutifully followed, his brow wrinkled as he considered a possible—and unwelcome—outcome he had not foreseen.

Dena had long since stopped tidying. She now sat by the hearth with Nell, telling stories about Lord Bromwell when he was a boy.

Nell wasn't surprised to learn that he'd always been kindhearted and generous, warm and loving. Unfortunately, he hadn't been a robust child and had spent many days ill in bed with various ailments. Dena told her how it had pained his mother to send him away to school; she'd insisted on getting the opinions of three different doctors before she'd allow it. But not only had Lord Bromwell survived, he'd thrived. He'd even flourished away from his father's overbearing hand and, Nell surmised, his mother's watchful, worried eye. He'd made good friends, too, "even if they all seemed like rowdy rascals the first time they came to visit. That Smythe-Medway, for instance. Now there was a boy needed a good thrashing! He put a snake in cook's bed and nearly scared the life out of her."

How she wished she could have seen Lord Bromwell as a boy, with big bluish gray eyes and tousled hair, studiously staring at a spider's web, or the other boys whose good opinion had meant so much to him.

A knock at the door ended their friendly tête-à-tête. "Oh, dear, I've been here too long!" Dena quietly declared as she hurried to open it.

A footman stood on the threshold. "If you please, my lady," he said, looking past Dena, "the countess wishes you to join her in her sitting room."

Nell rose, suddenly tense. What if the countess didn't want her to stay?

She managed to sound calm, however, as she answered. "Of course."

"Don't worry," Dena said in a confidential whisper as Nell went past her into the hall. "She likes you."

Somewhat encouraged but still full of trepidation, Nell followed the footman to the countess's sitting room.

She wasn't sure what to expect when she entered, but she hadn't anticipated finding Lord Bromwell and the earl. The viscount stood by the window, his hands behind his back, while his father was in the same attitude near the hearth.

Then Lord Bromwell smiled, and she immediately felt all would be well—or that at least she was going to be able to stay.

"Ah, my lady, here you are. I need to go to Bath to make the final arrangements for the orchestra for the ball," the earl announced as if they hadn't met earlier that day. "Since my son's off to London again, we're going to Bath in my coach and have to take our leave."

"You're welcome to stay here as our guest," Lord Bromwell confirmed. "My mother is pleased to have your company."

"Indeed, I am," Lady Granshire said with a smile, although her eyes were on her son, as if she was afraid she'd forget what he looked like all too soon.

"I shall only be away for a few days," the earl declared, obviously thinking he would be missed as much, and by both of them. "And my son assures us he'll return in time for the ball."

"Drury's going to bring me back," Lord Bromwell supplied, "and you mustn't have any fears for my safety, Mother. Drury hasn't tried to drive since he returned from the war, and I won't, either."

"Come, Justinian," the earl said. "We had best be on our way if we're to have a decent supper in Bath tonight."

The viscount approached his mother and kissed her cheek as she grasped his hand. "Goodbye, Mother. I'll be back before the ball. I promise."

"Then I know you will be," she said, dabbing at her eyes with a scented lace handkerchief.

He regarded Nell steadily as he bowed. "I look forward to seeing you again, Lady Eleanor."

"And I, you, my lord."

The viscount went to the door while the earl kissed his wife's hand. "Adieu, ladies," he said, bowing with a flourish before he followed his son out of the room.

The Viscount's Kiss

After the door had closed, Lady Granshire sniffled into her handkerchief, while Nell stifled a sigh.

At least the countess had the claim of love and family on Lord Bromwell, Nell thought as she walked toward the window that overlooked the drive. *She* could only be grateful that he didn't despise her for her deception, and she admired him all the more for offering to help her in spite of it.

The earl's coach was already waiting, as were the liveried driver and footmen. In a very few moments, the earl and his son appeared. The earl entered first and as the footman waited, Lord Bromwell put his foot on the step, then paused and looked back over his shoulder and upward. He must have seen her, for he gave a brief wave before embarking. The footman put up the step, closed the door and took his place at the back of the coach.

With the crack of the driver's whip, the four well-matched black horses leapt into motion, taking Lord Bromwell and his father away and leaving her alone with his quietly weeping mother.

"Perhaps you'd rather be alone," Nell said as she turned back into the room, "or would you like me to send for Dena?"

The countess wiped her eyes. "No, please stay. It's a comfort being with someone who shares my distress."

Nell wondered if she should say she didn't, or at least not to the same degree, but feared the countess would think she was making light of her dismay.

"He won't be gone for very long," she said, sitting across from Lady Granshire.

"This time," the countess added mournfully.

What could she say to that? She couldn't promise that her son would always return. "I must thank you again for your kind hospitality."

The countess waved a listless hand. "It's nothing, and I do like having a young lady nearby, especially one my son so obviously cares for."

Nell shifted uncomfortably. Clearly she was not doing enough to hide her growing regard for Lord Bromwell if everyone here could see it. She would have to be more careful when he returned. "I hope it doesn't cause you any trouble."

"Who last protected you, my dear?"

Nell glanced sharply at the countess, unsure how to answer that, or even what she meant exactly. A woman who was a man's mistress was said to be under his protection.

"My parents, of course," she said after a moment, "but I hope my godfather will come to my aid."

"And who might he be?"

"Why, Lord Ruttles," Nell answered, baffled by the question. Had Lady Granshire forgotten what she'd told them? Perhaps she really was ill…

The countess's expression didn't change as she regarded Nell with her son's eyes. "No, he is not, just as you are not Lady Eleanor Springford."

The breath fled Nell's lungs and her heart started to pound as if she were before a firing squad.

How did the countess know? Or had she guessed? Was it because of something she had said or done? And what should she do now?

Before she could decide, the countess leaned forward and put her hand on Nell's arm.

"Does my son think you're Lady Eleanor, or is he in on the ruse, too?" she asked. She didn't sound angry; she sounded merely curious, which confused Nell even more.

Yet one thing seemed clear—whatever she did and

whatever happened next, there was no need to lie anymore. "He knows who I really am."

Now.

The countess nodded, as if this was the answer she'd been expecting. "No doubt my son thought it best to pretend you were a titled woman to ensure that you could stay. Whatever the reason for that deception, however, I'm grateful you've come and have cause to hope I could be more grateful to you yet."

How could she possibly be grateful after Nell had tried to trick them?

"How long have you been my son's mistress?"

"I am not his mistress!" Nell cried, aghast and determined to make that clear.

"Please, my dear, there's no need to deny it if you are," Lady Granshire said with that same unexpected equanimity. "My son is comely, well educated and titled. What woman of sense *wouldn't* want him? And I've read my son's book, so I'm well aware that he's a grown man and an experienced one at that. No doubt you aren't his first lover."

She was probably right, and that gave Nell a different sort of pain.

"However, my dear, you *are* the first he's ever cared enough about to bring here, in any guise, which tells me his feelings for you must be beyond anything he's ever felt for his other mistresses."

"We aren't lovers," she helplessly replied. "It's just as he said—he came to my aid when the coach overturned and offered to help me."

Nell rose again, determined to leave this painful interview. The room. The house. Despite her promise to Lord Bromwell, she couldn't stay here. "I should go."

"Stay."

Lady Granshire shared something else with her son—a tone of command that was rare, yet thus all the more impressive when utilized.

Nell obediently perched on the edge of the sofa.

"I'm sorry if I've insulted and upset you," the countess said in a conciliatory tone. "I meant no harm or insult to you. Any woman who has earned my son's love is no common woman, and if there is a man's judgment I trust, it is his. So I'm predisposed to love you, too, and do all I can for you. Can you believe that, my dear?"

A few moments ago, she might not have, but as she regarded Lady Granshire now and saw her sincerity, she could. And did. "Yes."

The countess smiled and looked at her with hope. "So as you've been honest with my son, won't you trust me and be honest with me, too?"

It wasn't an easy request for her to answer, until she realized that Lady Granshire could have summoned the magistrate the day she first arrived and had her arrested for impersonating a duke's daughter. She had not.

Nevertheless, she still hesitated, until Lady Granshire leaned forward, took her hand and regarded her with a searching gaze that was also very like the viscount's. "If my son loves you, that's all I need to know."

After hearing the countess's heartfelt words, Nell's defences crumbled. She told Lady Granshire everything, just as she had told Lord Bromwell. Except for the kisses and other intimate moments they'd shared. Some things weren't meant to be shared, especially with a man's mother.

"So your son has offered to help me," she finished,

"and he goes to London in part to consult with his friend, the attorney."

"What a terrible situation! So much worse than the other!" the countess cried, patting Nell's hand and making her feel that it hadn't been a mistake to trust her.

"Rest assured, we'll see that Lord Sturmpole makes no more trouble for you," Lady Granshire continued. "My husband is not without some influence, too—and you mustn't even think of leaving until your situation can be sorted out."

"Thank you, my lady," Nell replied with gratitude. "You've all been so kind and generous to me, I don't know how I shall ever repay you."

Lady Granshire's eyes suddenly gleamed with a greedy, desperate light. "There *is* a way."

Chapter Thirteen

At this time, the method by which spiders avoid being trapped in their own webs remains one of nature's great mysteries. Is there something about the composition of their bodies, or is the immunity something to do with the strands themselves? This is only one of the questions regarding these fascinating creatures that has kept me watching them at work for hours at a time.

—from *The Spider's Web,* by Lord Bromwell

"I know the power certain feelings can exert over a person, how they cause them to make decisions that they wouldn't consider otherwise," Lady Granshire said. "I believe you can wield such power over my son. You can succeed where my husband and I fail. You can convince my son to stay in England, where he will be safe."

Nell immediately and vehemently shook her head. "No, I couldn't. I wouldn't. Please, don't ask such a thing of me!"

"Think of the dangers he will face if he goes on another expedition," the countess pleaded. "After all our kindness to you, and especially after his, is this how you would repay him? By not doing everything in your power to keep him here?"

"Even if I had such power as you think I possess, I wouldn't try to persuade him to give up his life's work."

"Instead you would let him risk his life wandering the world looking for bugs?"

Nell's heart broke to think of him so far away, or dead, but she would not put her fears before his aspirations. "Because it is his heart's desire, yes, I would."

The countess's face flushed and her knuckles whitened as she clutched her crumpled, damp handkerchief. "There are plenty of spiders in England he could study. If you could get him to stay in England, I will see to it that, whatever happens, you will want for nothing for the rest of your life."

How far was the woman prepared to go, what would she offer, to keep her son in England? "I notice you don't propose marriage."

"Since you aren't really a lady, my husband would never agree to a marriage," the countess grimly replied, "no matter what Justinian or I could say. And unfortunately, while the estate itself is entailed to Justinian, the income is not. My husband could cut Justinian off without a cent. If he marries a woman the earl considers unsuitable, he would."

"Even if your husband did as you say, do you doubt your son's capacity to earn a living?"

"Don't you?" Lady Granshire countered. "How much do you think his passion for spiders will pay? Consider what he will lose if he marries against his father's will."

"You do realize what it would make me if I accepted your offer?"

The countess drew herself up, reminding Nell that she

was a wealthy, titled lady. "Since you've lied so effectively to so many, you must forgive me if I thought your scruples might not be so lofty."

"Whatever I am, I am not a whore, my lady," Nell replied, stung by Lady Granshire's words and more by their truth.

The countess pushed herself up from the sofa, her whole body shaking, her lawn cap askew, the silken folds of her black gown quivering, as she upbraided Nell. "Have you no pity? No sympathy for a mother's love? You have not sat up all night praying for your baby's safety, fearing he will die at the dawn. You have not waited by that same bed listening to every breath, your own matching, as if you were breathing for him. You've never lain alone in the dark, unable to sleep, wondering where your child was. If he was alive or dead. Or ill in some godforsaken place calling out for you."

Nell *did* appreciate the countess's feelings, and her heart filled with pity for the woman's worried misery. "I do sympathize, my lady," she said, her voice gentle and quiet, although she was still firm in her resolve. "But your son is not a boy anymore. He is a man, and he has made a man's decision."

She took the older woman's thin hands in hers and looked into Lady Granshire's eyes that were the same cloud-gray as her son's. "When he sails, yours will not be the only heart breaking, nor you the only one anxiously praying for his safe return. But because I care, I *must* let him go. To hold him here, even if I could, would be to break his heart."

The countess leaned forward, her gaze intense. "What if you could be married to him? What if we could do away with his father's objections?"

"It would be no true marriage if I used a false name."

"No, I meant under your own." The woman leaned closer still, her eyes burning with fierce determination. "My husband wants one thing above all—a grandson, so that he can be sure his family name will continue. If you were to get with child, he might be willing to overlook your lack of family."

This was the most outrageous offer yet. Outrageous and impertinent and impossible and…tempting.

Very tempting.

"It would have to be a clandestine marriage," Lady Granshire continued in a rush as Nell fought the appeal of her suggestion, "but eventually, and especially if you provide the heir he so desperately wants, I think he would come 'round and forgive you."

Forgive *her?* That hadn't been her proposal, her scheme.

Yet more important than the countess's offer, or her own desire, was the viscount's happiness. Nothing else could take precedence over that, or the fulfilment of her own desire would have come at too high a price.

So Nell shook her head. "Knowing how much he cares about his work and his feelings about leaving a wife behind, I wouldn't marry him even if I could, just as I won't try to persuade him to stay in England. I wouldn't want to be responsible for the bitter resentment that would surely follow if I did."

Even then, the countess wasn't yet ready to surrender. "If he had a wife he loved, and children, surely they would be ample compensation for the loss of an expedition. After all, he's already been on one."

Nell refused to agree. "While he'd surely be an excellent husband and father, that lost opportunity would still be there, like a canker in his heart, so I won't ask him not to sail even if I never have a good night's sleep again."

When she finally realized Nell was adamant, the countess put her face in her hands, sank onto the couch and started to sob. "He won't come back if he sails again. I know he won't!"

Nell sat beside the older woman who loved her son so dearly and put her arm around her, trying to be strong, although she, too, could easily envision shipwreck or illness or some other disaster taking Lord Bromwell's life. "We shall have to hope and pray that he'll return as he did before, and remember that whatever difficulties he may face, he's a strong, brave, clever man."

Lady Granshire raised her tear-streaked face to look at Nell. "Will you stay here with me even after he's gone? My husband has little patience for my fears and even when he tries, he cannot comfort me. Nor the servants, although Dena has been with me so long. They try, but they don't love Justinian as we do."

Nell had never allowed herself to call what she felt for Lord Bromwell "love." But that was what it was. She knew it, felt it in the core of her heart. She loved him as she had never loved another, and likely never would.

"Or do you have family or friends with whom you'd rather reside?" Lady Granshire asked.

No, she did not, and if she stayed here, as his mother's companion, she would hear news of him as soon as she.

Yet there was another impediment to this plan. "The earl would surely object to my presence if he learns the truth about me."

A resolute gleam came to Lady Granshire's eyes. "Then we shall not tell him unless and until he needs to know, and

I shall also see that you have an income befitting a lady's companion out of my own funds."

The countess sank down on her knees and held out her hands. "I beg you to forgive me and forget the things I said today. Please accept my offer and stay here with me. We can comfort each other when he's gone because, like me, you love him."

Her own eyes filling with tears, Nell quickly stood, then reached down to help the countess to her feet. "I'm very grateful for your offer, my lady, and while I'd like to stay, I don't think I should make any more plans or promises until your son returns."

And then…?

She would not think about "and then" until she had to.

"Lord Bromwell to see you, Sir Douglas," Edgar Minor announced from the door of the study of Drury's town house.

After arriving in London, Bromwell had come directly to Drury's. He hadn't even stopped to change his clothes at his father's town house, and it looked like it.

"Good God, what's happened? Has somebody died?" the barrister demanded as he rose from behind his solid oak desk that was as large as a dining table for eight.

Unlike his father's study, Drury's was intended to be a place for work, not impressing other men, and the furnishings and decor reflected that. In addition to the massive desk, a comfortable chair was behind it for the barrister, as well as three other wing chairs for his guests or clients. Shelves of law books lined the walls, and a cabinet for papers stood near the desk. Two well-trimmed oil lamps, a silver inkpot, sand shaker and quill pens were also on the table, although the latter were rarely used.

Even if Drury was now able to write with more ease, he still preferred to prepare most of his cross-examinations in his head.

"No," Bromwell said as he handed his hat to the waiting butler, then closed the door so that they were alone in the room a short distance from the drawing room. "Where's Juliette?"

"Shopping with Fanny for fabric," Drury replied, his voice calm but his eyes full of concern. "Is it something to do with Lady Eleanor? Have her parents returned from Italy?"

Being an old friend, Bromwell didn't wait for an invitation, but threw himself into the nearest chair. "No, because she's not really Lady Eleanor."

For once in his life, Drury's reaction was unmasked and plainly visible, so great was his shock as he slowly lowered himself back into his chair. "She's not? Who the devil is she then?"

"Her name is Nell Springley and she was using a false identity to avoid being charged with a crime she didn't commit."

His composure apparently restored, although Bromwell could still see it was not by the set of his jaw, Drury folded his hands in his lap and regarded Bromwell steadily. "I await the details."

Bromwell was suddenly unsure how to begin, where to start and how much to say. He rose and walked to the window hung with dark green draperies, then back again.

"We aren't talking murder, are we?" Drury inquired.

"Gad, no!" Bromwell replied. "She is the victim of a crime."

He returned to the chair, sat and took a deep breath. Then he told Drury everything about Nell Springley, up to and including his decision to maintain the ruse that she was Lady Eleanor for the time being.

Drury would understand that. He and Juliette had pretended to be cousins so they could stay in the earl's town house not so very long ago, and Juliette had pretended that her maid had stolen her baggage and absconded, which was where Bromwell got the idea for the excuse they'd given his father.

Bromwell decided to leave out the full extent of his intimacy with Nell, for that could have no bearing on Drury's opinion of her legal predicament.

"What will the law say?" Bromwell asked when he was finished. "Could she be arrested and brought to trial for theft?"

The barrister nodded. "Unfortunately, yes. Her employer could bring charges—although he would have to prove them. However, under the circumstances, Miss Springley could also accuse him of attempted rape. It could be that the possibility of such a charge and ensuing scandal would be sufficient motive for Sturmpole to keep silent—or he may think the jury will take his word over Miss Springley's. In that case, he would likely accuse her of lying to cover up the theft."

Drury frowned ever so slightly. "It would have been better if Miss Springley had gone straight to the local magistrate after escaping Sturmpole's house."

Bromwell couldn't disagree, but he spoke in her defence regardless. "I think she wanted to put as much distance between herself and Sturmpole as she could and as quickly as she could."

Drury steepled his crooked fingers. "As understandable as that may be, it does make things more difficult. However, if Sturmpole was in arrears for her wages, he is hardly in a position to complain if she took a comparable sum. As such, it becomes a matter more for a solicitor than a barrister.

"Perhaps a letter from James St. Claire pointing that out and threatening him with a criminal prosecution for his attack and the confinement of Miss Springley will be enough to keep Sturmpole from pursuing the matter further."

"What if that doesn't work?" Bromwell asked. "What if Sturmpole wants her arrested?"

"If neither Jamie nor I can make him see why he should let the matter drop," Drury said, "he'll still have to find her. In the meantime, I'll have my men see what else they can find out about Sturmpole. He's likely the sort who delights in preying upon his servants, and if so, he will have done so before. And he should be in jail."

"As much as I find capital punishment barbaric, I believe that is one man I'd like to see hanged," Bromwell muttered as he got to his feet and stared, unseeing, out the window.

What he did not say, but felt, was that he might even have been able to put the noose around the scoundrel's neck himself. Never in his life had he been more enraged than when Miss Springley had told him what had happened to her.

And if the man had succeeded in his disgusting assault, the bite of a *Phoneutria nigriventer* would have been too easy a death for him.

"If Miss Springley goes with you when you sail, that will give me more time to find evidence against him," Drury remarked.

Bromwell started as if he'd been hit by a blow dart, then wheeled around to face his friend. "That is quite impossible."

Although the rest of him remained motionless, Drury's

expression flickered with surprise for the briefest of moments. "Why?"

"First, because my voyage is a scientific expedition, not a pleasure cruise," Bromwell retorted as he approached the massive desk. "Second, the accommodations aboard ship are primitive at best. Third, it would be most improper. No unmarried woman would dare risk her reputation in such a manner—nor should she."

"Forgive me for leaping to conclusions," Drury said, his eyes, like the rest of his face, inscrutable. "I was under the impression that you cared a great deal for her. Or do you intend to make her wait for your return for the wedding to take place?"

Bromwell stared at his friend as if he'd said the world was flat and he could prove it. His agitation as great as it had ever been in his parents' presence, he splayed his hands on Drury's desk and spoke firmly and decisively. "Gad, Drury, now that you've fallen in love and married, do you think everybody else is teetering on the brink? I have no intention of proposing marriage to Miss Springley—or anyone—before I sail. I would never ask a woman to wait for me, not even with the hope of marriage at my return."

Not even if it broke her heart. Better that than be the death of her.

He pushed himself away from the desk and walked to the window, trying to regain his self-control before he faced his friend again. "How many times must I say I won't marry before I sail and I won't ask a woman to wait for me before people believe me? Why can't anyone understand that it could be years before I return and there's always a chance I never will? It wouldn't be kind or fair to ask a woman to wait for me."

Drury leaned back in his chair, calmly regarding his indignant, dismayed friend. "You know, Buggy, I don't think I've ever seen you so upset."

"Because despite my excellent reasons for not marrying or proposing before I sail, everybody seems to think I should marry Miss Springley, preferably the sooner the better!"

"Everybody?"

"My parents are very keen—but then," he noted, "they don't know who she really is."

His father would surely rescind his offer if he did, and their newfound rapprochement would likely be destroyed, as well.

"So tell them."

Bromwell made no effort to hide his disdain for that ludicrous notion. "I can easily imagine my father's response. It would *not* be favorable."

"You've never let his disapproval dissuade you before."

"This is different."

"How?"

Bromwell realized he had no choice. As distressing as it was, he would have to tell Drury.

He slumped into the chair. "Because Miss Springley has already given me to understand that she would not be amenable to marriage to me."

Drury again raised an inquiring brow. "Is that all?"

Chapter Fourteen

For centuries, the spider has been the subject of fear and misunderstanding. Even one of their earliest admirers, the Reverend Topsel, in his History of Four-footed Beasts and Serpents, *considered them born of some sort of seeds arising from filth and decay, simply because they may be found in even the newest of houses, apparently neglecting to take into account that there will be a lapse of time between the framing of a structure and the final white-washing of walls.*

— from *The Spider's Web,* by Lord Bromwell

"All?" Bromwell repeated, dumbfounded. "Is that not enough? If she doesn't want to marry me, there's the end of it."

"For a man who can be stubbornly determined," Drury calmly replied, "I'm surprised you're giving up so easily. You didn't give up planning your first expedition when your father refused to fund it, did you? Or when the next five wealthy men laughed in your face? Yet you're willing to reject—"

"You aren't listening," Bromwell interrupted as he got to his feet again. *"She doesn't want me."*

Drury gave him a remarkably sympathetic smile. "I fear we men are not always the best interpreters of the feelings of women. You may recall my own road to domestic bliss was hardly a smooth one."

Yes, Bromwell did know that.

How easy it had seemed to solve all his friends' troubles when he'd been a dispassionate observer of their romantic dilemmas: Edmond and Diana Westover were two of a kind and had only to be made to see it; Brix had loved Fanny for years and only had to fear losing her to realize it; Drury had been attracted to Juliette from the day she saved his life with a basket of potatoes, even if he'd tried to deny it because she was French.

Now Bromwell knew better. When it came to affairs of the heart, things were not necessarily simple.

"Whatever I feel for Miss Springley," he said, "and I do not call it love, my road does not include marriage before I sail. I would never ask a woman to marry me, then wait patiently ashore for years, like Penelope pining for Odysseus, just as I'd never expect a woman to wait for me to return and then marry. It wouldn't be fair to her. And Miss Springley agrees with me."

"So you have discussed marriage with her?"

"I had to," he admitted. "My parents left me little choice. My father made her a most outrageous offer dependent upon marrying me. She refused, but it meant I found out how she felt.

"Besides, you know what this voyage means to me," he continued wearily. "How I've worked and planned and sought the necessary funds. I can't give it up now."

That, too, sounded simple—and it had been, until he'd met Nell Springley.

"I suppose not," Drury agreed, "especially now that Charlie will be able to captain your vessel. I had a letter from him today. He wrote to you at Granshire Hall, I expect, to tell you the news. He's resigned his commission and hopes to sail with you, whether as captain, or your assistant, or a bosun's mate or even a cabin boy."

Bromwell's dismay momentarily fled in the face of this good and welcome news. "That's marvelous! I was wondering whom I could get to captain the ship and now I have the perfect man! If only I could get the rest of the money as easily!"

"Your father still won't help?"

Bromwell flushed. "Miss Springley wasn't the only one he tried to bribe into marriage. He offered to fund the whole expedition if I married her before I sailed—although I'm sure he'd feel quite differently if he knew the truth about her. But there are others I can still solicit. However, that can wait for a little while. I'd rather consult with Jamie St. Claire immediately."

"Very well," Drury said as he rose and strode to the door. "We'll both go to his office, and then we can visit some other associates who inhabit the areas around Fleet Street. They can find out everything we need to know about the lascivious Lord Sturmpole."

"Good God, is that you, Titus?" the Earl of Granshire bellowed across the Pump Room in Bath.

Several people in the large room illuminated by tall windows turned. Curious whispers began as the nobleman headed toward the water dispenser and the tall, beefy, well-dressed, weak-chinned fellow leaning against the bar. The man addressed thus smiled, put down the cup of supposedly curative water, and straightened as the earl reached him and vigorously shook his hand.

"Titus, you old stick, why didn't you write and tell me you were coming to Bath?" the earl demanded. "It's been…what? Ten years since you last set foot here? How is your wife? Has she come to take the waters, too?"

"Alas, my wife is still too unwell to leave Staynesborough," Lord Sturmpole replied, straightening his waistcoat that was a rather bilious green.

"What brings you to Bath, then? You look healthy as a horse."

"A little matter of business," Sturmpole replied. "How is your charming wife? And your illustrious son? I congratulate you on his great success."

"Thank you," the earl replied. "The boy's done very well for himself, although I don't deny I would have preferred he chose another field in which to distinguish himself. But long gone are the days children heeded their parents, eh?"

"Indeed," Sturmpole agreed. "I fear too many young people today don't respect their elders, or their betters."

"Or do their duty," Lord Granshire charged. "In *our* day, a nobleman's son took his duties seriously. Married, had an heir, looked after the estate, respected his parents. Now they either indulge in gaming or wenching, or wander around the world discovering things nobody else much cares about."

As Lord Sturmpole chuckled and nodded his agreement, the earl seemed to mentally shake himself. "Of course, my son has our unqualified support, and his book was a great success, as is he. We're very proud of him, very proud. How long are you in Bath, Titus? My hunt ball is in a fortnight, and you would be welcome to attend."

"I had intended to stay in Bath for several days, so I would be delighted, if it's not too much trouble."

"Oh, no trouble at all! Where are you staying?"

"The Fox and Hound."

"Ah, yes, the good old Fox and Hound. Remember that maid—what was her name? With the large breasts?"

"Bessie."

"Ah, yes. Dead now, I think."

"In some sort of accident, I believe," Sturmpole concurred.

The earl slid his companion a sly smile. "Very friendly girl, poor Bessie was."

"For the right price. I gather your son has had a few adventures of that sort on his travels."

The earl flushed and looked around to see if anybody was listening, although whether he wanted them to be or not was open to conjecture. "Apparently. You've heard about his tattoo? It's a badge of prowess, although he doesn't say so."

"It's no wonder, perhaps, that he's not yet married," Lord Sturmpole replied.

"He's not married because he insists on going on another expedition first. But I'm not without hope," the earl added with a wink.

"Oh? Is there a young lady who's caught his eye?"

"Come to the ball and see for yourself. It only remains for me to get my son to see sense and propose. After all, he's had one expedition—what does he need another for, especially when he's got a pretty young lady from a most illustrious family who seems amenable to marriage just waiting for him to ask? I won't live forever and I need an heir, by God!"

The earl lowered his voice after several people had turned to look at them, albeit with the well-mannered pretence that they were not. "I'm sure Lady Eleanor will get him up to the post better than a father could."

"Lady Eleanor?"

The earl lowered his voice even more. "Springford. Remember her father, the Duke of Wymerton? Horrid bore even at ten and with a harelip, too, but his wife must be a beauty, for his daughter's quite lovely—which only goes to show how stubborn my son can be. He gets *that* from his mother. He met Lady Eleanor in a mail coach, of all places. Thank God it overturned, or he probably wouldn't even have introduced himself.

"I agree it's shocking they were in a mail coach," he said when he saw Lord Sturmpole's startled expression. "My son has some plebeian notions and she...Well, I suppose I shouldn't say any more about her family situation until matters are settled between them, but you remember her father? The fellow always was a dictator, telling us all what to do and making up ridiculous rules when he was prefect."

"Will Lady Eleanor be at your ball?"

"Yes. She's staying at Granshire Hall."

Lord Sturmpole drew his lips back in what was supposed to be a smile. "Excellent! I should very much like to meet her and hear how her father is these days."

Bromwell trotted up the steps to his father's town house. A few hours ago, he had read his paper about the *Phoneutria nigriventer* to the gentlemen of the Linnean Society. As always, they had listened with interest, and yet he had felt no excitement or pleasure in detailing the attributes of that dangerous arachnid. He hadn't experienced the usual delight, that spark of fascination, that desire to explain and illuminate.

It was as if he'd been waiting for Christmas, only to discover it had been indefinitely postponed.

He could guess why.

Despite Drury's offer of assistance and his belief that Miss Springley's difficulties with Lord Sturmpole could be resolved without too much trouble, he couldn't stop thinking about her. Memories of their time together, her face, her kiss, the feel of her in his arms, lingered on the edges of his mind when he was awake, and more than lingered when he was asleep.

During the last week, he'd had the same recurring dream, of Miss Springley dancing the *hura,* the sensual, erotic dance exclusive to the women of Tahiti, her hips swinging, her arms moving in graceful, wavelike motions, her breasts full and round and perfect above a flat stomach, her legs long and lithe.

And she'd been naked, save for a bridal veil and pantelettes.

He'd been thinking time and distance would make such thoughts and dreams recede. Unfortunately, he was forced to conclude that the old adage about distance making the heart grow fonder had some basis in fact.

"Thank you, Millstone," he said as the butler opened the door for him.

"You have a visitor, my lord, awaiting your return in the drawing room," the butler gravely replied as Bromwell handed him his hat, which was very like the one he'd been wearing in the mail coach that had wound up squashed flat beneath him, killing the spider. How surprised Miss Springley had looked when he told her where he'd put it! As if he'd announced he'd eaten it.

He brought his attention back to Millstone and the unexpected visitor. Perhaps it was someone he'd asked to sponsor the expedition, come in person to reply, and if so, that was a hopeful sign. "Who is it?"

Before Millstone answered, Drury appeared on the threshold.

One look, and Bromwell's heart beat faster, and not with joy. They were supposed to meet with Jamie St. Claire tomorrow. This early advent, and Drury's grim visage, probably didn't herald good news.

Drury, however, was his usual composed self as he addressed the butler. "Millstone, please tell the cook I'll be staying for dinner, if his lordship doesn't mind."

Bromwell was too anxious to find out why Drury was there to do more than nod his acquiescence before he grabbed Drury's arm and pulled him into the drawing room.

"There's no need to panic," Drury said before closing the door of the well-appointed room.

Lord Granshire rarely came there, but the earl was not one to live in anything less than the style and luxury his wealth afforded.

"I'm not panicking," Bromwell replied, although if he wasn't, he was very close to it. "What's happened? Miss Springley…?"

"Is safe in Granshire Hall, as far as I know."

Bromwell's relief was intense, but short-lived, as he frowned. "Juliette's not…?"

"She's fine."

"Is it Charlie, then, or Brix or Edmond?"

"No, all our friends and their families are fine," Drury assured him. "It's just that there have been some…developments. Tell me, Buggy, how much do you know about Miss Springley's family?"

Bromwell's brows drew together at the unexpected query. "As far as I know, she has none, or she would have sought their help," he replied. "She never spoke of brothers or sisters, her parents are dead and—"

"I think you'd better sit down, Buggy."

Bromwell was too taken aback by his friend's suggestion to heed it. "What? She has family after all?"

"Yes," Drury confirmed, growing grimmer. "Sit down, Buggy."

This time, the viscount obeyed, being too stunned to disobey. "Where are they?"

"Her mother is dead, just as Miss Springley said. She died of gaol fever in Newgate while awaiting trial. Her father was convicted on a charge of theft and sent to Botany Bay. Records show he was alive when the ship landed, and as far as I can ascertain, he's still there, serving out his sentence."

Bromwell felt curiously light-headed, as if he was again trying to drive the mail coach, only it was going much too fast. "She said they were dead. She didn't tell me they'd been arrested and charged with a crime."

More lies, in addition to the ones she'd already told him.

"Unfortunately, the evidence is incontrovertible, and if Sturmpole finds out about her family history, it will make his case stronger and ours weaker, provided things happened the way Miss Springley said."

Bromwell put his head in his hands and tried to think clearly, dispassionately, although he felt sick. How much could he trust anything she said? "Why would she tell me about Lord Sturmpole at all if she were guilty? She could have kept pretending she was Lady Eleanor. I didn't doubt her story, and neither did anyone else at Granshire Hall."

"That puzzles me, too," Drury admitted. "I can think of only one possible explanation. She confessed the truth—or part of it—because she didn't want to deceive you anymore and she truly felt justified in robbing Lord Sturmpole. However, if you knew about her parents' crime, you would be less likely to believe her version of events—and rightly so."

Bromwell got to his feet, too agitated to sit. "I should go home. I have to find out the truth."

"I thought you might feel that way," Drury said. "I've sent word to Juliette to be ready to leave first thing in the morning." He put his hand on his friend's shoulder and regarded him with sympathy. "Do nothing hasty, Buggy. Wait until we're sure we have all the facts."

Chapter Fifteen

There appears to be two primary responses to danger among all creatures—the urge to run or the resolve to stand and fight. I would say the first is the most natural, provided there is the opportunity to flee. The second impulse can be extremely strong among mothers, however, if they have offspring to protect.

Is this urge to save their children at all costs merely instinct, or is it love?

—from *The Spider's Web,* by Lord Bromwell

Nell smiled at Billings as he and Brutus walked beside her through the woods towards Lord Bromwell's laboratory. The countess was napping, and the day was fine, if cool, making Nell yearn for the fresh air and freedom of the forest. It was by pleasant coincidence that she met Billings and Brutus shortly after she entered the dim confines of the trees, or so he'd implied, although she seemed to encounter him every time she left the formal gardens to walk in the woods.

She enjoyed his company, especially when he told her some of Lord Bromwell's boyhood adventures, and she suspected he liked telling the tales as much as she liked to hear them.

Today was no different, for they hadn't gone very far before he said, "Did you know young Bromwell taught himself to swim?"

"No," she replied, although it seemed logical to assume he possessed that ability, or he might have gone down with his ship.

"Well, he did, when he about ten years old and home for the summer. He was sure his mother wouldn't want him to try, so he didn't tell anybody his plan. Then one day, I'm walking toward the pond and I hear this splashing. Odd sound it was, I thought, so I went to see if there was a wounded duck or sommat like that in the water.

"Instead, I seen him in the pond, his head bobbing along, as he's going from one side t'other.

"Well, my lady, you could have blown me down with a fa...feather," he amended. "And then I run over to where he'd end up.

"'What the devil are you doing?' I asked him. He climbs out of the pond buck naked, smiling like he's just found a pot of gold and says, 'Swimming.'

"'Where'd you learn to do that?' says I. 'School?'

"'No, Billings,' he says pulling on his trousers, 'I watched the frogs. It's quite simple, really.'

"Ain't he a wonder?" Billings concluded with that shy yet proud smile that often came to his face when he spoke of the viscount.

"I suppose his parents never found out about that?" Nell asked.

"Lord no! Although he told the countess he could swim before he sailed."

"His parents probably thought, as you did, that he was taught at school."

Billings sniffed. "If you ask me, he didn't learn anything useful there, just Latin and Greek—and a lot o' good that done 'im during his voyage."

"In his book he gives you credit for many of the practical skills that helped them after the shipwreck," Nell noted, shivering as she contemplated what might have happened if Lord Bromwell hadn't had such a friend in his childhood.

"Aye, he did," Billings said, blushing like a bashful girl at her first ball, "but he would have managed regardless. I never knew a boy so clever and at home in the woods, even if he is a viscount."

When they reached a fork in the path, one way leading to the laboratory, the other off between the shading beeches, ashes and oaks, Billings tugged his forelock. "Well, I'd best be getting over to the pasture. Set some traps there the other day, or rabbits'd be eating the earl's flowers. G'day, my lady."

"Good day, Billings," she replied as the man walked away, the dog trotting beside him.

The more she heard of the viscount, Nell reflected as she continued toward the laboratory, the more there was to admire. To be sure, he wasn't perfect—he could be stubborn and perhaps too preoccupied with spiders—but on the whole, he was one of the finest, bravest, kindest men she'd ever met.

She reached the stone building and, as she entered, thought again that it really should have a lock of some description. Rumors and the fear of large and poisonous spiders would be some deterrent and there wasn't anything of value to anyone but a naturalist or scholar within, but she would feel terrible if anything happened to his collection and he would surely feel worse.

Once inside, she strolled along the shelves, studying the jars and their contents. To be sure, she would hate to come upon some of those preserved specimens alive, but they were becoming like familiar faces and she no longer felt abhorrence when she looked at them. Indeed, she'd taken to studying the various living spiders in the building, noting when there was a new web and, as Lord Bromwell had done in his youth, marvelling at the delicate structures. How was it that they didn't become entangled themselves? And how did they manage to make the threads so evenly spaced?

She paused near the end of the shelves and for the first time noticed something behind two of the jars. Sliding the jars out of the way, she realized it was a dart or tiny, pointed arrow with feathers at one end. She put out her hand to bring it closer—

"Don't touch that!"

She whirled around at Lord Bromwell's command, nearly knocking one of the jars from the shelf. "You're back!"

He strode into the laboratory, looking like a vengeful god. "As you can see. What are you doing here?"

Why had he returned early? Why was he looking at her like that? Why was he speaking so harshly? "I sometimes come here to be alone and look at your collection."

She clasped her hands as her anxious gaze searched his face. "Has something happened, my lord? We weren't expecting you to return so soon."

She thought of his mother, with whom he might have already spoken, and an explanation for his altered behavior came to her. "Your mother told you, didn't she?"

"Told me what?" he replied with a frown.

He was going to find out sooner or later, so there was no reason not to tell him. "Your mother's met the real

Lady Eleanor. She knew I was an impostor from the start and thought you were lying because I'm your mistress."

His eyes flared with surprise, although it was quickly gone, replaced by an analytical expression devoid of emotion, as if she were one of his specimens. "Why didn't she tell me, or my father?"

"She thought you already knew and that we were both hiding the truth from them so that I could stay at Granshire Hall. I told her the truth, about what had happened with Lord Sturmpole, and that I was most certainly not your mistress."

In the stern line of his lips she saw Lord Bromwell's iron will, the same force that had kept him on his chosen path despite those who tried to stop him. What brought that to the fore when he looked at her now? "Since she already knew I wasn't Lady Eleanor, I thought it best to be honest."

Instead of relaxing, his expression grew even more stern and judgmental. "Tell only what is necessary when it's necessary, is that your theory? When were you planning to be completely honest with me?"

"I have been!" she protested.

Except on one point, her conscience chided—the depth and extent of her feelings for him.

"No, you have not."

She stared at him, aghast. What did he think she had kept back? "I told you everything that happened with Lord Sturmpole, exactly as it happened."

"I don't refer to the events with Lord Sturmpole, although what I've learned may have a bearing on that, as well," he said. He nodded at the sofa, addressing her as if he were her employer inquiring about her qualifications. "Please sit down."

"I prefer to stand," she said, straightening her shoulders as she faced him squarely. "I don't know what you've been told, my lord, but I *have* been completely honest with you."

"Everything you've told me about yourself and your history is true?"

"Yes!" she insisted. "I swear it!"

"Including what you said about your parents? That they died of a fever when you were at school?"

"Yes!" Was that the trouble? "I also told you my father gambled and died penniless. Did you learn something of his debts or his creditors?"

A horrible notion came to her. "Was Lord Sturmpole one of his creditors? Is that why he thought he could—?"

Lord Bromwell immediately shook his head. "No…at least, I don't think so." He reached into his jacket pocket and pulled out some papers. "Drury's men—and they are very good at ferreting out information that can be relied upon to be accurate—have discovered certain information regarding your parents that differs from that you've told me."

She sat heavily on the bench beside his worktable. "What information?"

"It is true that your mother died of fever." His manner softened slightly. "Gaol fever, in Newgate Prison."

"Prison?" she gasped. "What was she doing in prison?"

His visage relaxed even more, becoming less angry and more sympathetic. "She was facing the same charges of theft as your father, who is apparently alive and serving out his sentence in Botany Bay."

As Nell stared at him, too stunned to speak, not willing to believe she'd heard aright, he handed her the papers. "These are copies of the court record of his trial, conviction and sentence, the manifest of the ship he sailed on and a list of the convicts who survived the voyage."

As she looked down at the documents, the words on the pages swam before her eyes. Blinking, she looked up at Lord Bromwell. The spiders in their jars behind him began to shift and waver. Then the sheets of paper fell from her lap and spilled onto the floor, and everything around her went black.

Nell slowly became aware of a cool, damp cloth grazing her cheeks and forehead. Then she felt lips where the cloth had been, while Lord Bromwell's deep voice softly called her name and said he was sorry.

She opened her eyes and discovered she wasn't dreaming. Covered by a blanket, she was lying on the sofa in his laboratory, and he was seated beside her. A basin of water was on a low stool beside him.

"I'm so sorry. I shouldn't have blindly assumed you'd lied. I should have allowed for the possibility that you had told me what you believed to be true," he said, lifting the cool, damp cloth from her forehead.

About her parents. Who were not both dead, although she'd been told that they were.

"Are you certain that what you've told me is the truth?" she whispered, grasping his hand as if she'd been washed overboard and he was the lifeline.

Lord Bromwell nodded his head. "Drury's sources are always accurate and there is documentation. According to what was discovered, it's possible your mother might have been found innocent, but the evidence against your father was damning. Perhaps that's why he preferred to let you think he was dead."

"Perhaps," she murmured, wondering if that was true.

And no wonder Lord Bromwell had looked at her as he had when he'd appeared at the laboratory that day, believing that she'd lied. "Did he steal because of his debts?"

"That seems the logical explanation. Who told you he was dead?"

"I got a letter from a vicar in Bristol—or at least someone who claimed to be a vicar," she amended. How could she believe anyone or anything when it came to her parents now? "He said both my parents died of a contagious fever so they were buried right away. He regretted there was no money for a gravestone. I intended to purchase one after I'd earned the money from Lord Sturmpole, so I put off going there.

"I had no reason to believe what he wrote wasn't true. I didn't know my parents were even suspected of a crime, let alone arrested."

"Do you remember the vicar's name?"

"Smith."

Lord Bromwell frowned. "A common name, but we should be able to find out if there was a vicar by that name in Bristol at that time. It could be, however, that your father wrote the letter or had a friend do it."

To spare her pain and shame. "That could be," she allowed, remembering her jovial father and pretty mother.

Had they known arrest was imminent when they'd sent her off to school?

"I had no reason not to believe the letter," she said softly. "My mother, who had been a faithful correspondent, never wrote to me after I received it. Neither of them ever contacted me at all. If they had, I would have gone to them, no matter what they'd done. I would have tried to see them. To think of my mother dying in that awful place—"

She turned away to face the back of the sofa, choking back a sob.

"Cry if you like, Miss Springley," he said gently. "I certainly won't hold it against you. You've had a terrible shock, and my manner of telling you was inexcusably bad."

She turned back, wiping her eyes with the back of her hand. "I don't think it would have mattered how you told me. And I'm grateful to know my father is alive, however I heard it. If not for you and your friend, I might never have known."

"He's over half finished his sentence," Lord Bromwell noted. "He has only about three years left, and then he can return."

As if he were coming back from the dead.

How would her father find her if she was living under another assumed name? How could she find *him* if she wanted to seek him out in three years' time?

Lord Bromwell rose, taking the basin to the table. "So, my mother realized from the start you weren't Lady Eleanor," he said, clearly determined to talk of something else, "and she truly believed I would bring my lover home to meet my parents under an assumed name?"

She must put her father's possible return out of her mind for now and concentrate on the present situation. "Because she *hoped* I was your mistress and would have the power to persuade you to stay in England."

His eyes widened, and as if even his hair was surprised, that lock tumbled over his forehead again. "What did you say to that?"

"That I was not, and even if I thought I could convince you to stay in England, which I surely couldn't, I wouldn't."

"I see," he replied as he reached for the kettle and shook

it to see if there was water within, his expression as grave as if he were making medicine. "How did she respond?"

"She asked me to stay here as her companion. I fear your father is not the most comforting of men."

"No," he agreed as he added more water to the kettle from the pitcher on the sideboard, "and certainly not where I'm concerned."

He spoke calmly, matter-of-factly, telling her—if she had any doubt—just how little power she had over him, regardless of any tender feelings he might have for her.

Which was just as well. "I won't be able to stay now, of course."

He glanced at her before he put the kettle on the crane and pushed it over the fire he must have kindled. "Why?"

"My father is a convicted felon, and I'm in danger of being arrested, too," she reminded him.

"I don't think you need fear for your own fate. Drury and his solicitor friend are quite optimistic about your circumstances. They think Sturmpole can be persuaded to forgo any charges against you to avoid exposure of his own crimes. They're not going to leave it at that, though. They both believe we should be able to find other employees who've suffered the same experience. We're all determined to put a stop to the fellow."

Although she felt some relief, she couldn't be happy. She doubted she could ever be truly happy again. "I still think it would be better if I leave Granshire Hall as soon as possible, to spare you any difficulties that might ensue from your involvement with me."

"If that is what you'd prefer."

Prefer? She had no other choice. "I'm sure your mother can find another, more suitable companion."

"Perhaps," he murmured as the kettle began to whistle. "Where will you go?"

Somewhere. Anywhere. It didn't matter because he would not be there. "Ireland, perhaps. Or America."

"So far?"

"This from a man who plans to sail around the world again?" she asked, trying to hide her anguish even as she went toward him.

"I suppose it's different when you're the one sailing," he said, turning toward her as if they were connected by a strong, if slender, thread.

Their gazes met and held until he put up his hand as if to keep her away.

"I've been planning this expedition for months," he said, desperation in his voice, despair and determination warring in his eyes, "ever since I returned, getting the best crew and raising the funds to buy the ship. I've got the ship and the men I want, and it's only a matter of paying for provisions and setting sail. I've worked and planned for too long to abandon my expedition now. It's not just about the spiders. We could find new plants that will provide medicines and new foods that can help feed the starving. I *want* to go, Nell. I *need* to go."

"I know," she said softly. "That's why I would never hold you back, no matter how much I wished I could. Otherwise, you would surely come to hate me."

"*Hate* you?" He shook his head. "I could never hate you."

"Oh, yes, you could," she countered, putting her hands on his arms and gripping them tightly, feeling the strength of him, the power, the pure masculinity beneath the fine fabrics and expertly tailored clothes. "If you believed I'd kept you from your work, you'd eventually come to resent it, and me. As other men made discoveries, you would wonder what you might have found, if not for me. And who can say what achievements and discoveries my selfishness would have prevented? I won't have that on my conscience, not for all the world."

Or even your love.

She closed her eyes as he reached up to caress her cheek, his touch sending sparks of desire, slivers of need, along her limbs.

"You understand me better than anyone, Nell Springley. Better even than myself. Thank you for letting me go, because of all the women in the world, you are the only one who could have held me here."

His words broke her heart and filled her with pain. To know that she had that power, and that to use it would destroy him.

Yet they were together here, now. Alone. In this paradise of his.

She would make it hers, if only for a little while. She would not think of the future, or the world beyond the door. She would be with him here, now, as she yearned to be.

"Until you leave, until you sail, until then, let me be with you. Let me be your lover," she pleaded softly yet intensely, for she had a will of iron, too, and even though he must and should leave her, she would take what joy she could while she could, if he would agree.

He shook his head. "As much as I would like that, as much as I wish it, that would make our parting all the more difficult. And I would not want to leave you with child."

She wasn't willing to give up. Not yet. "The parting will be difficult whether we make love or not. As for children… There are ways to prevent that, are there not?"

"Theoretically," he replied roughly, his breathing harsh and heavy, as if he fought against an unseen opponent. "I cannot speak to their effectiveness personally."

"I'll take that risk, and if those methods fail, couldn't I go to your friends for help?"

Passion, desire, hope flared in his blue-gray eyes. "Yes—but as a gentleman, I should still say no."

In spite of his words, he didn't move, and she needed no more assurance than that.

"No, my lord, you should be quiet and kiss me," she murmured as she raised herself on her toes and kissed him.

Chapter Sixteen

Never have I known such unmitigated, overwhelming joy, such complete relief and happiness, as when we saw that the vessel making its way toward us. We were grateful to realize it was a British ship, but such was our condition by that time, we would have welcomed a garbage scow, French frigate, pirate ship, or even a well-made raft.

—from *The Spider's Web,* by Lord Bromwell

Bromwell was no fool. His teachers had told him he had a brilliant intellect and praised him for his ability to think clearly and rationally.

Today, rationally, clearly, the honorable thing, the best thing, would be to stop kissing Nell, to let her go and tell her to leave him. That he meant every word he'd ever said about his goals and plans for the future, and nothing she could say or do would change that.

But as always when he was with her, his rational mind was no match for his heart, or his burning desire. He was helpless to set aside his emotions and concentrate on anything except Nell and the feel of her in his arms, her lips on his.

It was so right, so perfect, so good, so meant to be.

Of all the women he had ever met, she was perfect for him. She understood his goals, his needs, his wants. She didn't think him eccentric or a fool because he like spiders and wanted to learn more about them. She was brave, independent, loyal, loving and strong…all the things he would want in a wife.

But most important of all, she understood why he wouldn't marry until he'd been on his expedition. She would give him the freedom to be about the work that meant so much to him.

Even so, a part of him ached to think she could let him go, even as the other part—that rational, scientific part—felt a vast and grateful relief that she would.

Yet whatever the future held, she was here now, kissing him with all the passion any man could ever hope for, and he discovered he was powerless to refuse what she so willingly offered.

His hands slid up her back, holding her closer, the sensation of her breasts against him exciting and arousing. He had seen women unclothed and doing the most heart-stoppingly sensual dances any man had ever witnessed. He had been there to see the feet-pounding, hip-swinging motions, the thrust of hips and breasts. He had been aroused and enticed, but never had he been so passionately excited, so full of desire and yearning and need, as he was now.

Surrendering to that need, and hers, he swept her into his arms and laid her on the sofa. Joining her, he covered her body with his, his hands and mouth seeking, tasting, stroking, caressing. She shoved at his jacket and he shrugged it off. She tore off his cravat as she arched, her breasts against him, her slender throat exposed to his eager, anxious lips and tongue.

Her fingers went to his shirt. After she got his buttons undone, he ripped it from his body. Then her hands were on his naked skin, while he kissed and licked the rounded tops of her breasts above her bodice.

She raised her knees, her skirts bunching about her hips, and he stroked her leg as he propped himself on his elbow and ran his hand through her hair while he kissed her ear, her cheek, her chin.

His erection strained against his trousers, and he wanted nothing more than to tear them off, too, and make love to her as if they were two wild animals in heat.

Except that they were not.

Did she not deserve better than some hasty rutting on the worn sofa of his lab? And what if he did get her with child before he left England? That was, after all, the natural outcome of what they were about to do, the reality rising up like a spectre to haunt him and douse his desire.

With a ragged sigh, he pulled back and got to his feet. "I won't do this, Nell," he said hoarsely, reaching for his shirt. "It isn't right, or fair to you."

She moved to sit up as he put on his shirt, then splayed her hands on his heaving chest. "You're an honorable man, my lord," she said, her voice low and husky. "I'm well aware of the consequences, and I accept them."

She inched forward on the sofa and ran her palms lightly over his nipples before moving toward the buttons of his trousers. "If you won't make love with me, we can still do…things. I've read your book."

His book? For a moment, he could scarcely remember writing one.

"The practices of some of the natives in the islands sounded very intriguing," she said as she finished undoing the buttons. He jumped when she slipped her hand inside. "Although you were not at all specific."

He closed his eyes as her hand encircled him. He knew precisely what passages she was referring to, the memories of what had happened on certain moonlit nights leaping vividly into his mind.

Only to disappear the moment Nell slipped from the sofa to her knees and took him into her mouth.

He groaned softly, cupping the back of her head, as she sucked and licked him, her tongue swirling around the tip until he thought he would burst. He'd never expected… dreamed….

All too soon, she stopped. He opened his eyes, to see her looking up at him with a shy smile. If she wanted to stop, he wouldn't…

And then her hand was around him, moving up and down along his shaft, grazing lightly. Faster and faster she stroked, the urge within him building, building and building until he was over the edge.

Gasping, jerking, he spilled his seed.

"I must have done that right," she said softly, a hint of triumph in her voice, as well as the heat of desire.

"Perfect," he murmured, blushing like a naughty schoolboy as he adjusted his trousers and did up the buttons, although his hands seemed inordinately clumsy. "I had no idea I'd been so…descriptive."

"You weren't. I guessed," Nell said, smiling, flushed with happiness and satisfaction. She had never even imagined doing anything like that, but it had seemed a natural way to give him pleasure, and since she had, she could only be pleased herself.

She rose as he reached into his trouser pocket and handed her his handkerchief.

"You are, without doubt, the most incredible woman in the world—and you have to stop calling me my lord. Especially after…after *this*. My name's Justinian, although that's quite a mouth…"

He blushed and began again, looking like the bashful schoolboy he must have been as he put on his shirt. "My father thought such a name impressive, especially if I became a politician. My friends call me Buggy. They didn't appreciate the difference between spiders and insects when they gave it to me."

She brushed that stray lock of hair off his forehead. "That sounds like something boys would call a schoolmate, but I don't think I could call you that. You're very much a man to me."

"Since you put it that way, I don't think I'd like you to call me that, either. I suppose my name will have to do and I'm suddenly reconciled to it," he said, taking her in his arms and pressing a kiss upon her soft lips. "But I can't continue to call you Miss Springley. Will 'my darling' do?"

"*My* friends call me Nell."

He sat on the sofa and drew her down onto his lap. "Well, Nell, this is familiar. I seem to recall a young lady in precisely this position not so long ago, resulting in a most interesting experience."

She loved it when he spoke with such apparent seriousness and answered him with the same grave tone. "It wouldn't surprise me in the least to discover that you deliberately put that spider in the coach in a crude attempt to seduce unsuspecting young women."

"If I'd had an inkling of your reaction, I might have, although upon further consideration, it occurs to me that there is no other woman in England I would care to have sitting on my lap."

"So you say now."

The merriment disappeared from his eyes. "So I truly believe, with all my heart."

She toyed with one of the buttons on his shirt, not meeting his steadfast gaze. "I'm flattered."

"It's the truth, and now, since I am a firm believer in fair play, I do believe we have something more to do."

"Such as, my lord?"

"You were going to call me Justinian," he reminded her as his hand began a slow glide up her arm.

"Such as, Justinian?"

"Such as…this," he replied, brushing his lips across hers lightly, as he had that first time. "And this." His lips continued to slide over her mouth.

"And this, too," he murmured as his hand grazed her bodice.

She wound her arms about his neck. "You are teasing me, my lord."

"Justinian. And I intend to do much more than that."

"Promise?"

"Oh, yes," he replied as he shifted and moved her down onto the sofa. "Much more."

Nell's heart raced and her body warmed as if he were sending out rays of light and heat like the sun. He shifted them so that he was again above her, his hips on hers, his weight on his knees between her legs and leaning on one elbow, while his other hand explored her.

His kiss deepened, and she responded with fervent excitement, pulling him closer as her palms slid over his back, feeling the muscles bunching and moving beneath the surface of his skin as he stroked and aroused her.

His mouth moved slowly down her neck, and below, to the soft roundness of her breasts and their pebbled peaks. Regardless of her gown, he kissed her there, too, and sucked and nibbled, the sensations incredibly arousing. The pressure of his hips increased slightly as he raised himself to slip one hand into her bodice to cup her. She sighed and gasped and squirmed with a growing craving as the pad of his thumb brushed over the sensitive tip.

His mouth caught hers again, but more aggressively this time, with more need, more longing, more urgency. She responded at once, rising to meet him, running her hands along his heated flesh.

His hand went to her stockinged shin, curling around her and moving upward in an excruciatingly slow progress toward her knee. He reached the garter holding her stocking and pulled the bow until it came undone and fell away. He pushed down the fabric with a caress that made her writhe with expectation. She would never have guessed so simple a thing—a thing she did every day—could be so exciting.

When he inched backward, she began to sit up, ready to help him remove her stocking or anything else he wanted, until he whispered for her to lie back and let him satisfy her as she had satisfied him.

Panting, heart leaping with expectation, she did as he asked and when she felt him untie the drawstring of her pantelettes and lower them, she raised her hips to help, sure she knew what he was going to do. What she would let him do. What she hoped he would do.

She gasped with both surprise and the unexpected thrill of his lips grazing her inner thigh. She had never even imagined being kissed there…or *there!* Or that he would do *that* with his tongue, licking her so intimately, making forays where his fingers had before.

She clutched her skirts, bunching the fabric as she parted her legs more, giving him room, writhing with the growing tension.

And then his hand was on her breast, stroking and touching, arousing her still more.

"Make love with me," she pleaded. "I want you. Oh, please!"

He didn't answer, but in the next moment, his finger glided inside her. She was slick and hot and so ready, the tension snapped almost at once. With a low, guttural cry, she half rose as her muscles pulsed and her toes curled, carried along on waves of blissful release.

When her body relaxed and she lay back, he pressed warm, soft kisses to her neck and the curve of her shoulder.

"*That* was not in your book," she said, wrapping a lock of his hair around her finger.

"Because I didn't learn that on my voyage," he replied as he moved back and got to his feet.

Some of her happiness dissipated, although of course she couldn't expect him to be inexperienced even before he sailed. He was a young, titled gentleman; he would have had plenty of opportunity to learn about women.

"Not every book I've read has been a classic or scientific one," he said as she pulled up her stocking and tied her garter. "You would be shocked if you knew what sort of books one can find in the less reputable bookstores, many of which are read by men who have no compunction about condemning other people for their licentious ways.

"Nor have I actually done that before," he admitted. "That was another experiment and I believe I can consider it a success."

"Very much so," she replied, wondering what else had been in those books.

He began to button his shirt. "We had best get back to the hall. Drury and his wife—who returned with me—will be worried, and my mother anxious. I fear Juliette and Drury half expect you to return in tears. I confess I was rather indignant when I thought you'd lied to me about your parents."

"Another man would have been far more than indignant," she replied, rising to kiss him again. "That's another reason I'm..."

She hesitated for a fraction of a moment, afraid to use that stronger word. "Why I care for you as I do."

"Do you really mean that?" he asked, his expression as studious as if he were taking an examination.

She had to kiss him again when he looked like that, before she wrapped her arms around him and regarded him just as gravely.

"I do. And I've never been happier in my life," she said, meaning it in spite of the undercurrent of sorrow she suspected she'd feel for the rest of her life. "Whatever happens in the future, I'm happier than I've ever been, because you make me so."

"I don't understand how," he ruminated aloud, his brows furrowed. "I am not handsome, or charming. Granted, the pleasure of sexual activity is certainly important, but—"

"You *are* handsome, and charming, and kind, as well as exciting. But more than that, you treat me as your equal, even though I'm so ignorant."

He looked at her with obvious bafflement. "You may not be as well educated—although that is the fault of a society that treats female offspring as incapable of comprehending as well as any male of the species and despite ample evidence to the contrary—but you are as intelligent as anyone I've ever met, male or female, as well as brave and resourceful."

He gave her a rueful smile. "And I might as well admit everything. You don't make me feel like I'm some sort of oddity because I'm so fascinated by spiders. Although…" He put his hands loosely about her waist and smiled. "I must say I find you infinitely more interesting than spiders."

She'd never had a more thrilling compliment. "You do?"

"Indeed," he murmured, leaning down to kiss her again.

The door to the laboratory burst open.

"Bonjour!" cried a merry, well-dressed young woman in a frilly, frothy pink gown and pink velvet spencer, as well as a delightful bonnet with a wide pink ribbon and fabric roses around the brim. "Are we interrupting? Should we leave?"

At the sound of Juliette's voice, knowing Drury must not be far behind, Bromwell quickly stepped away from Nell. Meanwhile, the heat of a blush travelled up his face, as if a description of their recent activity had been tattooed on his forehead.

"Sorry for barging in, Buggy," Drury said as he entered the laboratory behind his wife, who was smiling as genially as if she'd merely intruded on a tea party. "Juliette—"

"I thought you had been chastising and interrogating the

poor girl long enough," his wife interrupted with a smile, "although I see I was quite wrong. *Bonjour,* Miss Springley. I am Juliette, the wife of Sir Douglas Drury, who has not the manners to introduce me."

The dark-haired barrister scowled, although his equally dark eyes were far from angry. "Forgive me, Miss Springley. I am Sir Douglas Drury, and this is my charming and headstrong wife, Juliette."

"He calls me headstrong because I don't obey his every command," Juliette laughingly confided, "and while I am sorry to have interrupted, it is getting late in the day and unless you want the servants to gossip, we had better go back to the hall.

"Not that I care about gossip," Juliette said, slipping her arm through Nell's. "I am quite used to it, but dear Buggy is not, and neither, I think, are you."

As Juliette steered her out the door, Nell didn't even have time to look back as they left the two friends alone.

Chapter Seventeen

And then—oh woe!
The intruder comes
And all my hopes are dashed,
My desire thwarted,
My love denied,
I am again
Alone.
    —found among Lord Bromwell's private papers

Drury turned to Bromwell the moment the women were out the door. "I'm truly sorry we barged in like that, but Juliette was so worried about what you might be saying to Miss Springley, she wouldn't listen. She's a very stubborn woman when she thinks she's right."

"And yet you love her anyway," Bromwell noted as he went to his worktable and leaned against it.

"Can't help it," Drury replied with a smile as he sat in one of the chairs near the hearth. "And I think I'm not the only man here who's in love."

Bromwell didn't reply directly to that statement as he

ran his fingertips, which had so recently skimmed Nell's warm, soft flesh, over a long scar in the tabletop made when his knife slipped as he was attempting to carve a whistle several years ago. "Miss Springley didn't know her father was alive. She truly believed he was dead."

Drury's tone was noncommittal when he replied. "And you believed her, so you couldn't be angry with her."

"You would have believed her, too, if you'd seen her," Bromwell said, crossing his arms. "It was quite obvious she was shocked, so taken aback she fainted—and it was no false swoon, I assure you.

"I've had plenty of experience with those," he added, recalling certain episodes with his mother.

"That doesn't, unfortunately, erase the fact that her father is a convicted felon and she's been impersonating Lady Eleanor Springford."

"Whatever Miss Springley did, she was still attacked and held against her will," Bromwell replied as he reached for his jacket. "Sturmpole was more guilty of a crime than she. As for impersonating Lady Eleanor, I colluded with her in that, so if she's guilty of a crime, so am I. But there's been no harm done. Nobody knows save my family, and you and Juliette."

"I fear it may not be so simple. Did I not hear your father's in Bath? Don't you think he'll mention that there's the daughter of a duke visiting his estate?"

Bromwell felt for the bench beside the table and sat heavily. "Oh, God."

That truly hadn't occurred to him—and it should have.

"I don't want to upset you, Buggy, but we should be prepared. However, since your motive wasn't criminal or malicious and neither was Miss Springley's, it could be that Lady Eleanor won't prosecute, especially if she remains in Italy."

"If Lady Eleanor does prosecute, can we count on your representation?" Bromwell asked, trying to think clearly and plan for any eventuality.

"Of course."

"Thank you."

"As for Sturmpole," Drury said, "from what we've learned of the man, I'm fairly confident he can be persuaded not to press charges, so it's not Sturmpole I'm worried about. It's you. Are you still not willing to marry Miss Springley?"

Bromwell tried to mask the pain his question caused. "She must be free when I sail in case I don't come back. I don't have to tell you, Drury, that sometimes when ships go down, it can be years before the crew is considered lost for good. I won't put her through that."

"So you will break her heart before you sail, and for her own good?"

"If you wish to put it that way, yes," Bromwell said, heading for the door. "There's no point discussing that particular subject again, Drury. I won't, and that's the end of it."

Sighing softly, Drury rose and followed him.

Nell wished she was alone, or with Justinian, as she walked back to the hall, instead of in the company of a woman she'd only just met and in such a fashion.

"You are very fortunate to have won Buggy's heart," Lady Drury remarked as she walked beside Nell. "If I had not my Drury, I am sure I would be jealous."

Nell could hardly deny that there was something of an amorous nature between herself and Lord Bromwell when she'd been discovered in his passionate embrace, but she wasn't willing to encourage any discussion of the subject, either.

"I liked him much better than Drury when I first met them," Lady Drury confessed.

That got Nell's full attention.

"Buggy was kind and polite, even though I was only a seamstress and obviously French—both of which made it quite impossible for Drury to even like me, let alone love me, or so we both thought. Our hearts, however, would not listen."

Nell knew exactly what she meant. If her head could rule her heart, she wouldn't still be here, and she certainly wouldn't ever be alone with Justinian.

"You saw my husband's hands, I'm sure."

Nell had indeed noticed her husband's gnarled, twisted fingers. "Yes."

"He was tortured when he was captured in France during the war. By my brother."

Nell came to an abrupt halt. "Your brother?" she repeated incredulously.

"*Oui,* although it pains me to confess it. After the war, Drury found my brother and killed him for what he had done, not just to him, but others, too."

Her husband had killed her own brother? "And you still married him?"

"Because I love him more than I could ever hate him, and I could understand why he did what he did. But there was a time I was sure we could never be together, until we realized we loved each other enough to overcome what threatened to keep us apart."

Nell wondered why Lady Drury was being so forthcoming to a stranger, but it hardly seemed like a question one could ask. Nor did she wish to speak of her feelings for Justinian, or tell her that her father was a convict in Australia.

"You think I am forward, to tell you these things," Lady Drury said, answering Nell's silent query as they reached the terrace. "I tell you because I know who you are and what your father did. My husband has no secrets from me. And I speak to you this way, as if we are old and dear friends, because I want Buggy to be happy. I fear you might think your father and your rank mean you are not worthy to be his wife."

Lady Drury stopped and looked Nell steadily in the eye. "Buggy is not the sort of man who toys with a woman's affections, or makes love with them for sport. If I am any judge, he loves you very much. If he asks you to be his wife and you love him, you should accept him."

Nell didn't want to hear this. She didn't want to believe Justinian loved her, not when he was going to leave her. When he must leave her.

She turned toward the house. "Thank you for your advice, my lady. I will bear it in mind if he ever asks."

And for his sake, I will refuse.

Clad in her dressing gown and nightgown, her feet in simple slippers she had knit herself, Nell stood by the window of her bedchamber in Granshire Hall.

Her thoughts were not on the view of the formal gardens below, or the beauty of the clear night sky liberally sprinkled with stars. In her mind's eye, she was seeing her mother at their final farewell, when Nell had not known it would be their last.

Had her mother guessed it might be so? At the time, she had thought her mother's strained expression and tears were evidence that she would miss her daughter and because their next meeting was likely weeks away. She had even— to her intense regret—been ashamed of her sobbing mother at the main door of the manor house that had become a school, and prouder of her father's cheery manner.

He had always been a jovial, easy-going man. Never had the cares of earning a living seemed to weigh on him as managing the household did to her mother. She had supposed that her mother was simply a more sombre, serious character. It had never occurred to her that perhaps her father ignored their troubles, while her mother could not.

Had it been his idea to find a solution through thievery, a solution that had cost her mother her life, him his freedom and bestowed the stain and shame of their crime on their daughter?

If only she could see him again, to ask him about that, or even just be with him once more.

What might have happened if her mother had lived? Might she have been found innocent? If so, her daughter might not have had to accept employment with Lady Sturmpole and thus find herself deep in a mire of her own.

And yet, Nell mused as the moon rose full and bright over the wood beyond the garden, if she had not taken employment with Lady Sturmpole and been attacked by her husband, if she had not fled, she would never have met Justinian.

That was the one good thing that had happened to her in the past six months—except that the happiness she had experienced would bring her an equal, if not greater, measure of sorrow when it was time for them to part.

But not yet. Not yet.

She lowered her gaze to the dark garden. No light shone upon the terrace. No sound disturbed the silence, save for the occasional cry of a night bird or an owl swooping down in the darkness to catch a mouse.

Now she could go to him. He might think being together here too great a risk, too likely to cause gossip and scandal. If so, she would leave him, but if not…

Her eyes were already accustomed to the dark, so she needed no candle as she cautiously opened her bedroom door and looked into the empty corridor. Moving quietly, carefully, for old floors could creak—and loudly—she closed her door and made her way to his, easing it open.

She had never been in Justinian's bedroom before. It was a large chamber suited to the heir of a great house, with a huge, curtained bed with a set of bed stairs beside it at the far end. Those curtains were open, as were the draperies and shutters over the two tall, narrow windows that faced the front of the house and the long sweeping drive— the opposite view to hers, and away from his laboratory. Wondering if that was deliberate on the part of his parents, and if he liked to be awakened by the sun, she ventured closer to the bed.

Justinian lay sprawled diagonally on his back, his naked chest visible above the satin coverlet. He had one leanly muscular arm over his chest, the other slung out to the side. The rest of his body was hidden beneath the covers.

As she tiptoed nearer, she noted how Spartan the chamber was. Apart from the bed and a table beside it holding a lamp, there was a wardrobe by the wall to the left. A pedestal table with papers and ink and quills upon it, as well as a Chippendale chair, stood near the window, and a plain washstand and dressing table were half-hidden behind a folding screen. There was no looking glass of any kind, and the dressing table was bare of anything save a brush and shaving items.

Three more steps and she was beside the bed.

How young Justinian looked when he slept, with that lock of hair falling on his forehead! How sweet and innocent and boyish. If this was the way his mother always thought of him, no wonder she was so upset that he would leave England for unknown, dangerous parts of the world.

Yet he was no innocent, naive youth. He was a virile, experienced man who was showing her what true intimacy between a man and a woman could be.

And she wanted to learn more.

Untying her robe, she let it fall open as she took another step closer.

He moved and she froze. Still asleep, he sighed, muttered something and rolled away from her, the coverlet coming with him, but leaving his back exposed.

Three thin, parallel black lines in a pattern of slightly angular concentric circles had been drawn on his back. The majority of the design was still hidden below the coverlet; nevertheless, she could see enough to guess that she was looking at his tattoo and that it was a spider's web.

She should have known.

How low did it go on his body? Was there a spider, too?

Going to the other side of the bed, she took off her robe and laid it on the foot of the bed. Hiking up her nightgown of thin white linen, she climbed onto the high bed, which dipped so much she expected him to wake.

He didn't, so she leaned toward him and slowly pulled the coverlet down, until she could see the whole tattoo. It *was* a web and in the center was a small black spider.

She reached out to trace it, but as she put her fingertip

on his skin, he immediately turned over and she found herself beneath him, with her arms over her head, her wrists held in his vicelike grip. It happened so swiftly, she didn't even have time to suck in her breath.

"Nell!" he gasped, his eyes wide and vibrantly alert.

He let go at once, but didn't move from atop her as he ran his gaze over her. "What are you…?"

He paused when he realized she was wearing only her nightgown, then spoke with measured calm, although he didn't move. "Forgive my extreme reaction. As a result of my voyage and the situations I encountered, I tend to sleep lightly. You must have been very quiet."

Her breathing quickened when passionate warmth kindled in his eyes as his gaze moved slowly down her body in what was like a leisurely caress. "Or did you come here in a state of undress to alert me to some emergency? Perchance the house is afire?"

"The house is not ablaze, although I am rather… heated," she whispered in response.

He ran his fingertip around the neckline of her nightgown. "No thieves or poachers afoot?"

"None of which I am aware," she replied, sliding her hands up his lean arms to his broad shoulders.

Feeling bold and mischievous, very aware of his body above hers, she smiled. "Perhaps I came to see your tattoo."

"Ah, and did you?"

"Yes, so I could win the bet at White's, if I were a member."

He laughed softly as he leaned down to kiss the tip of her nose. "No one will ever win that wager, because the proof would require me to expose a portion of my anatomy to those I would rather not."

She reached down to the approximate location of the tattoo.

"Perhaps you would have been wiser to have it on your arm or chest, like a seaman."

"It was all I could do to get them to stop when they did. Among the Tahitians it's a sign of adulthood for the men to have that portion of their body covered completely by a tattoo."

She tried to imagine that. "Is it painful?"

"Less painful than having to sit so far from you at supper," he murmured, gliding his mouth over hers. "And only slightly more painful than having to make polite conversation afterward, when all I really wanted to do was this…." He kissed her lips. "And this." He kissed her neck. "And this…"

His lips slid downward toward her breasts as he undid the drawstring at the neck of her nightgown. "I suppose I should suggest that your presence here is highly improper and likely to cause a scandal should we be discovered *in flagrante delicto.* However, I find I am much too pleased and delighted to protest."

"Good," she said, brushing her fingertips along the dark T of hair between his nipples and down toward his navel, where she felt the growing evidence of his arousal.

He kissed her again, with more urgent need and she responded in kind. Bending her knees, she shifted so that she could feel all of him, while his hand slid inside the neck of her nightgown to her breast. As he gently kneaded the soft weight, she reached down to bring him closer, aware that her legs were bare, and her gown bunched about her hips.

His breathing heavy, he moved slightly to the side, so that he could caress her where she was moist, and ready.

She felt him hesitate. Knew what he feared and, for a moment, thought he meant to stop.

Whatever happened, she wanted him to love her fully, completely, as she would never love another. She didn't want to wait. She wanted to be with him now.

She reached for the neck of her nightgown. The fabric was old and thin, and with her own hands she tore it, until she lay beneath him naked and willing.

Chapter Eighteen

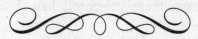

As in other cultures, the peoples of the South Seas have many rituals and beliefs about food, including the notion of tapu, or forbidden foods. For instance, bananas are forbidden to women, and the punishment, should a woman be seen eating one, is to be immediately clubbed to death.

—from *The Spider's Web,* by Lord Bromwell

Even then, Justinian hesitated as his heated gaze swept over her body.

Impatient, as determined as he could be, she seized his face between her hands and captured his mouth with fierce and hungry need. As she did, she wiggled closer and reached down, guiding him where she wanted him to go.

"Please," she pleaded, panting, her voice a harsh whisper. "Please. There are ways to prevent…aren't there? The girls at school said so. If you stop…"

"Yes, there are ways," he rasped even as he finally gave her what she craved and pushed inside. There was a pain, a moment's anguish, gone as soon as he began to thrust.

She felt the same tightening, the urgency, stronger than before. Anticipating that wonderful release, she arched against him, bare flesh to bare flesh.

His thrusts quickened and became more urgent, more powerful. The sinews in his neck grew more visible and his rough panting sounded in her ears.

Gasping encouragement or moaning softly, she wrapped her legs around him, instinctively locking her ankles to hold him close.

The sweet pressure, the glorious tension, grew. Muscles tightened. Toes curled. She clenched her teeth to keep from crying out…

And then—

And then, release, like a star shooting across the sky in the darkest part of night and she panted like an animal as her body rose of its own accord.

With an answering groan, he pulled back, head bowed, jerking as his seed spilled onto her naked stomach.

She caught her breath as he slowly sat on his haunches, bracing himself with his arms on either side of her while he drew in great gulps of air.

"My God, I've never…" He paused, then shook his head. "I've never felt anything like that."

"Because I was a virgin?" she asked, even more jealous of the other woman who had been in his arms.

He smiled and shook his head. "Because I've never cared more for a woman."

"Nor I for any man," she assured him.

She watched him as he climbed off the bed and went to fetch water in a Wedgwood basin and a towel of fine, soft linen.

"You've ruined your nightgown," he noted. "That may be difficult to explain."

"I have another just the same," she said as he returned. "Now I'm glad they're so plain. No one will be able to tell the difference. I'll hide this one beneath my other undergarments."

"I should have realized you'd have a plan," he said, sitting beside her.

He dipped the towel in the water. She held out her hand, but again he shook his head. "Let me," he said as he began to wash her stomach, and then between her thighs. "This provides more opportunity to observe your naked body— and a particularly fine naked body it is, too."

In spite of what they'd done together, she blushed as he washed her. "I feel like one of your spiders."

"You are even more lovely than an *Argiope bruennichi.*"

"Is that intended to be a compliment?"

"Oh, yes. It's a very beautiful spider."

"Then I thank you, sir."

"As I thank you."

Finished his ministrations, he turned to set the basin on the table beside the bed. "Do you know, I don't think I've ever enjoyed a visit to the ancestral acres more."

She sat up, then reluctantly rose and picked up the remnants of her nightgown.

"Are you leaving?" he asked, his brow furrowing as, still magnificently naked, he got up from the bed. "You've had your way with me so now you'll rush off?"

"I would rather stay, but if I'm found here, my lord—"

He took her in his arms and silenced her with a kiss. "There is a little time yet before that becomes a concern."

Taking her hand, he sat on the bed, then drew her down beside him. "But what is this *my lord?*"

"Habit, I suppose," she said, nestling beside him as they lay back on the soft pillows.

Habit, and because she couldn't ever really forget the gulf of rank, title and fortune that lay between them. Not even here. Not even now.

She ran her fingertip up and down the line of dark brown hairs from his navel to his chest. "I wish I could sail with you. We went to the Isle of Man once, in very rough weather, and I didn't get seasick."

Her tone was teasing, but she spoke only half in jest. She would gladly go with him to the ends of the earth, if he would ask her. "Perhaps I should stow away."

"You've never been in a ship's hold, have you?" he asked gravely. "There's scarcely room for a rat to run and the stench from the bilge would knock you flat."

Not willing to abandon that proposal just yet, and despite his grim tone, she said, "I could disguise myself as a boy and sign on with the crew."

"That would be even less likely to succeed. You are much too pretty and your figure would give you away."

"I could bind my breasts, cut off my hair and dirty my face."

"Which just goes to show how little you know of life at sea. There is no privacy on a ship the size we will have."

His chest rose and fell with a deep sigh. "I'm not happy to be leaving you and the thought of having you with me is very tempting," he said softly as he caressed her cheek, "but it's not just life on the ship that's difficult. There are storms and wrecks, islanders who may welcome you or decide you'd make a nice addition to the pot, and you don't know which until you land. And pirates aren't the merry brigands some ballads suggest. They are terrible brutes and a swift death would be a mercy if we were ever captured, especially if you're a woman. I've seen…" He drew in a ragged breath. "I would kill you myself before I'd let you fall into a pirate's hands."

"You make it sound terrible indeed," she whispered, her fears for him increasing, and she was tempted as she'd never been before to do what Lady Granshire had asked her to do, to use whatever means she could to keep him in England.

But what then? They could never marry and she would be the destroyer of his dreams.

She moved away. "It's time for me to go."

He laid a hand on her bare arm. "If I were going to the Mediterranean, or even the coast of Africa or the West Indies, I would take you, but not where I'm going. It would be far too much of a risk, and while I'm willing to take that gamble with my own life, I won't with yours."

She nodded and got out of the bed, the air making her shiver as she reached for her dressing gown.

"There's no need for you to get out of a warm bed to see me to the door," she said, trying to sound happy. "I can manage on my own."

"I want to see you to the door," he said, climbing off the bed.

"If the noblewomen of England had any inkling of the body beneath your clothes," she said as he pulled on a pair of trousers, "they would be even more eager to meet you."

He laughed, then pulled a face. "They torment me enough as it is. I certainly wouldn't want to encourage them."

Her torn gown over her arm, Nell went to the door. He met her there, and smiled down at her. "You're the most

wonderful, remarkable woman I've ever met, Nell Springley, and if ever I were to ask a woman to wait for me, it
would be you."

Ask me! she silently pleaded. *Ask me and I will.*

He took her hand and brought it to his lips, kissing the
back of her hand. "Good night, Miss Springley."

"Good night, my lord," she replied.

And as she slipped into the corridor, she was sure of one
thing:

Even if he didn't ask her, she would wait for him.

"You wished to see me, Mother?" Bromwell asked as
he entered his mother's sitting room a few days later.

As usual, she was reclining on her chaise, and this
morning, she looked pale, with dark circles under her eyes.

Remorse nipped at him. He hadn't yet spoken with Dr.
Heathfield about her treatment and he should have, regardless of his desire to spend every moment he could
with Nell. "Have you been drinking chocolate in the
evenings again?"

Although he had no scientific basis for his query, he suspected there was something in chocolate that affected
sleep, for he'd often noticed that his mother would become
more energized after drinking it, then complain that she
hadn't been able to fall asleep later.

Not unexpectedly, however, she always ascribed her
sleeplessness to a different cause, as she did today. "How
can I sleep peacefully when you're leaving England again?"

He had no answer to that, so he made none as he sat
across from her on a well-upholstered chair. He had to hide
a wince, for he'd pulled a muscle last night when demonstrating the *upa upa* for Nell. He'd been telling her about

the dances of the Tahitians, and she'd confessed to seeing him dance by the pond. Once he'd gotten over his initial embarrassment, he'd explained that he danced because it was excellent exercise.

She'd begged a demonstration, he'd complied, and somewhere between the dance, her attempts to imitate it and what had followed, he'd pulled a muscle in his side. It was a slight strain, and only hurt if he moved a certain way, but he didn't want to have to explain the source of that twinge to his mother.

He also sincerely hoped she hadn't summoned him here because his intimate encounters with Nell had been discovered.

"I've had a letter from your father. He requests that you join him in Bath as soon as possible. Apparently he requires your assistance with a financial matter."

His relief that her summons had nothing to do with Nell was swiftly overcome by baffled curiosity.

His father wished to consult with *him* on a financial matter? Despite his coming of age, his father had never shared information about his financial affairs or estate business before. "What sort of financial matter?"

"He doesn't say. Only that it's important, and he expects you to join him at The King's Arms this afternoon."

That was typical of his father—no explanation or opportunity to refuse, simply an order and the expectation of obedience.

However, he had no other pressing demands upon his time, except for wanting to be with Nell every available opportunity, and the request was so unusual he nodded his agreement. "Very well, Mother. I'll stay the night in Bath and return in the morning."

"I've already ordered a horse saddled for you."

Bromwell didn't think riding would aggravate his slight injury and so, dutifully, rose. "If you'll excuse me then."

"And would you stop in at the apothecary's? I need some more of my medicine."

"I'll visit Dr. Heathfield while I'm there. I'm concerned this latest medication is not as effective as it should be, considering your continuing sleeplessness."

"I feel quite wonderful after my morning dose."

Her comment led Bromwell to suspect the main ingredient in Dr. Heathfield's latest medication was some kind of narcotic that induced euphoria, possibly an opiate that could be dangerous if taken too long, or in too high a dosage.

"Nevertheless, Mother, I want to be sure it's not doing more harm than good." He gave her a loving smile. "After all, you aren't the only one who worries."

She reached out for his hand and pressed it to her cool cheek before she wordlessly let him go.

Bromwell found Nell in the garden, looking like a nymph in a gown of soft green, her overtunic dotted with small embroidered roses. Unfortunately, she wasn't alone, as he would have preferred even for this temporary and short-lived parting. Drury and Juliette were with her.

"Ah, Buggy, here you are!" Juliette cried when she saw him walking toward them on the gravel path.

"I hope your mother isn't unwell?" Nell said, blushing when their gazes met, as if recalling certain portions of the *upa upa* done while he was naked.

He found himself blushing, too, as he replied. "She's a little tired, but otherwise well. She's received a letter from my father asking me to meet him in Bath this afternoon. Apparently he has some business he wishes to discuss with me."

Drury, who was well acquainted with the earl, was as surprised as Bromwell by the request. "He's never discussed such things with you before, has he?"

Bromwell shook his head and, when he answered, spoke as much to Nell as to his oldest friend. "Not once, so I think I should go, and unfortunately it must be right away. I won't be back until tomorrow."

"Of course you must go if your father requests your help," Nell said quietly.

"It wasn't exactly a request," Bromwell replied with a wry smile. "A command, more like."

"Perhaps he has reconsidered and will sponsor your expedition," Juliette said hopefully.

Bromwell glanced at Nell before shaking his head. "I highly doubt it. It's probably something about the ball."

He started to bow in farewell, until Juliette grabbed her husband's arm and started to pull him toward the terrace. "Come along, my love. Let us leave them to say goodbye alone."

"As you see, Buggy, you aren't the only one who gets ordered about," the barrister remarked as he allowed his wife to lead him away.

With Bromwell's silent gratitude. He would much prefer to say goodbye to Nell in private.

"Since time is short, let's walk to the stables together," Nell proposed.

Bromwell nodded his acquiescence, remembering a part of the garden in that vicinity where they could take their leave without being seen.

"Is it really true that Lady Drury was a seamstress?" Nell asked as Drury and his wife disappeared behind a yew hedge.

"Yes, and living in deplorable conditions the first time we

met," Bromwell replied. "She saved Drury's life by hurling a basketful of potatoes at men who were attacking him."

"I can believe she's not afraid of anything."

"Like everyone, she has her moments of doubt and fear, although she hides them very well. She certainly did the first time we met, after Drury sent her to fetch me. She had to come get me at Sir Joseph Banks's house, and I'm sure that wasn't easy for her, and then Drury was remarkably rude to her." He smiled at Nell. "Afterward, I realized he'd been rude because he was so intrigued by her."

"He didn't do anything so insolent as kiss her, did he?" she asked archly, with the sparkle of mischief that he adored in her eyes.

"No," Bromwell said softly as they reached the little nook in the shrubbery. "Even though he hated the French, he wasn't *that* impolite, whereas I…" He gathered her in his arms and kissed her gently. "Find I have no memory…" She wrapped her arms around him and sighed as he kissed the lobe of her ear. "Of rules of etiquette and proper deportment…" Then her neck. "When I am with you."

"Clearly, my lord," she murmured as she relaxed against him, her body leaning into his, "I forget how a young woman ought to act with a gentleman when I'm with you."

He caught her mouth with his, and kissed her deeply. "I don't want to go," he whispered as he slid his mouth to her soft cheek, "not even for a single night."

"I don't want you to go," she murmured as he caressed her. "Not even for an hour."

They kissed again, deeply, passionately, as desperately as if this were their final parting, until he broke the embrace and stepped back, flushed and breathless. "If we don't stop now, I'm going to make love with you right here."

Exhilaration took hold of Nell as she spotted the back of the stables out of the corner of her eye, a place sheltered from the yard and the rest of the garden.

"Not here—there," she whispered.

Yearning to be with him intimately today if she couldn't be with him that night, she took his hand to lead him. He resisted a little, but not for long, as she pulled him toward the shadowed, sheltered spot.

Her back to the wall, she turned, to be engulfed in his embrace. "I'll miss you," she gasped as he spread kisses over her face and neck.

He regarded her with primitive, primal greed. "Promise me you'll wait. Promise me you'll wait for me to come back."

Was he speaking of this brief sojourn, or his longer voyage? Whichever one he meant, her answer was the same. "Yes!"

As if that single word released him from all restraint, he pushed her back against the wall and kissed her with fervent, heated ardour. As his hands boldly caressed her, he spread her knees with his. She thrilled to the pressure of his limb and leaned against it as she slid her tongue into his hot mouth.

With a low growl, he reached down to lift her gown and soon he was stroking her most private place with growing need as he kissed her, making her moist and ready while she ran her hands beneath his vest and shirt. The drawstring of her pantelettes snapped, then his hand slipped within.

All too soon he withdrew and she whimpered with the loss, until he cupped her buttocks and lifted her, so that she could hold him around the waist with her legs.

She wanted him with every fiber, every particle, of her body and her heart. "Yes, oh, yes," she hissed as she worked at the buttons of his trousers with one hand, the other around his neck, until he was free.

Holding him, she shifted, while he positioned himself. Then he was inside her.

This was no gentle lovemaking, no tender contact. He took her with primal, swift and hungry need as she responded, until he groaned and filled her, while she pressed her lips together to stifle her own triumphant cries of release.

Sated, panting, his head in the crook of her neck, he leaned against her. She slowly lowered her legs, only now aware of the rough brick behind her and that her pantelettes were that pile of white linen on the ground.

"Oh, God," he muttered as he moved back and his head bowed as he buttoned his trousers, raising remorseful eyes to look at her. "We shouldn't…" He shook his head. "I was too overwhelmed to stop."

She was as aware of that as he as she picked up her undergarment. "I've heard a woman can't get pregnant the first time," she said, hoping to lessen his obvious remorse because she felt none, except for his sake. To bear his child, whatever happened, no longer seemed a fate to be avoided.

"I fear that's an old wives' tale," he said as he tucked in his shirt.

"Sometimes those old wives were right, weren't they?"

"Perhaps. Let us hope so. But now I have to go. The groom will be looking for me."

"Justinian, I meant what I said," she replied, wanting him to know how she felt, needing him to, whatever happened. "I'll wait for you, wherever you go and however long it may be."

He simply nodded once and left her.

Chapter Nineteen

*The loss was a severe one, and may set back the
study of arachnology for years to come.*
—The *Bath Crier*

"Ah, Bromwell, here you are at last!" his father cried
from an upper window of The King's Arms when his son
rode into the yard beneath the high arched gate. "Hurry!
The banker has been waiting for over an hour."

Bromwell did as his father bid and soon entered a wain-
scoted, comfortably appointed upper room where the
remains of a large luncheon sat upon the table. A man
who looked every inch the prosperous, if somewhat un-
fashionably attired, middle-aged man of finance and who'd
been seated by the fireplace, rose when Bromwell entered.
His father, meanwhile, assumed his usual commanding
pose by the fireplace, one arm draped over the mantel.

"This is Mr. Denby, my banker," the earl announced.

"I'm honored to meet you, my lord," Mr. Denby said,
bowing. "Your book was wonderful, quite wonderful!"

"Thank you."

"Sit down, Mr. Denby, and you, too, Justinian," the earl commanded.

Bromwell obeyed, and when he did, he saw a copy of the *Bath Crier* near the bucket of coals on the tiled hearth, obviously intended to be used to help light the fire. It was open to the society column.

Then it was as if the bottom had fallen out of Bromwell's chair, for there, in the bottom paragraph, he read, *"Lately returned to London and reputed to be coming soon to our fair city, the Duke of Wymerton and his family. His musical daughters are sure to be a welcome addition to social gatherings in the weeks to come."*

Had his father seen that?

He couldn't have, or he surely would have said something at once, Bromwell realized with relief. He immediately and surreptitiously shoved the paper beneath the bucket with his foot. His father would never stoop to lighting a fire, so as long as the paper was beneath the bucket, he wouldn't see it…although his father was going to have to learn the truth about Nell soon. After all, she was going to be his daughter-in-law.

Of course he must and would marry her now. He had asked her to wait and she had agreed. How could he expect her to do that unless they wed? And she must have the protection of his name and rank if she got with child. He would never leave her here to bear his child out of wedlock.

And yet leave her in England he must. He couldn't take her with him, no matter how much he loved her. A voyage such as he planned might be the death of her, and he would die himself before he would put her in such danger.

"Well, Denby, give my son the documents," his father impatiently ordered.

The earl gestured at the table beside the hearth. In addition to several papers of legal size, there was a jar of ink, a quill pen, and some sand for blotting. Clearly his father had been signing papers of some sort, or preparing to.

"If you will be so good as to sign here, my lord," Mr. Denby said, presenting Bromwell with a raft of papers and pointing to the bottommost line, beside the current date.

"What is this?" Bromwell asked, flipping the pages held together with ribbon.

"Your father is giving you ten thousand pounds for your expedition, on the understanding that you will avail yourself of certain expertise I possess. I deal with many merchants who ship goods all over the world."

Bromwell couldn't quite believe what he was hearing. He turned his questioning gaze to his father. "You're giving me ten thousand pounds for my expedition? And all I have to do is avail myself of your banker's experience?"

"I'd rather be spending it purchasing a London establishment for you and a wife," his father growled, "but since you seem resolved to sail off again, you might as well go as soon as possible, so you'll be back all the quicker."

Bromwell put down the papers and faced his father. "Thank you," he said, overwhelmed and grateful—but not as happy as he thought he'd be.

As he would have been before he met Nell.

"However, no matter what reason you give for your generosity," he continued, determined to remind himself of the reason he had to leave her, "you aren't just helping me, you're contributing to the understanding of—"

"I'm upsetting your mother, that's what I'm doing," the earl declared, scowling. "She's going to faint when she hears what I've done."

"I'll try again to make her appreciate why I must go," Bromwell vowed, "and I'll send letters home whenever I can."

"Just come back safe and healthy," his father said gruffly. "And when you do, for God's sake, get married and make us grandparents."

"I will," Bromwell promised with every intention of fulfilling that vow. "Thank you."

Even as he said it, the vocal expression of his gratitude seemed far too cold and formal, so Bromwell did something he'd never done in his life.

He went to his father and embraced him.

Even more surprising, his father hugged him back.

After a moment, Bromwell pulled away and cleared the lump from his throat while, swiping at his eyes, his father strode to the window.

"I'd like to ask Mr. Denby to make an addition to the papers, if I may," Bromwell said.

His father, once more composed, turned to look at him.

"I want the funds to be a loan, not a gift, and one that I'll gladly repay." He addressed the banker. "Can we not set up a system whereby some of the royalties from my book can go to my father as repayment?"

Bromwell held up his hand when his father looked about to protest. "I insist, Father. And don't think it's going to be so very much. I daresay it won't even be enough to pay for the new fountain you want to put by the terrace."

He thought of something else Mr. Denby could do with another portion of the income from his royalties.

But that must wait until later, after he'd asked Nell to marry him.

And provided she said yes.

* * *

The next day, in her pelisse and with her shawl wrapped around her for extra warmth, Nell walked briskly along the fern-bordered path from the garden to Justinian's laboratory. Overhead, a wren flitted amid the branches of a lichen-coated ash surrounded by birch and alder trees. The day was cool, but no clouds threatened rain and the air was still, unlike her tumultuous mind. She wanted to be alone, away even from Sir Douglas Drury and his wife.

It was not that they were unpleasant, and it had been tempting to ask all sorts of questions about Justinian, but she found their mutual happiness and obvious love difficult to endure. It was too much a reminder of what she couldn't have with Justinian.

She wouldn't think about that, she told herself. She would think of something else. His father's summons, for instance. Justinian had clearly been taken aback by the earl's request for consultation.

She still couldn't understand how his father could have had so little regard for his son's intelligence in the past. On the other hand, she had never known Justinian as a child, and it might be difficult for some parents to see their child as an adult.

Her parents had only ever known her as a child. What would they think of the woman she'd become? What would they say if they knew she'd been so intimate with a man who was not, and never would be, her husband?

She'd accepted that as part of the price for being with him, and while she'd been thrilled he'd asked her to wait for him and she had every intention of doing so, there had been no talk of marriage.

They would be apart for so long, and there would be

many days she would never know how he was, or if he was well, or if he was even still alive. More and more she was sympathizing with the countess, and more and more she was tempted to beg him to stay.

"Well, well, well, who have we here?"

Nell's breath froze in her lungs as she spun around, to see Lord Sturmpole standing on the path.

How had he come there? Why had she not heard or seen…?

"You don't look happy to see me, my dear."

"I'm not," she retorted, backing away toward the laboratory. "What do you want?"

"Why, you, of course. It wasn't very sporting of you to run away like that."

"Sporting? You attacked me and then locked me in a room."

"Attacked? Ye gods, that's a bit strong for the demonstration of my affections."

She desperately wondered where Billings and Brutus were, and if they were within call. The gardeners wouldn't be so very far away, either. "If you don't leave, I'll scream!"

"I don't think so, not unless you wish to appear before the magistrate in Bath. There is the matter of the money and clothes you stole, not to mention impersonating Lady Eleanor Springford."

Of course if he knew where she was, he must have learned who she was pretending to be.

"So unless you wish to be arrested, you will do exactly as I say."

"How did you find me?"

"I was approaching the house on horseback to see if my suspicions were correct when I saw you cross the garden and come this way. You certainly didn't waste any time enticing another man after you left me, did you?"

His lips curved up in that familiar, terrible leer. "You can stop staring at me like that, milady. I wouldn't dream of preventing you from playing whatever game it is you're playing with that fool of an earl and his no doubt equally foolish son."

"Then what *do* you want?"

"What you wouldn't give me before, that's all. Just once, and I'll be satisfied, and we can call what you took payment for services rendered."

"That's…?" She couldn't call it *all;* to let him do what he would with her was very far from nothing.

His thick lips curved up. "Yes, my dear, that's all. Just once, and then I'll be on my way back to Staynesborough."

"Why?" she cried. "Why do you want me? What am I to you?"

"You're the little whore who dared to say no—to *me!*"

"But there are other women!"

"You underestimate your appeal."

"Or is it because I wounded your pride? I got away, so your arrogant conceit demands you come after me."

"Who do you think you are, to refuse me?" he retorted. "You are nothing—little better than a servant!"

Yet she was enough for Lord Bromwell to love, and that gave her confidence and the determination to stop Sturm-pole from ever attacking another woman in his employ.

"Have me arrested if you will, but if you do, I shall charge you with attempted rape and assault."

His eyes flared with anger even as he laughed with scorn. "Who do you think the authorities will believe?"

She put on a smile as false as his laugh. "Me, because

I shall have Sir Douglas Drury as my advocate, and he never loses."

To her surprise and growing dread, Sturmpole didn't look impressed. "You speak as if I would have the case tried in London. It would, of course, be heard in Staynes-borough, and there I *own* the magistrate."

It was possible that he did, at least in a sense.

Her throat dry, Nell could think of only one thing to do—she had to get help. Find Billings or Brutus, or run back to Granshire Hall.

Shouting for the gamekeeper and his dog, she broke into a run, heading for the garden.

But Sturmpole had anticipated her flight and he caught the back of her pelisse, then jerked her back to him.

"I don't think so," he growled as he roughly grabbed her arms and spun her around to face him, his breath reeking of stale wine. "One way or another, I'll have you. I didn't come all the way from Staynesborough for nothing."

"You did, you disgusting degenerate!" Nell cried, hitting him.

Holding her tight, he started dragging her toward the laboratory. "No woman says no to me. No woman refuses and robs *me!*"

"Billings! Brutus!" she shouted as she dug in her heels.

His face contorted with rage, Sturmpole struck her hard across the mouth, knocking her to the ground. Regardless of the pain, she scrambled to her feet, trying to run, but the ground was damp and muddy and she slipped.

"Shut your mouth!" Sturmpole ordered as he pulled her to her feet. "If you're calling the gamekeeper, he's on the far side of the estate. I saw him."

"You didn't—you're lying!" Nell retorted, hoping she

was right, her cut lip throbbing as blood trickled down her chin and onto her torn and muddy pelisse. "Lord Bromwell will kill you if you hurt me!"

"When he finds out the trick you've played, he'll be calling for your head," Sturmpole charged as he shoved open the door of the laboratory with his shoulder.

She grabbed the door frame with both hands. He pulled hard, forcing her to let go. Holding her with one hand, he raised the other to strike—then stopped and stared as he caught sight of the jars upon the shelves.

For that brief instant, his hold relaxed. She pulled away and grabbed one of the heavy glass jars. He realized what she was going to do and knocked it from her hand. The jar shattered on the floor, spilling its contents.

Nell tried to rush past him to the door, but Sturmpole grabbed her shoulders and threw her toward the sofa. She slipped on the wet floor and fell hard on her knees. Ignoring the pain and broken glass, she scrambled to her feet, aiming for the table and the candleholder there.

Again he saw what she intended and stepped in front of her to block her.

She moved sideways and grabbed another jar. She threw it at him, hitting him on the shoulder. She grasped another and threw it, too, narrowly missing him but making him duck before it, too, shattered. Another hit the side of his face before breaking on the floor.

The air reeked of alcohol, her eyes watered and her lip still bled; nevertheless, Nell kept throwing jars of preserved spiders, aiming for Sturmpole's head or chest, making him keep his distance as she worked her way back toward the hearth and the cupboard where Justinian kept the cutlery, including all the knives.

Chapter Twenty

My dear Buggy, what are you trying to do? Give your old friends attacks of apoplexy? Drive us to early graves? Is it not enough that we have to live in fear you'll be bitten by some exotic insect and die in fearful agonies, or that you'll be the main item on a cannibal's menu, that you must put yourself in harm's way in England, too?

—from a letter to Lord Bromwell, written by the
Honorable Brixton Smythe-Medway

It was breaking glass, Bromwell realized as he broke into a run along the wooded path. Breaking glass in the woods, where his lab was, and his spiders.

And Nell? God help him, was Nell there, too?

She hadn't been in the garden when he'd returned with the news of his father's unexpected generosity; he'd sought her out at once, while his father went to speak to his mother, as they'd decided in the carriage on their return from Bath. When he'd asked Fallingbrook where he could find Lady Eleanor, he'd said she'd gone out for a walk.

His heartbeat quickening at the louder and undeniable sounds of a struggle, Bromwell rushed into the building. He nearly slipped on the floor slick with alcohol and crushed specimens, and crunching with broken glass. A man he'd never seen before stood in front of Nell, who was by the hearth. Her lip was cut and bleeding, her gown torn and splattered with mud, and she held an upraised knife to protect herself from that lout who was obviously attacking her.

With a roar of pure animal rage, he launched himself at the attacker and tackled him to the ground, regardless of the broken glass. Straddling the man who did his best to buck him off, Bromwell got his hands around the brigand's throat and squeezed.

He was no chivalrous gentleman now. He was a primitive warrior prepared to kill to protect the woman he loved.

"Stop, stop!" Nell cried. "You'll kill him!"

The man's face was purple, his eyes bulging, as Nell's shouts brought Bromwell back to civilization—but only just. Spotting something lying on the ground amidst the ruin of his collection, he let go of the ruffian's throat with one hand and reached for it.

"This is a blow dart coated in the venom of a *Phoneutria nigriventer,* the most lethal spider yet discovered," he said, his voice hoarse with his barely suppressed rage. "I have only to break your skin with it to see you die in agony or, if you do not die, be painfully rendered impotent for life—a more fitting punishment, perhaps, for the likes of you."

Drawing in great rasping breaths, his eyes wide with terror, the man finally went still.

"Do you know who is this, Nell?" Bromwell demanded, glancing sharply at her.

Her face was palely aghast, the knife still clutched in her trembling hand. "Sturmpole," she breathlessly replied.

Bromwell moved the dart a little closer to Sturmpole's mottled skin.

"He came upon me in the woods," she continued. "He… he wanted me to…."

"I can guess what he wanted," Bromwell said, his voice slightly calmer, although he was even more tempted to put an end to this rogue's life. Or at least prick him with the dart so priapism would set in. "He's going to be arrested and charged with attempted murder."

"I wasn't trying to kill her!" Sturmpole protested, spittle on his lips.

"Whatever you were trying to do, you struck her and could have killed her. The evidence is there on her face. And there's the attempted rape at Staynesborough. You had better reconcile yourself to a long stay in a cold, damp prison, my lord."

Still holding the dart near Sturmpole's neck, Bromwell got up and pulled him to his feet. "Nell, perhaps you'd be so good as to tie his hands with that length of rope near the door. Be careful. The floor is slippery." He scowled at the nobleman, who kept his frightened, sidelong glance on the dart. "I'm going to charge you with destruction of property, too."

"I'm sorry about your specimens, Justinian," Nell said as she took hold of Sturmpole's hands to tie them. "I threw the jars at him to keep him away."

"Then the specimens are well lost," Bromwell replied, not regretting their destruction if it had helped her. "Nell, you hold the dart while I tie the knot. All those hours at sea have made me quite proficient in that art."

Nell did as he asked, gingerly taking hold of the weapon.

"It's not really poison," he said, his ire once more under control, and giving her the ghost of a smile when he saw her expression. "The only danger is its sharp point—which I would gladly have shoved into his neck," he finished truthfully, "if he'd succeeded in his disgusting quest."

Sturmpole emitted a moan, which Bromwell ignored as he started to frog march his prisoner outside. He halted when Drury appeared on the threshold.

The attorney couldn't have looked more surprised if he'd been told Nell was the Queen of England. "Good God, what's happened?"

"This oaf attacked Nell. I want him arrested and charged with attempted murder."

Drury's shock was swiftly mastered, replaced with his usual cool composure. "Of course."

Drury started to come inside, then realized what was on the floor. "Bring him here and I'll take him back to the hall." He turned to address Juliette, who had arrived behind him. "Juliette, would you help Miss Springley?"

"I'll do that," Bromwell said at once while wiping his hands on his trousers. Miraculously, he wasn't badly cut. "Juliette, perhaps you wouldn't mind going ahead and alerting the servants that we'll require assistance? And the apothecary should be sent for."

Juliette immediately hurried away, while Drury took charge of the damp, scowling Sturmpole, holding him firmly by the arm.

"Don't get any ideas about trying to get away, my lord," Drury said as he pulled him out the door. "My hands may not look strong, but I assure you, I am quite capable of incapacitating you and that prospect is far from disturbing."

When they were gone, Bromwell closed the door, went to Nell and took her in his arms.

"If you hadn't come…" she murmured, leaning against him.

He held her close, all too aware of what might have happened. "I'm so sorry I wasn't here sooner."

"You came before it was too late," she said, choking back her tears. "I was so afraid!"

"But not too frightened to defend yourself—and very well, too," he said, stroking her damp, matted hair, cherishing her, relieved beyond measure that she was safe. "You truly are the most remarkable woman."

Her body began to tremble, a natural reaction to the attack and the shock and the vital energy she'd summoned to fight Sturmpole off.

"We had best get you to the hall and see to that cut. Have you any others?"

"I don't think so…but Justinian, I've destroyed your collection!"

"Never mind that," he said, truly not caring as long as she was safe. "I'll get others. My father's agreed to fund the rest of my expedition—and I suspect his change of heart is due to a most remarkable young woman who championed me."

"Oh, Justinian!" she cried. "That's wonderful!"

And then she began to sob in earnest. Loving her, adoring her, cherishing her, he gathered her up in his arms to carry her to the hall, holding her close to his heart.

Where she belonged.

Where she would always belong.

Justinian carried Nell back to the hall and up to her bedroom, calling for the servants as he went and issuing orders like the aristocrat he was. She was too exhausted to protest, although he must be tired, and she didn't care what the servants thought. Dena came rushing up the stairs after them, all but ordering Justinian to let her take care of her.

Bromwell didn't stop until he set her gently on the bed. Ignoring the anxiously hovering Dena, he quickly looked at Nell's bruised, cut hands and even lifted her alcohol-scented, muddy skirts to look at her knees.

"I'll have to clean these abrasions later," he said, turning her hands over and kissing the back of them. "Fortunately, they aren't deep and there's no glass embedded that I can see. I'll use my magnifying glass to be certain, though."

"My lord, leave her to me," Dena said. "I'll look after her. She needs a bath and a hot cup of tea and some clean clothes. You can tend to her wounds later."

"I shall," he promised as he stepped back and Dena quickly ordered another maid waiting by the door to bring a bath and plenty of hot water.

"I'm going to make sure Sturmpole's under lock and key," he said, "then I'll return."

His pointed gaze silenced whatever protests Nell or Dena might have made.

When he was gone, Nell wrapped her arms around herself. He was going to leave her soon, for much longer. Now he would have even more reason to go, because she'd destroyed his collection.

"Let me help you out of those clothes," Dena said. "We'll get you washed and then you'll feel better."

Having no strength to refuse, Nell silently submitted until she was naked beneath a dressing gown and the bath was ready by the hearth. Another maid had carried in enough clean linen for the entire household, some of which now cushioned the tub, and Mrs. Fallingbrook herself had brought in two pitchers of water for rinsing her hair.

At Nell's request, only Dena still remained to help her.

"Thank you, Dena," she said wearily, more tired than she'd ever been in her life.

She let the robe fall and stepped gingerly into the bath. Her knees were bruised, and she smelled terrible, of alcohol and blood and sweat, so she was glad of the chance to get clean. With a sigh, she laid her head upon her knees.

How close she had come to what she'd prevented before! What might have happened if Justinian hadn't arrived when he did and her strength was failing?

"You may leave, Dena."

Nell's eyes flew open at the sound of Justinian's voice. He was standing by the door, looking marvellous and healthy, slightly damp hair brushing his shirt collar. Although she was happy to see him, she could unfortunately guess what Dena would make of this.

Yet she didn't ask him to go, or Dena to stay. Instead she watched as he closed the door behind the reluctantly departing maid and started toward the bath.

"Feeling better?" he asked.

"Now that my hero is here."

He stopped a few feet away. "You're going to give me an exaggerated sense of my own worth using such terms."

"Impossible," she replied.

He once again began to approach the tub.

"You might wish to reconsider," she warned, although her heartbeat quickened and that familiar yearning invaded her body. "I smell terrible."

"I'm quite used to the smell of that particular type of alcohol," he said. "It's like perfume to me."

Every ache caused by the attack began to diminish, while another sort grew. Well aware that he was watching her with the same intensity with which he studied his spiders, she reached for the lump of lavender-scented soap on the stool Dena had set nearby for that purpose, moving with slow deliberation. The warm water washed over her breasts and droplets fell from her outstretched arm. "I should wash my hair. Would you like to help?"

Justinian was immediately beside the tub, stripping off his jacket and rolling up his sleeves. "I hope your knees aren't too sore," he said as his gaze swept over her.

"Only a little," she said, looking up at him and smiling at the thought that if the tub were larger, he could join her.

He paused as he finished rolling up the second sleeve. "What are you thinking about with that devilishly sly look on your face?"

"That is for me to know, my lord, but I will say that it involves a tub. A larger one."

His eyes widened, making him look delightfully shy. "I see."

He knelt beside the tub. "Unfortunately, we shall have to make do with this," he said as he began to unpin her hair.

"Bend over, please," he said when he was done, reaching for the pitcher that was on the towel-covered floor beside the tub.

She did, gripping the sides of the tub, then gave a little yelp as cool water cascaded over her head.

"I'm sorry," he said as he began to soap her hair, massaging her scalp with his long slender fingers. "The other pitcher is likely to be just as cold."

"It's all right, as long as my hair gets clean," she said, leaning back with a sigh. She would put up with worse than that to have him wash her hair.

After what seemed a very little while, he picked up the other pitcher to rinse her hair. "Brace yourself," he warned before the cold water descended this time.

Spluttering and shivering, she put out her arm. "Towel, please."

He gave it to her, kissing her hand as he did. Smiling, she swiftly dried her face and rubbed her hair, then wrapped her head in the towel.

"You look nice in a turban," he remarked when she was finished. "But then, I'd think you looked nice in anything... and especially in nothing."

The water in the tub was much cooler; nevertheless, her body warmed. "Perhaps you should leave and let me finish my toilette in peace, before I do something that will really make the servants talk."

"That sounds promising," he remarked as he got to his feet and held open a large towel. "What did you have in mind?"

She gave him a wicked, wanton smile as she rose, naked as Venus, from the tub. "Come closer, my lord, and I'll show you."

"That cut on your lip might start bleeding again," he warned.

"I wasn't intending to use my mouth."

"My lord," Fallingbrook called from the other side of Nell's bedroom door sometime later, "supper will be served in half an hour."

"We'll be downstairs shortly," Bromwell answered as he

finished buttoning his trousers. He gave the blissfully sated Nell a rueful smile. "I wonder how he knew I was here?"

"A fortunate guess?" she suggested from where she lay naked beneath the rumpled sheets of the bed. What had started as one thing, intended only to satisfy him, had soon enough become another, although they were more careful than they'd been by the stables. "Or perhaps a logical conclusion."

Justinian pulled his shirt over his head. "I believe my feelings for you had not escaped the servants' notice prior to this, and I suppose Dena told him where I was."

Nell sat up and brushed her dishevelled hair from her face. "Dena once thought I was trying to seduce you into marriage. I hope she won't think she was right—although of course she's quite wrong."

He frowned as he walked over to her dressing table and ran her brush through his hair, and she instantly regretted mentioning marriage.

She got out of the bed and hurried to put on her chemise. "How soon before the magistrate's men can come from Bath, do you think?"

"They should be here before dark, but only just, even if they come at a gallop, and I'm sure Drury would make sure they did. They'll have to stay the night and keep Sturmpole under guard in the stable, then take him to Bath in the morning."

She went to the wardrobe and selected a gown, a simple one of light blue wool trimmed with brown piping. She stepped into it and pulled it up, then hurried to put her hair up in some semblance of a style. "Will you lace me, please?"

"Gladly, now and every chance I get," he replied,

coming behind her and doing as she asked, his deft fingers swiftly tying the knot.

She rose and turned toward him when he finished.

He reached out to take her hands gently in his. "Nell, you must know I love you," he said softly, the truth of that even more apparent in his eyes than in his voice and words. "So much so, I can scarcely believe it. For so long, and especially after my friends fell in love, I've feared something was missing in me, some capacity to feel deeply. That I was incapable of experiencing love and desire as they so obviously did.

"I told myself it was no great matter, because I had my work and that was more than enough to content me. Even so, I planned to marry someday. I believed I would simply select a woman whose temperament was the most compatible with mine, and one who wouldn't be jealous of my devotion to my work."

His grip tightened ever so slightly. "And then I met you, and discovered that it wasn't that something had been lacking within me. I simply hadn't met the right woman. Now I have, and I believe you love me, too, because I don't think you would ever have come to my bed otherwise."

"No, I would not," she whispered in confirmation.

He went down on one knee. "Then, Nell, would you do me the very great honor of marrying me?"

Chapter Twenty-One

There is much fluttering among the petticoats as the time draws near for the Earl of Granshire's hunt ball, especially as it has been confirmed by the earl that his son, the notable naturalist and author, will be attending.

—from the Social Circle column of the *Bath Crier*

A host of emotions ran through Nell at his softly, intently spoken request—joy, hope, fear, dismay, concern—while she gazed into his questioning face.

There was no doubt, no hesitation, in the eyes that regarded her so steadily. No worry, no concern, only love. Sincere, deep-seated love.

"I know this must come as a shock to you after all I've said about not marrying before I sail," he continued just as ardently and sincerely, "but seeing Sturmpole attacking you, I realized how very much I love you, need you and want you to be my wife. Nobody understands me, or loves me, the way you do. If we hadn't shared the same coach, if it hadn't overturned, I would still be thinking myself incapable of deep, devoted, passionate love. I would still be alone, and lonely."

Oh, how his words stabbed at her and made her long to ignore the world and all its restraints and conventions! If she could think only of herself, if she didn't truly love him, she might have been able to.

Since she did love him, she must think of him, and his future without her, because with her, he would suffer. Not at first, perhaps. But later. And she would not have him resent her for anything.

Not even his hand in marriage.

So she pulled her hands free and did what had to be done, even if it broke both their hearts. "No, Justinian, I won't marry you."

The dismay and disappointment in his eyes nearly weakened her resolve, but as he could be strong for what he believed necessary, so could she.

"I don't doubt that you love me as much as I love you," she said, "but I'm still the penniless daughter of a convicted felon. Such a marriage will make you a pariah to your friends and family, as well as other important, influential people who can aid you in your work."

"If it does, so be it," he returned, desperation furrowing his brow. "I would rather have you. Look at Drury, who married a seamstress—and a French one, at that. His legal career hasn't suffered. Surely to God I can marry—"

"Whoever you like, because you are famous, too? I'd like to think so. I'd like to believe that we may do as we wish with no thought to how it will change our lives, save for the better.

"But we both know that's not so. We aren't marooned on a deserted island, just the two of us.

"There is your work to consider—and we must—as well as your family. We can't ignore them, or pretend they don't exist.

"And there is something else to take into account. You're going to be gone for a long time, Justinian, and as strong as our love is now, I fear it will weaken with time and distance. Or worst of all, that you won't come back at all."

She put her fingertips on his lips to silence his protests. "I don't think it would be wise to bind ourselves in a marriage when you are leaving soon, and for so long."

"What if you're with child?" he protested just as fervently as he'd proposed. "We weren't careful before I went to Bath."

"I would not have you bound in a marriage you no longer wanted even under those circumstances. If that happens, your friends will help me, will they not?"

He nodded mutely, but his eyes were so full of anguish she couldn't look him in the face.

"My lord!" Fallingbrook called out from behind the door again. "Will you please come down? The countess is getting upset."

Still without speaking, his expression cold as stone, immutable as a rock, Justinian held out his arm to escort her from the room. "Since there is no more to be said, we had better go."

As she took his arm, she swallowed hard and choked back her tears, although she really wanted to throw herself on the bed and cry until she could cry no more.

Then run away and never look back.

"Sturmpole! By God, I went to school with him!" the earl was all but shouting as Bromwell and Nell reached the threshold of the drawing room. "He was a fine fellow, so whoever would have guessed…?"

Standing beside the hearth, arms crossed over his chest puffed out like an enraged rooster, Lord Granshire fell silent when he saw Nell and his son. Juliette sat on the Grecian couch beside the countess, and Drury was by the windows, his ruined hands clasped behind his back.

The countess immediately got to her feet. "What is it? What's wrong?" she demanded, glancing uneasily from her son to Nell.

In that instant, in that precise moment, as his mother looked at him with worry, as Nell's grip tightened on his forearm, Bromwell knew what he must do. And in that instant, that precise moment, he was equally certain it was the right, best, only thing to do.

"Be happy, Mother," he said, smiling at her and everyone else gathered there. "I'm not going on another expedition."

"What?" Nell cried, her hand dropping as she turned to stare at him.

"What?" his father roared as if Bromwell had lost his mind.

"What?" his mother gasped, sitting heavily.

"Why?" and *"Pourquoi?"* demanded Drury and Juliette in unison.

Bromwell ignored them, speaking only to Nell as if they were alone, because right then, they might as well have been on that deserted island.

Regarding her with all the love he felt, sure of his decision as he'd never been so sure of anything in his life, not even his desire to study spiders, he said, "I've been a stubborn, selfish fool. If I must choose between my expedition and you, I gladly, happily choose you. And you mustn't fear that I'll come to resent you or regret my choice. How can I regret anything that will make me so happy and so blessed?"

Still doubtful, still unsure, Nell didn't reply as her anxious gaze searched his face.

"I mean it, Nell," he assured her. "I think marriage—provided it's to you—will be even more interesting than any expedition could ever be."

"Not to mention vastly more entertaining and comfortable," Drury said from the sofa, where he now stood behind Juliette.

"But your studies, your plans, the spiders!" Nell protested in astonished, uncertain gasps, as if she still couldn't believe he meant what he said.

"As my mother has noted on more than one occasion, there are plenty of spiders in Britain. I shall devote myself to studying the local arachnids. After all, some things are common to all the species, such as the navigation and construction of their webs and—"

"By God, *now* you see the light?" his father demanded abruptly and loudly, coming out of his shocked stupor. "After refusing to listen to sense all these years?"

"Oh, be quiet, Frederic!" the countess ordered, leaping to her feet and more animated than Bromwell had seen in years. "Miss Springley has not yet accepted his proposal."

"Miss Springley?" the earl cried. "Who the devil is Miss Springley?"

"I am," Nell said quietly. "I'm not Lady Eleanor Springford, but Eleanor Springley, the impoverished daughter of

Edward Springley, who's been convicted of theft and transported to Botany Bay."

"Oh…my…God!" the earl choked, reaching for the mantel to steady himself. "Is that *true?*"

"Yes, but I don't care," Bromwell firmly replied.

"Whereas I do," Nell said, louder and with more confidence, her eyes shining not with unshed tears, but fierce determination. "I'm well aware of what marriage to a woman like me will cost your son, so no, Justinian, I still won't marry you and be the ruin of your career."

"What do you mean, *ruin?*" Juliette exclaimed with disbelief. "Buggy is famous for his work, and justly so—work he can continue to do. And he will always be received by the people who matter. As for those small-minded people who will not because of the woman he loves, he does not need their friendship or support."

"She's right," Drury said calmly. "In fact, those of a romantic bent will likely be even more inclined to buy your books, wondering if they'll be able to see hints of the sentimental lover in the naturalist."

"You're being ridiculous," Bromwell said, too upset by Nell's continuing refusal to be amused.

He turned to Nell and grasped her cold hands. "Except for the part about not being received by fools and idiots. I don't care about that."

"Do you mean to say," his father said as if the point was finally penetrating his gray matter, "that this young woman is not the daughter of the Duke of Wymerton?"

"No, she isn't," his wife affirmed, "but if she makes Justinian happy—"

"And she's got no dowry or property at all, nor likely to?"

"Father, I don't care if she's poor," Bromwell said. He

looked down at Nell, his eyes pleading. "Please, Nell, won't you accept me?"

She shook her head, her eyes bright with unshed tears. "To give up your expedition for me…it's too much, Justinian. I won't have that on my conscience."

Juliette sighed with exasperation. "Why must he give it up? Can he not take his wife on the expedition with him?"

Bromwell shook his head. "I wouldn't subject my wife to the deprivations and dangers."

Drury tilted his head to one side and gave Bromwell his Death Stare. "Do you know, Buggy, there are times you sound remarkably like your father? How many times have you told me that he wouldn't see you as an adult with the capacity to decide your own fate? What are you doing but taking the decision to choose her own fate out of Nell's hands? Are you not treating *her* like a child rather than an adult?"

If someone had shot a cannon at Bromwell's head, it would hardly have been more disturbing. Because Drury was right. He had never seen his urge to protect Nell in that arrogant light.

A sudden vision, previously unimaginable, came to him—of having his work as well as Nell for his wife, of facing the future, whatever it held, with her by his side, to love, to cherish and to comfort all the days of his life.

If she would only say yes.

Nell felt poised on a precipice between hope and dismay, longing and fulfillment. Even if Justinian loved her enough to marry her regardless of what society might think, if she couldn't sail with him, she must hold firm and refuse to marry him in spite of the urgings of her heart. Too much could happen between the time he sailed and when he returned, and she would not have him bound to her under those conditions, no matter how much she loved him.

"The voyage will be dangerous and uncomfortable," he said slowly, regarding her steadily, "and the ship cramped and the food terrible and there is always the threat of illness, but if you would like to marry me and come with me under those circumstances…?"

If she would like it? "Are you sure, Justinian?"

The look in his eyes alone would have been enough, and then he said, with all the conviction of complete truth, "Yes."

"Yes!" she cried, throwing herself into his arms, laughing and crying at the same time, overwhelmed with joy and relief and hope and happiness. "Yes, I'll marry you!"

He drew back and regarded her with his most studious expression. "You truly mean that? You will accept me?"

As if she was the one making concessions! "If you'll really marry me in spite of my father's crime and my lack of fortune and rank."

His answer was a passionate kiss, until his father drew everyone's attention away from the young and happy couple.

"Do you expect me to contribute the necessary funds to your expedition if you marry this…this *woman?*"

Bromwell regarded his father with calm acceptance. He should have realized his father's support would be conditional, capricious and liable to be withdrawn if he was displeased.

However, he no longer cared, because Nell had agreed to marry him.

"If that's how you choose to respond to my happiness, so be it," he said evenly, his arms still around her. "I shall find other sponsors, as I did before. However, since Nell's agreed to be my wife, nothing you or anyone else can say will deter me from marrying her."

The countess rose, hands clasped, her expression desperate, and Bromwell feared he was about to hear more pleas to stay in England, especially if he had a wife.

"Frederic, you *must* provide the funds for his expedition, and especially whatever money they require to make their accommodation aboard ship more comfortable."

Bromwell and everyone else in the room regarded her with incredulity, not just for what she said, but because of the firm tone with which she said it.

Lady Granshire went to her son and, taking his hand in hers, looked at him with tears running down her cheeks. "Naturally I would prefer that you stay in England, but it is finally clear to me how much this voyage means to you, and what it would mean if you didn't sail."

Taking one of Nell's hands, too, she addressed her with a smile, although her lips trembled and her tears still flowed. "I'll be a little less worried, though, knowing he has someone who loves him to look after him."

She drew in a ragged breath, then spoke to her son again with that unexpected resolve. "You must promise me, though, Justinian, that you'll be even more careful, because you'll be responsible for your wife as well as yourself."

"You have my word that I'll protect Nell with my life," he vowed.

"And I shall do the same for him," Nell added, equally sincere.

The countess embraced her, and Bromwell's heart swelled not just with joy because he was going to get to spend the rest of his life married to Nell, but because his mother had come 'round—if not completely, at least to acceptance.

"My dear, surely you cannot countenance such a union!" her husband protested. "She is nothing, a nobody—worse than nobody, if her father—"

The countess whirled around to face her husband. "She is the woman your son loves—the son you've belittled and derided even after his great success."

She walked up to her husband and poked him in the chest as she spoke. "You care more about your precious estate, this house and your blasted garden than you ever have for us. I've put up with that, and you, for thirty years for the sake of our marriage and our son, because I was afraid of gossip and scandal. But no more, Frederic. If you don't accept this marriage, I shall leave you and reveal certain details of your life that will cause a scandal such as you have never even imagined!"

The earl blanched, but haughtily demanded, "What *details?*"

"There are certain books—illegal books—you keep hidden in the library, books of such a lewd nature, you should be ashamed to even touch them!"

Bromwell glanced at Nell, who raised a brow, wondering if this was the reading material he'd been referring to that wasn't of a classical or scientific nature. His answering rueful grin told her that it was.

"You…you…know about…?" the earl spluttered, his face as red as his scarlet waistcoat.

"I believe, my love, that we should retire from this family gathering and await the butler's summons to supper elsewhere," Drury said, taking his wife's hand and leading her, somewhat unwillingly, from the room.

"What sort of books are they talking about?" Juliette whispered as she gained the hall.

"I'll explain when we're alone," Drury murmured as he closed the door behind them.

Chapter Twenty-Two

It has recently been brought to our notice that a certain Lord from the north has been arraigned on a charge of assault, as well as other crimes of such a nature that we shall refrain from disclosing them in their entirety lest we upset our female readers.

—The *Bath Crier*

By the time the door had closed, the earl had managed to recover some of his composure. "My dear wife, no doubt you're overwrought, a condition not unexpected given the startling and shocking events of the day. I'm sure upon further reflection, you'll see that I'm quite right to oppose a marriage that can only humiliate our son and cause him difficulties in the future."

"You certainly ought to be an expert on humiliating our son," his wife retorted. "You've been doing it for years, and heaven only knows how he might have turned out if not for *my* love and comfort."

"For which I'm exceedingly grateful," Bromwell interjected, hoping to end this distressing confrontation. "And if you truly wish to leave Father, Mother, I won't question your decision."

How could he, when her unhappiness, anger and resentment must have been building for years? "However, with regard to his reaction to my marriage and the withdrawal of his financial support, you may set yourself at ease. Nothing he says or does will deter me from marrying Nell, and I'm sure we'll be able to sail with or without his help."

In spite of that determination, he regarded his father with genuine, heartfelt sorrow. "I wish it could be otherwise, Father. I was happy and proud when you offered me the money without conditions, and enjoyed our journey back to Granshire when we talked like friends. I would that we could continue in such a way. But I won't give up Nell because of your fears of what society will say, any more than I gave up going on my first expedition because you thought it the height of lunacy.

"The choice is yours, Father. Accept my wife or not as you will, but we *shall* marry and we *will* sail."

Whatever Bromwell had expected his father to do, it wasn't to walk slowly up to his wife and look at her with genuine distress. "You would really do that, Susanna? You would really leave me?"

"I would," she said, her voice wavering a little. "You should be proud of our son and happy that he's found a woman who loves him and isn't after his money, or his title. How many young women do we know would refuse him because she thought it was best for *him?*"

The earl looked from his wife to his son and the woman standing anxiously beside him as if he'd never really seen Nell before. "I do want you to be happy, Justinian."

He turned back to his wife. "I didn't realize how much

I was distressing you, Susanna. I will accept Justinian's choice, and if he wants to sail off to some godforsaken…" He reined in his temper. "Whatever he wants to do, he'll have my full support, both in good wishes and funds."

"I'll stay. Oh, Frederic, I'll stay!" the countess cried, pulling him into her arms. "Although you must also get rid of those books."

"Anything for you, my dear," he replied, kissing her fervently.

Nell grabbed Bromwell's arm and pulled him toward the door. "I think we should leave them alone for a little while."

Fallingbrook, as stunned as Bromwell, was standing in the doorway. "Dinner is served," he whispered as Nell closed the door behind them.

"Tell the cook dinner will have to be delayed a little while," Nell told him. "You'll find us in the garden."

"Congratulate me, Fallingbrook!" Justinian said merrily. "I'm getting married."

"Are you indeed, my lord?" the butler murmured absently, his gaze still on the closed door of the drawing room. "When might we meet the fortunate bride?"

The night of the Earl of Granshire's hunt ball, Granshire Hall was ablaze with light from nearly a thousand candles. Music from the orchestra drifted from the ballroom into the rest of the house, and outside, several carriages lined the drive. Coachmen, footmen and linkboys clustered in small groups, occasionally quaffing mugs of mulled wine and ale brought to them from the kitchen.

Inside the manor, finely dressed men and women milled about, awaiting the start of the dancing. Torches had also been lit in the garden, and the night was warm enough that a few couples drifted to the terrace for a breath of fresh air or more intimate conversation.

Inside, near one of the French doors leading to the terrace, a group of three couples watched as the earl, his wife, his son and his son's fiancée greeted the arriving guests.

Lady Francesca Smythe-Medway wore an evening gown of pale pink taffeta, the bodice trimmed with lace as was the hem, and she had diamonds in her ears and around her throat. Standing beside Fanny and dressed in deep blue satin with tight sleeves and sapphire earrings set in silver was Diana the wife of Viscount Adderley. Next to her was Juliette, in a fashionable concoction of Nile green that she had made herself, the bodice embroidered with golden leaves. Their husbands were much more plainly attired in black formal evening dress, but even so, they were the object of many admiring glances from other women, as their wives were the object of many men's.

All of whom they ignored.

The Honorable Brixton Smythe-Medway, whose straw-colored hair defied the efforts of comb, brush and valet to lie flat, declared, "I've never seen Buggy looking so…so…"

His brow furrowed, Brix turned to his wife with a pleading look. "What's the word I'm looking for?"

"Happy?" Fanny proposed.

"Heroic?" Diana supplied, her eyes twinkling.

"Triumphant?" suggested Edmond, Viscount Adderley.

"Successful in life and in love," Drury said in a tone that implied the matter was settled.

"You're all right," Brix replied with a grin. "Good ol' Buggy. I always knew he'd find the right woman someday. I just never expected it would be in a mail coach."

"I daresay neither did he," Edmond said. "Which goes

to show we never know where we'll be when Cupid aims his arrow."

"Don't go all poetic on us," Brix warned. "I'm glad the earl has seen the light at last about Bromwell's abilities, and his mother's looking very pleased."

"Who could not be pleased with Nell?" Juliette asked. "She's a lovely girl. And see how she looks at Buggy! *That* is love."

"See how every other young woman here is looking at him," Brix said, waggling his brows. "Egad, he was popular before but he looks a very Adonis now. It's a good thing Miss Springley snatched him up when she had the chance."

His wife swatted Brix lightly with her fan. "I wouldn't be speaking of missed opportunities, if I were you," she warned.

Brix rubbed his arm as if she'd hurt him and put on an aggrieved face. "Yes, but I made no claim to being observant. How could I, when I couldn't see the rose right under my nose?"

His wife smiled and stroked his arm with her fan.

"My dears, I tell you, it's really true," a woman noted in an excited whisper as a gaggle of women passed by, her voice audible as the orchestra took a short break to get out new music. "Not of the first rank, or indeed, any rank at all. And her father—"

As one, Bromwell's friends turned to look at the speaker with varying degrees of scorn. The woman flushed and fell silent, then moved swiftly away, trailed by her equally silent companions.

"So it begins," Edmond noted with a sigh.

They all looked serious for a moment, for each had been the subject of rumor, gossip and speculation.

"I find it fascinating that the faces of gossips possess

the same bovine aspect," Brix said, doing a very passable imitation of Buggy at his most studious. "It is easy, if one has a creative cast of mind, to imagine them as cows standing in a field chewing their cud."

The tension eased, and they shared a smile.

"Where's Charlie? I thought he'd be here," Drury said, surveying the ballroom. "Buggy's anxious to talk to him about the ship's provisions."

"There he is now, waiting at the end of the receiving line like a dutiful officer," Edmond said, nodding at the tall, commanding figure in the line moving slowly toward the earl and his family. "Even without his uniform, he's every inch the officer, isn't he?"

"I'll sleep better knowing he's in command of Buggy's ship," Fanny said, earning nods of agreement from her companions.

"He's not the only other late arrival," Diana noted as a beautiful young woman dressed in the height of fashion in a gown of jonquil silk with ruffles from hem to knee, lace around the bodice and a necklace of garnets, appeared at the entrance to the ballroom. Pearls and more garnets were in her ornately dressed hair. The older gentleman with her, however, was dressed in what would have been appropriate for a ball fifty years ago. "Who is that?"

"The Duke of Wymerton and Lady Eleanor Springford!" Fallingbrook announced.

Nell started and Bromwell stared, while his mother smiled and his father cleared his throat.

"Gad, Snouty, how are you? It's been years!" the earl said as he moved toward the older man.

Meanwhile, Lady Eleanor let go of her father's arm

and gracefully approached the countess, who was looking better rested than she had for many months since Bromwell had found out exactly what was in her medicine, which was mostly comprised of caffeine, and put a stop to it.

"I was delighted to receive your invitation," Lady Eleanor said in a musical voice and with a smile which revealed that even her teeth were lovely. "As well as your letter."

Nell stared at the countess, and so did her son. "Letter?" Bromwell murmured.

"Yes," Lady Eleanor said, turning to him. "I understand I've been of great assistance to you both, although I didn't know it."

Nell wondered if she should say something—anything— or just be quiet and let Bromwell, who looked equally lost, speak.

Lady Eleanor solved her problem for her. "I'm not at all upset that you felt it necessary to use my name. Indeed, when the countess told me of your predicament, I was quite happy to oblige."

A hint of merriment sparkled in her bright blue eyes as she ran a swift gaze over Bromwell, then addressed Nell. "I can't say I blame you a bit for wanting to accept his invitation, even if it required pretending to be someone else."

By now, Bromwell's face was scarlet, while Nell was more sorry than ever she'd used Lady Eleanor's name.

The orchestra's leader looked at the earl, who nodded at Bromwell. "It's time."

"I say, Charlie!" Bromwell called to a tall young man with a regal bearing who was standing near the earl, who was still talking to the duke while his wife looked on.

The younger man skirted the older three and hurried to join them. "Aye aye, sir!" he said, saluting as he came to a halt.

"Lady Eleanor, Miss Springley, this is Charles Grendon, late of His Majesty's Navy and my very good friend. He's going to captain our ship when we go on our expedition.

"Charlie, would you be so good as to engage Lady Eleanor for the first dance? He's a most accomplished dancer," he assured her.

"I'd be delighted," Grendon replied with a polite bow.

As grim as if he were about to be executed, Bromwell took Nell's arm. "I wish we didn't have the honor of leading the first dance," he said as they started forward.

"Smile, my lord," she whispered. "It's easier than the *upa upa*."

"I thought I was going to swoon when Lady Eleanor was announced!" Nell said later that evening as she and Justinian strolled on the terrace.

"I was shocked myself," he replied. "To think my mother had written to her and told her everything—and she wasn't angry or upset. Indeed, she's a very agreeable young lady. I note Charlie seems quite taken with her."

"She's very beautiful."

Bromwell laughed softly. "She's pretty, I suppose, and well dressed in a gown that fits, but…" He took her hands and held them out in front of him so he could survey her in the lovely gown of pale blue silk she wore. "Her beauty is nothing compared to yours."

Still holding his hands, Nell leaned back against the balustrade. "I fear your mother's a very sly woman in some ways."

"I suppose she's had to be sometimes, to get around my father. I must say, she seems quite a different woman now that I'm getting married."

"If we were staying in England, she'd be even happier."

"No doubt, but she'll have plenty of time to spend with us when we return."

"And our children, if we are so blessed," Nell said softly, turning so that her back was to him. "Show me again how the women of Tahiti give birth, without the crouching, of course, or you'll crease your breeches."

"We can't have that," he said with a low chuckle as he came close behind and put his arms around her.

With a sigh, she relaxed against him as he ran his hands down her stomach.

"Are you sure about the expedition? What if you get with child on the voyage?"

She turned in his arms so that she was facing him. "There'll be a physician on the ship, won't there?"

"Yes. Dr. Reynolds is a very competent, open-minded fellow who wishes to learn about native medicines."

"And if we're in the islands, there are midwives, are there not?"

"Yes."

"Then since you will be with me, too, what need have I to fear? I will be in the best possible hands, and so will any children we may have."

"You are the most amazing woman I've ever laid eyes on. Such a pity you don't appreciate spiders."

"I don't hate them anymore," she protested. "I'm even beginning to like them."

Bromwell smiled broadly. "I knew you were different from the moment you landed in my lap."

"I knew you were different the moment you told me you'd put that spider in your hat." She caressed his cheek. "I also thought you were the most handsome man I'd ever seen."

In his evening dress, he looked as comely as any man in the ballroom, and given what else he had accomplished, he was superior to most. "I still find it hard to believe such a clever, famous, handsome man wants to marry me."

"Believe it, Nell," he whispered as he pulled her into his arms, "and believe that you are the one blessing me by accepting my hand, for that is the truth."

His lips met hers with the same gentle, wonderful tenderness of their first kiss, and then, as always, desire unfurled within her, fueling the undercurrent of passion between them.

She guided him back into the shadows and the vine-covered walls, out of sight, away from the illuminated windows and the people inside.

He laughed softly. "This is hardly the time or place for an intimate encounter."

"I only want to be alone with you for a few moments," she replied with bogus innocence. "Not so long we'll be missed."

"I may not be able to tear myself away."

"Oh, very well," she said with a disappointed sigh. "After all, we'll have the rest of our…"

He was staring at something over her shoulder and she twisted to see what it was. "What are you looking at?"

"There's an *Araneus diadematus* starting to build a web in the vines," he admitted sheepishly, nodding toward thin white filaments barely visible among the green leaves. "There's the bridge line, and the start of the spokes."

Smiling, happier than she'd ever been, looking forward to the future and the adventures yet to come, she slipped her arm through that of the famous Lord Bromwell and leaned her head on his broad shoulder. "Let's watch it together, shall we?"

Epilogue

The Explorer docked on Wednesday, August 5, the entire crew intact after a successful voyage. The Earl of Granshire has confirmed that his son, the famous naturalist, will be publishing a new book on the venture.

—Bath Crier

Plymouth, 1825

"Make way there! Demme, let me through! I want to see my grandson!" the Earl of Granshire cried as he pushed his way through the crowd of seaman, navvies, families and friends of arriving passengers at the Dover wharf.

His wife, holding a scented handkerchief to her nose to cover the odors of tar, hemp and sweating men, followed in his wake. Despite the crowd and the stench, however, she was no less excited than her husband.

Lord Granshire halted and pointed at the small boy in the bow of an approaching longboat. "There! There he is!"

Shouting hellos, the earl took off his hat and waved. "And there's Justinian!"

He turned to his wife, who was jumping up and down trying to see over his shoulder. "He looks very healthy and so does Nell and—good God! Is that a baby in her arms?"

With an excited cry, Lady Granshire shoved past him, nearly sending the earl over the edge of the wharf into the water below. "It *is* a baby! And look at little Douglas—how sturdy and brown he is!"

"Buggy!" the Honorable Brixton Smythe-Medway shouted from among the crowd a few feet closer to the end of the wharf. "Nell! Charlie!"

"Watch what you're about, Brix," Drury warned as he moved away from his friend and nearly collided with Edmond beside him. "Sorry, Edmond, but our friend is a little overenthused."

Edmond gave Drury a sardonic smile. "Just imagine if our wives were here. It's a fortunate twist of fate that they're all expecting again. Otherwise we'd never have been able to convince them to wait for us at the earl's town house."

"It looks like Buggy hasn't been remiss in that aspect. Did *you* know they'd had another baby?"

Drury shook his head. "They must have wanted to surprise us."

"They've succeeded," Edmond replied.

The longboat reached the wharf and a general hubbub ensued. Charlie, sun-browned and showing some gray at the temples, was the first over the thwarts and onto the wharf. Buggy handed his son over to him, then turned to take the baby from Nell's arms while Charlie helped her onto the wharf. Once Nell was on the wooden platform, Buggy gave her the baby, then climbed out to stand beside them.

The countess got to them first and she threw her arms

around her son. "Oh, my boy! My blessed, blessed boy! You're home and you're never leaving again!"

"No, I'm not," he assured her before turning to another older man in the longboat, his face deeply tanned by the sun, his slender frame and gaunt face hinting at years of deprivation, as if returning from long and weary exile. The old man rarely took his gaze from Nell unless it was to look at her children. "This is Nell's father, Edward Springley."

"Delighted, I'm sure," the countess murmured, barely looking away from her son.

"Hello, young man," the earl said to the little boy standing with his arms crossed, surveying the chaos as if he found it fascinating until the earl interrupted his study. "Can you guess who I am?"

"My other grandfather?" the lad replied warily.

"Other grandfather?" the earl repeated.

"Yes, that's my Mama's papa there. He's been in Australia. It's a marvelous country. I'm going back when I'm older."

"I sincerely hope not," the earl muttered.

"You're also the Earl of Granshire and a very important man, Papa says," the little boy added, which brought a beaming smile back to the earl's face.

"As clever as his father, by God!" the earl proudly exclaimed to everyone within earshot.

"And a fine healthy child he is," Bromwell said as he managed to disengage himself from his mother.

"As is his sister," he finished with a nod and a smile at the baby cradled in Nell's arms.

"A granddaughter! Let me see her!" the countess cried.

Nell gently moved the blanket away from the slumbering infant's face and exchanged happy and proud smiles with her husband and father as the countess and his male friends clustered around.

"My God, she's a beauty!" Brix declared as he studied the slumbering infant with dark brown curling hair and plump cheeks. "I claim her for my Harry."

"If she's anything like her parents, I think my Brom might do well to consider her when the time comes," Drury mused aloud, "but don't any of you tell Juliette I said so."

Edmond leaned close. "Such a charmer will break a lot of hearts," he said gravely, "although being Buggy's daughter, she's bound to be a bluestocking. If so, she'll never do for my rascal D'Arcy, or his brother, either."

Nell laughed heartily. "She's only a baby! Let her grow up and she shall make her own choice—and it may be none of your sons."

"May I hold her?" the countess asked, reaching out eagerly.

"Of course," Nell said. "I haven't got my land legs yet."

"Papa says you have lots of horses," little Douglas said to the earl. "Can I ride one?"

"Certainly!" the earl replied. "And one of my best bitches just had a litter, so you shall have a puppy, too."

"Papa, did you hear!" Douglas cried with delight. "A *Canis lupus familiaris!* He's going to give me a *Canis lupus familiaris!*"

"Yes, Douglas, I hear you, and so can the whole wharf. Now, where's Charlie got to?" Bromwell asked, looking around. "He said something about not coming for dinner and I…oh, isn't that…? Egad, it is!"

They all stared at Charlie, who was over by a stack of barrels kissing Lady Eleanor Springford as passionately as any of them had ever kissed their wives, which was very passionately indeed.

"Yes, well, I suppose we can leave him here," Bromwell said, turning to lead the way from the wharf to the area of the docks where carriages could wait.

"You and the children shall come with us in the barouche," his father announced, taking his grandson by the hand.

He glanced at Nell's father and gave him a smile. "Mr. Springley, too, of course."

"As you wish. And you'll come to call tomorrow?" Bromwell asked his friends.

"On the contrary," Brix merrily replied. "We're following you, for our wives are already there, anxiously waiting and probably complaining about all our faults."

"The children are there, too," Edmond added, "the ones already born and the ones who will be within the next few months."

"Oh, how wonderful!" Nell exclaimed as she gripped her husband's arm to steady herself as she also took her father by the hand. "I have so much to ask them—and tell them, too. I'm thinking of writing a book about our voyage, but unlike Justinian's, mine will be a romantic novel."

"Excellent!" Edmond cried. "Diana will be pleased. She's been saying you should be a writer ever since your first letter arrived. She found it delightful."

Nell beamed with pleasure and Buggy's face shone with pride as they all followed the earl to the waiting carriages, until the countess came to an abrupt halt and turned to her son and his wife. "You haven't told us her name! What is my granddaughter's name?"

"We named her after the woman the goddess Minerva turned into a spider," Nell said.

As the younger men and Mr. Springley smiled, the earl and the countess looked baffled.

Viscount Bromwell, known as Buggy to his friends, grinned from ear to ear. "Her name is Arachne Juliette Diana Francesca."

"Well now," Sir Douglas Drury said gravely, "*that* is what I call a name."

"Here, here!" his friends agreed.

* * * * *

The World of Mills & Boon®

There's a Mills & Boon® series that's perfect for you. We publish ten series and with new titles every month, you never have to wait long for your favourite to come along.

Blaze® — Scorching hot, sexy reads

By Request — Relive the romance with the best of the best

Cherish™ — Romance to melt the heart every time

Desire™ — Passionate and dramatic love stories

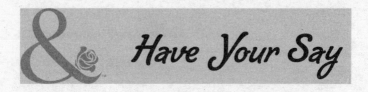

Have Your Say

You've just finished your book.
So what did you think?

We'd love to hear your thoughts on our
'Have your say' online panel
www.millsandboon.co.uk/haveyoursay

- 🌹 Easy to use
- 🌹 Short questionnaire
- 🌹 Chance to win Mills & Boon®
  goodies